I0689621

# Blowin' in the Wind

## A Novel by

# Joel Samberg

Black Rose Writing | Texas

© 2019 by Joel Samberg
All rights reserved. No part of this book may be reproduced, stored in a retrieval system or transmitted in any form or by any means without the prior written permission of the publishers, except by a reviewer who may quote brief passages in a review to be printed in a newspaper, magazine or journal.

The author grants the final approval for this literary material.

First printing

This is a work of fiction. Names, characters, businesses, places, events, and incidents are either the products of the author's imagination or used in a fictitious manner. Any resemblance to actual persons, living or dead, or actual events is purely coincidental.

ISBN: 978-1-68433-363-9
PUBLISHED BY BLACK ROSE WRITING
www.blackrosewriting.com

Printed in the United States of America
Suggested Retail Price (SRP) $19.95

*Blowin' in the Wind* is printed in Palatino Linotype
Please note there is a Yiddish/Hebrew glossary at the back of the book.

*As a planet-friendly publisher, Black Rose Writing does its best to eliminate unnecessary waste to reduce paper usage and energy costs, while never compromising the reading experience. As a result, the final word count vs. page count may not meet common expectations.

"To find joy in work is to discover the fountain of youth."
—Pearl S. Buck


My thanks to Victor Jaccarino and Roslyn Newman, high school teachers who truly cared and helped me find my own fountain of youth; and to Bonnie, with whom I've been fortunate to share that fountain for all these years.

# Blowin' in the Wind

# One

How did an eighteen-year-old boy who never before had a girlfriend learn to kiss that way? Maybe it's from all the television shows that Daniel watched when he was little and all the books he's read over the last few years. I wonder if it can be traced to the boost of confidence and serenity he seems to have absorbed since he moved to my house in New Jersey from our childhood home on Long Island more than a year ago.

Is it genetic? Could it merely be that Daniel comes from a family whose members are bestowed with a healthy dose of passion that explodes when the time is right? (If that's the case, as his sister it's nice to know that I'll have much to look forward to as time goes on. From my lips to God's ears.)

I suppose, though, that the real answer might be deceptively simple: Daniel could just be very much in love with Marissa, the girl I saw him kissing as I glanced through my living room window last week. Marissa is a pretty redhead who walks home from school with him most days. That particular day she was carrying a tambourine that she wasn't supposed to have taken out of the band room. Perhaps I should have been embarrassed to watch the two of them on the front lawn; after all, it was one hell of a kiss. But I wasn't embarrassed at all. I was happy for Daniel. It had been a rough few years. To me, the kiss meant that he is at peace. He deserves to be.

After the kiss, he took Marissa's tambourine away from her and gently tapped it against her butt.

"Hey, Mr. Tambourine man!" Marissa complained. "Why'd you do that?"

I'm sure she used those words because she knew it was a line from a famous Bob Dylan song. Daniel undoubtedly had told her everything he knew about the famous songwriter and folksinger. After all, music used to be the focus of his life.

"Why'd I do that? Because if Mr. Paisley sees that you took the tambourine out of the band room," Daniel explained, "he'll give you detention. I'm just looking out for you. That's all."

"I took it out of the band room because you distracted me, Daniel," Marissa insisted. "I forgot I was holding it when I left the school."

"How did I distract you?"

"Are you serious? You don't remember yelling up to me from the courtyard when I was in the band room, next to the window?"

"No."

"Of course you remember. You yelled, 'Hey Marissa, hurry up! I want to take you home and make mad passionate love to you before I do my homework!' I mean, come on, Daniel, nobody does that in front of a million people."

"Well," Daniel smiled, "the times, they are a-changing."

At that point, Marissa went home. Daniel came into the house to read a book at the kitchen table. I sat there, too, doing my own work. I glanced up to look at him. I needed a break anyway; I had just finished rereading a long essay called *The Mystery of Jewish Mysticism*, which is part of my preparation for the most important exam of my life. It was written by one of my instructors, Rabbi Joseph Kaufman, which made it all the more imperative for me to absorb it cover to cover.

I closed the essay booklet. Daniel looked up at me.

"Why are you staring at me?" he asked.

I apologized and quickly looked down. The word *mysticism* on the cover of the booklet caught my eye. Suddenly I wondered if that's what life is all about—a little bit of mystery, regardless of what you try to do or how fate decides to intervene. Is that what ultimately led me to New Jersey in the first place? Is that why Daniel ended up here not long afterward?

Daniel glanced up again, and I could swear he was wondering the same thing—or at least something similar. His glance turned into a stare. I summoned all my courage and stared back.

"What?" he asked, even though I hadn't said a word.

"Nothing," I responded.

"Bullshit."

I smiled at him.

"It's just that you look so absorbed in that novel. I can see the wheels turning in your head while you're reading. Like you're writing one of your own in your head at the same time. It's interesting," I said.

"Intriguing. In a nice way, I mean. It's your new reality, and I like it."

"Intriguing? My new reality? Holy crap, Lori, you're talking like one of those doped-up psycho-hippy freaks that you probably humped at Woodstock after you danced topless during an acid trip."

"Daniel!"

It was a shock to hear him use those words to paint such a scene with me at its core (a completely inaccurate scene, I might add)—but I enjoyed it nonetheless.

"Well, Daniel, you have to admit that things are miles from the way they used to be. Light years."

I suppose that Daniel didn't quite know what to say, which is why he didn't say anything. I continued to stare. To avoid a protracted and potentially embarrassing silence, Daniel decided to turn it into a joke by pretending to be a television narrator with a comically deep and earnest voice:

"Nine years ago," he announced, "Daniel Hillman was a nine-year-old musical prodigy on Long Island. But the assertive and ambitious Daniel of 1963 is almost nothing like the mellow and contemplative eighteen-year-old of 1972. And by the way, ladies and gentlemen, don't ever ever *ever* use the word 'prodigy' in front of his mother, the one and only Beverly Hillman. You'll live to regret it!"

I doubt I ever laughed so loud and for so long as I did after Daniel's impromptu performance. My laughter made *him* laugh.

"Well, it's true, Daniel," I continued. "It really is. I mean, just nine years. And not just *any* nine years, but nine years when it never felt like it would be really nice outside. Like it was always in between fall and winter."

"Jesus, Lori!" Daniel said. "Between fall and winter? When did you become Elizabeth Barrett Browning? Do you mind if I use that phrase somewhere?"

"Be my guest."

"You changed a lot in those nine years, too, you know," he said. "I can tell just by the weird way you're talking."

He was absolutely right. Daniel wasn't the only Hillman who had a transformation. Some people would say my own was truly remarkable. I'm not prepared to make that determination on my own. Not yet, anyway. (Modesty forbids it.) Since Daniel already invoked 1963, I'll use that year as an example of how things have changed. Back then I was an intelligent, trim, fairly attractive teenage girl with green eyes and brunette hair who should have been running around from one Sweet Sixteen party to the next, giggling, yapping up a storm, and being completely delusional with my giggling, yapping, delusional friends. Instead, I never wanted to leave the house, cried in school almost every day, and was always ready to expect the worst. By contrast, today I have my own house, my own life, a great circle of friends, and might possibly make history. (Well there goes the modesty!)

"Yes. I've changed," I acknowledged to Daniel. "Maybe we should talk about it a little more."

"Oh my God," he exclaimed loudly. "Now all of a sudden you're the female Sigmund Freud?"

"Blame it on my years of therapy, Daniel. It's just interesting, that's all. I mean, the way things changed for you between then and now..." I looked off to the side. "Was it all your own doing? Did it happen by chance? Was there some divine intervention? Was it all those things?" I looked back at my brother. "That's what I like to believe—that it was all those things combined. Maybe *that's* the mystery. But whatever it is, I admire you for it."

"Admire me? Why?"

"Because God gave us free will, and you chose to end up who you are."

"Holy Moses and Jesus friggin' Christ, Lori! Are you listening to yourself?"

"I know, I know," I admitted. "I speak in sermons now."

"Damned right you do."

Perhaps I did speak in sermons. But I also spoke the truth, which only a visit to the past will prove. I think a good place to start would be the day of my other brother's bar mitzvah, which was also in 1963. For Steven, Saturday, November fifth of that year was a glorified thirteenth birthday party, but for Daniel it was another mile marker on what we all regarded as his preordained road to success as a professional musician. He knew he'd be asked to sing and play at the reception. The entire family knew it.

So, as Rabbi Joseph Kaufman might like to hear me say:
'In the beginning...'

.    .    .    .    .

First of all, please forgive me for starting out with an anecdote of such inelegance. Childhood does provide many inelegant memories, and I suppose it's up to each of us to decide which ones to share and which ones to keep hidden. I think this one should be shared. It was an important part of an important day, and both Daniel and I remember the incident as if it happened yesterday.

On the back lawn of our home, Steven took a break from a game of one-on-one touch football with Daniel so that he could urinate into the snow next to the huge weeping willow tree. He made two big yellow circles, one inside the other.

"A little pee for big ol' tree," Steven said as he zipped his pants.

"But—but..." Daniel sputtered. He was concerned about what he thought might be an act of sacrilege on Steven's part; after all, it was the day of his bar mitzvah, and Daniel wondered if there would be any dire consequences.

"But nothing," Steven responded to his little brother—with complete confidence. "Someone told me there's fertilizer in pee. Bet you didn't know that. Mom loves that damn tree, and my pee will help it grow big and strong. And now, since I've already peed, I won't have to schlep any snow through the house just to go to the bathroom, which would drive Mom and Grandma nuts. See? Everyone's happy!"

"But what if God gets mad?" asked Daniel. "It's your bar mitzvah today, and Mom told you not to pee outside anymore."

"God won't get mad," Steven assured him. "I bet if God came down to play, he'd have a peeing contest just to see who could make the biggest circle. I bet God's a lot of fun."

Daniel decided to agree with him.

"Me too!" he smiled. "I bet you can name more places on Earth than he can."

"And I bet you can play more instruments than him," Steven replied. "Except the harp. You don't play the harp yet, but God does. Someone's gotta teach all those fat naked angels how to play." Steven inflated his stomach and puffed out his cheeks to impersonate a fat naked angel.

Thanks to Steven's silliness, Daniel felt giddy enough to make up a song from the top of his head called "Yellow Circles in the Snow," and he sang the impromptu thing out loud. Steven and Daniel laughed for a long time. Daniel felt good about that; when you're nine years old, thirteen is an entirely different generation—yet there they were, my two brothers, Steven and Daniel, in a kind of youthful, impertinent partnership despite their age difference. Steven said "Yellow Circles in the Snow" could win an award one day.

Daniel looked up to him, literally and figuratively; he was four years younger and a foot and a half shorter. But they shared the same kind of passion and conviction about life. Daniel loved to listen to the stories Steven told of the places he would go one day and the things he would do. Daniel soaked it up. Sometimes he even wrote songs based on Steven's wild ideas and crazy commentaries, though most of the time he just kept it all in the back of his head for use later on, although exactly for what purpose, he didn't know at the time.

Steven's passion and conviction could be traced to a single goal: to become a famous explorer by the time he graduated high school. A world adventurer. Although officially a teenager by only three weeks, and not to be deemed a man in the eyes of God for another hour, Steven had already driven a motorboat around the Great South Bay, ridden his bicycle from the north shore to the south shore of Long Island, and studied enough books to fly a single-engine airplane. As he liked to say, he thrived on speed and uphill climbs. More than one relative remarked that Steven would kiss the North Pole long before he ever kissed a girl. The agreement between Steven and our parents was that if he could raise and maintain his grades in school, he could take flying lessons when he turned seventeen. He was counting the days.

The walls of Steven's bedroom were covered with maps of the United States and all the countries of the world, and all the maps were dotted with pushpins to show all the places he planned to visit by air, land or sea. He could tell you how many miles away each place was from Westbrook Hills, and approximately how long it would take to get there, depending on the mode of transportation. A few years ago, our mother took down all the maps so that his room could be painted, but our father had to buy a can of spackle first because of all the holes made by all the pushpins. Dad went through half a can of spackle and was not too pleased. "Flying lessons?" he yelled in frustration at the time. "Forget it, pal. My entire income is being spent on spackle because of these damn pushpins. I never want to see another pushpin as long as I live." Mom told him that if pushpins were the extent of his troubles, he should just calm down. "If you had to choose between cancer and pushpin holes," she said, "which would you choose?" Dad finished spackling and painting in complete silence.

As for my younger brother's passion and conviction, everyone, not the least of whom was Daniel himself, believed that it was his destiny to become a successful musician by the time his own bar mitzvah rolled around; he was convinced he'd be the first boy in history to write, arrange, sing, and play his own songs on a bestselling 33⅓-rpm album. Certainly this aspiration came from the proficiency he had discovered early on, a proficiency that gave him the comfort to sit behind a piano and play for anyone, anywhere, anytime, or stand with a guitar strapped around his neck and strum with the confidence usually attributed to people much older. It was that same proficiency and confidence that allowed him to sing without a note of embarrassment, unlike many of his classmates (and me), who blanched at the thought of having to croon in public.

Daniel's bar mitzvah was still four years away. He had plenty of time to reach his goal.

As Daniel explained to me much later on, he gladly accepted what he felt was his destiny at the time because he enjoyed all the comedy, drama and emotion that he knew were part of the troubadour lifestyle. Our Grandpa Jesse—our father's father—had been a professional musician when he was younger, and his stories of the road were always so compelling. (Grandpa Jesse was a colorful storyteller.) Daniel daydreamed constantly about the captivating chronicles that he would live out in his role as a professional musician. But there was something more to it than that: the stories told within each song that he performed, and the tales behind the creation of each composition, were often even more intriguing to him than the process of actually performing them. Daniel didn't quite know what to make of that perception at the time. So he just put it in the back of his mind and continued to study his instruments and practice his composing and performing with all the seriousness of a professional-in-waiting. Besides, it all came so easily to him.

Heredity undoubtedly played a big part. Like Grandpa Jesse, Dad was also very musical. He sang well and was a skilled trombonist. Daniel had shown a flair for music since he was a toddler. He played a toy piano and a Hohner harmonica with remarkable precision while still in diapers. By the age of five, he could already play sophisticated compositions on the upright piano in our living room, as well as the guitar and xylophone. The music teacher at our elementary school, Mr.

Hammel, gave him private saxophone lessons starting in third grade when he discovered how well Daniel played after just one lesson. (Students usually started lessons in fourth grade, but the school band desperately needed a saxophone player, so Mr. Hammel, who had heard rumors about Daniel's skill, bent the rules.)

By the age of eight, Daniel had already composed more than a dozen songs and taught himself how to write musical arrangements. He also found harmonizing an almost intuitive sport. Most people in the family assumed that his professional goal was not merely self-selected, but divinely inspired. I particularly enjoyed hearing that.

Music took up much of Daniel's time. He played wherever he could. People took enormous pleasure listening to him perform. They called him special, delightful, remarkable, and a prodigy. Those were the times when Mom would pull him aside to warn him that being special, delightful, and remarkable was fine as long as he also realized that things can change, that things can happen, and that he should always be ready to accept an alternate plan, if necessary. What's more, Mom despised the word prodigy. She said that being deemed a prodigy was often more a "useless nuisance" than anything else.

That morning—the morning of Steven's bar mitzvah—neither Steven nor Daniel wore winter coats while outside playing. Steven had on a new blue suit. Daniel's suit was brown. If Mom or Grandma Rose (Mom's mom) had looked out the kitchen window at the time, they would have shouted out to the boys loud enough for half the neighborhood to hear. Although the temperature was mild that morning, Mom and Grandma were of one mind when it came to the belief that multiple layers of clothing were required from September through April, regardless of the actual weather outside. Steven always said that if a single freak snowflake fell on the lawn in the middle of summer, Mom and Grandma would race to the basement to dig out a dozen pairs of thermal underwear, some vinyl coats, hats with earmuffs, plenty of woolen scarves, leather gloves, rubber boots, and a few cartons of Goodman's Chicken Soup.

While Steven and Daniel played in the backyard, the rest of the family was busy inside getting ready to leave for temple. I watched my brothers for a while through the kitchen window. They could easily have spotted me there since I wore a blouse and dress combination that was far more colorful than anything I had ever worn before. (Mom insisted and overruled my many objections.) Had they spotted me, the boys would have seen the worry on my face, for I was concerned about the reaction Mom and Grandma Rose would have once they realized that Steven and Daniel were in the backyard without coats. Then again, to be honest, I worried about almost everything. I didn't want to hear Mom yelling about 'those two dodo degenerates' outside, which is something she might actually have said. (She loved a good turn of phrase.) Certainly she regarded them neither as dodos nor degenerates. Nor did they look the part. They were both adorable. Steven, with his slim frame and long legs, had the air of an athlete, and his dark, wavy, well-mannered hair gave him a look both of roguishness and refinement at the same time. His appearance was a bit of a contrast to Daniel's, whose arms, legs and torso, thanks to his age, still were not properly proportioned. The freckles across the bridge of his nose made him look even younger than his nine years, and his sandy hair always had a few strands that stuck up in the back. Daniel was cute, but Steven was handsome—though if anyone mentioned to him that he was handsome, he'd have walked away in disgust and threatened to not come back until the conversation turned to something far more important, like cockpits and horsepower.

"Maybe we should put on our coats," Daniel said to Steven as if he had read my mind. "I don't want Mom to yell and then see Lori cry."

Had I been outside with the boys, you can pretty much bet I would have bundled myself up from head to toe. I was different from them. At least that's what I thought at the time. Unlike my brothers, I seemed to lack any specific passion at all. Nothing drove me to plan for the future, and I certainly had no intention to be 'the first' anything. I was frightened of growing up. It was almost as if I believed that if I stayed a child eternally, nothing bad would ever happen to me or to anyone else in the family. Everything was good the way it was; why risk it by growing up? I wanted everyone to be happy, yet could find very little joy for myself. I wanted very much to be loved, yet spurned attention. Even something silly like a birthday party made me uneasy. Two months earlier, Mom insisted I should have a Sweet Sixteen party. I begged her not to plan one. Steven would have asked for a hot-air balloon ride in the Catskill Mountains with a few of his friends. Daniel would have thrown a concert for the neighborhood. All I wanted was a simple dinner at a small restaurant with just the family—which is exactly what we ended up doing.

"Lori will be fine," Steven said to Daniel. "Mom and Grandma are too busy screaming at mirrors to worry about us. Lori knows it. So stop worrying."

They continued to throw snowballs at the utility pole in the corner of the yard. (They were hardly snowballs, for there was hardly any snow; they were more like snow marbles.) We were supposed to be at Temple Beth Shalom at ten o'clock. It was nine-forty.

I sat down at the kitchen table. Dad called out to me from the bathroom, where he was putting on his tie.

"Sweetheart," he shouted through the wall, "can you find the boys for me? They have to do a few things before we leave, and if we don't leave now, Steven won't have his bar mitzvah, and if he doesn't have his bar mitzvah, he won't become a man, which is okay with me, but I don't think it would be okay with him. Vishtayst?"

"They're in the backyard," I called back. "I'll get them."

Steven and Daniel walked in just as I opened the back door. They stomped their feet on the mat to get rid of any betraying evidence of snow on their shiny black shoes.

"You look pretty, Lori," Daniel said.

"Yeah, you sorta do," echoed Steven. "You look like that fake Marc Chagall painting in the hallway. Very colorful."

"Thanks, I think." I smiled at Steven. "How do you feel?"

"About what?" Steven asked.

"About your bar mitzvah."

"Oh, you mean that thing that starts in about nineteen minutes?"

"That's why I asked. Are you nervous that we might be a little late?"

"Nervous? Who do you think I am—you?"

He instantly regretted it and touched my shoulder.

"Sorry. I didn't mean that. Besides, I'd bet a million bucks that when you grow up, you'll become a cruise director who can get a thousand people to Italy on time. Mom and Dad can't even get seven people to a temple that's a mile away."

But Steven smiled when he said it because he knew there was really no question that we would get to the temple on time. Ours were competent parents who had always planned carefully and tried never to be frivolous with their actions or deeds. They had a good and loving marriage and made everything work out for the best.

•    •    •    •    •

I always loved the story of how Mom and Dad met. Daniel loves it too. I used to think about it whenever my friends (few though they were) came over our house to play. They knew them only as Mr. and Mrs. Hillman—as Lori's parents. But to me it was always a classic love story about two very special people.

Murray Hillman saw Beverly Gersh for the first time in 1944 at a USO show where Dad was playing the trombone in an army band. Dad had been drafted into the service but deemed unfit for combat because of poor eyesight. When his superiors discovered that he was a talented musician, he was asked to join a swing band that traveled to bases throughout the country and overseas. He eagerly accepted the assignment. His next-to-last show was at a ballroom in Manhattan. Mom, a photographer for the Brownsville Democrat, a weekly newspaper in Brooklyn, was sent over the bridge to cover the show.

Mom had actually been pursued by the publisher of the Democrat after she entered three editorial essay contests sponsored by the newspaper when she was a senior in high school. All three essays won first prize. The publisher nicknamed her the Brownsville Wunderkind. As the story goes, Mom's job as a photographer was foisted upon her (not very delicately, as has been hinted) by that same publisher, who thought that if he had a 'good-looking dame' behind the lens, he might be able to get pictures that the other newspapers would miss. Mom had actually wanted to be a reporter for the paper (which would have made her the first female reporter in Brooklyn), but the publisher was unrelenting. So Mom grudgingly accepted the assignment and went to photograph the USO show. Before long, the young trombonist eyed the auburn-haired photographer with such intensity that "Begin the Beguine" began without him. She stared back. Dad was a solidly built man, a few pounds heavier than he wanted to be. His army band uniform was a bit snug, but he looked dapper in it anyway. He had wavy black hair, which Mom liked. He despised the thick glasses he had to wear, but she thought they made him look intellectual.

The trombonist went over to the photographer during a break in the music and boldly predicted out loud that she would be fired from her job and married to him all within the same month. Beverly Gersh told Murray Hillman that he was certifiably crazy.

Mom and Dad became Mr. and Mrs. Hillman on January 14, 1945.

Both were just twenty-three years old.

Dad didn't pursue music as a career. He had little faith in the profession's ability to provide a good living, despite how much he loved his trombone, and how good a player he was. Although he had scant interest in electrical engineering, he had made sure to study it in the service and was convinced by his instructors that employment at a public utility was the way to go. After his discharge from the army, he bought a house on Pearl Drive in Westbrook Hills, a New York City suburb several miles east of Brooklyn, and got a job as an assistant supervisor at LILCO, the Long Island Lighting Company. By 1954 he was a supervisor, and in 1961, on his thirty-ninth birthday, he was named Director of Operations for the Western Region. Mom was proud of him. She always said that his decision not to pursue music was a smart one. She was convinced that too many musicians suffered the type of professional and financial heartache and frustration that skilled engineers seemed somehow better able to avoid. She was glad he didn't feel the need to become a professional trombonist just because his father, who played trumpet in several bands and knocked around for years as a songwriter and occasional singer, told him he should.

Mom never picked up a camera again, which was probably a blessing for the art of photography. She still had the urge to write, but felt she would never be taken seriously. She had planned to go to college to study literature, but when World War II broke out she felt compelled to go to work instead to help her family. When she married, she decided that life as a full-time housewife and mother was the right thing to do. I was born two years into the marriage, and Steven three years after that. Daniel came along four years later.

All the kids in the neighborhood liked Murray Hillman. He was a far less imposing figure than some of the other fathers on the block, yet could still get angry if he had to—like when Steven and two friends hitched scooter rides off the back of an ice cream truck and nearly impaled themselves on a fire hydrant. Dad screamed at Steven, screamed at his friends, and screamed at the poor ice cream man who had let them do it. (That particular ice cream man never returned to Pearl Drive; the rumor was that he gave up his route after the incident and moved to Maine to work on a lobster boat.)

In addition to raising the three of us, Beverly Hillman kept busy with many other pursuits—although they weren't always the most practical of endeavors. She watched *Search for Tomorrow* every weekday after lunch and went to Alberto's Beauty Salon every Saturday morning. But she also volunteered as a writer for the monthly PTA newsletter, attended most of the quarterly meetings of the neighborhood improvement society, and argued stridently about Long Island politics during a weekly mahjong game with friends from the temple.

Mom also forced Dad to dress up in a suit and take her dancing and dining in Manhattan twice a year. "Let me at least *pretend*," she'd always grumble at him when he whined about it—although she never explained exactly what it was she needed to pretend.

On one hand, Mom was fiercely protective of her three children, even to the point of telling little white lies to teachers and other mothers if it served her purpose. On the other hand, in the house, she was always brutally honest, which made for bruised feelings every once in a while. She might tell one of us, for instance, that a picture we drew of the United States for a social studies project looked like "a pig about to have a baby," and that if we didn't draw it over again, "and make it look like a country instead of a fat pig this time," we could just forget about dessert for a week. In a way, I suppose, that, too, was a protective measure.

Mom was adamant that the three of us do well in school, for that, she believed, was the best way to be prepared for any eventuality. "It may not open any of the doors you want opened, but it couldn't hurt, either," she often said. "There are no guarantees in life" was also a line she repeated from time to time. "Expect the worst, but hope for the best" was yet another.

My grades were always excellent, so Mom had no issues there. Her greatest challenge was to have me go through an entire week at school without crying for one reason or another and asking to be sent home. With Steven, there was a bit more of a problem because his grades were never very good. He did well in geography, though, and his guidance counselor at Westbrook Hills Junior High School insisted that his interest in travel and his enthusiasm for all modes of transportation would take him far one day. So Mom decided not to worry too much. As for Daniel, his grades, like mine, were always good. Mom was also quite aware of how popular he was at school because of the music he played at concerts and special events, though it's also true that she fussed over it much less than other mothers fussed over their own children who showed various talents. She warned Daniel from time to time to drop any idea he might have had of running away to Manhattan or Hollywood to make his mark before he finished college. "After you have your college diploma and get a good job," she said to him on more than a handful of occasions, "*then* you can run away wherever you want."

• • • • •

"You look beautiful," Dad said to me as I stood by the kitchen table staring at the clock on the wall.

"Thank you," I said. I was embarrassed. "Mom made me wear this."

"Only because you're so pretty, and she wants people to notice you, and we both want you to learn how to take compliments!"

"If I'm so pretty, why do I have to wear something so loud to prove it?"

Dad chortled.

"Lori, Lori, Lori... Always a good rebuttal. Maybe you'll be a lawyer one day."

"I don't want to be a lawyer," I insisted.

Dad wore a new suit, similar in color to Daniel's, and he smelled of English Leather. He always seemed a little younger, a little taller, and a little slimmer when he dressed up like that. If not for the belly that had gotten a bit larger lately, and a bald spot at the top of his head that hadn't been there three years earlier, he would still have looked like that trombone player at the USO show. The three of us—Steven, Daniel and I—loved, respected, and admired our father very much, though Steven always said he wished he had been a little more of an adventurous sort. I appreciated Dad's unwavering faith in traditional things and his uncompromised trust in fate—though it also frightened me at times, as if it were deceptive, hiding something, blocking some other potential outcome. I distinctly remember thinking that I was the only girl in America who loved and despised English Leather at the same time. (Daniel swears he heard me say that out loud one day and wrote it down on a scrap piece of paper to keep hidden away.)

"Steven," Dad called out, "go downstairs and make sure the lights are off down there. Daniel, go see if Ashler's car is blocking the driveway, and if it is, tell him to get his big fat tuchis outside and move it."

Henry Ashler was our next-door neighbor, a sixty-year-old widower who was a hundred pounds overweight and never without a cigar in his mouth, sometimes lit, sometimes not. Steven called him Havana Fats. Mr. Ashler had a habit of parking his huge yellow Cadillac so that its rear end, with its pointy fin taillights, partially blocked our driveway, which made it difficult for Dad to pull in and out. Daniel looked through the living room window and saw that the driveway was clear.

Despite living next door to us for fifteen years, Mr. Ashler was not invited to Steven's bar mitzvah. Months earlier while making out the invitation list, Mom said,

"No one called Havana Fats is going to my son's bar mitzvah. It's just not right."

Daniel ran from the living room back to the kitchen and was intercepted by Grandpa Sol. That was Mom's father. He put his hands on the sides of Daniel's face and said,

"Dan'l Boone, is there any schmutz on my punim? I just noshed a bagel. Don't tell your grandmother. She'll holler at me."

Grandpa Sol loved to play with names and enjoyed using as many variations of Daniel, Lori, and Steven as he could come up with. Sometimes I was Lorelei, other times Flora Laura. Dan'l Boone was the one he had selected for Daniel that week.

"No Grandpa," Daniel reported dutifully, "no schmutz. Your face is as clean as your tuchis."

"Tank Gut," Grandpa said—which was 'Thank God' with a Yiddish accent, an accent as fake as it was predictable. "Ve go to shul now, yes?"

"No. Mom and Grandma aren't ready yet. I don't think they're happy with their dresses."

"Oy, vey is mir," Grandpa whined as he scratched his bald head. "I'll read maybe the paper then."

Grandpa Sol put on the Yiddish accent whenever he wanted to be funny, which was all the time. At seventy, Solomon Gersh was as lovable as they come, and we all adored him. He and Grandma Rose were at our house several times a week. They had their own apartment in Middle Village, Queens, but for all intents and purposes, they also had a house in Westbrook Hills, Long Island. I'm sure many people on Pearl Drive thought they lived with us, that everything we ate was prepared by Grandma Rose, and that all of the laughter that came out of the house was traceable to something silly Grandpa Sol had said. And none of those thoughts would have been very far from the truth.

In the kitchen, Grandpa Sol went to the pile of old newspapers that Mom kept in a shopping bag by the basement steps (mostly for him) and grabbed the previous Sunday's New York Times. Then he sat down by the table to read, just as Steven returned from the basement, and just as Dad called out from somewhere else in the house to urge Mom and Grandma Rose to please hurry up.

"It's getting late," Dad pleaded.

"Two minutes," Mom hollered from her bedroom.

Meanwhile, Grandpa Sol found something of interest in the newspaper.

"Ah-hah!" he declared loudly. "Here's one."

Steven and I went over to him in the kitchen to see what he had found, just as we had done hundreds of times before. Grandpa Sol always read the wedding announcements to see if he could put a bride's first name together with a groom's last name to come up with an entirely new name that was funny and whimsical.

"Look here," he said as he pointed to one corner of the page. "See? Miss Lotta Vukovich from the Bronx, and down here, Mr. Lawrence Paine from Glen Cove. Vishtayst?" Grandpa looked at us to see if we could make the connection on our own. "No? You don't see?" He waited another moment while we thought about it. "If Lotta Vukovich married Lawrence Paine…"

"She'd be Lotta Paine!" Steven announced proudly. "That's one of your best ones, Grandpa."

"Best shmest," Grandpa Sol said. "I'll do better yet one day. You'll see."

Dad came into the kitchen, grumbling under his breath that he couldn't find his car keys.

"Murray," Grandpa said, "your mother-in-law and your wife and their fekakta dresses will make us late for the bar mitzvah. No?"

"What will be, will be," Dad said, with little patience for his father-in-law at the moment.

"What will be, will be? Now all of a sudden you're Doris Day?"

Dad went to the closet and found his keys in his coat pocket. Daniel and I went to the living room to wait. Grandma Rose finally came out of my parents' bedroom and into the living room. She wore a purple sequined dress that was a little too tight.

"Such gorgeous children," she said. She put her hands over her heart, then straightened out the thick straps of my dress (even though they didn't need to be straightened), and finally rubbed her thumbs along each side of Daniel's nose and under his eyes as if to spread his freckles further onto his cheeks.

"Let's go, Beverly," Dad called out from the front hallway one more time.

"Okay, Murray. Please, I'm hurrying. Two minutes."

"That's what you said two minutes ago."

"Just two minutes. I promise"

Under his breath, Dad muttered,

"From your lips to God's ears."

Ten minutes later we left for temple.

•          •          •

I sat between Dad and Daniel in the front seat of our 1957 Ford Galaxie. Mom, who managed to slip on the last of her accessories—a pearl necklace—just before we turned off Pearl Drive, squeezed into the back seat with Steven, Grandma Rose and Grandpa Sol.

Mom wasn't happy with the way she looked. She had complained all morning about the thick, black patent leather belt that came as part of her blue dress ensemble. She said it made her look "as fat as a house," and that without it, she looked even fatter, "like a whole fat neighborhood of fat houses." That wasn't true. Although she had lost her hourglass figure, she was still beautiful—but it always took an hour of pleading from others just to get her to grudgingly accept the compliment. "I won the life I won," she often said, with neither a smile nor a frown. "And the hips."

On the short ride to temple, Daniel wiggled his fingers as he played an imaginary piano, with the upper keys on his lap and the lower ones on mine. Instinctively I knew that in his head he was rehearsing the theme from the movie *Exodus*, which I had overheard was on his playlist for Steven's bar mitzvah reception after the ceremony.

"What are you doing?" Dad asked, seeing Daniel's busy hands out of the corner of his eye.

"Practicing," Daniel said.

"Why? It's just our family there, not the President of the United States."

"I still have to practice."

"You never know," Steven piped up from the back seat, "maybe President Kennedy heard about my bar mitzvah and is gonna show up to give me a medal."

"For what, getting a D in American history?" Dad said.

"Ha ha ha," Steven remarked.

That little burst of quirky chatter reminded me of the time we all sat in the living room, almost three years earlier, during John F. Kennedy's inauguration. As we all watched it on our little black & white TV set, Grandma Rose said,

"It's a shame we don't live in Washington. I bet they would have asked Daniel to play for President Kennedy. Oy, how I'd love to meet him."

"What—and have him think we're asking for favors?" Mom sniped. "I'd rather just be invited to the inauguration so that I can shake his hand. That's all."

"I'd love to go to Washington," Steven said. "Did you know that President Kennedy has a bunch of boats? Maybe he'd let me see them. Or drive them! Maybe we could take a trip there one day. To Washington. You think, Mom?"

"First of all, sweetie, his boats aren't in Washington. And anyway, who has time to take a trip?" she chided. "Dad works, you go to school, I have to take care of the house…"

We never went to Washington.

But we *did* make it to Temple Beth Shalom—on time. The temple was on Suburban Avenue, on the border of Westbrook Hills and a town called Northwood, and it served families from both communities. It was built in 1954 when two smaller synagogues joined forces to create a bigger and more modern one. Dad was a founding member, which gave the Hillmans a place of distinction among the congregation. One of Daniel's best friends was Glenn Sheldon, the rabbi's son. The Sheldons lived down the block from us, at the east end of Pearl Drive. Glenn and his mother Helene attended many of the bar mitzvahs over which Rabbi Sheldon officiated at Temple Beth Shalom, as well as many of the receptions that followed. Steven's would be no exception.

Our family, like many others, attended temple services only a few times each year. But Mom and Dad believed that Rabbi Sheldon knew in his heart where we stood in ours, in the spiritual sense. We were good

Jews, if one were to base that on the fundamental moral principles and family values long attributed to the Jewish people. In my heart of hearts, I had always wanted to go to Hebrew School at Temple Beth Shalom, but worried deeply that as one of the very few girls who would have been enrolled I'd have a spotlight on me that I was ill-prepared to face. As it turned out, though, Mom and Dad never even asked me if I wanted to go.

Steven and Daniel, however, were among the Hebrew school's most active students. Rabbi Sheldon said that was a reflection of good Jewish nurturing in our home. Steven led many youth group activities on hikes and bicycle rides, and Daniel played the piano and sang at countless Brotherhood and Sisterhood meetings. We were, in effect, among the Temple Beth Shalom elite, even though we were basically only High Holy Day Jews.

The parking lot was already full by the time we arrived. Dad had to park next to the dumpster at the side of the building, which wasn't really a parking spot. Ned Early, the temple's long-time maintenance man, stood by the front door as we approached. He opened it for us, smiled, and wished us all a hearty mazel tov.

"A colored man knows from mazel tov?" Grandma Rose whispered to me.

"He's worked here for years," I explained quietly.

Rabbi Sheldon was in the lobby. He was a very popular leader because of his engaging personality, curly brown hair, and handsome face. It was not unusual to hear Rabbi Sheldon referred to as the Jewish John Kennedy. He was extremely kind and gentle to everyone in our family. For me, he validated the English translation of Beth Shalom: House of Peace. Although I liked being home more than any other place else in the world, I always felt relaxed at Temple Beth Shalom. Rabbi Sheldon spoke to me as if I had been one of his favorite students, even though I had never been a student there at all. By his presence, he somehow made the temple a citadel of trust, comfort, and security, and by his sermons he made us feel that if somehow we got lost in a scary, remote corner of the world, as long we could find a Jewish family, we'd be home.

"Shalom, Hillman clan," Rabbi Sheldon said cheerfully. His white knit yarmulke practically glimmered on top of his dark brown hair.

He put his hands on Steven's shoulders.

"Those mischievous eyes," the rabbi said. "They look at us today and say, 'A man? You think today I am a man? I've been a man for the past year and a half, you stupid idiots! Today's just the day I get all the gelt!' That's what you're thinking, Steven. Am I right?"

There were three or four other families behind us, and they all enjoyed the rabbi's wit as much as we did.

Rabbi Sheldon moved over to Daniel.

"So, my little chazzan—my little cantor," he said as he put his hands firmly on Daniel's shoulders, "soon it will be your turn. Cantor Goldstone is looking forward to beginning your bar mitzvah lessons. And on the day of your bar mitzvah, no one will sing but you, maybe not even Cantor Goldstone himself, because why compete with an angel?"

Finally, the rabbi turned to me and gently took hold of my hands.

"Lovely Lori," he smiled, "I have no doubt that you will give your parents and grandparents more nachas than they can possibly handle. I can tell simply by talking to you. We'll just have to wait and see which path you choose. Doctor? Architect? Governor? The possibilities are endless, Lori. Don't you agree?"

"Yes," I said, embarrassed to have to speak with so many people around. Dad gently stepped in front of me, I suppose fearful that my self-consciousness might reveal itself in a discomforting way. I let him.

Rabbi Sheldon stepped backward and looked at us all.

"You are a beautiful and handsome family," he said. "Nice work, Murray. Not that you had anything to do with it." Rabbi Sheldon winked. Everyone laughed. "You'll be shepping nachas till the cows come home."

"From your lips to God's ears," Dad said.

"They're wonderful kinderlach," Grandma Rose interjected. She pushed her way to the front of the crowd because she, too, wanted to be warmed by the glow of Rabbi Sheldon.

Within a half-hour, the ceremony was underway. Relatives, friends, and congregants occupied every seat in the sanctuary. Steven, up on the bimah—the raised platform at the head of the room from which Rabbi Sheldon and Cantor Goldstone conducted all services—stood confidently behind one of the two lecterns and chanted a specially-selected portion of the Book of Prophets, which all bar mitzvah boys have to do. Cantor Goldstone stood behind the other lectern, and Rabbi Sheldon waited at the back. Although Steven had had trouble memorizing his portion when he first began his bar mitzvah lessons, he did reasonably well.

Mom and Grandma Rose cried.

Several men stared at Helene Sheldon, the rabbi's beautiful red-haired wife, throughout the entire service. She sat at the side of the sanctuary. One of the white stripes on her tight black and white dress soared like a comet diagonally across her chest, which made her breasts appear as if they had no choice but to get out of its way. Although the men tried desperately to make it seem as if they were merely glancing around to see who was at the temple that morning, everyone knew they were mentally undressing the rabbi's wife over and over again.

Dad's parents, Grandma Leah and Grandpa Jesse, were on the other side of the room, chatting with relatives they hadn't seen in a while. Marty Warshaw, the bombastic president of Temple Beth Shalom, hurried over to tell Grandma and Grandpa to please keep quiet, although he didn't do it very quietly. "Shhhh, please," he implored, with one finger up against his nose. "Rabbi Sheldon is about to deliver his invocation."

"It is a blessing to me to have such a wonderful and devoted congregation," Rabbi Sheldon began. He had taken Cantor Goldstone's place on the bimah, but almost immediately took a spot in the center of the two lecterns and then walked to the edge of the platform. That's where he stood for the invocation. He didn't need a microphone. His sermons were performances as much as they were discourses.

"Yes, it is a blessing," he continued. "And it is especially nice since we are in a country where we are not made to feel like outcasts just because we are Jews. As Americans today, we can experience the blessings of peace, tolerance, brotherhood, and humanity. So we must sing the praises of our faith and the praises of our country. These blessings must go on.

"But they don't come cheap. We must be persistent in earning our blessings. We must dream hard, we must be patient, we must have good hearts, and we have to be easy on ourselves when we stumble or fall. And if we stumble or fall, we must pick ourselves up and move on, even if we don't know exactly where we're going. We must follow our hearts, and sometimes our instincts, in order to navigate toward safe, sensible, and peaceful waters, where all dreams can ultimately come true. And we must reach, sometimes high, sometimes far, sometimes even further within ourselves, to find the answers to life's toughest questions. To find our way."

Rabbi Sheldon had looked straight at Daniel, who sat next to me in the front row, when he uttered the line about singing the praises of our faith and our country. His eyes met Steven's, next to him on the bimah, when he described how we must navigate toward safe and sensible waters. And he glanced at me when he said we must look within ourselves to find answers to life's toughest questions. Rabbi Sheldon spoke directly to each of us individually; how could the Hillman children not believe that we had a page reserved for us in God's book of special families?

•  •  •  •  •  •

"And because of me," Grandpa Jesse explained to Fred and Ed, two of Dad's colleagues from LILCO, "my friend Benny Sapperstein accidentally killed Houdini." It was a story our family had heard many times before.

We were at the Huntington Chalet, a catering hall several miles from the temple, for Steven's bar mitzvah reception. Another bar mitzvah was being celebrated in the hall's second ballroom, so the entire building was alive with the sounds of music, talkative guests, and busy silverware. About an hour had passed since we arrived. Hors d'oeuvres and drinks were served while a five-piece band played popular hits of the day and Jewish ceremonial songs. The leader of the band announced that the ritual candle lighting and slicing of the challah bread would begin in twenty minutes, followed by the formal meal.

Daniel and I left the ballroom for a few moments to get away from the cigarette smoke and found Grandpa Jesse in the lobby with Fred and Ed. It was nice to see how easily sixty-eight-year-old Jesse Hillman got along with people so much younger. Fred and Ed hung on to his every word. They knew they were in the presence of a master storyteller, a man still young at heart. Grandpa Jesse didn't even look like an old man; he was taller than Fred and Ed, rail thin, and had better posture than both of them. His hair, while thinning, still had a youthful yellow tint to it and a bit of a curl in the back, which he refused to let the barber cut back. He said it made him look jazzy.

"You see, we were in Canada," Grandpa continued. "Benny was visiting relatives, and I was working a small club in the Jewish ghetto in Montreal. One day Benny sees a poster about a famous magician who's playing at a theater near the ghetto, but he can't remember the fella's name. But I knew who it was."

"Are you sure it was Houdini?" Fred asked.

"Who then? He was the only famous magician that played Canada in those days. Everyone knows that. And the poster billed this guy as the strongest man alive. Had to be Houdini. Anyway, Benny liked to go backstage whenever he saw a show, no matter what theatre. I never wanted to. I worked in enough theaters on my own—I was never interested. But Benny?—he loved it and he could get into any dressing room, anywhere, anytime. I called him Slip, not Benny. Slip Sapperstein. He was able to slip in no matter where he was. He was like soap, that guy. So anyway, I says to him that while he's back there he should see just how strong Houdini really is. So he goes backstage, right up to Houdini, and belts him in the stomach with all his strength. Boom! Just like that. But Houdini isn't ready for him, see. The next day, Houdini's dead."

Fred and Ed remained silent. They stared at Grandpa Jesse in awe.

"How does Slip feel about that now?" Fred asked. "About killing Houdini? Does it bother him?"

"Who knows? He's been dead twenty years. Slipped through the railing on the roof of his apartment building. Fell eighteen stories. Squished like a Jewish bug, the poor schmuck."

At that point, Glenn Sheldon, the rabbi's son, walked out of the ballroom and came over to us. He was sweating; he had been running around grabbing rolls off people's plates.

"I didn't even see Lori and Daniel standing there," Fred grinned as soon as he noticed Glenn stop next to us.

Grandpa Jesse put one arm on Daniel's shoulder and one on mine.

"So quiet," echoed Ed, "listening to their grandfather like that."

"This is my doll face," Grandpa said as he looked at me. "She's bad for blood pressure because she's sweeter than sugar, this one. And this guy," he said, turning to Daniel, "he's *my* little Houdini. He does magic with his fingers—on the piano."

"And xylophone and saxophone," Daniel added proudly.

"And he sings and writes songs! Takes after his old grandpa. I gave him his first instrument. A toy piano. Real wood."

"Murray should have hired him to play at the bar mitzvah instead of that band inside," Ed said. "Could've saved a fortune."

Grandpa Jesse shrugged. "Bar mitzvahs these days! See that guy over there? He does a puppet show. You think God knows from puppets?" We all looked at the other end of the lobby, where a young puppeteer was emptying the contents of an oversized trunk. On the recommendation of the banquet manager, the parents of the other bar mitzvah boy agreed to have a puppeteer entertain their family's younger guests, of which they had far more than we did.

"You don't like puppets?" Fred asked Grandpa Jesse.

"It's not that," Grandpa answered. "I don't think sticking your hand up the tuchis of a sock is what Abraham, Isaac, and Joseph had in mind when they invented bar mitzvahs."

Fred and Ed weren't sure what Grandpa meant, but they laughed anyway. Then the three men returned to the ballroom, and so did I. Glenn and Daniel remained in the lobby and walked over to where the puppeteer was setting up his show. He was a tall man with a bushy beard and moustache. He appeared to be very serious about his work.

"When you gonna start?" Glenn demanded of him.

"I'm really not sure," the man replied gently. "I don't usually do these kinds of events. I'm just doing it for a little extra money. In fact, this is my first bar mitzvah."

"I've been to a hundred," Glenn strutted.

"Really? A hundred?" The puppeteer had a skeptical look on his face.

"His father's a rabbi," Daniel clarified on Glenn's behalf.

"Oh. That explains it."

The man had already set up a cardboard puppet stage. He picked up two puppets, one of which was a fuzzy blue sock with buttons for eyes and the other a stringy mass of rag strips with little white ropes for arms and legs.

"Weren't you on *The Jimmy Dean Show*?" Daniel asked.

The puppeteer looked up and smiled broadly. "Yes, I was! My first time on network TV." He offered his hand to Daniel. "What's your name?"

"Daniel."

"Mine's Jim." They shook. "So, you've seen me on TV?"

"He sees all those stupid shows," Glenn said. "He knows every dumb show."

"No I don't. Just the ones with music. Jackie Gleason, Ed Sullivan, Red Skelton, Garry Moore, Andy Williams—"

"Wow!" Jim said. "Why do you watch all those shows?"

"So that I know what it's like to be on them."

"Doing what?"

"Playing music."

"Very nice," Jim nodded. "Are you doing anything about it now?"

"I take lessons," Daniel said, "and I play all the time. I'm gonna be the first person in my family to be on television show, even though my mom says I should wait."

"Why does she want you to wait?"

"She says that anything can happen and that I shouldn't act like I know everything's that's gonna happen."

"Well, anything *can* happen, you know," the puppeteer smiled. "But that can be a good thing, too. You just never know. Sometimes you have to follow your heart, even if takes you somewhere else."

"Somewhere else? What do you mean?"

Jim smiled and shrugged his shoulders. Daniel was disappointed; he wanted to hear what the man had to say.

"Come on, Daniel," Glenn called out impatiently. "Let's play hockey. I got something we can use for a puck. Let's go back inside."

Daniel glanced at the puppeteer.

"It's okay," Jim said. "Go play with your friend."

Back in the ballroom, Glenn and Daniel began to kick a small, round disc across the shiny floor. The six-piece band was in the middle of "It's My Party." People danced. Mom and Dad walked around holding hands. Rabbi Sheldon went from table to table to chat with guests. Steven was with three of his school friends at the dais, making a single liquid concoction out of six or seven multicolored beverages. (I remember thinking to myself, Are we absolutely certain that today this boy is a man?)

Glenn kicked the little black disc in the direction of his parents' table, and the disc hit Helene Sheldon's right foot. Mrs. Sheldon stood up and then bent down to retrieve it. As she did, a dozen weary men at nearby tables suddenly perked up.

As soon as Glenn and Daniel reached her table, Mrs. Sheldon turned around and glared at her son. She looked at the little black disk.

"Where did you get this, young man?" she demanded.

"We're playing. It's our hockey puck," Glenn said.

"That wasn't the question. Where did you get it? Were you just in the lobby?"

"Yes."

"Come."

Mrs. Sheldon led Glenn out of the ballroom. Daniel followed; I'm sure he was slightly concerned for his friend, but more importantly, he realized that some sort of interesting story might soon unfold for him to store away in his memory. Once in the lobby, Mrs. Sheldon walked over to the puppeteer. She held out the little object in her hand.

"By any chance," she said to him, "is this yours?"

Jim took it from her, examined it, rubbed his beard, then bent down in front of his cardboard stage. One of its four little wheels was missing.

"Hmmm…. I wondered why this thing was so wobbly all of a sudden. How in heaven's name did you get it off?" he said to Glenn, with more curiosity than anger.

"Glenn, what do you say to this man?" his mother demanded.

"Sorry," Glenn responded, almost under his breath.

As she retraced her steps back to the ballroom, Mrs. Sheldon saw Daniel by the entranceway. She leaned over and cupped his chin in her left hand.

"I don't know what to do with that boy," she whispered to him. Then she kissed him on the cheek. "Why can't he be more like you?" Mrs. Sheldon smiled and went back to the party with Glenn.

A few minutes later, Steven and his friends stood in the middle of the floor mocking the current dance crazes with comically exaggerated dance moves of their own. The members of the band were willing accomplices to their shenanigans. At one point, a friend of Steven's named Billy grabbed a girl and spun her around so hard that she slammed into the dais and fell on the floor. Her long skirt slid all the way up her thighs and exposed her underpants. She turned red with embarrassment. I felt for her with all the sympathy and compassion I possessed; I could only imagine the state of sheer mortification I'd be in had it been me. Probably clinical shock. Mom rushed over to the poor girl to help her up, and then told Steven to make sure that his friends behaved. At the same time, Dad went over to Billy to ask him to please tone down his behavior.

"I can hardly afford this bar mitzvah," Dad said to Billy, who was a year older than Steven and very self-possessed. "I really don't want to pay for someone's hospital bills."

"I'm sorry, Mr. Hillman," Billy said. "It won't happen again." Billy shook Dad's hand and walked away.

I went to sit with Grandma Leah for a while. Daniel came by moments later and sat on my lap. Unlike Grandpa Jesse, who was tall and thin, Grandma Leah was short and stout. Her hair bore the same yellowish tint as Grandpa's, although I'm fairly certain that hers was not entirely natural. She coughed a lot, the result of her thirty-five-year smoking habit. She had smoked at least three cigarettes at the temple alone, and another two or three at the Huntington Chalet. "It's just not right," Mom had whispered to me a half hour earlier when we saw Grandma Leah lighting up for the second time since we had arrived. At the table, she was talking to her cousin Ida from the Bronx, who sat on the other side of her. That's how her cousin was always referred to in our house: Ida from the Bronx. They were chatting about Nat Hillman, Grandpa Jesse's younger brother.

"He's not here, Leah?" Ida asked. "Your brother-in-law Nat's not coming?"

Grandma Leah shrugged.

"He never says anything one way or the other," Grandma responded. "Maybe he'll come later. Who knows?"

I had seen Uncle Nat just a handful of times over the years. He was really Dad's uncle, of course, not mine, but that's what we always called him, Uncle Nat. He was only thirteen years older than Dad. When Uncle Nat was sixteen, he left home and wasn't seen again for several years. It was said that when he was in his twenties and thirties he did 'something in finance' and had business all over the world; that's why he was frequently absent from family functions, or so it was said. I remember Grandpa Jesse telling a story once about how his mother was pregnant with Nat very late in life, and that she kept it a secret until the ninth month. Nat was an unwanted child and apparently knew it. To me, it was and still is an incredibly sad story.

"Shayna punim," Grandma Leah said to me, effectively changing a subject on which she preferred not to dwell, "you didn't invite a friend to the bar mitzvah?"

"No," I said. "I didn't want to."

"Lori, darling," interjected Ida from the Bronx, "don't worry. You'll be in high school soon, you'll make plenty of nice friends. No?"

"Ida!" Grandma Leah barked in her gravelly voice. "She's sixteen years old! She's *in* high school already. What's the matter with you?"

"Oy. Forgive me. I'm such a dope."

"Daniel," Grandma said, "you'll play a few songs later?"

"After dinner," Daniel explained.

"Leave him alone, Leah," Ida from the Bronx admonished. "He's having fun."

"He wants to play, Ida. My Daniel knows what he wants to do."

"But it's not his bar mitzvah."

"Steven doesn't mind, and everyone wants to hear. Am I right, Daniel?"

"Yup."

"Are your friends here to see you play?" asked Ida from the Bronx.

"Just one. Glenn Sheldon. The rabbi's son. My other friends are home. They'll come to *my* bar mitzvah."

"We should all live and be well," Grandma Leah said.

The bandleader announced that the candle-lighting ceremony was about to begin. The photographer positioned himself in front of the purple velvet-covered table. Daniel and I were called up to light two candles. Steven stood between us as together we used a tall white candle to light two other shorter ones. We all smiled. (I still have that photograph in my house, prominently displayed on the fireplace mantle.)

Our parents lit two candles, and so did both sets of grandparents. Then Uncle Milt and Aunt Paula—Milt was Mom's brother—lit a candle. They looked joyful and seemed happy. Dad's brother, our Uncle Jack, and his wife, Aunt Gloria, were up next. What a stark contrast between the two uncles; while Uncle Milt's smile was bright and genuine, Uncle Jack seemed totally incapable of forming a smile. (Grandpa Jesse once said about his son Jack that he was born without lip muscles.)

Finally, in one big group, all of Steven's friends lit the last three candles.

Dinner was served. Afterward, Glenn Sheldon once again recruited Daniel to leave the ballroom with him, but this time they went outside to the back of the building. First, they crossed a large brick patio and then they entered the parking lot beyond it, where two valet attendants eyed them suspiciously. It was only five o'clock and already dark outside, although dozens of tall poles with lights on top put the entire parking lot into an artificial daytime. Daniel and Glenn zigzagged through rows of cars pretending they were cops on motorcycles, and when they came to the Sheldons' white Plymouth, Glenn pulled something out of his pants pocket, opened the back door and threw it in.

"What was that?" Daniel asked.

"Nothing," Glenn said.

Glenn moved on, but Daniel glanced inside the car and saw a fuzzy blue sock puppet on the back seat.

Glenn stopped by a silver Cadillac. Its sleek shine under the mechanical glow had stopped him in his tracks.

"I found a Matchbox car yesterday that looks exactly like this," he stated proudly. "Want to come over tomorrow and see it?"

"Maybe after lunch," Daniel muttered. "Sometimes, I watch *The Bowery Boys* on TV with my dad."

"Really?"

"Yeah. Why? Don't you ever watch TV with your dad?"

"He's not home a lot."

Steven's friend Billy and another friend named Mike stood by the chain-link fence at the edge of the parking lot, smoking cigarettes. Daniel had assumed (as did I) that neither Steven nor any of his friends smoked. So the sight of the two of them puffing away on cigarettes, especially Billy, who Daniel knew and liked a lot, was a bit jarring for him.

"Don't worry, kid," Billy said. Apparently he had recognized the apprehensive look on Daniel's face. "Steven doesn't smoke. I swear to God, cross my heart, and hope to die."

"I know," Daniel said.

"Hey, Daniel," Billy continued, "did I hear that you're gonna play the piano?"

"In a few minutes, I think."

"Good. Can't wait. Just don't be better than me, or I'll have to kill you."

Just then, Dad came outside looking for Daniel. It was time for him to perform. So Daniel ran back inside and took his place behind the baby grand piano that was positioned to the side of the band platform. Over the microphone, the bandleader introduced him as "the little brother with a big surprise." Everyone stopped what they were doing. Daniel knew, having listened to the band earlier, that the rhythm section—the bass player and the drummer—would be able to back him up, even though they had neither rehearsed nor discussed the songs. He nodded to them; they seemed to have the same confidence.

Daniel began with "Where Is Love?" from the recent Broadway show *Oliver*, then played the theme from the movie *Exodus*. Several of the adults in the room had tears in their eyes when he reached the crescendo. That made him happy; it meant that what he did was working the way he had intended. Next, he played the popular ballad, "Roses are Red," and ended with an up-tempo composition of his own called "Little Star," which was basically a jazzed-up version of "Twinkle, Twinkle, Little Star."

Dad, at his table not far from the band platform, watched Daniel and the musicians on either side of him with an almost wistful look on his face. Mom chatted with her sister-in-law Paula, but glanced Daniel's way every once in a while to smile. The applause after the final number was loud, and several shouts of "Encore, encore" followed close behind.

The only off-key note was Steven's sudden absence.

When Daniel had first taken the platform, Steven had been sitting at the dais table with his friends. When "Where Is Love?" began, he walked out of the ballroom. I saw him leave and was certain that he merely had to go to the bathroom because of the limitless quantity of soda he drank all day. I'm sure Daniel felt the same. But as it turned out, Steven didn't return until long after "Little Star" had faded into memory.

.   .   .   .

Daniel was able to overlook the disappointment of Steven's sudden disappearance because in the days that followed the bar mitzvah, Rabbi Sheldon's promise of good things to come for the Hillman family did indeed seem to go from his lips to God's ears. We all took little steps forward—even me!—and that kept us all satisfied, for a few days, at least.

Dad's little step was a $350 holiday bonus that he received from LILCO, which he bashfully told us was the largest bonus any middle manager at the utility had ever received. He immediately put it in the family savings account.

A day later, Mom received a ten dollar Macy's gift certificate and a letter of appreciation from the PTA on behalf of the volunteer writing and editing she did for its newsletter. She used the gift certificate to buy picture frames for Steven's bar mitzvah photos, which she had picked up in the morning from the photographer's studio.

Steven's step was more like a leap: his second-semester report card had the best grades he had received in years. After he absorbed the good news, Steven folded the report card into a paper airplane and gave it flight whenever Mom and Dad walked by as a not-so-gentle reminder of their promise to let him take flying lessons when he got a little older.

Daniel's step was in the form of a paid performance. He was asked to lead a sing-along for youngsters at the opening of a new children's reading room at the local public library, which the library decided to call The Green Eggs and Ham Corner. The library paid Daniel one dollar, and the Westbrook Hills Times ran an article about it and a picture of Daniel by a piano surrounded by giant cardboard cutouts of Dr. Seuss characters. I hung the picture on the refrigerator between Steven's report card (which I rescued from being a paper airplane forever) and a menu from Mr. Wong's Chinese Restaurant (upon which Steven had written "For Jews Only" in magic marker).

My own modest stride concerned a new friend I had made on the block, Carla White. Carla, whose family recently moved to Westbrook Hills, didn't mind coming to our house to talk and do homework with me, and never once complained when I refused to go to hers.

"Very nice grades, Steven," said Grandpa Sol as he looked over Grandma Rose's shoulder at the report card taped to the refrigerator. "An A, two B's and three C's."

"And not a single solitary D or F!" Steven said.

I was in the living room with Daniel, who was practicing the piano. When he heard Grandpa Sol's comment about the A, two B's and three C's, he began to play the first few notes of a song called "The ABCs of Love" (which, as the story goes, was one of the songs he pounded out constantly on his toy piano when he was two).

"Not now, Daniel," Mom called out from somewhere else in the house. "I have too much to do."

"Let him play, Beverly," Grandpa urged.

"No. It's nice outside. It's like spring. Sixty-two degrees. Absolutely beautiful! Go find a friend, Daniel."

"I haven't finished practicing," he complained.

"Then finish and go outside. And bundle up! It's winter."

   •   •   •   •   •

Our family had known the Sheldons—the rabbi, his wife Helene and son Glenn—since I was nine years old. Daniel and Glenn first became friends when they were two, and then, as time went on, four other boys were added to the Pearl Drive group of friends. The others—Doug Kelleher, the twins Johnny and Joey DePuzo, and Craig Stuart—all lived within a few houses of each other on the block. They all were the same age. After he slipped out the front door of our house without bundling up, Daniel went to see which ones wanted to play with him.

Doug Kelleher lived directly across the street. He was the older of two boys in a family of five children. Steven called Doug's three older sisters N.I.T.s, for Nuns-in-Training. That stemmed from the fact that they wore uniforms to the Catholic schools they attended; also, on the few occasions our families saw each other at parades and other town events, the Kelleher sisters seemed to Steven to be overly prim and proper. Doug's five-year-old brother Michael suffered a crippling accident when he was a baby, and as a result had to spend his life in a wheelchair.

Johnny and Joey DePuzo lived further down the block, in a brick house that was the largest on Pearl Drive. It was owned by their grandfather, Salvatore Bonomo. The house had life-sized marble lion statues on either side of the cement driveway. Next to the garage was a brick archway over a path that led to the granite patio in the backyard. In essence, the DePuzo twins didn't live in a house as much as they lived in a twenty-four-hour showroom for Cross Island Mason Supply, the brick, stone, and concrete business run by their grandfather.

Craig Stuart lived three houses down. He had been left back in third grade. Dad once commented that Craig must have been held back because instead of books, his school bag was always packed with Twinkies, Yodels, Oreos, Tootsie Rolls, Drake's Cakes, and Ring Dings. I inadvertently glanced into Craig's school bag when he stopped at our house after school one day, and I'm afraid that Dad's quip wasn't too far from the truth.

At Doug's house, Alexis Kelleher, the oldest of Doug's three sisters, was at the side of their house when Daniel arrived there. She had just placed a kitchen garbage bag into a big silver trash can, and she told Daniel to follow her inside through the back door. In the kitchen, Mrs. Kelleher was combing Doug's light brown hair, even though it was so short that the comb hardly accomplished anything at all. Daniel asked Doug if he wanted to go with him to the elementary school to play on the hill.

"Hello, Daniel," Mrs. Kelleher interjected. The interjection was her way of telling Daniel that he was rude for not saying hello to her first when he had entered the kitchen.

Mrs. Kelleher wasn't particularly tall, but held her head so high and stood with such regal posture that she had a stately presence. Most kids on the block were intimidated by her. Mrs. Kelleher's manner was so cold that it was impossible to warm up to her, even though she was a pleasant-looking woman who never raised her voice. I hadn't become friends with any of the Kelleher sisters, and whenever I saw their mother in the front yard of their house, I silently prayed that I would never *have* to become friends with them.

"How was your brother's bar mitzvah?" Mrs. Kelleher asked Daniel.

"It was nice," he said.

"I'm sure you performed."

"Yes, I did."

"And I'm sure you made everyone happy."

"I guess."

Doug grabbed his coat, and he and Daniel walked to Craig's house. When they arrived, Craig stood behind the glass storm door eating an oversized frosted chocolate donut.

"We're going to the hill," Doug said. "Wanna come?"

"Can't," Craig said between bites. "We're having company. I'm making the dessert."

Craig's father suddenly appeared behind him.

"Hi, boys," he smiled. He was missing several teeth. "Craig can't play. We're having company over to eat."

"That's okay," Daniel said.

"See you around… Oh, hey—Daniel, how was your brother's party?"

"Really nice."

"Good food?"

"Yup."

"Did you play?"

"Yup. Four songs."

"Four? That's all?"

"It wasn't my bar mitzvah."

Mr. Stuart smiled again. The boys caught a whiff of freshly-baked corn muffins as they left the front steps.

At the DePuzo house, Joey opened the door just as Daniel and Doug arrived on the front stoop. They told him they were going to the hill.

"Where's Johnny?" Doug asked.

"He's sick," Joey said.

"Then how come *you're* not sick?"

"It doesn't always work like that. Everybody thinks that. I hate that. Meet me in the back. I have to get my coat."

The two boys ignored the gigantic lions as they walked through the brick archway. The lions may have been imposing long ago, but were now just lifeless blobs of stone. Sal Bonomo came out of the back door soon after Daniel and Doug arrived in the yard. He carried a box that said 'Christmas Lights' on the side. As always, Mr. Bonomo was impeccably dressed, with a black woolen sweater that had a double white stripe across the chest, and spotless black pants. His silver hair, which was still thick for a man in his upper sixties, was brushed straight back.

"Hello, boys," he said.

"Hi, Mr. Bonomo," Daniel and Doug said in unison.

"Hey, Daniel, how was your brother's bar mitzvah?"

"Good," Daniel said.

"Where was it?"

"The Huntington Chalet."

"Huntington Chalet... hmmm... let me think... crumbling stone wall along the circular driveway... brick patio in the back with weeds sticking out all over the friggin' place? Am I right?"

"I think," Daniel said.

"You played?"

"Yup."

"What you play?"

"'Where is Love' 'Exodus,' 'Roses Are Red' and one of my own songs."

"Next time you throw in some Sinatra. Kapish?" He pointed his finger at Daniel and winked. "By the way, how's your Uncle Nat? Was he there?"

"No. He was away on business."

"Oh yeah?"

"But he sent Steven two hundred dollars in the mail."

"Good. Family's important. Well," Mr. Bonomo grunted, "gotta go untangle these friggin' lights. Have fun, fellas." He disappeared into the garage.

Joey came out of the back door, and the three boys crossed the street to the Sheldon house. They knocked. Glenn opened the front door and said he'd be out in a few seconds. Even though he was no stranger to that front stoop, Doug for the first time noticed the little wooden ornament on the left side of the door, which had what to him were strange markings upon it. He asked Daniel if he knew what it was.

"It's a mezuzah," Daniel explained. "We have one on our front door, too. Haven't you ever seen it?"

"No," Doug said.

"It has a Hebrew message inside. It's for good luck. We're supposed to kiss it whenever we go in or out."

"That's disgusting," Doug sneered.

"No, it's not. My sister said that it's like a tiny shield that protects Jewish families. She even has one on her bedroom door."

Doug had already stopped listening to the explanation.

Glenn finally came outside, and the four boys walked to Westbrook Hills Elementary School, where they rolled down the steep hill at the side of the school building over and over again, like human logs. The ground was coarse and muddy in spots because of the recent snow flurries. But the hill was also speckled with fallen autumn leaves from the dozens of trees that lined each side of the hill, and those clusters of leaves gave them the momentum they needed. It was almost as if the leaves tried desperately to stretch out the hill's usefulness for fun, now that winter was approaching. The crunchy noise of the brittle brown leaves as the boys rolled over them seemed unusually loud, like hundreds of busy crickets. The four of them had fun but soon began to tire. Also, the temperature was dropping, along with the sun. Daniel was very cold.

"I think I'll go home now," he said.

"Not yet," Glenn urged.

"But my grandparents are over."

"Your grandparents are *always* over."

"Just ten more times down the hill," Joey suggested. "Till it gets a little darker."

"Okay."

It was at that moment that Daniel realized how it was not only the exhaustion and the chill that urged him home. The truth was that he felt slighted by his friends. Alienated. Different, somehow. He had been asked about his performance at Steven's bar mitzvah at each of the houses at which he stopped on the way to the hill, but by one mother, one father, and one grandfather—*not* by Doug, Craig, or Joey. And this despite the fact that Daniel always made sure to comment on Doug's G.I. Joe collection, Craig's experimental desserts, and the twins' backyard clubhouse (which, not surprisingly, was made of brick and sat on a cement platform).

"I think it just got a little darker," Daniel said after two more tumbles down the hill. "I'm going home."

"No, it didn't," Glenn muttered.

"Yes, it did. A little bit."

"Not yet," Glenn said. "Stay a little longer, Daniel."

"How about till it gets just one more darker?"

"Okay. Just one more darker."

It was a compromise on which they both could agree, though Daniel wasn't very happy about it.

Ten minutes later, Daniel walked home. But before he went into the house, he sat on the front lawn. A breeze picked up, which prompted him to sing "Blowin' in the Wind," a song that had been popular on the radio during the summer. Daniel liked the group that recorded it, Peter, Paul, and Mary, particularly their three-part harmony. But on the cool, damp grass, there were no other voices. Just his own. Even if Glenn or one of the other boys had been there with him, harmony would still be lacking, simply because they had no interest in what interested him.

> *"How many times must a man look up,*
> *Before he can see the sky?*
> *How many ears must one man have,*
> *Before he can hear people cry?*
> *The answer, my friend, is blowin' in the wind,*
> *The answer is blowin' in the wind."*

As he sang, Daniel looked up as the darkening sky started to obliterate whatever moonlight there was that night. It would have been nice for him to have someone with whom to harmonize.

"Why didn't you bundle up?" Grandma Rose shrieked from the front door, which she had opened wide after spying him through the living room window. Daniel went into the house. "Look at your cheeks," Grandma said, her voice tight and angry. "Red like tomatoes. And at nighttime yet. Oy gevalt, you'll catch pneumonia. What's the matter with you?"

"Geeve him a bisl soup," Grandpa Sol said from the kitchen, heaping on the Yiddish accent. "And a piece bread vit a schmear butter. Good for a cold."

Even though it was just forty minutes before dinner, Grandma forced Daniel to drink a bowl of chicken noodle soup at the kitchen table. She also wrapped a wool sweater around him and pulled it tightly across his chest. "Just to be sure," she said.

In the kitchen, I helped Grandma Rose prepare a pot roast. Mom rearranged the photos on the living room wall so that she could include Steven's bar mitzvah portrait. Steven was in the basement, building a glider for his junior high school science fair. The phone rang. Dad called out from the bedroom that he'd pick it up. He grumbled loudly that it was probably a crew chief at LILCO again. Twenty minutes later, he came out of the bedroom and seemed very annoyed.

"Morons," he said. "They can't even change a light bulb without an instruction book. You know, Beverly, when I go to the big generator in the sky, Long Island will be in the dark for months, until they figure it out for themselves." I despised hearing him use words like that, even in jest, and I told him so. He smirked.

Daniel finished his soup and went to the piano in the living room.

"Is it okay?" he asked Mom. "Can I play? Because yesterday you made me stop."

"Yes. Just not too loud," she said. "Maybe in five minutes you can go downstairs and practice your xylophone instead. Don't you have a lesson tomorrow?"

"Day after tomorrow," he said.

"Oh, that's right."

Mom had been warning him lately to keep the volume down, or to practice only when Grandma and Grandpa were back home in Queens, or when Dad was at work. What had once been a normal occurrence in the house had become something of an off-key refrain. So Daniel sat down at our black upright and, within ten minutes, wrote a song called "Whatever Happened to Harmony?"

•   •   •   •   •

As it turned out, Daniel's idea for a song title was prophetic: the following week there were quite a number of discordant notes for the three Hillman children.

My note was the bloodiest, though the blood, thank God, wasn't mine.

There was a new girl at my school named Adrianna Scutter. Adrianna began classes at Westbrook Hills High School in late November, even though there were only a few weeks left of the semester. She lived in Old Manor, a depressed residential area several miles to the north of Westbrook Hills, known for its ramshackle homes and garbage-littered playgrounds. No one seemed to know exactly why Adrianna transferred to Westbrook Hills. Like me, she was a junior. Starting on Adrianna's very first day, kids made fun of her clothes, which were torn, and her hair, which was unkempt. But she was courageous in the face of it all. I admired that and summoned all the courage I could find to approach Adrianna in the hallway and introduce myself. As Adrianna and I began to talk, two seniors, a short one and a tall one, started to taunt her. Adrianna ignored them at first, but after a few more minutes of the most demeaning insults, she hurled both of the thick textbooks she was carrying directly at their faces and shouted,

"Shut the fuck up, you fucking asshole lesbian bitches."

Blood poured out of the nose of the short girl, and the tall one fell down and twisted her ankle so severely that she screamed out "God fucking dammit!" in agony. The hallway filled almost instantly with giggling students and outraged teachers. One teacher grabbed Adrianna and me by our arms and dragged us to the main office. The teacher forced us onto the notorious wooden bench just outside the principal's door. We were told to sit there until Dr. Donaldson came out of his office, and that we would have detention that afternoon and probably for several afternoons even beyond that. I cried. The tears were swift and automatic. Adrianna, who at first had seemed appreciative of my effort to be friendly, moved to the other side of the bench and ignored me.

Then there was Steven, over at the junior high school.

He was sitting in Mr. Berger's history class racking his brain for a good way to explain to Mom and Dad why he received an F that day on his World War II report. Steven truly thought that Mr. Berger, who was known for his love of cars and trucks, would appreciate all the information he provided in the report about Jeeps, Sherman tanks, and Flying Fortresses, even though the assignment had nothing to do with Jeeps, Sherman tanks, and Flying Fortresses. Steven worried that the F would be looked upon as a signal that his recent report card was a fluke, and he feared Mom and Dad's disappointment. He knew their promise to let him take flying lessons would be in serious jeopardy.

Finally, there was Daniel's own installment of The Day Without Harmony.

He had signed up to sing and play the piano for the elementary school's annual talent show that day. Miss Sang, his fourth-grade teacher, a former professional violinist, had started the tradition a few years earlier. To most students, Miss Sang was a drill sergeant, a humorless, no-nonsense classroom witch who made every day longer than it really was. But to Daniel, she was a warm and friendly mentor, for she recognized from the first day of school that he was the only one in her class with whom she could have a conversation about three-quarter time and diminuendos. At least once a week, Grandpa Sol asked Daniel, "So, did Miss Sang sing today?" He adored her name as much as Daniel treasured her friendship. Daniel considered Miss Sang a very special friend.

School legend had it that Miss Sang became an accomplished violinist in her native China, but in college, she developed a rare muscle condition in her left hand that prompted her family to come to the United States for treatment. Unfortunately, she was never able to regain full dexterity in that hand. She stayed in America to become a private music teacher. But she had difficulty even with that, so she became an elementary school teacher instead. As the story goes, she was bitter about that, which triggered the harsh personality for which she had become known at Westbrook Hills Elementary School.

Early in the day, no one in class knew that Daniel was going over the lyrics of "Loco-Motion" in his head while the class recited "The Pledge of Allegiance." Like everyone else, he stared at the American flag so that no one would catch on. To the right of the flag were portraits of George Washington, Abraham Lincoln, and John F. Kennedy, and to the left of the flag was the public address speaker. Daniel knew that just after lunch, an announcement would come over that little speaker about the talent show. He was ready for it. The speaker was nearly invisible because it was up high and painted the same light green color as the walls. But *he* knew it was there, and he considered it his *other* secret special friend in the classroom.

In the middle of a multiplication lesson, the speaker finally crackled with the formal and familiar voice of the principal, Dr. Eugenie Smith:

"Will those students who signed up for the talent show please report to the gymnasium."

A girl named Betsy Rossi (another name Grandpa Sol loved) grabbed her flute from under her desk and popped up from her chair. Daniel also stood up, and together they walked to the door.

"Good luck, children," Miss Sang called after them.

Daniel and Betsy quickly made their way to the gymnasium, which doubled as the auditorium. As they arrived, two janitors were wheeling an upright piano onto the little stage in the front of the room. One pushed, the other pulled. Metal folding chairs had already been set up in fifteen rows across the gym floor. Within two or three minutes, all twelve students who had signed up for the talent show had arrived, followed by the principal.

Dr. Smith had been the principal since Westbrook Hills Elementary opened in 1952; some people joked that she hadn't changed her clothes, shoes, or hairstyle since the day she arrived. Dr. Smith always seemed on edge, as if too many people were constantly asking her too many questions. (I was well aware of this personality trait, having been a student there for six years, plus kindergarten. Whenever I had a crying incident, which was almost daily, being forced to explain why to Dr. Smith made me cry even more.) After the principal gave some instructions to the twelve students who were to perform in the talent show, she asked if everything was clear.

"Will someone be able to test the mike for a level before we start?" Daniel asked.

"Daniel," Dr. Smith said as she closed her eyes, "the microphone will be fine."

Over the course of the next ten minutes, every class at the school was ushered into the gym and seated row by row. Daniel waved to Miss Sang when he saw her walk into the auditorium with the class. Once all the chairs were filled, the teachers stood against the side wall, though none of them too far from the row of students for which they were responsible. Then the show began.

With a toy maraca in hand, Timmy Ziegler, a first grader, accompanied himself to "Old MacDonald," and he did it with much spunk, although in his version the cows quack-quacked here and the ducks woof-woofed there. The students laughed, but little Timmy didn't seem to mind. Pamela Bellachanski, a fifth grader, played "Oh, Susanna" on her accordion, and she did it well—although the silences during which she carefully repositioned her fingers on the keys and chord buttons made the song three times longer than it should have been. Carolyn Clarke danced to the "Sugar Plum Fairy" movement from *The Nutcracker* ballet. A record was played from backstage, and Carolyn's performance was marred only for a few seconds when she had to do three double pirouettes to the part of the record that skipped. Betsy Rossi played "I Feel Pretty" from *West Side Story* on her flute. A sixth-grade boy in the audience whispered to the boy next to him that Betsy may have *felt* pretty but sure as hell didn't *look* pretty. Miss Sang heard the boy's whisper and sent him to sit in the main office for the rest of the talent show.

Daniel was introduced next and performed "Loco-Motion." It was a good choice because, while it was a simple tune for him to sing and play, it was also a natural audience pleaser.

After Daniel performed, seven other students took the stage. When the talent show was over, Daniel joined his class in the hallway outside the auditorium. Miss Sang assembled them into two even lines to lead them back to the classroom. Several classmates told Daniel that he did a good job. When she was convinced that everyone else was preoccupied, Miss Sang rubbed Daniel's head and gave him a smile and a wink. He looked forward to a few more of those smiles and winks before the day was over.

As the double line turned from one hallway to another, Miss Sang stopped to let the stragglers catch up. That's when a boy named Randy Brogan leaned over to Daniel and said,

"I heard your foot. It was really loud."

Daniel continued to look straight ahead.

"You were tapping loud," Randy continued. "Your foot was tapping really loud. Like this—" and he proceeded to pound his foot several times onto the tile floor with heavy thumps. "You looked retarded. It was louder than the piano. It sounded really stupid."

Daniel turned toward him.

"My foot wasn't tapping loud at all," he said.

"Yes, it was. Boom boom boom. That's all I heard. Boom boom boom. You sounded like a moron or something."

"Randall," Miss Sang said sternly, "please stop talking. Come along, class."

Back in the classroom, Miss Sang began a lesson on the continents. Usually, Daniel asked and answered many questions, but suddenly felt like doing neither. He kept quiet. Miss Sang glanced over at him once or twice but said nothing.

Moments later, the loudspeaker crackled once again with Dr. Smith's voice, which was unusual for that time of day, especially since there were no more special events, and dismissal was more than an hour-and-a-half away.

"Boys and girls," the principal began slowly, "teachers and all staff members… I have a very important announcement." She cleared her throat—twice. "President Kennedy… President Kennedy has been shot. I am sorry to say… I am sorry to say that he has died." Daniel looked at Miss Sang. She had put her hand over her mouth, and it froze there. "We are therefore dismissing classes early today. Any student who knows their mother will not be home, please report to the main office before you leave the school. Bus students, please meet at your normal spot in the circular driveway. Everyone else, walk home safely. And please—I would like for all of us to pray for Mrs. Kennedy, for her children, and for the United States of America."

Then the bell rang.

A similar announcement had been made at my school and also at Steven's. Since Westbrook Hills High School was closer than the others, I arrived home first. Mom was in the living room, staring blankly at the black & white television set. I walked over to her but didn't quite know what to do. I cried, and when I saw *her* crying, I cried even more. Steven walked into the house five minutes later, and Daniel a few minutes after that. We all stared at the television set in dreadful silence. On channel two, an emotional Walter Cronkite struggled to listen to reports coming into his headphones and to choose the right words to report to his listeners across the country.

"Awful. Just awful," Mom said as I held her. Her words clearly had anger as much as sadness in them. "Disgusting, what people do. Disgusting." She had a tissue in one hand and wiped her eyes and nose with it repeatedly.

"I'd like to find out who did it," Steven said. "I'll kill the fucker with my bare hands."

"Steven—" Mom said.

"I would. I swear to God. I'd snap his goddamned neck. I'd snap it in half."

Mom said she was going to her bedroom to rest. That was something she had never done before in the middle of an afternoon. She left the three of us alone in the living room. It was difficult to see her so full of sorrow—more painful, perhaps, than the news itself.

Certainly my brothers had seen me cry a thousand times before, but this time there was an extra element of misery about it, which I suppose made it seem to them an even more desperate situation. Neither knew how much I had already wept in school that day because of the Adrianna Scutter incident, but I'm certain it was obvious to them that *something* had happened to make these newer tears all the more bitter.

Steven, in that moment, became much more than just a new teenager; now he was a teenager with an almost stereotypical fury and resentment brewing inside. Maybe it wasn't that moment that did it; maybe it had started in school when he received a deplorable grade simply for following his instincts and exploring his passion. Or maybe it had started even earlier than that. We'll never know.

Daniel felt suddenly very lost and all alone. Originally his plan had been to come home from school and tell the entire family about his performance at the talent show, and about the special smiles and winks that Miss Sang shared with him until the final bell. He had always been able to count on our family to listen and to appreciate these things as much as he did. But Mom was behind her closed bedroom door, Steven seemed on the verge of exploding, and I was entirely helpless. Besides, the school day ended early; there *were* no additional secret smiles and winks to tell anyone about. There was nothing to share.

Things had changed. But who was to blame? I'm not sure that Steven took even a moment to consider anyone in particular, for he was too full of rage to think rationally. I remember asking God for some advice, but my head was so achy that I was unable to imagine a response. As for Daniel, many choices swirled through his mind. He could blame Randy Brogan if he wanted to, or perhaps Dr. Smith. Walter Cronkite was another possibility, or even Miss Sang, whose only crime was to dismiss class after the announcement was made. There was even Mom, who made the awful mistake of keeping the television on after Walter Cronkite had interrupted *Search for Tomorrow*.

So he decided to blame them all.

# Two

Elvis Presley was next on Steven's neck-snapping wish list.

Steven had a crush on Ann-Margret, the shapely actress who was very popular at the time. I might not swear to it, but I was fairly certain that Dad and Daniel were equally infatuated with her. As a family, we had seen Ann-Margret in the movie musical *Bye, Bye, Birdie*, and in the spring of 1964, we went to see another musical, *Viva Las Vegas*, in which she starred with Elvis Presley. A few weeks later, Life magazine arrived in the mail with an article about the two stars, and one of the photos showed Elvis and Ann-Margret resting comfortably on a park bench, his greasy head on her lap. Elvis looked quite content. It's important to note that Steven didn't like Elvis to begin with. He didn't like the way he sang, the way he twitched his hips, or the way he snarled his lip. He didn't like the fact that girls who had not yet jumped on the Beatles bandwagon considered Elvis a deity, or that Elvis got to drive trucks, race speedboats, tool around on motorcycles and fly airplanes in all of his movies. So when Steven saw that photo in the magazine, he decided that Elvis's neck had to be snapped in half. He said so half a dozen times in the house.

Daniel wasn't much of an Elvis fan, either. I don't think he cared much one way or another about the records; I do know that he had an interest in discovering how stars like Elvis Presley became stars in the first place. It was clear to me that articles about his rise in fame were more appealing to Daniel than the fact that he could carry a tune and curl his upper lip. As for me, I still mourned for President Kennedy and looked forward to hearing Rabbi Sheldon talk on the High Holy Days in September; there just wasn't room on my list to like or dislike Elvis Presley.

One Saturday, after her beauty parlor appointment, Mom stopped at the five-and-ten-cent store on Miller Avenue to buy a dozen magazines to take with us on our summer vacation, which was about to begin. That would help pass the time on the long ride up to the Catskill Mountains, and it would also come in handy if there were any rainy days while we were away. Mom knew that Steven had a crush on Ann-Margret, and she assumed that Dad and Daniel were smitten, as well. So she purchased five magazines that featured the sultry redhead on their covers. But Mom was unaware of Steven's bloodthirsty tendencies toward Elvis Presley, and what she didn't know was that two of the magazines also talked about the actress's relationship with him. I discovered Mom's faux pas before the trip and tried to hide those two magazines, but she found them and returned them to the carrying bag that was eventually placed on the back floor of the car.

We were scheduled to stay at Ehrlich's Hotel and Bungalow Colony for nine days. Ehrlich's, which had been a popular Catskill destination since 1939, was in a village called Kiamesha Lake. Dad, busier than ever at LILCO, planned to stay with us for the first three days and last two. He'd remain on Long Island for the four days in between so that he could go to work. Mom thought that he should put his foot down and tell his boss at LILCO that he deserved nine full days of vacation. Three days before our scheduled departure, Mom and Dad had an argument about it.

"It's just not right, Murray," she had complained that afternoon, while Daniel and I sat with them in the living room.

"Beverly," Dad sighed, "the reason the rest of you can go for nine days is because I work hard on four of them to make the money it costs to go in the first place."

"I know that Murray, but what about you? Your mental health? Spending time with your family?"

"Beverly—"

"Murray, it's not like you're asking for something you're not entitled to—"

"Lori will graduate high school soon, Beverly. What then? Can we afford college right now? Is the College of Pearl Drive in our basement and I just never knew about it? Then Daniel's bar mitzvah is in three years. Where do you want to have it—at Howard Johnson's? You keep talking about tutors for Steven. What'll we pay with—your mother's kreplach? And do you want to be the one to tell Daniel that he can't take piano and guitar and xylophone lessons anymore? We can hardly afford them *now*."

"Murray, you still deserve a vacation."

"Stop Murraying me!"

"I'm not Murraying you. Forget it. It's over."

Daniel and I left the living room to go to our separate bedrooms.

"I hate it when Dad yells," I whispered on the way.

The fact was that it happened so rarely that whenever it did, it was usually accompanied by a wounded look on Mom's face, which I hated even more than the yelling itself.

"Are you gonna watch *Hollywood Palace* with me tonight?" Daniel asked when we reached our respective bedroom doors. I sensed his desire to hold on to as many comforting traditions in the house as possible, one of which was watching variety shows on television. I, too, adored traditions. Until recently, Dad and I, and sometimes Steven and Grandpa Sol, watched at least two variety shows on television with Daniel every week. Often we would ask him questions about songs and instruments and other musical matters from those shows, and it always made Daniel feel special and proud to be able to answer them with expertise. He was especially eager to watch *Hollywood Palace* that night because a new rock 'n roll group called the Rolling Stones was scheduled to be on. The Beatles, who had appeared on the scene only a few months before, were already enormously popular, but it had been rumored in the newspapers that this new group of shaggy-haired young men from England might soon rival John, Paul, George, and Ringo in popularity. Daniel wanted to see what all the fuss was about. So later that night, with Mom and Dad's little fight forgotten, we all met in the living room. Dad turned on the television. After several commercials, Dean Martin, the host of that night's episode, introduced the band.

"So this is the group that you and the rest of the world want to see, Daniel?" Mom asked as she settled into the couch. "The Falling Rocks, or whatever? Well, I guess I'll see this nonsense for myself."

"Rolling Stones," I corrected her.

"Falling Rocks, Rolling Stones, what's the difference?"

The Rolling Stones, whose manner and appearance seemed to alarm and annoy even the typically cool and suave Dean Martin, played a song called "I Just Wanna Make Love to You."

"It's just not right, singing a song like that on television for everyone to hear," Mom complained. "It's just not right."

Steven rolled his eyes and left the living room. He went to the basement to work on a model of the PT-109, the torpedo boat that John Kennedy had commanded in World War II. Dad nodded off in the easy chair. Mom picked up Good Housekeeping magazine and started to flip through. I watched with Daniel for a while, but then quietly picked up a book that I had earlier placed on the end table next to the couch. It was by the Yiddish author Sholem Aleichem; Rabbi Sheldon stopped by the house one day to loan it to me. But I didn't divert my attention to the book entirely because I didn't want Daniel to think that I was disinterested in the show.

"Well?" Daniel asked to no one in particular when the Rolling Stones left the stage. "What did we think?"

I looked up from my book and smiled. "Interesting," I said. Mom looked up from the magazine and yawned. Dad snored.

•          •          •

We piled into the Galaxie on a hot August morning for the two-hour trip to the Catskill Mountains. Ehrlich's Hotel and Bungalow Colony had been our vacation destination every summer since 1958. Grandpa Jesse and Grandma Leah drove up to the Catskills the day before we left Westbrook Hills and said they'd meet us in the lobby at Ehrlich's when we arrived.

This vacation was to be a little different from Ehrlich getaways of summers past, simply because this time it was also the site of a Lebitz Family Foundation reunion. Lebitz was Grandma Leah's maiden name and the name of the family organization founded by her father and uncles in 1911 as a way to help their Eastern European relatives assimilate into American life. And although the founders were dead and the assimilation complete, the Lebitz Family Foundation was still very much alive. Dozens of Grandma Leah's relatives would be at Ehrlich's that week, and many of the events would be geared exclusively for the extended family.

Grandpa Jesse was friendly both with the owner and the entertainment director of Ehrlich's, and he performed at the hotel's nightclub, The Bluebird, once or twice every summer. It was not uncommon for Old Man Ehrlich to ask Mom or Dad if Daniel could also perform one night during our annual summer stay. Mom never had the heart to refuse, although I'm sure she was tempted.

Steven enjoyed our Ehrlich vacations, too, because he loved to hike in the woods behind the hotel and drive the electric golf cart that the maintenance man used on the grounds. Steven would drive the cart up and down hills (he flipped it over once, but thank God wasn't hurt) and around the ponds and sometimes through the woods. He usually did so without permission, which Old Man Ehrlich did not much appreciate.

I hardly ever made a friend at Ehrlich's, but I very much enjoyed the clean, pine-scented air as I read books on the white, deeply reclining Adirondack chairs on the grounds and listened to the adults chat. They chatted mostly in Yiddish, and while I had never been taught the language, I picked up enough over the years to be able to make out the gist of most of their animated and often very funny conversations. It's such a comforting language. The guests, all of them Jewish, were comforting, too, in their way, which made me feel at home, as Rabbi Sheldon had once suggested.

In the car on the ride up, I continued to read my Sholem Aleichem book while Steven and Daniel flipped through most of the magazines that Mom had bought along. At one point, a little more than an hour into the trip, Steven saw a photo of Elvis Presley and grumbled "Goddamn snake" under his breath. Dad told him to watch his language. The magazine Daniel was reading had an article about Ray Bradbury, an author he had recently discovered in the library. (Daniel had finished reading Bradbury's "Something Wicked This Way Comes" the day before we left for vacation.) On the facing page was an article about a new passenger jet called the Boeing 727. When Steven glanced over at Daniel's magazine and saw the headline and a photo of the jet airplane, he lost even more interest in Elvis who, of course, didn't interest him at all in the first place.

"Give me that magazine, and you can have this one," Steven demanded.

"In a little while," Daniel said. "I'm reading something interesting."

"Two minutes," Steven countered. "You have to listen to me because I'm older."

"Well, since you're older, you should take out the garbage more than I do."

"What does that have to do with anything? Stop being a jerk."

"You stop being a jerk."

"Boys!" Dad snapped from the front. "Stop it! Now! Daniel, give Steven the magazine. Steven, give it back to Daniel in five minutes."

Both did as instructed.

Usually, the three of us grew excited whenever we started to see the first of several billboards that dotted the highway as we got closer to our destination. The billboards had giant photos or caricatures on them of Jerry Lewis, Patti Paige, Alan King, Eddie Fisher, Totie Fields, and dozens of other performers who urged us on up to one hotel or another. That meant that we were finally *in* the mountains. But this time, Jerry Lewis didn't do the trick. Nor did Patti, Alan, Eddie, or Totie. The reason was that Steven had refused to give Daniel the magazine back after five minutes, and Daniel screamed at him and called him an asshole.

"I said stop it, you two," Dad warned, "or you'll both stay in the room for the first two days. Understand?"

"Murray," Mom said, "stop yelling."

"Then tell your sons to behave."

"We'll be there soon."

"Forty-five minutes is soon? Not when kids are acting like animals. Then it's not soon."

"Murray—"

"Stop Murraying me, Beverly."

• • • • •

When we arrived at Ehrlich's, Grandma Leah and Grandpa Jesse were waiting for us in the lobby, as they promised they would. I sat with them while Mom got the key to the room, and while Steven and Daniel helped Dad unload the car. Once all the suitcases had been brought to our third-floor room, the family joined forces to put things away in dressers and closets as quickly as possible.

The room, which was in the main building, was really two bedrooms connected by a tiny hallway. The hallway had a small bathroom on one side. Mom and Dad's was the larger room, which had a television set; the room I shared with Steven and Daniel had two beds and a fold-away cot.

"Listen, children," Mom said when we were all assembled in the big room, "you'll be nice to all the relatives. Steven, don't treat everyone like they're boring you to death. Daniel, don't hang out by the piano all day long. Lori, you'll try to make some friends."

"Not a lot of crying this summer," Dad said to me as gently as possible.

"Come on, Lori," Steven said as he pulled me into the hallway. "Let's go see if they did anything new to the pool."

"What about Daniel?" I asked.

"He won't want to come. He's still mad at me about that stupid magazine."

Daniel was just five feet away from him when he said it. He sat on the oversized windowsill and looked out at the parking lot—but said nothing. Neither did I, which almost instantly I regretted. I left the room with Steven. Daniel remained, forced to listen to Mom tell Dad which of his relatives she hoped to see and which ones she hoped would get sunstroke so that they'd have to go home early to seek medical help.

"From your lips to God's ears," Dad said.

While Steven and I looked over the outdoor pool (which hadn't changed at all since the summer before; the broken blue tiles on the floor along the shallow side were still broken), Daniel went on his own to the lobby, where Grandma Leah chatted with her sister Greta. Grandma kissed him, and Greta told him how big he was getting. Then he went to the other side of the lobby and was grabbed by Grandpa Jesse, who was quick and agile for his age. Grandpa had been talking to two distant Lebitz cousins from Boston.

"Come, sit, schmooze," Grandpa said to Daniel, "I want to tell you something, but let me finish my story first." He turned back to the two Boston cousins. "Where was I? Oh yeah—the club. So I'm in this jazz quartet downtown. Playing trumpet. I'm on a break, talking with the drummer. Ziggy Cohen. Suddenly these old fellas come in. Some Jews, some Italians. They take a booth in the back. So Ziggy and me, we sit behind the divider, where we can hear everything they're saying. And what do we hear? Guess. You'll never guess. They're planning to fix the 1919 World Series. Must've been Arnold Rothstein and his men. You know—Arnold Rothstein, the Jewish gangster!"

"No!" exclaimed one of the husbands.

Grandpa Jesse raised his right hand.

"As God is my witness," he said.

"They could've killed you."

"What are you talking, kill us… They never knew we were there. Right after, we went back to play a few tunes. They sat and listened. They liked us."

"Where was Nat at the time?" the other cousin asked.

"Nat was a kid," Grandpa said. "Nine, ten years old. He was probably in school—if he wasn't stealing candy from another store."

The cousins laughed.

"I heard Nat might be here this weekend," one of them added.

"Oy gevalt," the other replied.

Grandpa Jesse finally let go of Daniel's arm and introduced him to the two distant cousins.

"Having a good time?" Grandpa asked.

"Not yet," Daniel responded.

"You will. Take a look at The Bluebird when you get a chance. You'll plotz. Old Man Ehrlich finally fixed it up. New lights, new sound system. You'll feel like a real pro in there. He said you can perform Tuesday night, before the comedian. He asked me to do a few numbers Wednesday night. They got some lousy dance act—he wants me to save the night."

Daniel returned to our room. Mom and Dad were gone, but I walked in just as he climbed up on the windowsill. Steven wasn't with me; he had gone off on his own to look for the electric golf cart to commandeer.

"That's exactly where I left you," I said in an attempt to make it sound lighthearted.

Daniel didn't look at me.

"What's the matter?"

"Nothing…."

"Something."

"How come you didn't ask me to go see the pool with you?" he asked. He had finally glanced my way.

"You were resting," I said. "I thought you were tired."

"Liar. I heard Steven say he didn't want to ask me. I like the pool too, you know."

"I know you do," I said. "I'm sorry. I really am." I backed quietly into the smaller room, certain my tears would begin to flow. I managed to hold them in. But then I heard Daniel crying in the bigger room, and that was the end of that.

• • • • •

We both tried gallantly to forget that first afternoon and start fresh in the morning. Daniel, Mom, and I went for a walk around the hotel grounds before breakfast. It was already warm outside, but Mom didn't complain, nor did she mind the gentle hills over which the paths rose and fell. In the half hour it took us to circle the few acres of property, Mom covered at least half a dozen topics, such as which college brochures I should write away for, which of Steven's courses next term might require tutors, whether or not it was right to have Daniel play the piano at a PTA meeting that she was helping to plan, and what could possibly encourage Helene Sheldon to wear such provocative clothing.

"Does she want to be fruitful and multiply with all the men in the congregation? Because with her bosom sticking out to here, that's just what they'll want to do," Mom said as we completed the course. "I don't understand some people. It's just not right."

"But she's nice," I said. "Isn't she? I don't think Rabbi Sheldon would marry someone who wasn't nice. Do you?"

Mom simply smiled. "Lori, Lori, Lori," she said. "Let's talk about something else."

So she changed the subject and then surprised us when she said that she was pretty confident about the way things would turn out for everyone.

"*Pretty* confident?" I asked.

"I never like to sound *too* confident," Mom replied. "God doesn't like too much confidence. I know that for a fact. It's just not right."

But beyond that simple piece of advice, Mom didn't lecture us. Other mothers might have found an opening for a good old-fashioned lecture about one thing or another, and other mothers would have been zapped of strength by then and forced to retire to the lobby to sit out the rest of the day. But our mom was thoughtful and strong, and we were proud that she was our mother. I even told her that.

"Well," Mom sighed, "I'll just be very happy if everyone stays healthy."

"Why?" I asked, suddenly a bit anxious. "Is someone sick?"

As curiously as the day had begun, it got more interesting as the hours moved forward. First, I made a friend named Rebecca Fishbein, a sixteen-year-old who seemed ready to take on the world. Although that was an aspect of her personality that scared me, I tried hard to keep up with Rebecca. Then, Steven paired off with a boy named Drew Friedman, whose father was a famous ophthalmologist in New York City. Dr. Friedman gave Drew and Steven forty dollars worth of quarters to play the pinball machines in Ehrlich's concession room. They were gone for hours after that.

But most importantly, Daniel met Carol.

•     •     •     •     •

We had lunch with Grandma Leah and Grandpa Jesse. When we were finished, Daniel left the dining hall and walked down the hotel's long dirt driveway to a duck pond a few yards in from where cars turn off the main road. Carol appeared as if out of nowhere. They introduced themselves, and then Carol asked Daniel if she could sit with him. They sat on one of the many algae-green boulders that surrounded the pond.

Carol wore white shorts and a blue sleeveless blouse, and Daniel had on blue shorts and a white polo shirt, which made it seem as if they had somehow coordinated their clothes earlier that day. Carol's blouse, however, was patched in several places, and her shorts were ripped. She had faded pink ribbons around each of her pigtails and was barefoot. Daniel knew she wasn't a guest at the hotel; after all, Carol was black, and in all the years we had been going to Ehrlich's there had never been a black family that stayed there.

She said that her father was the new maintenance man at the hotel, and that she lived with him in a small cabin about a mile away, but that they ate and often even slept in a little maintenance shack on the outer edge of the Ehrlich property. Carol said that her father called the maintenance shack The Chapel because of the angular way it was built; the front of it, she said, looked like a little, broken-down church. As soon as she finished her explanation, Carol began to sing a song that was popular on the radio at the time called "Chapel of Love." Daniel knew in an instant, beyond any doubt, that he had just made a new best friend—at least for the next eight days.

"The Dixie Cups!" he announced when Carol started to sing the song. That was the name of the group that recorded the song.

"Yup," Carol responded. "I love them!"

They sang the rest of the first verse together:

*"Goin' to the chapel and we're*
*Gonna get married.*
*Goin' to the chapel and we're*

*Gonna get married.*
*Gee, I really love you and we're*
*Gonna get married.*
*Goin' to the chapel of love."*

"Sometimes listening to the radio is the only thing I can do in The Chapel," Carol said—and there was no sadness in her voice when she said it. "I know all the songs and who sings them and everything. Sometimes I make up songs. Sometimes, when I miss my mama, I sit on the grass and look up at the sky and make up a song, and that makes me feel better."

"Me too," Daniel said excitedly. "Except my mother doesn't like it when I lay on the grass because my clothes get stains on them."

"My daddy don't care about that."

"How come?"

"We ain't got no washing machine anyway."

Together they watched the sun disappear behind a thick cumulous cloud and then reappear with such intensity that Carol had to shield her eyes. The sudden brightness reminded Daniel of a song that Grandpa Jesse always sang called "You Are My Sunshine." He began the verse and, a moment later, Carol joined in with the harmony:

*"You are my sunshine, my only sunshine.*
*You make me happy when skies are gray.*
*You'll never know, dear, how much I love you.*
*Please don't take my sunshine away."*

In the second verse, Carol sang the melody and Daniel harmonized. When they finished that verse, Daniel felt as if he had sailed through that cumulous cloud and went right to heaven, and that Carol, whom he had met only ten minutes before, was the ray of sunshine that propelled him there.

As the afternoon wore on, Daniel and Carol finally left the pond and began to walk along one of the paths that surrounded the property. (I saw the two of them out of the lobby window and was struck by the unplanned synchronization of their outfits.)

"Do you write your songs down?" Daniel asked Carol. "The ones you make up?"

"Sometimes," she responded. "But I remember most of them, anyway. Do you write yours down?"

"Yup. Music and lyrics."

Carol picked a small pine branch off the ground as they walked and twirled the needles between her fingers. "Do you keep pencils and napkins in your pocket?" she asked.

"No. Why?"

"So's you can write down songs when they pop into your head. That's what Chubby Checker does. He said so on the radio. Who teached you how to write songs?"

"No one, really. We just always had a lot of instruments and stuff. My grandfather was a musician, and so was my father."

"No one teached me, either. But everyone always sings in my family. Hey, what's the last song you wrote?"

"I was gonna write something about grandmothers. But I didn't even start it yet."

"I got a grandma in Georgia. I was gonna write a poem about her cause she likes to write poems."

"Really?"

"Actually, I guess they ain't poems. She writes down things that happen to her, and then she reads them like they's poems."

"I thought of doing that, too."

"My grandma even writes down her dreams. Do you dream a lot, Daniel?"

"I don't know if they're dreams or if I'm just thinking about things before I fall asleep. I think about all kinds of things. I guess I'll turn them into songs one day. Or stories. Or something. I don't really know."

The hotel's lone little playground appeared in the distance when they rounded a corner of the property.

"Wanna play?" Daniel asked Carol. He pointed toward the swings.

"Sure!" Carol said.

Before long they tried out every ancient piece of equipment in the playground while they talked and harmonized to songs they both knew from the radio.

"You're interesting," Daniel said to her.

Carol lowered her head. She was embarrassed.

A few minutes later, on an old wooden seesaw, Carol said,

"I had a dream last night that my daddy got me a new white dress and that I wore it to the church in Georgia where my grandma lives, and that they let me sing all by myself in front of everybody for hours and hours. And everybody was happy, and kids came over to me because they wanted to play with me, and all the grownups were nice to me…"

"I bet that will happen one day," Daniel said. "Even if you don't get the dress. And anyway, you can always sing in your *own* Chapel right here!"

"I guess…" she smiled faintly.

Up and down they went, slowly, on the old, splintered seesaw.

"Who's your favorite singer?" Daniel asked.

"I got lots," Carol answered. "Chubby Checker. Bobby Darin, Ray Charles. A bunch of others. What about you?"

"I like Bobby Darin, too. And Pete Seeger. And a lot of groups, like the Beach Boys and the Yardbirds. Sometimes I make believe that I'm playing with them—that I'm the first kid to be in a grown-up band."

"Is that one of your dreams?"

"I don't know."

"Isn't there a song about dreams?" Carol asked.

"Yes! The Everly Brothers."

Carol was on the up end of the seesaw, and Daniel kept her up there while he sang:

*"When I want you in my arms,*
*When I want you and all your charms,*
*Whenever I want you, all I have to do is dream.*
*Dream dream dream. Dream…"*

He let the seesaw down, and Carol joined him in the song as they continued to go up and down, singing in perfect harmony:

*"When I feel blue in the night,*
*And I need you to hold me tight,*
*Whenever I want you, all I have to do is dream.*
*Dream dream dream. Dream…"*

When they both slid off the seesaw, Carol noticed a huge stain under her arms. "Jeez Louise," she smiled, "I'm sweating like a pig."

Daniel looked under his own arms. "Me too!" he said. "Maybe we should go swimming to cool off."

"In the pond?"

"No, silly. The pond's too slimy. In the pool."

Carol's face dropped. "I can't," she said.

"Why not? It's so hot. And there aren't a lot of kids here this summer. The pool's almost empty."

"Think it would be all right?" She kept her chin down but raised her eyes, as if she had done something naughty.

"A pool's for kids, isn't it? And we're kids," Daniel said.

"I got a bathing suit in The Chapel. Sometimes I go in the pond at night when everyone's at dinner."

"Go put it on," Daniel urged. "I'll meet you at the pool in five minutes."

And with that, Carol ran across the field toward The Chapel. Daniel went back to our room in the main building to put on his own bathing suit.

I was at the pool with Rebecca Fishbein when Daniel arrived. We were not yet in the water but merely trying to decide if we wanted to make the effort. Mom, Dad, and several Lebitz relatives were also there, on chaise lounges, chatting in the shade under the green and white awning. After a few moments, Carol bounded down the hill in a faded, threadbare yellow bathing suit. The chattering stopped.

"Ready?" Daniel called out to her.

"Yup!" Carol said—and they jumped into the water together.

I watched them splash around for a moment, but out of the corner of my eye I saw Lenore Zwick, a very pale Lebitz cousin from Larchmont, stand up and walk stiffly through the screen door that led into the exercise room. At the same time, Mack Rubin, a fat Ehrlich old-timer, rose with difficulty from his lounge chair and shuffled off toward the lawn. I wondered what had prompted them both to leave so hastily. Rebecca, meanwhile, stared at a muscular young man (not part of our extended family) who sat by the deep end of the pool

"Wanna play a game?" Carol shouted to Daniel. "I'll act out something and hum the line, and you have to guess what song it is. I'll go first."

Carol slapped the water several times with her open palms and hummed eight notes.

"'Splish Splash,'" Daniel said. "Is that it? Am I right?"

Carol smiled and nodded yes.

"My turn, my turn," Daniel said eagerly. With one hand he pointed to her and then with the other he pointed away from her with a make-believe angry expression on his face while humming six notes at the same time.

"I know! I know!" she exclaimed, "'Go Away, Little Girl.'"

"Yup!"

The two of them giggled and fully enjoyed their silly little game—but were abruptly halted by a tall, thin man in tennis whites who briskly walked onto the pool deck and called out in a loud voice:

"Little girl… little girl…"

Carol looked at the man. So did everyone else.

"Yes, sir?"

The man was Denny O'Connell, the athletic director at Ehrlich's. As Denny made his way to the edge of the pool, Lenore Zwick appeared in the doorway of the exercise room and stopped there with her arms folded. She had a scowl on her face. Denny sputtered a few incomprehensible syllables; had he not looked so panicked, it might have been humorous. No one understood what he was trying to say. Suddenly, someone in the distance hustled down the hill and called out Carol's name. Denny was saved the impossible chore of finding the right words, and undoubtedly was relieved. The man in the distance was Carol's father. Mack Rubin was several steps behind him but made no effort to keep up. Instead, Mack found an empty folding chair on the hill and wedged himself into it.

"Carol," her father shouted once again near the bottom of the hill, "what you doing there, girl?"

"Swimming," she said. "I made a friend."

"You come out of there right now, you hear?" Carol's father looked incredibly hot. He wore long brown pants and a thick gray pullover shirt, both of which were dirty and wet with perspiration. Large, yellow work gloves hung out of his back pocket. "Go on up to the shack. Right now."

"But daddy—"

"No lip, child. Go on. Now! We'll talk later. Go!"

Without another word, Carol swam to the ladder, climbed out, and hugged herself from the sudden chill. She had no towel, and no one offered her one.

"Sorry, Mr. O'Connell," her father called out to the athletic director. "It won't happen again." Then he and Carol rushed off in the direction of The Chapel. Carol didn't look back.

Daniel remained in the pool, but neither swam nor played. He just bobbed there silently and moved his legs slowly under the water to remain in place. I wanted to call out to him but didn't know what to say. I walked to the edge of the pool.

"Why'd she have to go?" Daniel said, as he looked up at me with gloomy eyes.

"I don't know," I said softly. "I really don't know."

"Daniel," Mom called out, "you'll get a chill like that. Move around in the water. Let me see your fingers."

But instead of showing her his fingers, Daniel climbed the stairs, grabbed a towel, and went back to our room.

•    •    •    •    •

The next day, Rebecca Fishbein told me that since she had to spend the entire day in the village with her parents, she wouldn't be around to play with me. That was a lie. I saw her through a line of trees playing badminton with three other teenage girls. I mentioned it to Mom and begged her not to make an issue of it. As it turned out, Mom felt it best to let the incident pass. "There are all kinds," she said. "Besides, Lori, you're better off without this Rebecca person."

Just before dinner, I went to the lobby and saw Grandma Leah in an alcove just off the lobby entrance. She was smoking and coughed incessantly. Daniel roamed aimlessly around the lobby. I caught up to him, and the two of us went to say hi to Grandma. She stubbed out her cigarette as soon as she saw us.

"I don't like it when you cough," I said. "Either does Mom or Dad. Or Steven or Daniel."

"Me neither, sweetheart. Terrible habit, smoking," she said. "Your father doesn't smoke anymore, does he?"

"No."

"Good. Are you having fun?

"Yes."

After a short coughing spell, Grandma asked if we had met anyone new. Daniel didn't say anything about Carol. He did tell her about Steven's friend Drew, the ophthalmologist's son. Daniel mentioned how interesting it was for the son of a famous eye doctor to have such a problem looking anyone in the eye. Grandma chuckled. Then I told her about Rebecca and how she didn't seem happy to be a teenager. I said I wasn't ready to give it up yet. Grandma smiled and shook her head.

"You two are something else," she said. "I love the way you tell stories, Daniel, and I love the way you try to understand people, Lori. You've both been that way for years. The two of you have gifts. Maybe more than your parents know. You know what mediocre means?"

"Yes," I said.

"It means not you two—that I can tell you. You'll both make your mark."

"How?" asked Daniel.

"Who knows? You'll do something, you'll try something, you'll ask something, you'll become someone. I don't know. You just won't accept and give up. Vishtayst?"

Grandma Leah sounded so pleased and assured that it felt foolish to disagree.

"Vishtayst," I said.

On our way back to our room, Daniel spotted Carol through a lobby window. She was sitting on the side lawn. Daniel told me that I should continue on without him and ran off.

Daniel and Carol walked slowly through the woods behind Ehrlich's.

"Are you okay?" he asked.

"I guess," Carol said. Her face was pensive.

"Can you play?"

"I guess. A little."

"Is your father mad at you?"

"A little," Carol said. "I don't like it when he gets mad at me. Is your daddy mad at you?"

"No... Does your father get mad a lot?"

"Sometimes. What about yours?"

"Sometimes. Not too much. My mom always tells him to calm down."

"It's just me and my daddy," Carol said, "so when he's mad, he don't got no one to get mad at but me."

Daniel felt the urge to console her with a hug, but he didn't, just in case her father lurked somewhere nearby.

"Everybody here has a happy family," Carol said softly.

"No they don't," Daniel responded. "You know the Rosenthals? In the stone building next to the main house? The grandmother walks around with an oxygen tank and makes babies cry just by looking at them. Last summer, Gary Rosenthal told me he can't stand her. And he has an older cousin who got pregnant when she was sixteen! Nobody in *his* family is happy." A gentle breeze blew by. "And you know that weird Hershorn family, with the loud brown car? Mr. Hershorn has a gigantic tattoo of a mermaid on his arm, and my mother heard Mrs. Hershorn say that she hated it. And they have that fat baby who everybody says poops in the sandbox."

"I know. My daddy gotta clean up that poop every day."

"So I don't think *every*body here has a happy family."

Carol smiled.

"I guess me and my daddy ain't too bad," she allowed. "'Cause when he's happy, he's really nice to me. I bet your family is nice."

"At least we don't have oxygen tanks or babies that poop in the sandbox. Hey, Carol—you think you might be able to come see me play in The Bluebird?"

"When?"

"Tomorrow night. Maybe your dad could take you."

Carol chewed on a fingernail.

"I don't think so. I don't think I could even ask him," she finally said.

"Well, will you think about it? About asking him?"

But before she had a chance to respond, the two of them felt pine needles fall on their heads, so they moved a few steps further down the path. Then they heard branches rustle and looked up. There were two people up in a pine tree. One of them was Steven. The other was Drew Friedman.

"Scaredy cats," Drew called down, as Daniel and Carol moved away.

Daniel called up to Steven.

"What are you doing up there?"

"Nothing," Steven replied. "Go back to the main house. Mom wants you."

"No she doesn't. You haven't been in the main house since this morning."

"Just go!" he yelled.

"Hey, Steven," Drew asked, "is that your little brother? Hey kid," he called down, "who's your little nigger friend?"

Steven began to climb down the tree.

"Where the hell you going?" Drew asked.

"Back," Steven said.

"Why?"

"Because."

"You gonna play with the little nigger girl, too?"

Steven lowered himself onto a branch about six feet off the ground and let go—but hit the ground hard and landed on his side. Daniel went over to him, and Carol took a few steps closer. There was a cigarette butt beside Steven on the path, with a tiny ribbon of smoke that still wound its way out of one end.

"Are you okay?" Daniel asked. Steven's right arm was caked with dirt, and there was a little patch of blood by his elbow.

"Just go back to the main house," he said crossly. Then he stood up and walked away.

"Baby," Drew sneered at Steven from up on his pine perch.

Steven went in the direction of the main building. Daniel and Carol stood on the path and didn't quite know what to do. Drew swung himself down from branch to branch and landed in the same spot as Steven, but on his feet. He had a cigarette in his hand.

"What the fuck's the matter with him?" Drew asked—although his eyes completely averted Daniel's. Before Daniel could answer, Drew walked away.

"Do you have to go with your brother?" Carol asked.

"No," Daniel said.

"What do you wanna do?"

"Let's go to the duck pond."

"Was they smoking up in the tree?" Carol asked as they made their way down the hill toward the pond.

"I don't know. Probably just that other kid was. Not Steven."

"My daddy says it's bad for kids to smoke. He says they can go to a special jail for children. Do you think your brother's friend will go to jail?"

"I don't know. My rabbi says that if we fall, we can pick ourselves up again. He says that God understands."

"Understands what?"

"That we can fall."

"You mean on the ground?"

"No. By making mistakes. By doing something bad."

There was a large boulder by the side of the pond. They climbed on. But then Carol slid down again when she noticed something nearby.

"Look!" she shrieked. She pointed to a puffy white cluster of dandelion seeds that floated over the path. "If you catch it and make a wish, your wish will come true."

"Really?" Daniel slid off the boulder to stand beside her.

"Yup. Those are little stars that come down from heaven. And if you wish on them and then blow them back up to heaven, your dream will come true. My mama told me that just before she died. Let's share it."

Carol returned to the boulder and stood up. She reached out to try to grab the cotton-like cluster of seeds as it passed by. She had called them little stars that came down from heaven, and Daniel vowed to remember that phrase forever. He fell in love with the words. With the idea. He smiled and urged Carol on as she stood tall on the boulder.

"Careful," Daniel said. "Don't fall."

The cluster of dandelion seeds seemed to come closer to her almost on purpose as she leaned over. She stretched out her right arm to clench it in her fist. To Daniel, they *were* stars, each one a tiny sun with orderly rays that reached out as far as they could. But before Carol was able to grab it, her father's voice rang out from the dirt road just beyond the pond.

"Carol? Is that you? What you doing there, girl?"

"Just playing," she called back.

"What did I tell you? Don't you ever listen to me no more? We're going home now. Come. Now. You hear me?"

Without another word, Carol jumped off the boulder and hopped over a rotted, dismembered branch on the ground to join her father on the road. The two of them disappeared around the bend. Daniel looked for the cluster of dandelion seeds near the pond, in the trees, even by the road. But he couldn't find it.

•    •    •    •    •

"You've became Lori," Steven said to Daniel the next day.

He said it when he noticed that Daniel had spent the entire morning and afternoon alone in the room, ignoring Mom and Dad's request to look for a boy with whom to become friendly. I had been out for another walk with Mom but heard the exchange through the door as Mom and I were about to walk in.

Daniel decided to leave the room. He exited the building and walked around the grounds, in almost the same route as Mom and I had just completed. He spoke to no one. He spent a few minutes at the pinball machine in the concession room, again alone, and then listened to a portable radio that someone had on in the lobby

After dinner, back in the room, Mom ordered Steven to dress extra nicely for the show at The Bluebird. She didn't have to tell me, for I was conscientious enough not to have to be reminded, and she certainly didn't have to tell Daniel, either, because he was on the bill and was predisposed to dressing nicely for performances anyway.

Although Daniel was pleased to have once again been given a spot on The Bluebird stage, the thrill was somewhat less than it had been in previous summers. For one thing, being asked was now predictable; for another, no longer was it one seamless day after another of boundless optimism and carefree contentment at Ehrlich's, as it had been in summers past.

Steven stood by the windowsill as he buttoned a new shirt. He called me over to look at something out the window.

"You know whose car that is?" he asked as he nodded to the dirt parking lot below. "That big white Impala? I think it's Uncle Nat's."

"Probably not," I said. "We would have heard."

"I think it is. Look—it has Ohio license plates, and the last I heard, Uncle Nat was living in Ohio."

Grandpa Jesse and Grandma Leah knocked on the door and walked in. They had planned to accompany us down to The Bluebird.

"What's his name again—the comedian?" Mom asked Grandpa Jesse.

"Riggler? Wrinkles? I can't remember," Grandpa said. "It's on the billboard downstairs. You'll see it in a few minutes."

"You don't remember his name? I thought you said he was famous."

"He is famous! Jewish fella. Big head. Small eyes. Insults people. A real nut."

"Well," Mom said, "*that* narrows it down."

"Three numbers of your own choice," Grandpa said to Daniel for the third time since we had arrived in the Catskills. That instruction was from Old Man Ehrlich himself. Either Grandpa Jesse forgot that he had mentioned it twice before, or he was just making sure to follow orders so that he and Daniel would continue to be invited back to perform. "Three—unless the audience demands an encore, of course. Then all bets are off. You'll have the full band behind you. I know most of those guys. Same from last year. They're good. They'll follow whatever you do, so don't worry about arrangements. You'll knock 'em dead, kid."

"I don't want him to knock anyone dead," Mom said.

"It's a showbiz expression," Grandpa grinned.

"I know, I know. I wasn't born yesterday. And I married a trombonist, remember?"

"Who maybe should have stayed a trombonist," Grandpa said, almost under his breath.

"Yeah—" Mom sneered under her own breath, "and I should have been Virginia Woolf. Without the headaches."

"Who?"

"Never mind," Mom said.

•    •    •    •    •    •

Grandpa and Daniel walked to The Bluebird ahead of everyone else. Daniel wanted to relax backstage before he went on to perform. The rest of us planned to go down to the lobby a little later, closer to curtain time. I told Daniel I'd save him a seat in the nightclub so that he could join us for the rest of the show after his performance.

As Grandpa Jesse and Daniel approached the stage door in a hallway adjacent to the lobby, they saw an old hotel clerk named Al who had been at Ehrlich's since it opened in 1939. Al always asked Grandpa about the music business, and this summer was no exception. He requested a story about the first band Grandpa was ever in, a story he had asked for twice before. (No one knew if Al was just overly accommodating to an important guest like Grandpa Jesse, or just very forgetful.) Grandpa told an abbreviated version of how he quit high school to go on the road as a trumpet player with a ballroom orchestra.

"Excuse me, Al," Grandpa said toward the end of the story, "I just want to tell my grandson something before I forget."

"That's okay, Mr. Hillman. I gotta get back to the desk anyway. That skinny kid we hired away from Grossinger's, Jeff Toppleman—it's like trying to teach a puppy to change the oil in a Studebaker, if you know what I mean."

Al departed. Grandpa turned to Daniel.

"Did you see the billboard?" he asked. "Old Man Ehrlich, that son of a gun… First, he says that union rules won't allow him to put your name on it, which I know is baloney, then he goes and does it anyway. It's in the lobby. Go take a look."

Daniel had already seen it, as had Grandma Leah and I when we sat in the lobby for a few minutes late in the afternoon. But Daniel went to look once again, mostly because Grandpa Jesse was so excited about it.

It must have agonized Grandpa to have to abbreviate the tale he had been sharing with Al, for one of his greatest joys was talking about his old days in show business. Every once in a while he would tell us stories of his life, from his birth in Romania through his years on the club circuit, and little by little my brothers and I were able to piece together the entire story. Grandpa Jesse went off on many tangents—but Daniel and I were eager to remember each one. For some reason, I thought they might have life lessons in them that could come in handy one day. Daniel seemed to enjoy the tangents for their narrative drama and distinctive humor.

Grandpa Jesse's father and mother, Zalman and Reza Hilzatz, along with their first child, Yussel, emigrated to New York in 1907 from a city called Breaza, just north of Bucharest. In Breaza, Zalman Hilzatz owned a small furniture shop. He talked of striking it rich in the New World with his own chain of luxury department stores. His father before him, in Romania, was a tailor named Yitzhak who had often talked of the affluence that would come from designing clothes for the aristocracy. He was such a skilled clothes stylist that the aristocracy surely would ask him to work for them exclusively.

As it turned out, Yitzhak became an itinerant tailor, not a clothes designer for the aristocracy, and Zalman, when he finally made it to America, worked as a junkman on the streets of Manhattan, not as the proprietor of luxury department stores.

Dad was fond of saying that not being wealthy was the Hillman destiny.

When they left Ellis Island, Zalman and Reza Hilzatz saw on their papers that they had magically become Saul and Rita Hillman and that their eleven-year-old son Yussel had become Jesse. They moved into a tenement on Hester Street on the Lower East Side. Despite their papers, they remained Zalman and Reza, and Yussel stayed Yussel until he was sixteen.

The musically-inclined Yussel was forced to accompany Zalman as he walked around Manhattan six nights a week to collect the artifacts and scrap that he would refurbish and sell during the day. As the story goes, Yussel tried every trick in the book to avoid these long walks, which he found tedious—that is, until he discovered the speakeasies, vaudeville houses, jazz bars, and blues clubs along the route. Then he began to look forward to the journeys and never missed an opportunity to sneak inside to listen to the musicians play. He had to think quickly and be creative in order to create opportunities to slip inside, for Zalman tried to never let him out of his sight. Several times a week, little Yussel would disappear, and his father would have to search for him. Zalman used to complain that he'd have been a millionaire by the time he was thirty-five had he not been forced to spend so much time in search of Yussel inside of dim, smoky rooms when the two of them should have been collecting junk on the sidewalks of New York.

Jesse was the first Hilzatz—now Hillman, of course—to come close to living his dream. At seventeen he was already writing songs and playing trumpet for the popular Ben Selvin Orchestra, and he traveled across the country with an interesting assortment of men, all of whom were more than twice his age. His future wife, Leah Lebitz, lived in the tenement two buildings down; the two had been keeping company since they were thirteen. Leah was the smartest girl in the neighborhood. They married on Leah's eighteenth birthday.

Jesse was a good enough songwriter, trumpet player, and arranger to work full time in the music business from 1920 to 1927. He and Leah started a family right away, moved into a small apartment not far from the block on which they grew up, and made plans for an exciting future that had no place for tenements. But Jesse quickly grew tired of the uphill climb. He saw too much greed in the music industry, too much immorality, too much mediocrity, and he blamed it all for his inability to rise up in the musical ranks. His standards were high, and his patience low. It wasn't the Great Depression that ended Jesse's professional music career, but a depression of his own.

Jesse and Leah's apartment wasn't quite a tenement, but it wasn't very comfortable, either. Jesse's income wasn't deplorable, but it was close to deplorable. So in 1930, with two sons and his widowed, sickly mother living in the apartment with them, Jesse decided to take a job as a salesman at Marcus Suitcases in Brooklyn. His income there—a modest salary and a small commission—helped them scrape by. Sometimes Leah tutored children on the block, and those were the times they had a little extra money for a night out or to put away for a rainy day. Jesse said he took the position at Marcus Suitcases because it was the only job that afforded him enough time during the week to write a song or two, which he still liked to do. He had a dozen or so notable clients from the entertainment world who returned to Marcus every so often not just for a suitcase, but also to hear a funny verse or an absorbing story about the old days. Jesse stayed with the store until his retirement at the age of sixty-five. That was just four years before the Lebitz family reunion at Ehrlich's Hotel and Bungalow Colony, where he was always asked more about music than suitcases.

●   ●   ●   ●   ●   ●

Daniel paced backstage for about twenty minutes as guests started to fill the seats in The Bluebird. Grandpa Jesse had often told us that it was one of the largest hotel nightclubs in the Catskills. I remember when he once explained to Al how different Ehrlich's was from the first place he had ever played in the mountains, back in 1928. "That was a toilet of a hotel, five miles from here," he said. "Which is funny, since they didn't even have a good toilet."

Milt Seebach had been the emcee at The Bluebird ever since I could remember. He came out on stage in an ill-fitting tuxedo. His jet-black toupee always looked as if he had plopped it onto his scalp moments before coming onto the stage. Holding a corded microphone close to his mouth, he first told a few jokes, then asked the orchestra conductor in the pit and the lighting director in the booth if everything was in order. He followed that with a few announcements about other events at Ehrlich's. Then he began the show.

"It is my pleasure to announce that we have a very special guest with us tonight, as we do every summer—a little musical marvel directly from the extended family that has more or less taken over our fine hotel this week, the Lebitz Family. Ladies and gentlemen, from the Lebitz Family Foundation, I bring to you, Mr. Daniel Hillman!"

Daniel trotted to the stage from the right wing. The spotlight had erased whatever shadows might have hung over his head for the past two days. He sat by the piano (a phone book had been pre-placed on the bench for him), repositioned the microphone, looked at the black and white keys as if they were old friends he hadn't seen in a while, and began to play. He first performed "On the Street Where You Live" from *My Fair Lady*. A few members of the band provided simple yet effective backup. Then he sang "Up the Lazy River," which was one of Grandpa Jesse's favorite songs. He added a four-measure, ragtime-style closing of his own creation that the audience seemed to particularly enjoy. He announced as his third and final number a recent hit by Ray Charles called "I Can't Stop Loving You."

"This one's for Carol," he said into the microphone.

And then he sang:

*"I can't stop loving you, I've made up my mind,*
*To live in memory of the lonesome times.*
*I can't stop wanting you, it's useless to say,*
*So I'll just live my life in dreams of yesterday."*

When Daniel finished the song, the audience roared its approval, Lebitzes and non-Lebitzes alike, and before long it evolved into a standing ovation.

Dad leaned over to me and whispered, "Who's Carol?"

Daniel stood up, took three steps away from the piano, and bowed. Then, mimicking the way he had seen singers and pianists act on television hundreds of times, he commended the orchestra for their work with a few gentle claps of his own. Someone in the audience shouted, "One more!" and that was echoed by several others who made the same request. Daniel glanced at Milt Seebach, who was by the stage left wing, just to confirm that it was okay. Seebach nodded. But just as Daniel was about to take three steps back to the piano, the evening's featured comedian walked onto the stage from the other wing, unannounced. Grandpa Jesse was right about the way he looked—short, with a large, egg-shaped bald head that in itself was very funny, and small, darting eyes. He, too, wore a tuxedo, though it fit him well. He carried a microphone with him and swung the cord skillfully so that he wouldn't trip as he approached center stage.

"A little musical mensch, this guy, huh?" the comic said. He stared at the audience with a look that was both incredulous and ridiculous. "Daniel Lebitz, is it?"

"Hillman," I said.

"Hillman Lebitz? What the hell kind of name is that?" The audience laughed. "Can I call you Dan?"

"Yes."

"Good. On behalf of the entire Lebitz Family Foundation—which, by the way, paid for this cheap, second-hand tuxedo—let me just say that you were terrific. Now give me my seventy-five percent, and I won't report you to the musician's union, you little squirt."

There was more laughter. Daniel stood there straight-faced because he didn't know what else to do; it was all so sudden and unexpected.

"Ladies and gentlemen," Seebach said from the wing on his own microphone, "please welcome—" But the comedian shut him down.

"They know who I am, you dummy," the comedian said, looking toward the wing. "And if you interrupt me again, I'll feed your toupee to my dog. He'll probably want to bury it." Seebach smiled and then remained quiet. The comedian turned back to Daniel. "Lebitz!" he continued, which halted the audience's laughter. "Sounds like something to eat. 'Excuse me, waiter, I'll have a bagel and Lebitz.' What the hell's a Lebitz? What does a Lebitz do, for Christ's sake? Can you tell me that, Dan?"

From somewhere in the middle of the audience an old man stood up and shouted,

"Some of us are in cabinets."

The comedian shielded his eyes and looked into the crowd. "Cabinets?" he repeated.

"For the kitchen," the man quickly added. "Kitchen cabinets."

"I know what a cabinet is, you moron." More laughter. "I know some other guys who are in kitchen cabinets… at the bottom of the East River. And I know the guys who put 'em there, so don't mess with me, fella. They all look like this." With one index finger he bent his nose to the side. "Are you one of them? Do you know my friend Frank Sinatra?"

"No," the man called back.

"No? You don't know any of those guys? I think there's one sitting next to you, in the shiny suit? Because I don't know any Jews who wear shiny suits like that."

Everyone looked, including me. It took a second to recognize him, and another second to believe it; the man the comedian referred to was Uncle Nat. There were several nervous giggles in the audience, but only for a moment—until Nat himself threw his head back and laughed. That seemed to be the cue that allowed everyone else in the nightclub to laugh.

At that point, Milt Seebach joined the comedian on stage.

"Let's have one more big hand for little Daniel Hillman," he said.

The audience applauded. The comedian glared at him.

"I'm not finished with this kid yet! Go away." He turned back to Daniel. Seebach slithered back to the wing. "You're not going into cabinets like that dummy out there, are you, Danny?" Daniel shook his head. "Good. Where's your mom and pop?"

Daniel pointed to the third row. (I slid down several inches in my seat.)

"Mom? Dad?" the comedian said, "Can I take him back to Hollywood with me? You know why? 'Cause I think I can make a lot of dough off this kid. What do you say? We'll split the profits right down the middle—sixty-forty."

"No thank you," Mom said. She didn't shout, but her voice carried well. "We'll keep him."

"You're the mother?" The comedian turned back to Daniel and pretended to whisper in his ear: "I'd run away if I was you. I'd go with the guy in the shiny suit. Maybe he could build you your own casino in Las Vegas."

The audience hung onto every word the comedian said, and as a result, Daniel realized that his own performance was now history. The encore would never happen. Milt Seebach returned, and he and the comedian verbally sparred for a few more moments while Daniel slipped through the wing and out to the lobby.

I watched as Daniel left the stage and sensed that he was upset. So I, too, went to the lobby. I called his name and went over to him. That's when we saw Uncle Nat. He had left The Bluebird through another door.

"Lori, Lori, Lori" Uncle Nat smiled. "Oh my God, how you've grown. And into such a pretty young woman." He put his hands on my shoulders and kissed my cheek.

"Hello, Uncle Nat," I said.

"And Daniel… little musical mensch is right. How are you, kid?"

"Fine. I'm glad you got to see the show."

"Wouldn't miss it for the world."

Uncle Nat was a little shorter than Grandpa Jesse, his hair wavier, his build much broader and, being fourteen years younger, he had far fewer wrinkles on his face.

"I hardly know the two of you," he said, "and God knows it's my own fault. I'm very sad about that."

"Is everything all right with you?" I asked. Although he was one of the more mysterious members of the family, he wasn't difficult to talk to. Maybe it was that his eyes were kind. Tired and guarded, but kind.

"Pretty good, Lori, thank God. I'm busy. Doing well. After all, like the man said, look at this fancy-schmanzy shiny suit. Huh?"

"You look very nice," I said.

"And so do you. That's a beautiful dress. But it needs a necklace."

"I was supposed to wear one, but we were late coming to the nightclub."

"A nice gold Jewish star, I would think."

"Well," I admitted, a bit embarrassed, "I don't have one. I just have a little pearl. But I didn't have time to put it on."

"Pearl-schmerl. A Star of David. Or better yet, a chai. That's what you need, Lori." He turned to Daniel. "And chai means what?"

"Life," Daniel said.

"That's right. Life. Hey, Daniel—you shouldn't have let baldy upstage you in there. I wanted to belt him."

"I know," he said. "But I couldn't do anything."

"You're too nice. Sometimes it pays not to be too nice."

"How long are you staying?" I asked.

"Not long, I'm afraid," Uncle Nat replied. "I only came up for a few hours, to see everyone. In fact, I'd better go back in to watch a little bit more of the show, or everyone will wonder what the hell happened to me. Which I guess is the way things have been for years. Huh? Why should this night be different from all other nights?"

He kissed me on the head and shook Daniel's hand.

"What's the matter, Lori," he said. "You look so… what's the word… melancholy."

"Melancholy?" The word took me by surprise. "No, I'm fine. Really."

"Really my tuchis," Uncle Nat said. "You're sad when you see me because you want us all to be one big happy family. Am I right?"

"I'm fine."

"You're a terrible liar, Lori. Don't be a lawyer when you grow up." He smirked and lifted my chin. I smiled—at least to the best of my ability. For a moment it seemed as if I had been thinking of the past, present, and future all at once, and that put me in an odd, almost surreal mood—melancholy was probably accurate—which must have registered on my face. "You'll see," Uncle Nat continued, "things will be okay. And if I don't see you both later, remember that I'm thinking of you and I promise I'll try to come out to the Island to visit. Vishtayst?"

Uncle Nat went back into The Bluebird. Daniel and I returned to our third-floor room and sat in Mom and Dad's side of the suite.

"You were great," I said.

"That idiot ruined it," Daniel mumbled.

"The comedian? No he didn't."

"Yes he did, Lori. Don't try to make me feel good about it. Carol wasn't there, and that jerk ruined it. I didn't even get to do an encore."

Then Steven walked through the door.

"Nice show, Daniel," he said in a voice so low that we hardly heard him. He plopped himself down on the master bed. He looked miserable. He had had a rough day. First, Drew spread stories to the other teenagers at Ehrlich's about Steven's poor school grades (which Steven had regrettably shared with him when they had still been friendly), and then Old Man Ehrlich had the electric cart locked up for the remainder of the summer. So Steven felt as if all he could do on this Catskill vacation was watch television, which he was able to do on Long Island where reception was much better.

Steven glanced at me. He hadn't yet turned on the set.

"Why do *you* look so sad?" he asked.

"Probably because the two of you are so sad," I said.

"Oh. I thought it was because this is the stupidest vacation we've ever had."

I took the initiative to turn on the television set. *The Red Skelton Show* had just begun. On the show, one of Skelton's characters, a drunk called Willie Lump-Lump, made believe he was in a fancy restaurant with a woman, although he was really alone on the street. Willie had neither silverware nor a glass, just a bottle of booze. "Guess I'll have to sip," he said daintily to his imaginary date—and then took an incredibly long swig from the bottle. The studio audience roared with laughter. In the old days, Steven, Daniel, and I would have laughed, too. This time, we didn't.

•     •     •     •     •

"If Ella Conners married Peter Vayda," Grandpa Sol announced as he scanned two separate wedding pages in the Sunday newspaper, "she'd be Ella Vayda."

We had returned from Ehrlich's the week before.

Steven, who was in the basement, overheard Grandpa's resounding voice and called up,

"Grandpa, I think that's the best one ever!"

"Pretty good, no?" he said to me.

"*Very* good," I agreed.

Grandpa Sol and Grandma Rose stayed over to watch the three of us because Mom and Dad had gone away again, thanks to a sudden turn of events at Dad's company. Two days after we returned from the Catskills, he received a phone call from the personnel department requesting that he and Mom chaperone a trip to Aruba that several LILCO subcontractors had won from the company. All expenses would be paid. The original LILCO chaperones had suddenly taken ill. Mom considered it a little gift from God for all of Dad's hard work. "And such gifts don't come too often, Murray—so accept the responsibility, and that's all."

Dad grudgingly accepted, though it was the responsibility part that troubled him. He said he knew nothing about being a chaperone. It wasn't part of his makeup, he said.

"I'll bring the makeup," Mom countered, completely dismissing his concern. "Just smile and follow the schedule that they'll give you on a piece of paper. Easy as pie."

They left for the Caribbean two days later.

"Ella Vayda, Rose! You hear?"

"I hear, I hear," Grandma said, unimpressed. She was cooking a brisket for dinner and didn't like to encourage her husband of forty-nine years in his silly name-play endeavors. She wished on him nobler ways to pass the time.

"Vat you tink of your old zaide now, huh? A regular Jack Benny?" he said. "See? Somebody up there likes me. That's vy he puts deez tinks in the paper—so I can find them. Steven!" he called down to the basement, "vat you doing down there? Building a spaceship?"

That wasn't far from the truth. Steven was assembling a model rocket. Although he had casually followed the Gemini and Sputnik programs, recent news accounts that showed close-up photographs of the moon taken by Ranger 7 truly ignited his passion, and he now added spaceflight to his list of travel goals. Steven started to sprinkle words like zero gravity and light years into his conversations. The Ranger 7 photos, Steven said, were a thousand times clearer than those that could be taken by any telescope on earth. "Sometimes earth just isn't good enough," he said later on, while we ate Grandma's brisket.

That evening we all watched *Saturday Night at the Movies* on TV. The featured presentation was the musical *Gigi*. Grandma said that she would have liked to have seen the original Broadway show, but Daniel explained to her that *Gigi* had never been on Broadway, that it had been written directly for the movies. "Maybe I can do something like that," he said, almost under his breath. (I saw the creative wheels turning behind his eyes even as he whispered; it was almost as if he had put himself into a trance.)

Daniel went to his bedroom to begin work on something that he eventually called *The Little Girl in the Chapel*. Over the next few days, he composed seven songs and crafted a story to go along with them.

So Steven had his project and Daniel had his own. I had one too, which was to help Grandma Rose with all the household cooking, cleaning, and sewing while Mom was in Aruba with Dad. I truly enjoyed it. I asked Grandma many questions as we went about our chores—about Jewish cuisine, how to clean different kinds of fabric and furniture—and Grandma appreciated the chance to share her knowledge. At one point, we spent several minutes discussing how to clean our two mezuzahs, the one by the front steps and the other next to my bedroom door. Those little religious ornaments were no bigger than a single piece of ivory on the key of a piano and should have taken no more than three seconds to clean. Still, I spent more than two minutes on each one.

Daniel didn't let anyone know why he hid away so quietly in his room every day. He came out every now and then to play a few notes on the piano in the living room or the xylophone in the basement. Neither did he want Grandma to worry about him, which she would, especially since the weather outside was gorgeous. It was one of the most glorious weeks of the summer, weather-wise, and Daniel knew that Grandma would make a full report to Mom. So he decided to spend a little bit of time with his friends simply to avoid any motherly criticisms later on. *The Little Girl in the Chapel* was still his priority, but Glenn Sheldon and the other boys on the block were his insurance policy.

"I'm going to Glenn's house," he called out from the hallway. He placed the screenplay underneath a stack of novels he had on his desk, and then went to the front door.

"Is it chilly?" Grandma called back.

"No."

"What are you wearing?"

"Shorts. It's hot."

"Eat something first."

"We had lunch twenty minutes ago."

But she gave him a kreplach anyway to eat on the way to Glenn's house.

Doug Kelleher and Craig Stuart were already there when Daniel arrived. Craig had chocolate fudge on his teeth.

"Where were you all week?" Glenn asked.

"I was doing something," Daniel told him.

"What?"

"Something."

Glenn, Doug, and Craig had just finished watching a baseball game on TV between the Yankees and the Cardinals. Then Glenn led the boys to his basement, where most of his toys were kept.

"I was writing a movie," Daniel said on the way down the steps. "It's about a poor little girl who feels like the richest person in the world only when she's alone in her house singing, which makes her want to grow up to be a singer. But her father—"

"I got five new Matchbox cars and two new G.I. Joes yesterday," Glenn interrupted.

"Can I see them?" Doug asked.

"You know who I'm gonna send it to?" Daniel continued. "MGM. Do you know what MGM is?"

"My mom put my favorite Matchbox car on top of a cake she made for my stupid cousin," Craig complained. "There's chocolate all over the wheels. I keep licking it off, but some of it is stuck way inside."

Daniel sensed it was hopeless. He understood now that he would never get to tell them about *The Little Girl in the Chapel*. On the other, he no longer cared.

Moments later, Helene Sheldon, the rabbi's wife, came downstairs carrying the dishes her family had used on Friday night. They were kept during the week in a special cabinet in the basement. Her red hair was wrapped and pinned in a circle above her head. The basement ceiling was low, and the lights were bright, and the effect made her hair look even fierier than Ann-Margret's in *Bye, Bye Birdie*. In fact, Mrs. Sheldon wore tight pink pants and a yellow blouse that ended just above her navel, strikingly similar to what Ann-Margret had worn in the movie.

"Hi, boys," Mrs. Sheldon said. "What are you playing?"

"Racing with Matchbox cars. And war with my G.I. Joes," Glenn explained.

Mrs. Sheldon put the dishes away.

"Well, I don't mind the cars, but war..."

"War's neat," Doug said.

"War's neat? It won't be so neat if we go to war," she said as she closed the cabinet door. "Do your parents tell you what's going on in the news, Douglas? What President Johnson just did in North Vietnam? We might have to send boys not much older than Daniel's brother to fight. You wouldn't want that, would you?"

"I'm gonna be on the Yankees when I grow up," Glenn said, unconcerned with his mother's fears.

"What about you, Douglas?" she asked. "What do you want to be when you grow up?"

"A policeman or a garbage man."

"Okay. Very nice. What about you, Craig?"

"A pastry chef."

"Of course."

Mrs. Sheldon turned to Daniel.

"I don't have to ask you, do I, Daniel?"

"I want to be a rabbi," he said. She looked surprised. Mrs. Sheldon smiled and took a few steps over to Daniel. She bent down and cupped his chin in her hand.

"A rabbi? Not a musician? Well, I bet you would make a wonderful rabbi, Daniel. One who can carry a tune *and* can keep a promise." She kissed him on the forehead. The boys were too busy to notice. That was probably a good thing, for Daniel had little patience for their sarcasm.

Mrs. Sheldon went back upstairs.

"Hey!" Doug suddenly shouted to Glenn, "where'd you get that Mustang? That's mine!"

Glenn ignored him and drove the Matchbox Mustang across the floor and over to the couch. When he was by the couch, he picked up a small pillow and held it to his chest.

"Look!" Glenn called to the other boys. "A tittie." Doug and Craig giggled. Glenn took a matching pillow from the other end of the couch and held it to the other side of his chest. "Look! My mommy's titties!" He was closer to Daniel than the others. "Wanna touch my mommy's titties?" he said as he shoved the pillows toward Daniel's face.

"Stop it, you jerk," Daniel said.

"Touch my mommy's titties, touch my mommy's titties."

"Shut up."

Daniel lurched forward and grabbed both pillows out of Glenn's hands. Glenn reached to grab them back, but Daniel resisted. They went at each other like schoolyard rivals, and it was unlike any encounter they had ever had in all the years they had known each other. Glenn took a hold of Daniel's arm and spun him around. Daniel tripped over the leg of a chair and fell to the floor, and when he was on the floor, Glenn grabbed his shorts and pulled them down over his sneakers. Daniel sprung to his feet, but he did it so quickly that he felt dizzy and fell back onto the floor. When he got up, he looked around frantically for his shorts, and out of the corner of his eye, he saw Doug roll them up into a ball and pitch it toward Glenn.

"Strike one!" Glenn announced. Then the three boys ran upstairs, laughing.

"I hate you!" Daniel shouted after them.

Daniel thought that Glenn had taken his shorts with him, so he ran upstairs to get them back. The kitchen was empty. Apparently, the boys were hiding somewhere else in the house. He heard a door close down the hall, so he ran to check. The bathroom door was shut. It usually was open. He thought that Glenn and the others were hiding in there, so Daniel opened the bathroom door. The moment he opened it, he felt his body jerk backward as if he'd been struck by a bolt of lightning, and his eyes shut tightly with the force of two opposing magnets. What he had seen for a split second before they shut was Helene Sheldon in the middle of the bathroom floor, completely naked.

"Daniel!"

"I'm sorry," Daniel stammered through sudden tears. "I'm sorry. I'm sorry."

"It's okay, sweetheart. Just give me a moment...okay. You can open your eyes." He did. "Is something wrong? What happened down there to make you run upstairs?"

While Daniel's eyes had been closed, Mrs. Sheldon put on a tan brassiere and white panties.

"Glenn took my shorts," he said, his head still lowered. "I thought he was in here. I'm so sorry. I'm sorry..."

Mrs. Sheldon walked over to him and got down on her knees.

"It's okay. It's okay. Don't worry, Daniel. Everything's fine... How do you put up with those boys? They're so foolish sometimes." She stood up and called out loudly,

"Glenn, wherever you are, come over here and give Daniel back his shorts, right now! Do you hear me? And then I want to talk to you." She touched Daniel's head. "It's all right, honey. Go get your shorts, and then I'll have a talk with the boys."

Glenn found Daniel's shorts in the basement and muttered an apology when he gave them back. "It's okay," Daniel mumbled back, and reluctantly he sat with the three boys in the kitchen to have milk and cookies. Then Rabbi Sheldon came in through the front door and went into the kitchen. He had just returned from officiating at a funeral and asked if he could sit with the boys. First he poured himself a glass of milk and grabbed two cookies.

"How's your little brother?" Rabbi Sheldon asked Doug.

"Okay, I guess. It's just hard when he has to pee and poop because of the wheelchair."

"Two very important things at the beginning of life, peeing and pooping," Rabbi Sheldon said. "Actually, now that I think about it, not too different from the important things at the *end* of life, too."

"Do you get sad at funerals?" Craig asked as he started on his fifth Oreo.

"Sometimes," Rabbi Sheldon explained. "But today... well, Mr. Bessler lived a long, full life. He had three children, eight grandchildren, and five great-grandchildren, and they were all there. It was actually very nice. A few years ago, when I first moved here, Mr. Bessler told me that the only thing that ever mattered to him was having children, because maybe, just maybe, he said, one of his children or one of his children's children might just be the one to fix this fekakta world once and for all. Isn't that something? Who knows?—maybe one of them *will* fix the world one day. There are certainly enough of them to make the odds pretty good!"

"That's nice," Daniel said, as he tried to imagine Mr. Bessler watching his own funeral as Rabbi Sheldon had described it. Glenn, Craig, and Doug were bored with the story and went back to the basement. Daniel stayed behind.

"Sometimes, Daniel," Rabbi Sheldon said, "a rabbi becomes a good rabbi only because the people in his congregation are good people. Vishtayst?"

"I think."

"How are your grandparents treating you while your mom and dad are away? Are they keeping you busy?"

"I spent all week writing a movie musical," he said.

"A movie musical? No kidding? That's wonderful, Daniel! What's it called?"

"*The Little Girl in the Chapel.*"

"What a wonderful title! I love it. I hope something good comes of it. Did you show it to anyone?"

"No. I don't want to. I just want to send it to some people who make movies. That's all."

"I think I understand that," Rabbi Sheldon whispered. "Then just stick it in the mailbox and don't show it to anyone else. You don't have to mention it to anyone, either. It will be between you and me. And a movie producer—from my lips to God's ears, as your father would say. And God will know too, of course, since he knows everything anyway. But don't worry—he loves stories about churches. Churches are so much prettier than temples, don't you think?—and the bells sound so nice. I wish we had bells."

Daniel smiled.

Rabbi Sheldon said he wanted to change into comfortable clothes and then do some paperwork in his office. He told Daniel to take care, then left the kitchen. Daniel went to the basement door and listened to the boys and their nonsense chatter for a few moments. It hardly interested him. He wanted to go home. For a moment, he considered finding Mrs. Sheldon to say goodbye. But he was actually frightened to walk through the house. So he simply went home. But he did turn back to look down the block once or twice.

•　　　•　　　•　　　•　　　•

The next morning at breakfast, Daniel asked if I could walk with him to the public library. It wasn't far from the house, but there's a four-lane thoroughfare you have to cross to get there, and Daniel knew that Grandma Rose would never let him go alone.

"Take Lori with you," Grandma said—even though Daniel had already told her that he had asked me. "Put on a sweater and butter yourself a bagel. You call fruit and cereal a breakfast?"

Daniel looked up at me.

"Isn't it?" he whispered.

"Yes," I whispered back. "But she's a grandma. So just go along with it."

"Okay," he called out, "I'll butter myself a bagel."

He didn't have to. Grandma did it for him. Then we left the house.

I took the opportunity at the library to look up some books that I had recently read about in a literary journal I had stumbled upon at school. While I searched for Henry Roth's *Call It Sleep* and Philip Roth's *Goodbye, Columbus*, Daniel approached a reference librarian and asked for help. He told her he wanted to find the address of MGM Studios in Hollywood and a list of its executives. Within minutes the librarian found what he wanted. Both Daniel and I had always considered librarians among the few adults in the world who would never look at us oddly if we asked an unusual question—as we both had done from time to time. In this case, the librarian smiled and seemed to instinctively know that Daniel was attempting to act on a literary compulsion—and that there was nothing wrong with that.

On the way home, Daniel said he wanted to stop by the post office. He asked me if I had any money. I had a few dollars with me and asked him what he needed it for. Stamps, he said. I saw no reason to question him further, so I purchased a few stamps, and then we walked home.

Later that afternoon, Grandma Rose told us to get ready to go to the airport to pick up Mom and Dad. They were scheduled to return from Aruba at four forty-five. Steven asked if he could stay home. He said he'd keep an eye on the house. Grandma didn't like the idea, so Steven appealed to Grandpa Sol. First Grandpa spoke up in Steven's defense. Then he did something that interested him even more: he tested out another name concoction from the wedding section of the newspaper.

"If Rhoda Shapiro married Harold Ruder," he said from the kitchen, "she'd be Rhoda Ruder."

"Sol!" Grandma yelled by the sink. "Stop it already! I don't think Steven should stay here alone. Don't you agree?"

"He's not a baby, Rose. What can happen? He had his bar mitzvah. He's a man. It's a quiet day."

When he argued with Grandma Rose, he never put on a Yiddish accent.

"What do you think, Lori?" Grandma asked

"I think Mom and Dad would like it if we were all there to pick them up," I said as diplomatically as possible.

Steven stayed home anyway.

Our destination was the newly-renamed John F. Kennedy International Airport, in Queens. Grandpa drove. On the ride over, Daniel asked Grandma to turn on the radio, and we listened to Cousin Brucie, who was a popular, amiable, motor-mouthed disc jockey on a New York City station, WABC. He talked a lot about all four Beatles. Grandma Rose wondered aloud how any mother could name their son Ringo.

"Ringo is at least a name," Grandpa Sol said. "How a mother could name her son Cousin Brucie—*that* I don't understand."

Kennedy Airport was busy. It always was. As we walked from the parking lot to the International Arrivals Building, we had to step aside dozens of times to let people pass who walked in the same direction, but more hastily. We were early enough so that we didn't have to rush. When we arrived in front of the terminal building, we saw two teenagers on the sidewalk by the entrance doors, a boy and a girl, campaigning for Barry Goldwater, a senator from Arizona who was running for president against Lyndon Johnson. Johnson was completing the term begun by John Kennedy. The teenage boy and girl held up signs and handed out buttons and bumper stickers. A poster was set up behind them that had a picture of Goldwater with the slogan, "In your heart, you know he's right." I heard Grandpa Sol mutter, "In my heart I know he's a Republican."

The teenage girl was in front of me. Her name tag said Hillary.

"Hi!" she said. "May I give you a Goldwater button?" She was practically giddy at the prospect of being able to put her candidate's name on my sweater. She looked to be about my age, was of similar height, and held back her light brown hair with a black beret, similar to the way I wore my hair that day. But in other ways this girl could not have been more dissimilar. I would never have approached a stranger with such brashness. Her assertiveness actually startled me for a moment. Daniel stood by my side, more curious than startled, and spoke up on my behalf.

"We're Democrats," he said. "I think we'll be voting for President Johnson."

"That's okay," Hillary said. "Everyone is entitled to an opinion. But everyone is also entitled to having their opinion challenged, based on the facts!"

I must admit that while my natural inclination was to pull away, I suddenly and secretly admired this girl's theatrical zest for what she was doing. Despite thick glasses and a prominent overbite, her spirit and confidence were undeniable. I wanted a little of that to rub off on me.

Grandma Rose and Grandpa Sol, already several steps ahead of us, turned around to see why Daniel and I had stopped following. Just then, an older man in front of us said to Hillary,

"Leave well enough alone, girlie. Go somewhere else."

The teenage boy who was with Hillary looked nervous.

"Come on, Hill," he said. "We're not supposed to get into fights."

"If we leave well enough alone," Hillary countered, "we'll all be communists soon, whether we like it or not." She forcibly put a Goldwater bumper sticker into the man's hand.

"You're very cocky," the man stated. "Why don't *you* run for president."

"Maybe I will one day," the girl said. Then she started to say something else, but her campaign buddy put his hand on her shoulder to compel her to stop.

Grandma insisted that Daniel and I speed up and join them as they approached the doors that led into the building. They didn't want to be late for Mom and Dad's arrival.

The International Arrivals Building was a small universe onto itself. There were people of all different shapes, sizes, colors, and temperaments, with all manner of personal styles and accessories, some with exotic luggage, others who pushed carts or carried handbags or boxes. There were trails of perfumes and colognes from all over the world. Steven would have loved it. I was sad he hadn't come along.

Grandma Rose kept a tight grip on Daniel's hand as we walked through the building in search of gate twenty-seven. Grandpa Sol always was a few steps behind. We found the gate and settled in by a cluster of blue plastic chairs at the end of the hallway that were all connected to one another. It was fifty-five minutes before the flight's scheduled arrival. The chairs were uncomfortable and slippery, and Grandma accepted the fact that it was all but impossible to keep Daniel sitting still for more than a few minutes at a time. So she grudgingly agreed to let him wander just a few yards in either direction, as long as I kept a strict eye on him.

A group of Hasidic men approached our gate, where Daniel now stood, all with long black coats and wide-brimmed black hats. Most had thick beards and moustaches and the long curly sidelocks that are common among them. From comments I had heard in the past, I knew that Grandma Rose and Grandpa Sol, and even Mom and Dad, were somewhat bothered, at times even repelled, by the outwardly archaic ways of the Hasidic Jews—Jews who believed in the literal truth of the bible and tenaciously held onto their ancient ways. I recall having discussed it with the family a few months before when we saw a group of Hasidic men on a Brooklyn street during a visit to Grandpa Jesse and Grandma Leah's apartment. I was in the back seat of the car and said that I believed that devotion and good hearts on the inside were far more important than customs and appearances on the outside. I said I neither despised nor approved of their attire, but simply accepted it. "Well," Mom said from the front seat, "accept it from a distance. If they're good people, fine, but to me, it just doesn't seem right. It makes it difficult for the rest of us."

Neither Daniel nor I felt any cause for concern when we saw the Hasidic men in the International Arrivals Building. What with the vast sea of human diversity flowing through, these quiet, antiquated men seemed incapable of creating difficulty for anyone. Most of them searched their pockets for notes and papers. Two of them, one fat and the other skinny, chatted in Yiddish. Daniel noticed that the skinny one carried sheet music under his arm. The man saw Daniel's head cocked almost sideways, trying to glance at the top page, which hung to the side.

"You read music?" he asked, in a real accent that resembled Grandpa Sol's fake one.

"Yes," Daniel replied.

"Your mama and papa know where you are?"

"My grandmother's right over there," he pointed.

"Look here. Can you read this?" The man took the sheet music out from under his arm and held it in his hands. Daniel hummed the first two staff lines. Both men watched and listened.

"You sight-read very well," the fat one said.

"Thank you," Daniel responded.

"Can you read Hebrew?"

"A little."

"Can you read this?" He pointed to the Hebrew words under the first staff line. Daniel studied them carefully for a few moments and put into play all the Hebrew school lessons he had absorbed for about a year now.

"*Hazzor i-yim bed-heem ah-berinnah yiktsoru,*" he sang slowly.

The two men looked at each other, smiled, then clapped their hands. A few of the other Hasidic men turned toward them when they heard the applause, and the skinny man asked Daniel to sing it again.

"*Hazzor i-yim bed-heem ah-berinnah yiktsoru. La la lu, la la lu, ah-berinnah yiktsoru,*" he repeated.

The entire group of Hasidic men now applauded loudly with smiles and cheers. Grandma Rose heard the commotion, looked up, saw Daniel surrounded by the ancient cult, and shouted,

"Daniel! Daniel! Get away from there! Now! You hear? Lori—why did you let him—? Oy gut..."

A baby held by a young mother on a chair next to Grandma's started to wail. The mother stood up abruptly and glared at Grandma.

"What's the matter with you? Are you stupid?" she barked and stormed away.

I don't know which embarrassed me more—Grandma's frightened shout or the young mother's nasty insult; all I knew was that I wanted to disappear. Daniel quickly sat down next to me and rested his head on my arm. That helped calm me down. We stayed there, the two of us, silent and still, for what seemed like an eternity.

"Rabbi Sheldon would have let me talk to them," Daniel whispered to me sadly.

"I know," I whispered back.

The flight from Aruba finally arrived. Mom and Dad hugged and kissed us, and then we all went to the baggage claim area two flights down. After all the luggage had been collected from the circling carousel, we made our way back to the car and headed east on the Belt Parkway toward Westbrook Hills. Dad drove. Mom told us she missed us and had presents for us, and she asked what we did while they were away. I told her about the two books I had taken out of the library and how Grandma and I had finally gotten the dirt and grass stains out of Steven's baseball uniform. Daniel said he watched a new family move into a house down the block that had been for sale for many months.

"Jewish?" Dad asked.

"I don't know," Daniel said.

"I hope you didn't spend too much time in your room," Mom said to Daniel. "You want to turn into a skinny, pale man like your Grandpa Jesse? He stayed inside and wrote songs all day long. I want you to look like a mensch, not a songwriter."

"Guess who we saw in Aruba?" Dad said as we turned onto Pearl Drive. But we never found out who they saw in Aruba because Mom, in the front passenger seat, let out a terrified shriek when she saw two fire trucks, three police cars, and an ambulance in front of our house.

"Steven!"

"What? What? Oy gut!" Grandma screeched next to me in the back seat. "Oy gutenyu. I told you, Sol! No one listens to me."

Dad sped up the car and screeched to a halt in front of the Kelleher house, where there was an open spot on the street. Several neighbors stood around watching the activity by our house. We saw no fire, nor any smoke, but a hose from one of the fire trucks snaked across our front lawn toward the driveway. We all jumped out of the car.

Steven came to the front from the side of the house, accompanied by two firemen. Dad ran over to them. Mr. Ashler was there, too, talking to one of the policemen. He was shirtless and wore red bathing trunks. His huge stomach hung over the top of the trunks.

"I'm sitting in the sun in my backyard," Mr. Ashler said to the policeman, "and suddenly I hear this hissing sound and then a loud crack, and I hear shingles fall off the house and crash onto the driveway cement. Sounded like big dominos. So I ran inside and called the fire department."

As we soon learned, Steven had fastened three model rockets together with duct tape, believing that would make the conjoined missile go faster and higher than they would have one at a time. He set it up in our driveway. But the contraption blasted off at an angle instead of straight up, and smashed with tremendous force into the shingles on the side of the house, just to the right of the chimney. The collision was so powerful that eight shingles shattered and exposed the black tarpaulin beneath them, and splintered the wood even behind that. The remains of the three rockets, in several dozen pieces, were scattered all over the driveway, and even onto Mr. Ashler's back lawn.

"He was alone, Mr. Hillman?" the policeman asked.

"Just for a little while," Dad said. "My in-laws picked us up at the airport. He's almost fourteen."

"I'm not sure that was such a good idea."

A fireman joined them on the driveway.

"No fire?" Dad asked him.

"No fire. The good news is that your son is a quick thinker," he said. "The moment it happened, he turned on your garden hose and wet down the entire area. There *could* have been a fire, though. Those little rockets are very powerful. They can be quite dangerous under the wrong circumstances."

Dad turned to Mr. Ashler. "Thanks for calling it in, Henry," he said.

"Kids," Mr. Ashler responded. "I'd have a serious talk with him if I was you, Murray."

Dad didn't need advice from Henry Ashler, and everyone knew it, probably even Mr. Ashler himself. We all knew that Dad would handle the situation in his own way—seriously, yet without much yelling. And absolutely no striking. (Mr. Ashler, it was rumored, had been a yeller *and* a striker when his children were young.)

"Owning these rockets," the policeman said to Dad, "is perfectly legal, Mr. Hillman. But you need a permit from the county to set them off, and it must be done under adult supervision."

"I understand, officer."

"So it'll just be a verbal warning this time. Next time it could be a little more serious."

"Thank you. Thank you very much."

Mom hugged Steven and thanked God that he was all right. Grandma Rose smothered him with kisses and gave him an extra large white fish sandwich on Italian bread that she seemed to have whipped up in the house even before the fire trucks left the block.

Steven's punishment was the cancellation of an overnight bike trip he had planned to take to the North Fork of Long Island with one of his friends. It was actually the harshest penalty Dad could have dispensed, because Steven had talked about that trip for months.

"Don't write a damned song about this," Steven snapped at Daniel as he went into the house to spend the rest of the afternoon in solitude.

Early the next morning, Daniel put *The Little Girl in the Chapel* and a handwritten letter into a large manila envelope, put five stamps on the envelope, and went outside.

"I'll be right back," he called out to no one in particular.

He walked down the street toward Miller Avenue. There was a mailbox on the corner of Pearl Drive and Miller. He dropped the envelope into the mailbox.

Suddenly, a single cluster of dandelion seeds flew by. Daniel thought instantly of Carol. Little suns bursting with rays. He also thought of them as tiny white firecracker explosions frozen in time. Miniature propellers that took all wishes to heaven... That's how it went—assigning all kinds of fictional imagery to it—which he had time to do because the cluster of seeds hovered in front of him for a long time. Daniel stretched out his arm and gently grabbed it, hoping not to crush it beyond usefulness. He held it in front of his face for several moments, made a wish, and with a single puff, blew it into the sky.

# Three

I had applied to five colleges, all within driving distance of Westbrook Hills, and was accepted at all five. I selected Adelphi University. My first semester was to begin on Monday, August 30, 1965.

"I'm gonna go to the University of Colorado," Steven announced the day a class catalog arrived in the mail for me. This was in the middle of June. We were all in the living room. (Grandma Rose and Grandpa Sol weren't there that day. Rare—but it happened from time to time.) Steven, who had a little league game later on, was hunched over tying his sneakers.

"Colorado..." Mom murmured—not as a question, but an attitude. "Why Colorado?"

"Because I read somewhere that students there hike all the time, ride motorbikes, jump off mountains with parachutes—"

"They also attend classes," Dad said. He didn't look up from his newspaper.

"Hardy har har," Steven smirked. Dad looked at him over the rim of his glasses and smirked in return.

"You don't have to jump off any mountains," Mom said. "You can jump off your own bed if you want. As long as you take off your sneakers."

"I guess I'll go to NYU," Daniel said moments later, unceremoniously, while he flipped through the TV Guide. "They have a good arts program."

Mom, a laundry basket by her feet, gave up looking for a matching sock to the one on her lap. She seemed slightly exasperated.

"You know, Daniel," she said, "there *are* other things to study in college besides music. And that would be the smart thing to do anyway."

"I know that," Daniel said. "I didn't say 'music program' anyway. I said 'arts program.' Literature. Creative writing. Film. Theater. If you listened to me every once in a while, you would've heard that."

Mom threw the lone sock that had been on her lap into the laundry basket and looked at Daniel with a furrowed brow.

"Literature? Creative writing? Where did *that* come from? That's not exactly what I had in mind, either. Oy gevalt."

Mom seemed to have added the 'oy gevalt' simply because Grandma Rose wasn't there to do it. It didn't really sound like her, and we all knew it.

It occurred to me at that moment that although Steven was soon to enter his sophomore year in high school and Daniel was soon to start junior high, it was the two of them talking about college careers, and not me, even though I was the one who was actually on the way to college. I sat alongside them, in the living room, with an Adelphi catalog, and no one said anything about that. Did it occur to no one but me? If I were to psychoanalyze it I suppose I'd deduce that Mom and Dad were worried about how I would fare in the college environment; after all, my junior high and high school days were fraught with more social and emotional insecurity than most other students seemed to endure.

Dad always had the option to request the use of a company car, though he never sought it for fear of appearing greedy. But just before the fall semester began, he filled out the paperwork, was given a three-year-old Chevrolet Malibu (with the LILCO logo painted on each side), and let me have the old Ford Galaxie so that I could commute to Adelphi. Not long after the semester started, I took Daniel with me to campus one day when Westbrook Hills Junior High School was closed for a teachers conference. I thought he'd like to see the way so many students played instruments outside. While we walked around, Daniel noticed handwritten fliers all over campus that announced the next meeting of a special program called Camp Campus. "Don't be shy! Stop on By!" one flier urged. "Don't be a snail. Come tell your tale," said another. Daniel chuckled. That's when I confided in him that I was a participant in Camp Campus.

"Seriously?" he asked.

"Seriously," I assured him.

Camp Campus was an experimental program designed to help timid students adjust more easily to the college environment. It was actually Mom and Dad who suggested it in the first place after they heard about it from a friend at Temple Beth Shalom. I had joined on my second day as an Adelphi undergrad. Mom and Dad were quite surprised that I did so without serious reservations. While my academic performance at school was excellent, Camp Campus actually caused me to miss many classes because of all the therapy sessions I attended with the group's faculty advisor, Dr. Vincent Yaccarini, who was also chairman of the Psychology Department at Adelphi.

Adelphi had recently been endowed with a grant that allowed the department to test the new program, which combined group meetings with private sessions. If Camp Campus was successful, the college would get additional grants to help modernize the financially threadbare psychology department. The experimental program was given just one year to succeed. Which, in a way, meant that I could help out my department by skipping some of my regular classes.

As we strolled from one cluster of buildings to another, I confided to Daniel that what Mom and Dad didn't know about the sessions was that I had come to depend upon them to help me start my day the way some people depend upon their first cup of coffee.

"That's a good line," Daniel said. "Can I use it?"

"For what?" I asked.

"I have no idea."

"Okay."

I told him that the sessions helped me stay calm all afternoon on campus, regardless of who I met and what I had to do. I made Daniel promise not to tell Mom and Dad any of what I shared and warned him that if he did, I'd tell them about the secret package he put in the mailbox.

"You *know* Mom won't like to hear that," I said. "She'll say it's just not right."

Daniel promised—as long as I told him a little more about the Camp Campus sessions.

"Why?" I asked.

"Maybe it will make a good story one day."

"Fine."

So I described my first session where, at the end of it, Dr. Yaccarini asked me why I spoke so easily to him yet claimed to have difficulty speaking with everyone else. I told him that I always felt more comfortable around people whose job it is to help other people—like him. Maybe it was because deep down, I felt that people like him have heard and seen it all.

"But you talk to me about lots of stuff," Daniel said, "and *I* haven't seen it all."

"But you listen well," I told him. "Dr. Yaccarini said that maybe I should choose to become a professional whose job it is to listen. To help other people. Maybe a guidance counselor. Or a psychologist."

"Dr. Lori Hillman!" Daniel announced. "Maybe you can help explain why Mom says Murray every time he asks her to stop Murraying him."

We walked through an outdoor quad where many undergrads lounged around. One student played a guitar, another one played a flute. Next to the fine-arts building a girl stood by an easel painting the scene in front of her, and at another end of the quad, by the cafeteria, a boy sat cross-legged on the grass with a small typewriter on his lap, oblivious to all else going on as he furiously pressed key after key.

"Don't you think Mom and Dad listen?" Daniel asked, having picked up on a part of the conversation that had ended several minutes earlier.

"Sometimes. With them, one day it seems like it's all hope and optimism, and the next it's like all the hope and optimism are just delusions. I'm learning how *not* to think that way."

We walked around some more. The guitar player's instrument had one string that was out of tune. I could see Daniel blanch. I'm sure he was tempted to ask the guitarist if he could tune it for him—but the guitarist did it on his own just as we passed by.

A girl with a fancy camera around her neck—she looked like a younger version of Mom—walked in front of us and said hi. I said "Hi" back. It felt good to be friendly so easily.

"Do you know what autistic means?" I asked Daniel.

"I read a little about it somewhere," he said. "Why?"

We sat down on the grass.

"A long time ago," I explained, "when I was in junior high, I started to cry because I misunderstood what my teacher told me to do, and I thought the other kids were making fun of me. I was a mess. Completely miserable. A few days later, one of my teachers told me to stop by the school psychologist's office. So I did. Mom was there. I overheard the school psychologist whisper to her that there was a small possibility that I might be borderline autistic."

"Did you tell that to Dr. Yaccarini?"

"Yes. He said that was ridiculous. He said the school psychologist was an idiot. I also told him that Mom called the guy a fat dope right to his face. Then at home, she called him 'a stupid ass with an IQ of minus a thousand.' I remember it word for word. How could you forget something like that?"

"What did Dr. Yaccarini think about that?" Daniel asked.

"He said that with a mother like that, how could I have any problems at all?"

We drove home. When we pulled up in front of the house, Daniel said he felt pretty good because he knew that I'd be fine in college. Whatever made things easier at home, he said, was okay with him. That proved to me either that Mom and Dad talked a lot about me when I wasn't there, or that Daniel had suddenly aged a few years and was secretly studying to be a psychologist himself.

Whatever it was, I, too, felt pretty good.

But then Grandpa Sol passed away, and I realized how we were all still so vulnerable. When Rabbi Sheldon visited our house, he tried to put it in perspective by reminding us how almost everyone on earth will one day lose not just one grandfather, but two. We all appreciated what he said, but it was painful, nonetheless. Grandpa Sol had been the first member of our immediate family to die.

•     •     •     •

Grandpa Sol had come down with what everyone thought was the flu. A week later, he was dead. He had never gone to the doctor. He was rushed to the hospital by ambulance from our house about ten minutes after he put together two names, Mora Connelly and Herbert Less, from the wedding section of the newspaper. Mora Less was the last thing he said before he died.

To decide who in the family was hit the hardest would be an exercise in futility. Grandma Rose lost an entirely devoted, if not completely dependable, companion of fifty-five years and suddenly felt like a newcomer all over again in a strange and not very friendly new world. Mom was embittered, all too well aware of the fact that there were so many mean, bigoted, humorless, unworthy, even sick old men who hung on for years, while her sweet, gentle, life-loving father had been taken away so unexpectedly. She treated it not simply as an injustice, but as yet another preordained misery. "First my brother Howard, now this," she moaned a number of times the week we sat Shiva in our house. Dad tried to be patient and understanding but was so worn out at the end of the day that he was able to offer little comfort either to Mom or Grandma Rose. His constant weary appearance didn't help.

I tried to imagine that Grandpa Sol was happy wherever he was. I also tried to avoid Grandma Rose because she refused to entertain the notion that anyone could be happy anymore. I asked her once if she remembered Rhoda Ruder, but Grandma looked at me as if I had just arrived from Mars.

At the funeral, Rabbi Sheldon talked about Grandpa's journey to America, and his mission in life to laugh and make others laugh along with him. In the days that followed, Steven poured himself into atlases and maps, ostensibly to trace our family's transatlantic voyage, but more likely to escape all the new emotions that had suddenly invaded our home on Pearl Drive.

Daniel was affected more by Mom and Grandma's constant crying than by the permanent absence of the grandfather he had seen almost every week since he was born.

I stayed at Adelphi as much as I could.

$$\bullet \qquad \bullet \qquad \bullet$$

Daniel received a second sour note a few days later. It was in our mailbox. A rejection letter arrived from MGM about *The Little Girl in the Chapel*. The note acknowledged that Daniel had "a tremendous amount of talent," but that it would be "virtually impossible for us to produce the work of such a young person, especially one without professional representation." Daniel felt it was a gross hypocrisy: if he had the talent, what did it matter about his age or lack of representation?

Meanwhile, Grandma Rose moved in with us, even though she still had the apartment in Queens. In addition to all the crying in the house, sometimes now there was shouting, too, mostly between Mom and Dad about what course of action would ultimately be best for Grandma. To break her lease in Queens and move in with us permanently was the quickest and least costly option, but it wasn't necessarily the one that would suit everyone's sensibilities. There was another option: Grandma Rose had a widowed sister and a widowed sister-in-law at a senior condominium complex in Pompano Beach, Florida. If Grandma decided to move in with them, there would be plenty of help with the relocation arrangements, and there would always be someone around to keep an eye on her. Mom and Dad gently pushed her in that direction, insisting there were more people her age and that the weather was good all year long. "But it's hot like soup," Grandma said. "And there are bugs and little lizards, and there are old men who might think I have a lot of money because my clothing always looks new, which it's not and I don't have a lot of money. but they'll think I do. And who needs that aggravation from old men?"

She decided to stay with us in Westbrook Hills.

After a few weeks in our house, Grandma Rose settled into a sort of functional misery. She spent her days cooking, cleaning, and sewing and frequently sprinkled a little complaining into the mix. Everyone in the house did their best to accept it. Steven said it was like living in a soap opera called *As the World Kvetches*.

•  •  •  •

Steven was on the Junior Varsity baseball team at Westbrook Hills High School and practiced with the team every Saturday after breakfast. One morning, as Grandma drank a cup of tea in the kitchen while looking at the newspaper, Steven walked into the house after practice and said to her,

"See any good names to put together?"

"I don't know what you're saying," Grandma snapped. "You walk into the house with filthy shoes like that?"

"Hello to you too," Steven grumbled. Over Grandma's shoulder, he noticed an article about the conflict in Vietnam.

"If I'm ever drafted," he muttered "I'll move to Canada and explore the Canadian Rockies on a Harley Davidson. Far away from here."

"Don't talk nonsense," Grandma said. "Canada. Oy gevalt..."

"Oh—*that* you understand... Okay. I'll go to Cambodia instead. Would that be better?"

"You'll go nowhere. You want I should be *more* miserable, thank you very much?"

"In three years they can draft me. I might *have* to go somewhere."

"Oy gevalt."

Steven came into the living room, where Daniel finally practiced the piano after having been told not to three times earlier that morning.

"Where's Mom?" he asked.

"The beauty parlor," Daniel said.

"I need to get out of Temple Oy Gevalt, or I might kill myself. I'm going to Billy's house. When Mom gets back from the ugly parlor, tell her where I am."

"Can I come with you?" Daniel asked.

"To Billy's? No."

"Why not?"

"Because you can't."

"Fuck you, asshole."

Steven's mouth hung open in bewilderment.

"Excuse me?" he finally said, with a tone that seemed mature beyond his years. For all his new-found teenage impertinence, Steven still toed a fairly straight line, and Daniel's words bothered him. Even Daniel wasn't entirely certain where those words had come from; it seemed as if some sort of secret cauldron of frustration had somehow developed deep in his subconscious, primed to bubble over at any moment.

"Sorry," he said to Steven. "It's just that nobody lets me do anything anymore."

Billy, who had been at Steven's bar mitzvah, lived in Hicksville, two towns away. The two had met at a local summer camp a few years earlier. Billy was in a rock 'n roll band that was fairly successful around Long Island. Though Steven didn't play any instruments, he liked to help the band set up their microphones and amplifiers and also to help navigate them to gigs around the Island. One of Billy's older friends had a Volkswagen van and a driver's license.

I had met Billy two or three times. I wanted to say hello to him at Steven's bar mitzvah but found too many excuses not to. Although he was two years younger than me, I'll admit to being a bit mesmerized both by his looks and the confidence he exuded. A few years ago he had seen the mezuzah on my bedroom door when he was over our house and complimented me on it. In fact, I believe he may even have been flirting with me. I said I had homework to do and quickly retreated into my bedroom.

Billy liked Daniel, too, which is just one reason why Daniel wanted to accompany Steven to Hicksville. The other reason was that he simply needed to get out of the house. A trip to Billy's would have given Daniel a way to play some music on his free time while averting any musically-related criticism at home. His weekly piano and guitar lessons had already been cut back to twice a month, ostensibly because of finances, but more likely because Mom wanted the house to be quieter more often. She had suggested selling the xylophone, which she said was collecting dust in the basement (it really wasn't; Daniel played it two or three times a week), and also requested that Daniel play the piano and guitar only when Grandma was away at other relatives (which was almost never). Finally, Mom urged him to go to school a little early or to stay a little late so that he could practice the saxophone for the school band in the music room instead of at home.

But Steven refused to let Daniel go with him to Billy's house. Mom and Dad were not home to intervene, Grandma Rose was in no position to make decisions, and I wasn't around to mediate, either. (I was at Adelphi.) So as Steven rode to Billy's house on his bicycle, Daniel went into the kitchen to see if he could at least find something to say to Grandma Rose that wouldn't cause an immediate Oy gevalt.

"Can you tell me the story one more time about the village in Poland where you and Grandpa Sol met?" he asked her gingerly.

We had first heard the story about six years earlier and enjoyed it so much that we requested it about once a year—at least while Grandpa Sol was still alive.

Grandma Rose glanced up from the newspaper.

"Poland?" she said. "Oy—I don't remember."

"I do," Daniel muttered on his way out of the kitchen. He knew it was useless to press her on it. He went to his bedroom instead, already replaying the story in his head, just as Grandpa Sol had told it half a dozen times before.

Grovitsz was the name of the shtetl where Grandpa Sol and Grandma Rose grew up. Most of the adult citizens were friends of Grandpa's at the factory where he and Grandma worked beginning in 1909. The factory made very simple window shades, curtains, and louvers. To call it a factory was a bit of a stretch, for it was not automated in any way whatsoever. Grandma and Grandpa and about two dozen other poor Jews made all the products by hand, including the tools used to assemble the raw materials and connect all the parts. When they both came to America in 1915, Rose Lashinsky married Solomon Gersh and begged him to open up his own window factory, or at least a window retail store. But Sol said he had worked hard enough between the ages of nine and nineteen for five careers. "I worked harder than a doctor, a lawyer, and a blind cab driver put together," he was fond of saying. Also, he had been so sick on the boat to Ellis Island that he was convinced he had to take it easy for the rest of his life. "Diarrhea, vomiting, you name it. I didn't know one end from the other."

So Sol worked as a window sill cutter and polisher at a factory—a *real* factory this time—in Long Island City, for forty-seven years. Grandma worked at the same factory as a seamstress during their first few years in America, which in effect duplicated their lives together in Grovitsz, although with better working conditions and higher wages. Rose often complained that her beloved Sol had never really left the shtetl.

We all loved that story, despite its relatively gloomy tone.

As a result of Sol's chosen career and attitude, his income was meager and his prospects for the future dim. Sol and Rose did what they could for their three children, Beverly, Milton, and Howard, to help them explore their interests and find their strengths. Both Beverly and Milton had music lessons for several years and were given as many books as they wanted to read, at least until the apartment began to grow smaller. The family even took several road trips so that the children could see famous sites in Philadelphia, Hartford, and other cities. Beverly loved to buy out-of-town newspapers and survey their stories and columns. Milton loved to walk into tall, austere office buildings to explore their lobbies and hallways. Their little brother Howard, who Beverly adored profoundly, hardly had a chance to explore anything at all; he died suddenly of diphtheria at the age of six, when Mom was just fourteen years old. I heard her say a number of times that a part of herself had died that day, too.

$$\bullet \quad \bullet \quad \bullet \quad \bullet \quad \bullet$$

On Sunday, the day after Steven refused to let his brother tag along to Billy's, Daniel went to a party at Joey and Johnny DePuzo's house—although he hadn't actually been invited.

Mom was in the kitchen arguing with Grandma Rose. Daniel knew that Mom and Grandma considered October to be a winter coat month, but with the two of them so preoccupied with their kvetching, he managed to slip out of the house without one.

Craig Stuart couldn't play. He had eaten three chocolate doughnuts after breakfast and had a terrible stomachache. His older sister Linda came to the door to explain that to Daniel. Linda was my age but attended parochial school. Only her large brown eyes gave any evidence at all that she was related to the other brown-eyed Stuarts. All of them were plump with poor complexions and bad teeth; Linda was beautiful. Her features were well-proportioned, and she was without a blemish. (That's what I was truly jealous about; acne at that time seemed to adore my chin.) Linda's teeth were white, her hair jet black and shiny, and her lashes long. Even her cheeks were rosy. We all knew her to be popular and outgoing. Despite the dreadful stories we had all heard over the years about parochial school kids who rebelled against treacherous nuns and repressive rules (and rulers), Craig's sister embraced her religious upbringing. She went to mass every Sunday and was involved in many church activities. I admired that.

Daniel left the Stuart house after he talked with Linda for a few moments. He skipped the Sheldon house because he wasn't in the mood for Glenn. He went to the Kelleher house, but Doug was at a wedding in Rhode Island. That left the DePuzo twins.

As Daniel approached their house, he noticed several cars on either side of the street—shiny Buicks, Lincoln Continentals, and Cadillacs. They were parked bumper to bumper along the curb in order to squeeze four cars between two driveways where normally only three would fit. Two men in dark suits sat quietly on the front steps as Daniel came closer. They stared but remained silent. Suddenly, Joey came from the side of the house, chased by Johnny, each brandishing a brand new water rifle.

"Daniel!" Johnny called out, "come to our party."

"What party?" he asked.

"My grandfather is having a party for the business."

"But I'm not invited."

"So what? We got a million cousins here. No one's gonna mind."

"No one's gonna know, either" echoed Joey.

"I'm not dressed for a party."

"Who cares?" Joey said. "You look fine. Besides, my grandfather likes you. He says he wishes you were one of his grandsons."

"He does?"

Salvatore Bonomo, Johnny and Joey's maternal grandfather, was often heard crooning old Italian love songs in his backyard, despite the fact that he was entirely tone deaf. A widower who, at sixty-nine, was still as vigorous as ever, it was not hard to imagine Sal Bonomo tell his family something as impertinent as wishing for another grandson, a *different* grandson, a *musical* grandson.

Daniel followed Johnny and Joey into the backyard, which was crisscrossed by strings of small yellow lantern lights. Although it was still daylight, the lanterns were lit. A bed sheet was draped over the tall brick border of the patio, and hand-painted on it were the words: "Cross Island Mason Supply: 25 Successful Years." Men and women, all in elegant coats, stood on the back lawn. They talked and laughed, and nearly every one of them held a drink. Most of the men also had cigars, some lit, others simply being chewed. A portable bar had been set up at the side of the patio. There was a tuxedoed bartender behind it. A Dean Martin record played in the background. The stereo system was behind the bar, and the speakers were on the ground by each end of a long table that was covered by a white tablecloth. On the table were trays of cold cuts, sausages, meatballs, breads, dips, pretzels, nuts, and fruit. And stacks of record albums.

"Johnny, Joey, the two of you's put those guns away," someone yelled from the kitchen window. "This is your grandfather's party, for Christ's sake." It was their mother, Felice DePuzo.

Johnny opened the garage door, and he and his brother threw the water rifles inside. The toys hit an old window pane or an old picture frame; Daniel heard the sound of shattering glass.

"I'm gonna kill you's both," Mrs. DePuzo shouted, even though she hadn't seen exactly what had happened. "Clean it up now, whatever the hell it is—or else! You hear me?"

Without an argument, Johnny and Joey rushed inside the garage. Daniel sauntered over to the end of the long white table, where the record albums were stacked high, and looked through. A man joined him there and looked through a different stack of records. He was about as tall as Dad, though more solidly built and at least fifteen years younger. He was impeccably dressed in dark gray pants and a white v-neck sweater. Each strand of his jet black hair was firmly in place. He wore no coat.

"How you doing, kid?" the man said to Daniel.

"I'm fine," Daniel responded.

"You a friend of Felice's boys?"

"Yes. I live down the block."

"What's your name?"

"Daniel."

"You like music, huh?"

"Sometimes."

"Sometimes? I think you mean *all* the time," he said. "You've been going through this here pile of albums like you was picking out a new suit."

"That's because I can't play records at home anymore," Daniel said.

"Your old man's on your case?"

"No. It's something else."

"Sorry. I shouldn't pry. Not my place." He grabbed a roll and took a bite. "You play an instrument?"

"Yes," Daniel said. "Piano, guitar, xylophone, and sax."

"Jesus friggin' Christ. You write songs, too?"

"Yes."

"Holy mother of God! You're a regular Paul Anka. Anything you *don't* do?"

"I haven't made a record yet."

"You want to?" the man asked.

" Maybe. I guess."

"Piano, guitar…" the man repeated. "No ukulele? Like Arthur Godfrey?"

"No," Daniel said. "But they're pretty neat. I saw someone in the Lovin' Spoonful play one on television last night."

"The Lovin' who?"

"It's a new group."

"You'd like one of them things, huh? Think your folks will get you one?"

"No. They don't even like the instruments I have now."

"Maybe you can ask someone else for a ukulele. How about Sal?"

"Mr. Bonomo? My parents would kill me."

"You think? Too bad. Hey—who's your favorite singer, kid?"

"Solo or group?"

"Solo."

"I've actually been listening to Bobby Darin and Nancy Wilson lately. But that changes."

The man laughed.

"Group?" he asked.

"The Beatles. But that changes, too."

"You're a real pisser kid." The man stuck out his arm. "Call me John. From Howard Beach. I do a little work with Sal from time to time. It's nice to meet you, Daniel." They shook hands. "Maybe I shoulda been a musician, like you. Actually, you know what I wanted to be? A priest." He laughed again. "You believe it? I didn't quite make it, though. I ain't no angel, and if you ain't no angel, you can't be no priest."

"I used to think about becoming a rabbi."

"No shit! Sorry—" The man covered his mouth. "I gotta watch my language in front of you's kids."

"Shit's okay. I use it all the time now," Daniel said, and the man's smile grew even wider than it was before.

"You could be a singing rabbi! Not a bad idea, huh? Anyways, I better go mingle… You're a real pisser, kid."

The man winked and left the patio to join a small crowd of people on the lawn.

Daniel walked back to the garage to look for Johnny and Joey but bumped instead into Felice DePuzo, who was now on the back-door steps holding another tray of cold cuts.

"Oh, Daniel!" she said, "I didn't know you were here, hon! Where are the boys? Are they ignoring you?"

"No. They're still cleaning up in the garage."

No one knew what happened to Frankie DePuzo, Felice's husband and Johnny and Joey's father. No one even speculated anymore. I think I had seen him a total of two times in my life when I was little and wouldn't even be able to describe him if I tried. Whatever his fate, Mrs. DePuzo went on after his disappearance as if nothing at all had happened. She looked the same, talked the same, and acted the same after Frankie was gone as she did when he lived on Pearl Drive. Felice DePuzo was always blonde in the summer and brunette in the winter, and in the spring and fall you could see a little bit of summer and winter in her hair at the same time. She always smelled of cigarettes, despite an extraordinary amount of perfume. And although she was a year or two younger than Mom, her perpetually tanned skin was almost completely covered with wrinkles. To be honest, her looks had always scared me a little bit.

"I think they finished cleaning up in the garage, hon," Mrs. DePuzo said to Daniel. "I heard them in the house. Go inside. There are other children in there. It's boring out here for kids, anyway."

Daniel went inside the house, looked in all the bedrooms, but found no one. He called out Joey's name and then Johnnie's. There was a large crucifix on the wall between two bedroom doors. A loin cloth-covered Jesus writhed in pain upon it. For no apparent reason, Daniel shrugged at it and said, "I have no idea what the fuck's going on."

He backtracked to the kitchen. Annette DePuzo, the twins' fifteen-year-old sister, was in there grabbing a handful of paper towels from the counter by the sink.

"Daniel!" she said, surprised to see him there. "What are you doing here?"

"Looking for Johnnie and Joey."

"They're probably hiding. They're so fucking immature." She covered her mouth. "Sorry."

"Fuck's okay," Daniel responded. "I say it all the time now."

Annette smiled.

Like Linda Stuart, Annette DePuzo had gone to parochial elementary and junior high school, but switched to Westbrook Hills High in her freshman year. She was what I suppose would be called a tomboy, with a brown shag-cut hairdo that was always a little messy and a full-lipped smile that was always a little crooked. Steven once told me that most boys at the high school thought she was sexy.

"We're downstairs," Annette said to Daniel. "Me and my cousins. Wanna come? I'll introduce you."

"But what about Johnnie and Joey?"

"What about them? Did they wait around for you? Why should you wait around for them? Fuck 'em."

Annette turned around to go back downstairs, and Daniel followed. He, too, felt her understated allure.

One half of the basement, the carpeted half, had chairs, a couch, and a pool table. The other half had all the typical basement utilities. The sun filtered in through the small windows near the ceiling and provided the only light in the room because none of the electric lights in the ceiling were on. Three girls sat in a semi-circle in the middle of the carpet. When Daniel's eyes adjusted to the dimness, he saw that they all were about the same age as Annette and dressed very similarly in flowered knee-length skirts with thick blue plastic belts. He saw that one held a magazine and another smoked a cigarette. In front of each girl was a wine glass that sat on a little wooden coaster. A bottle of wine was in the middle of the circle.

"That's my cousin Gina, and that's my other cousin Gina," Annette explained. "And that's my friend Gail."

With the paper towels she had taken downstairs with her, Annette began to dab at the carpet where a drink had apparently spilled earlier.

"This is my brothers' friend Daniel. He's okay. Not one of the idiot kids."

"I think I'm drunk," said one of the Ginas.

"Ever see a picture of two people fucking?" Gail asked. She pointed to Gina's magazine.

"Sure," Daniel lied.

"Ever feel anyone up?" the other Gina asked.

"Sure," he lied again.

The girls giggled.

Annette sat down on the carpet and Daniel sat next to her, completing the circle, with Gail on one side and the two Ginas on the other. The Gina with the cigarette passed it to Annette, who took a deep drag and then passed it to Daniel.

Daniel was entirely familiar with the smell because of Grandma Leah. Mom and Dad had warned the three of us on a number of occasions not to be tempted to take up the habit, that it was very bad, even though Dad used to smoke and Grandma still did. Dan and I had once wondered together what prompted some people to smoke, particularly *good* people like Dad and Grandma Leah. I must admit, though, that I once almost tried it myself, when I was twelve or thirteen, out of sheer curiosity. Dad had left a half-spent cigarette in an ashtray at home. Ultimately, I decided not to. Perhaps I feared God's watchful eye. Surely he would punish me in some way, even if it was merely to make sure that pimples never disappeared from my chin.

Daniel, too, was curious because he had seen so many photographs in music magazines of pianists and guitarists he admired smoking cigarettes, not to mention actors like Sean Connery and Dick Van Dyke, both of whom he had seen smoking in movies and on television shows. There had to be *something* that coerced good people to do something bad.

Was this unexpected basement powwow—in the presence of four older and not-at-all unattractive girls—the *something* in question? Daniel could only wonder. Could this, too, be one of the stumbles that Rabbi Sheldon mentioned from time to time? The rabbi had often said that God accepts a few wrong turns on the road of life, as long as you agree to pick yourself up and head in the right direction. What's more, if the reason for the stumble in the first place is to make new friends, well, isn't that one of the best reasons to stumble? After all, if there were any certainties at this time for Daniel, it was that he felt the need for new friends. The old ones were neither interesting nor encouraging. He had outgrown them.

So he took a drag of the cigarette. Then he handed it to Gail.

Annette looked at Daniel.

"You won't tell my mother, will you?" she asked.

"Tell her what?"

"That we're down here smoking and drinking."

"Not if you don't tell mine," Daniel said.

The girls giggled again.

Annette leaned into the center of the circle to retrieve the bottle of wine. It was half empty. She passed it around.

"I don't have a glass," Daniel said when the bottle came his way. "Guess I'll have to sip." So he took a marathon swig right out of the bottle, which the girls enjoyed immensely. Then he passed the bottle to one of the Ginas, and it made its way around again, eventually back to him. Without a moment's hesitation, Daniel swigged the rest of the wine in three large gulps. Almost instantly, his tongue and throat started to burn, and tears bubbled into his eyes. His head felt light and heavy at the same time. All four girls stared at him in what he later described as 'curious delight.' He handed the empty bottle to Annette.

"Holy fucking shit," Daniel said, "I *love* seeing pictures of people fucking. Give me the goddamn magazine."

The girls broke into laughter, but Annette quickly quieted them down. Daniel's eyes were completely used to the darkness by now. He stared at one girl after the other, starting at their eyes. Then he focused on their bosoms, and finally gazed down at their bare legs.

The cigarette made its way back to Daniel, and he took another drag. Someone had put the magazine on his lap, and he started to flip through but was too dizzy to make much sense of the fleshy photos. The girls chattered and giggled among themselves. Daniel drew another deep drag on the cigarette. When he exhaled, he glanced across the circle and saw one of the Ginas yawn. When she yawned, he saw her bosom stretch the material of her yellow blouse, which helped him imagine the size and shape of her breasts.

"I want to feel you up now," he said.

Without waiting for a response, Daniel lurched forward on his knees with his open hands outstretched. But because of his awkward position and lack of control, he missed Gina's breasts and landed his hands on her stomach instead. Then he fell sideways into the center of the circle. The giggles swelled. Daniel straightened himself up and made another lunge for the same Gina, but this time went for her bare legs. This, too, was an awkward lunge, and his nose and tongue met her exposed skin. Gina stood up brusquely, backed away, and wiped her leg with her hand. The sudden movement disoriented Daniel even more, and he fell onto his side into the middle of the carpet.

"We should go up," Annette said.

The game was over almost as quickly as it had begun.

Daniel, down there on the carpet, on his side, in his haze, considered the entire affair completely unfair: if it was okay to drink and smoke with girls, why was it against the rules to feel them up? Besides, wasn't it one of the Ginas who mentioned it in the first place? More hypocrisy, he thought to himself. Just like MGM. It was a realization—as cloudy as it was—that tasted to him as bitter as the cigarette.

The girls departed. Daniel sat for a while longer, trying to will himself to feel normal. It wasn't easy, and he wasn't entirely successful. But after five minutes or so, he at least felt confident enough to go outside. He climbed the basement stairs, drank a glass of water at the kitchen sink, rubbed his face with a wet paper towel, dried it with another, and went into the backyard through the kitchen door. Johnny and Joey stood at the rear of the garage. Joey had a tennis ball.

"Let's have a catch," he said.

But the catch was short lived because Sal Bonomo took his place on a short limestone bench in the middle of the lawn to make a speech, and everyone in the backyard stopped what they were doing. Two men tried to help Mr. Bonomo get up on the bench, but he stubbornly refused the offer.

"Ladies and gentlemen," he began as he smoothed out his black jacket by pulling at the waist, "it has been a wonderful and very successful twenty-five years, thanks to the help and dedication of my family, my friends, and my associates. I expect each and every one of us to be here for our fiftieth anniversary, with a few more children and grandchildren and maybe even great-grandchildren, God willing. Even as we stand here today, three of you's out there are pregnant, and in the words of my wonderful accountant, Manny Levine, kinahura and mazel tov."

There was laughter, followed by applause.

"We all built this company together, not just me. And it gives me great satisfaction to see how many of my dearest friends accepted my invitation to be here today. A beautiful fall day. I ordered it special."

There was more applause.

"When I came here on the boat from Palermo in 1907, just eleven years old, I didn't know a word of English, and alls I could do was carve a ship out of a piece of wood. I was scared, but full of dreams. My uncle Francis, rest in peace, took me in. One of the best brick and stone masons in the city, no can tell me otherwise. He helped build the towers of the Brooklyn Bridge. Used to drag me all over Manhattan, Brooklyn, Queens, showing me the buildings he worked on, the overpasses, the tunnels in Central Park... I hated it at first. Bored out of my friggin' skull, those damn walks... But after a while, I saw that it's a real skill. An art. Not everyone can do it. He taught me about brick and stone and concrete and got me a job with a company in Brooklyn. I learned a lot, made friends, saved some money, and in 1940 I started my own business. Cross Island Mason Supply, which back then, of course, was called Flushing Cement. Small office, five people. Remember?" A few elderly men nodded their heads and smiled.

As Sal Bonomo continued the historical account, Daniel's attention wandered—perilous though that may have been, given that every other pair of eyes was sharply focused on the man on the limestone bench. Daniel's attention wandered not out of boredom or disinterest in Mr. Bonomo's story, but *because* of it. In his mind's eye, he imagined a little boy from Italy carving a ship out of a piece of wood as he waits to step ashore in New York City to make his fortune. Somewhere else in the city is Solomon Gersh, who is just three years older and had also recently arrived in the New World after his own perilous journey. But instead of trying to make his fortune, Sol decides to make up funny names from the wedding section of the newspaper, like Frieda Livery and Anita Bath. They were two young men from different parts of the world who had both arrived at Ellis Island probably wearing similar clothes and carrying similar baggage—but with ideas and ideals that could not have been more dissimilar.

Daniel was startled out of his flight of fancy when someone touched his shoulder from behind. It was Steven.

"What the hell are you doing here?" Daniel whispered.

"What the hell are *you* doing here?" Steven answered in a much harsher whisper.

"Shhh. Mr. Bonomo's talking."

They quietly moved off to the side of the garage, beyond the view of anyone in the backyard.

"No one knew where you were," Steven explained. "Mom made me look all over the friggin' neighborhood for you."

"How'd you know I was here?"

"I didn't. I looked everywhere else first. I wasted the whole damn afternoon because of you. I have better things to do than to look for a jerk like you."

"Fuck you, Steven."

Steven smacked the side of Daniel's head.

"Watch your mouth, you little punk."

"What makes you think you can hit me?"

"Because you're eleven and I'm fifteen. Who are all these people, anyway?"

"They work for Mr. Bonomo."

"Oh, terrific, Daniel. Great place to spend a Saturday afternoon."

"What does that mean?"

"Nothing. Go home. Mom wants you."

Daniel started to walk away.

"Hold it!" Steven said sharply. He turned Daniel around by his shoulders and smelled his breath.

"Jesus Christ," Steven said.

Daniel walked home without another word. Steven followed. When he walked through the front door, Daniel saw the mezuzah nailed to the doorpost, shrugged, and said,

"I have no idea what the fuck's going on."

    •    •    •    •    •

I had not yet declared a major at Adelphi and continued to resist more invitations to parties and dates than I accepted. But I was trying hard, and things seemed to be evolving. I was also quite pleased with the progress I had made in my private therapy sessions.

One morning I asked Daniel if he wanted to help me write an opera called *Oy Traviata*. He said no thanks, without even bothering to question the strange title—but I explained it to him anyway.

In my private sessions, Dr. Yaccarini often asked me about my studies. I told him how much I enjoyed the work of Yiddish author Isaac Bashevis Singer in my Comp Lit class. He, in turn, told me that my love of literature reminded him of his own love of Italian opera. He quipped that we should combine our passions and write a Yiddish opera called *Oy Traviata*.

There was a time, of course, when Daniel would have thoroughly enjoyed the idea of an *Oy Traviata*, or something like it. This time, however, he gave me merely a pinch of acknowledgement and barely a smile. That made me a bit gloomy.

But later on, he did feel badly for so easily dismissing my *Oy Traviata* story, so to make up for it he asked me to pick him up after Hebrew School and drive him to the library. He knew that would give us a chance to chat. But we never did make it to the library. It turned out to be a terrible day for him: that was the day that Daniel lost all musical privileges both at Westbrook Hills Elementary School and Temple Beth Shalom. Although music as an obsessive foundation of his life had already begun to show a few cracks, until then it had still at least been a companion he could turn to in order to sooth his nerves.

Daniel lost another companion that day.

The first musical penalty was the result of a nasty exchange that Daniel had with a boy named Brendan. Brendan, who sat next to him in Mr. Valentine's sixth-grade class, had a slight speech impediment that some kids joked about from time to time. He responded to the taunts by misbehaving and became quite a disciplinary problem. Brendan saw Daniel write something in his notebook instead of taking notes from Mr. Valentine's classroom lesson. That apparently bothered him very much because Brendan's father demanded to see his own copious handwritten classroom notes every evening. Brendan didn't want Daniel to get away with what he could never get away with on his own. So he called the offense to Mr. Valentine's attention. Mr. Valentine asked Daniel to stop doodling. That infuriated Brendan even more since he often got in trouble simply for talking out loud without raising his hand. Brendan then decided to complain about something else. *Anything* else. He said he wasn't able to concentrate in class because Daniel constantly used pencils as drumsticks on his desk. This newest accusation put Mr. Valentine in a tough position. Brendan's father was a wealthy businessman who sat on the Board of Education, and an important school board meeting was only days away; it was possible that Brendan might tell his father that Mr. Valentine—who was not yet tenured and was always worried about his job—played favorites with some students. So Mr. Valentine had no choice but to respond to Brendan's complaint.

"Daniel, are you tapping on the desk with your pencils?" he asked reluctantly.

"No," Daniel said.

"Yes you were. Before!" Brendan protested. "You do it all the time. And you make fun of the way I talk every morning during the Pledge of Allegiance."

Mr. Valentine looked at Daniel.

"Daniel?"

"No I don't!" he insisted.

"Yes he does," Brendan said. "And he keeps telling me that I stink in music and that he's great."

"I never said that. Not even once!"

"You say it every day, Daniel. Every day!"

"Fuck you, Brendan, you asshole," Daniel shouted.

The class was stunned. So was Mr. Valentine.

"Daniel, I'm afraid I'm going to have to ask you to go to Dr. Smith's office," he said. "And please take this note with you." He quickly wrote out a note.

After Dr. Smith read the note, she leaned back in her chair and considered it for a while. She admitted that Brendan was often a problem student, but added that the outburst in Mr. Valentine's class was indefensible. Punishment would have to be severe "in order to be fair and effective—for you and all the other children," she said.

Daniel was told that he wouldn't be allowed to stay in the school concert band for the remainder of the term, nor would he be able to participate in the winter talent show.

Then, at Beth Shalom, Daniel inadvertently angered his Hebrew school teacher, Mrs. Weinstock. She frequently asked Daniel to play the classroom piano to help her describe the unique styles inherent in many Jewish songs and prayers. As he played a piece called "Yom Shaket," Daniel realized that the left-hand bass line resembled the bass line from a Beach Boys song that was popular at the time called "Help Me, Rhonda." Daniel allowed the thought to stay hidden in the back of his mind during the class lesson. But then Mrs. Weinstock was given a note from the temple secretary to come to the main office, so she told Daniel he could play a few songs while she was gone. That's when he decided to transform "Yom Shaket," into "Help Me, Rhonda." His Hebrew school classmates stood up and began to dance as Daniel pounded the keys. The kids boogied as if they were on some sort of Jewish-American Bandstand, and made a complete mess of the classroom in the process. (Ironically, yom shaket means quiet day in Hebrew.) By the time Mrs. Weinstock returned, there were books, papers, chalk, chalk board erasers, and magic markers all over the floor, the desks were scattered haphazardly in no discernible arrangement, and several coats hung off the American and Israeli flags on both ends of the blackboard. Mrs. Weinstock was appalled and barely able to speak. When she found her voice, she screamed at the entire class but saved an extra dose of anger for Daniel.

"What's happened to you?" she asked.

All Daniel could do was shrug his shoulders. He had no adequate response.

Mrs. Weinstock left the room again and returned a minute later with Ned Early. With a distressed look on his face, Ned wheeled the piano out of the classroom. Mrs. Weinstock said the music portion from her lessons would be eliminated for the next few months. She made Daniel sit in a corner of the room until dismissal.

After class, as Daniel left the building to walk to my car, Ned Early stopped him by the door and said,

"I heard why Mrs. Weinstock made me put the piano in the auditorium." He stooped over to whisper. "Betcha they'll tell me to move it back in before you can say Good Shabbos. You'll see."

Daniel was so frazzled from the day's events that he asked me to take him home instead of to the library. Later that night he told me that he planned to quit Hebrew school. We were in the living room watching television. He had already told me what had happened that day.

"Quitting? Just because of the piano?" I asked. "It wasn't even your fault. It was the other students who made the mess."

"I'm quitting because I hate it, and I hate Mrs. Weinstock, and I hate Mr. Valentine, and I hate Dr. Smith. They're all assholes."

"Please don't talk like that, Daniel."

"I hate school. Even Hebrew school. And I'm not going back."

"But you like Rabbi Sheldon, don't you?"

"He's not my teacher."

I stared at the television. I didn't know what to say.

"I used to get in trouble, too, because of something I loved," I finally shared. "Just like you got in trouble because of music. We're not so different, Daniel."

He looked at me dubiously, obviously in need of a deeper explanation.

"We're not so different," I repeated. "You know how much I love to read, right? Remember all the books I used to carry? In sixth grade, I used to sneak little peeks at some of my books, on my lap, after I finished the class assignment. One day Mrs. Fischer asked me a question while we were studying the Pilgrims, and I didn't hear her because I was so involved in what I was reading. She got mad at me. I'll never forget it. I remember the book, too. It was *Catcher in the Rye*. Mrs. Fischer must have asked me three times what I thought about the Pilgrims before she yelled at me to pay attention. I cried like crazy—as if that's a surprise."

"That's different," Daniel said. "She didn't stop you from ever reading books again, Lori."

"And nobody's stopping you from playing music."

"Oh no? I can't play in school anymore, I can't play in temple, and Mom doesn't let me play here. Where should I play—in the cemetery where Grandpa Sol is buried? Actually, I don't know why I care so much. I don't even *want* to play music anymore. That's the funny part."

"But you can't quit Hebrew school, Daniel."

"Why not? *You* never went to Hebrew school. Why do you care?"

"But I wish I *did* go. And I care because I think you'd be making a mistake."

Daniel stood up.

"Then *you* go!" he said and then hustled off to his room. On his desk was his Hebrew School notebook with a Temple Beth Shalom sticker on the cover. Temple Beth Shalom... House of Peace... Neither the temple on Suburban Avenue nor our home on Pearl Drive seemed to fit that bill much anymore.

Grandma Rose went to Yonkers to stay for a few days with a sister-in-law she despised. Grandpa Sol's sister Yetta cackled like a chicken, Grandma Rose insisted. "A sick chicken. It makes *me* sick to hear it." But Mom forced her to go. When she packed, Grandma stuck five of our towels in her suitcase because she was convinced that Yetta's towels would smell of mothballs.

Just before she left for Yonkers, Grandma Rose made a pot roast for the rest of us to have that first night without her. As we all dug in, Mom said to Daniel,

"Why don't you put on a concert for the neighborhood?"

For a moment, we thought we saw a ghost—the Ghost of Mother Past.

"It's just not right," she continued. "You come home from school every day and lock yourself in your room, and you never see your friends, and you look so miserable all the time... Do you feel all right?"

"Yes," Daniel said.

"School's okay?"

"I can't be in the band anymore. The kids stink. I'm bored out of my head. Other than that, sure, it's fine."

Dad looked up from his plate. "I'm still gonna fight that stupid decision," he said. "Taking you out of band. Stupid decision! What kind of school does that?"

"Dr. Smith's a moron," Steven added. "You should run over that little midget with a Mack truck until she breaks into a million pieces. Want me to do it?"

"Thank you, Mr. Subtle," Dad said to him. "When I want your help..."

Mom continued to stare at Daniel.

"Did you have an argument with your friends?" she asked.

"No.

"Well, that Craig isn't quite right anyway, and those twins—I just think they're nogoodniks."

Mom was not aware of how far Daniel had drifted away from his friends. But he had indeed drifted—not just because of their lack of interest in him, but because of his lack of respect for them. Doug had developed a serious case of vanity. He was in his church's production of *Oklahoma!* as Curley, the main character, and wasn't shy about letting everyone know how good he was. Glenn's penchant for pilferage, which was a secret to no one, reached a crescendo when he took one of Daniel's harmonicas, which had been a present from Grandpa Jesse, and stubbornly claimed it as his own. But it mattered little that Craig was not quite right or that the DePuzo twins were nogoodniks, for they had all found other friends in the neighborhood who were even duller and more irresponsible.

"Remember the little show you gave when you were or six or seven?" Mom continued. "That was so nice. The whole neighborhood came. Remember? Do it again, Daniel."

"I don't want to give a concert," he said.

"I'll help set it up," I offered.

"Of course you want to give a concert," Mom persisted. "You love to put on concerts. Don't play the martyr with me, young man. Daniel, sweetie, I know things haven't been easy, with Grandpa Sol passing away, and Grandma Rose always being in a mood, and Dad working so hard. And I know I haven't been a barrel of laughs lately, either, and that your father and I have been having a few little fights lately—but it doesn't have anything to do with you. You know that, don't you?"

Despite Daniel's repeated objections, Mom decided to plan a concert in the living room. It was to be held the following Saturday afternoon at two o'clock. It would be an open invitation for everyone on the block. Mom made a few phone calls, I bought snacks and drinks at the supermarket, and the two of us dusted off the old bridge chairs from the basement.

Dad signed on to work a half-day shift that morning so that he could be home to see the concert. He said he'd finish up with a half-night shift after dinner. I asked him why he couldn't just take the whole day off.

"And make everyone think that I'm leaving my job to go into showbiz management? You want me to get fired? You think Adelphi is free?"

Steven said he'd be at the concert. He also accepted an invitation from his friend Richard to go to Grumman Airport early Saturday morning, where Richard's father worked, to see a new military jet take a test flight. The flight was scheduled for eleven forty-five; Steven said he'd come home right after that.

Mom had a beauty parlor appointment that morning. She rarely missed a Saturday. She said it was her one luxury—a treasured indulgence that no one could take away from her. But appointments rarely lasted more than an hour, so she assured us she'd be home by noon.

Only Grandma Rose would miss the concert. She'd still be at Yetta's apartment trying to avoid all the mothball towels.

On Saturday morning, I put out the drinks and snacks, set up the chairs, and Windexed the large living room mirror. At ten to two, Doug Kelleher's father rang the front doorbell. Dad opened the door and invited Ken and Doug into the house.

"Hi, Ken," Dad smiled.

"Hi, Murray," he nodded back. "Hi, Lori." Mr. Kelleher was taller than Dad. As always, a few stiff strands of his dark brown hair hung over his forehead. Dad often joked that he always had an incredible urge to brush back those strands since Mr. Kelleher never seemed to want to do it himself.

"How are things at LILCO?" Mr. Kelleher asked.

"Busy," Dad said. "People still want their lights on. How's the pharmaceutical business?"

"Good. People still get sick. Hey, Murray," he said, "I hope Daniel's not upset that it's just me and Douglas. My wife and the girls took Michael on an outing. They went to the North Fork to pick vegetables. They have a farm out there that's easy on wheelchairs."

"I'm sure Daniel will understand," Dad assured him.

Daniel came out of his bedroom and went over to Doug.

"You don't have to stay if you don't want to," he whispered.

Moments later, Craig Stuart and his sister Linda arrived. Through the living room window, I saw them approach and opened the door just as Linda was about to ring the bell.

"Hi, Lori," Craig said to me. "Hi, Daniel."

"Hello, Craig," I smiled. "How are you, Linda?"

"Fine," she said. "It's so nice to see you, Lori."

Linda wore a blue cotton skirt and a lightweight gray vest over a white blouse. For a moment I thought she was dressed for church, but realized it was only Saturday afternoon. She had apparently selected the outfit specifically for Daniel's concert. I suppose she thought it was only right. I admired her conviction, not to mention her sense of style.

"Sorry, my mother and father couldn't come," Craig explained. "We're going to my Aunt Alice's tomorrow, and they're making a huge bread stuffed with all kinds of cheeses and dressings and junk."

"Lori, I wanted to thank your mother for inviting us," Linda said. "Is she here?"

"Not yet," I explained. "She'll be here any minute."

"Okay. Well, I'll tell her later, then." She turned to look at Daniel. "I love your music," she smiled. "That's why I didn't want to miss the concert."

I went back into the living room, and Dad walked over to me.

"Where's Steven, for Christ's sake?" he whispered. "Where's your mother?"

"I don't know," I said. (I, too, was very nervous about how close the two of them were cutting it.)

It was a minute past two o'clock. Daniel walked over to the piano and adjusted the lamp. Dad looked at his watch. Doug and his dad and Craig and his sister sat quietly, though the two boys were fidgety. Then Helene Sheldon walked into the house with Glenn. She didn't ring the bell or knock on the door. That was her way. Even had there been a big crowd, Mrs. Sheldon would have stood out. She wore a black, button-down shirt and tight, white pants. Dad went over to greet her as she stood to the side of the Marc Chagall reproduction in the foyer, and Mr. Kelleher sprung out of his chair to join them there.

"Sorry I'm late," Mrs. Sheldon said to Dad. She kissed him on the cheek. "But I wouldn't miss it for the world." She glanced at Daniel by the piano. "You know that, Daniel. Don't you?"

"How's the rabbi?" Dad asked.

"The rabbi? The rabbi's the rabbi," she smiled. "He's in Philadelphia. Temple business of some kind. Beverly didn't tell you?"

"No. That's fine. I'm glad you're here."

Dad told Daniel to start the concert. "Let's not keep everyone waiting," he said.

Daniel played the song "Downtown" as an instrumental, followed by "Pretty Woman," to which he sang along—listlessly, but entirely on key. He looked behind him to acknowledge the applause (though it seemed to me he glanced only at Linda and Mrs. Sheldon). Doug, Craig, and Glenn played with a marble on the carpet. Dad looked at his watch. Mr. Kelleher stared at the rabbi's wife.

When "Pretty Woman" was over, Mrs. Sheldon asked Daniel to play "The Wedding Waltz," which she said she had particularly enjoyed when he performed it at a temple event three years before. So he did.

Steven came through the front door just as he played the final measure of "The Wedding Waltz." When the song was finished, Daniel stood up and said that he wasn't feeling well. He thanked everyone for coming, said goodbye, and went into the hallway.

Steven was in the foyer at that point. His clothes were filthy, and he smelled of oil. He wore a little pendant on his lapel—gold pilot's wings—that his friend's father had given him, but he took it off and put it on the shelf in the foyer. Both he and I followed Daniel into his bedroom.

"Okay, McCartney, what's up?" Steven asked as he closed the door behind him.

"Nothing," Daniel said. He sat at his desk.

"Nothing? You walked out of the living room like it was full of farting skunks."

"It was."

"What's the matter, Daniel?" I asked gently.

"Just leave me alone. Both of you."

"No can do, little boychick," Steven said. "Tell me what's wrong, or I'll wring your scrawny little neck until you sound like Wayne Newton."

I glared at Steven. He ignored me.

Daniel continued to stare at the wall. It took me a moment to realize he was crying. I covered my mouth with my hand, trying fiercely not to break into tears myself. That's when Steven noticed it, too.

"Jesus," he said to Daniel, "it's that serious, huh?"

"Mom wasn't even here," Daniel said. "It was her idea! And Dad looked at his fucking watch the whole time."

"Then you must be mad at me, too," Steven said, "because I came in on the last note—although it was a *very* good note."

Daniel stood up and went to the window, hardly in the mood for Steven's feeble attempts at humor.

"Sorry," Steven quickly added. "I'll stop. Sit down."

"Please, Daniel," I echoed. "Sit down. Let's talk. That's always the best way."

He sat on his bed but didn't talk.

"Listen," Steven said, "you, and God, know what you've got inside of you, and so do the rest of us, for that matter, and God will make sure that your life isn't a whole lot of quickie little Pearl Drive concerts for the next fifty years. Today doesn't mean a damn thing."

"How is that supposed to make me feel better about Mom and

Dad?" Daniel asked.

"Well, you got me there, kiddo. Give me an hour to think about it. Okay?"

"Whatever."

"They probably don't even know what they did," I said—though I realized as I said it that as an explanation or excuse it was woefully inadequate. "They're confused about a lot of things lately," I added hastily.

Steven motioned for me to come into the hallway with him and to leave Daniel alone for a while. Once in the hallway, I closed the door behind me.

"I'm sure he'll be all right," I said to Steven. "Don't you?"

"What would've helped," Steven said, "is a mother who shows up when she's goddamn supposed to, and a father who didn't worship LILCO like it was the Messiah." He paused. He knew how hard I worked to keep it together. I *was* keeping it together—but barely. "Don't worry, Lori," he said. "He'll be fine."

I walked with Steven back to the living room. He stopped at the foyer shelf where he had previously placed his pendant from the airport.

"Who the hell took my pilot's wings?" he yelled.

I looked out the living room window and saw Mrs. Sheldon and Glenn walk down the block toward their house. I had a pretty good idea where Steven's pilot pendant had flown off to.

*     *     *

Mom finally came home at three o'clock. Steven ran outside to meet her at the curb when he heard her car pull up. He wanted to talk to her in private. Her hair appointment had run late, she explained, and then someone at the beauty parlor mentioned a phenomenal sale on towels at Macy's at the Roosevelt Field Mall. She wanted to buy some new towels since Grandma Rose had taken most of ours to Yetta's apartment. The mall was exceptionally crowded; Mom said that in her frustration, she lost track of the time.

Dad had already left for LILCO, even though he didn't have to be there until seven o'clock.

I stayed in my room. Daniel stayed in his.

As a result of her faux pas, Mom was so attentive to Daniel over the next week that it was almost comical. He could easily have taken advantage of it, but instead simply did what he was supposed to do and asked for no special privileges. He went to school, did his homework, ate his dinner, even played "Exodus" for Grandma Rose, at her request, when she came back from Yonkers.

The next Friday afternoon, a United Parcel Service truck stopped in front of the house. The driver knocked on the door, and I opened it. He had a package addressed to Daniel. The return address said Howard Beach, NY, and nothing more. I took the box to Daniel's room and asked if I could stick around while he opened it to see what was inside.

It was a ukulele.

# Four

Grandpa Jesse and Grandma Leah gave Daniel a drum set for his twelfth birthday. Since they never gave a gift to one grandchild without giving one to the others, they presented Steven with a pair of binoculars (he had two already) and they gave me a beautiful sweater to wear around campus.

Daniel hadn't actually asked for a drum set, but Grandpa Jesse always had it in his head that it was a logical progression for what he saw as his youngest grandson's inevitable career in music.

As a present of their own, Mom and Dad agreed to let Daniel take drum lessons, at least for a few months, to see if he took to the instrument and enjoyed it as much as he once claimed he would. His first lesson, on July 10, 1966, was the same day that NASA launched Orbiter 1 to the moon. Steven threatened to burn the new drum set down to the ground if the lesson in the basement coincided with the televised launch, which he planned to watch in the living room.

"Be a Gene Krupa," Grandpa said to Daniel. "Not so much a Ringo."

"How about just a Daniel," Grandma Leah added. "That's all he needs to be."

Mom wasn't thrilled with the idea of a drum set, though when she learned that Daniel's present had five fewer pieces than a typical full set, she decided to feel fortunate. She said that if all went well (which meant that Grandma Rose didn't mind the noise too much), the lessons could continue.

But all did not go well.

The problem was the drum teacher, Randy Werner. Mom had found his name in the classified section of the local newspaper. I suspected something was wrong after Daniel's very first lesson.

"Well, that's lesson number one," Daniel said to me after Randy Werner had left the house—and to make his point, Daniel held up the middle finger of his right hand.

"Daniel!" I said.

"Sorry. But it's the truth."

Werner, whose scraggly hair always looked wet (I don't know why I remember that more than anything else), was the author of three of the most popular drum instruction books on the market at the time. At first, Daniel thought that was impressive, but as it turned out, the man was as unpleasant as he was skilled. He smacked the back of Daniel's head with an open palm whenever he misplaced a beat, and while that wasn't very often, it was often enough to give Daniel a headache before Werner even arrived at the house for the second lesson.

As the beginning of the first lesson, Werner had asked Daniel whether or not he had ever played the drums before. Daniel said he had and explained that whenever he saw a drum set, he'd sit down behind it and try it out.

"That ain't music," Werner said demonstrably. He shook his head, which in turn whipped his hair left and right. "That's a kid trying to be cool."

"But I got the hang of it."

"What you got the hang of was a lot of hooey noise. You know what hooey noise is?"

"No."

"It's kids who have big heads because they think they can play music when all they can play is bupkis. I don't teach hooey noise. I don't teach bupkis. I teach music. Kapish?"

"I guess," Daniel said.

"You guess?" That made him mad. "You listen to the rock 'n roll? Jazz?"

"Both," he said. "Folk and classical, too."

"You have a lot of albums? Listen to the radio?"

"Yes."

"So you think you're better than Buddy Rich?"

"No."

"No?" (Did Werner expect Daniel to say yes?)

"No," Daniel repeated.

"I bet you do."

Daniel couldn't stand Werner from that very first lesson—and from having overheard a little bit of it from the kitchen, neither could I. Still, after three lessons, Daniel was able to play better than the "Randy Werner Pre-Pro Guitar Method Book One" said a student should be able to, and that annoyed Werner very much. He took it out on Daniel with a few additional slaps to the back of his head.

The fourth lesson began safely enough, but then, when Werner asked Daniel to play "Circles and Curves," he played it rapidly because the instruction book said it should be played "at the fastest tempo with which the student is comfortable." The tempo Daniel selected wasn't the tempo that Werner had in mind.

"Don't show off," he barked.

"I'm not showing off," Daniel insisted. "The book says to use the fastest tempo you're comfortable with, and this is the fastest tempo I'm comfortable with. I practiced it this way, and I can do it. Watch."

"No."

"But it works. Just listen."

"No."

Daniel ignored him and began to play "Circles and Curves" the way he had practiced it. Werner cut it short with a slap on the back of Daniel's head.

At that point, Daniel sprung up off the chair and threw his drumsticks against the wall.

"Stop hitting me!" he shouted.

"Then stop showing off," Werner shot back.

"I'm *not* showing off, you jerk! I'm doing what I *can* do and what I *want* to do. So why don't you just stick your fucking head in a fucking bass drum on the fucking moon."

Daniel stomped up the stairs and barreled through the kitchen. I had been on my way out the door to go to an Adelphi event, but out of both concern and a bit of shock I stayed behind to see if there was anything I could do. Grandma Rose was at the kitchen table and muttered "Oy gevalt." Mom was putting dishes away and said, "It's just a joke, right?" as Daniel continued to his bedroom. He slammed the door behind him hard enough to cause several pictures to fall off the wall in the hallway. I went to see if there was any shattered glass. Werner arrived at the top of the stairs a minute later, and Mom realized by the look on his face that it was no joke.

Whether or not there would be a fifth lesson was not discussed that afternoon. But it hardly mattered, for three days later Mom was told by Dr. Lewis that Daniel would have to be admitted to Meadowbrook Hospital as soon as possible to have his tonsils removed.

Mom always said that the first four things she did when we moved to Westbrook Hills were sweep the floors in the house, clean the inside of the refrigerator, buy groceries, and make an appointment to see Dr. Irving Lewis.

It was 1954. I was seven years old. Daniel was an infant. We had had been living in an apartment in Rego Park, Queens, and moved to Pearl Drive on a September weekend. Mom had heard wonderful things about Dr. Lewis from a friend at the apartment complex who had already moved to the Long Island suburbs. Dr. Lewis was forty-five years old, smart, well-liked, personable, and funny. His office was close to Westbrook Hills, and he made house calls whenever necessary. Mom wanted him as our family pediatrician and determined that she would refuse to take no for an answer. Although the doctor's practice was already very busy, Mom got her wish. Irving Lewis was our family physician from that time on. He was also a friend. That's why Steven, Daniel, and I tried to ignore the fact that it was his job to jab us with needles and shove sticks down our throats. Of course, we couldn't ignore it when he was actually doing it, but we could easily forgive him afterward because he was very nice and kept us healthy.

Dr. Lewis decided that Daniel needed a tonsillectomy because he had been in for exams four times in just the first six months of 1966 with sore throats and swollen glands. The hospital stay would be for only a day and a half, but Daniel would have to rest for several days after that, which meant no outdoor play and no music lessons. So Randy Werner was history. We heard no complaints about that from Daniel.

At the final visit to the doctor's office prior to the hospital stay, Dr. Lewis asked to speak to Daniel alone for a moment. Mom went to the waiting room.

"Daniel," Dr. Lewis said in the examination room, "I'm a doctor. I can tell. You've been smoking, haven't you? Probably not a lot, but with your friends every once in a while. Am I right?"

"A little," Daniel admitted.

Even though the act of smoking was something he neither craved nor particularly enjoyed, it was something he could *choose* to do, and get away with, which to his way of thinking was an antidote to much of what had been going on in his world. After all, he didn't *choose* to outgrow his friends; he didn't *choose* for Grandpa Sol to die; he didn't *choose* for our parents to become a little more remote, or for music to become a source of some distress. But he *could* choose to smoke. So a few times a week he hung around with some older students who smoked regularly behind the stores on Miller Avenue. Daniel didn't know them well, but they didn't mind having him around because he was able to keep up with their banter about rock bands. He was also able to talk a bit about football and baseball since he absorbed a little from Steven, who was a fan of both and watched many games on television. In addition to smoking with those students, sometimes Daniel relit the cigarette butts that he stole from ashtrays at home whenever Grandma Leah visited.

"You're not an irresponsible kid, so please don't smoke," Dr. Lewis said. "It's not worth it, Daniel. Believe me. Besides, it will affect your singing voice. You wouldn't want that, would you?"

"It was just a few times," Daniel said, decisively putting it in the past tense. "With some new friends I made at school. I was bored and a little frustrated. It's stupid. But that's why."

It wasn't entirely a lie. Dr. Lewis grinned.

"Bored? You? With the way you attack a piano? I doubt it."

"I've haven't been playing a lot lately."

"Still..."

Dr. Lewis called Mom back into the exam room.

"Daniel will come out of that hospital with a dozen new hit songs," he smiled. "I'm sure of it."

Daniel was to be admitted to the hospital on a Wednesday night, and the operation was scheduled for the following morning. Steven begged Mom and Dad to wait until the TV show *Honey West* was over before they drove to Meadowbrook Hospital. He had a crush on the pretty actress Anne Francis who played the sexy private eye on the series. Mom and Dad said no.

I had planned to attend a concert at Adelphi that night but decided to go to the hospital with the family instead. I drove home from campus late in the afternoon. Mom, who hadn't seen me leave the house that morning, criticized my blouse and told me to change for the hospital. My yellow blouse accentuated my bust just a trace more than what she had been used to. I had selected it on purpose because it seemed like a harmless way to more easily be accepted into groups of students (particularly male students) without the need to assume an overtly more social personality. What was interesting, though, was that it didn't necessarily make me feel comfortable, and I didn't really crave the attention. I just knew I *needed* some attention to feel more normal.

I was happy to change my blouse for the hospital.

Dad had insisted on an early evening arrival at the hospital so that he wouldn't have to leave work early. We stayed at the hospital for about an hour-and-a-half, and then the nurses informed us that we had to leave. It was nine forty-five. Daniel would be asleep soon, anyway.

At ten o'clock, another boy was wheeled into his room.

"Daniel," said the elderly nurse who pushed the wheelchair, "this is John. I think he's the same age as you. He was on the fourth floor, but we've decided to let him share a room with you tonight. Isn't that nice?"

Neither Daniel nor John responded.

The nurse placed a little case of John's belongings on the table beside his bed, then helped him climb in.

"Do you need anything?" she asked, looking first at John and then Daniel. "Anything at all?" The boys remained silent. The nurse sighed, smiled, and left the room.

Like Daniel, John was in pajamas, but Daniel's had blue clouds on them, and John's had large black stripes. Daniel thought it made him look like a convict.

Both remained silent for a while. There were framed paintings of flowers on the wall above both beds; Daniel and John looked above each other's heads instead of at each other's faces.

Five minutes later, John spoke.

"What's that?" he asked.

He was looking at the little table next to Daniel's bed, upon which were get well soon cards that had been mailed or dropped off at the house. Mom had brought them from home.

"Cards," Daniel said.

"What about that one?" John asked as he pointed to the card from Rabbi and Mrs. Sheldon. It had a drawing of a Star of David on the cover. "Is that a Jew thing?"

Daniel remained silent.

"Are you a Jew boy?"

Once at Westbrook Hills High School, a student I didn't know asked me if my little brother was "that little Jewish kid that plays all the instruments." When I mentioned it at home, Daniel said that someone at his school had asked him the same thing. Occasionally someone in school asked me if I knew "that Jewish language," or if my other brother had "one of those big Jewish birthday parties" when he turned thirteen. Daniel and Steven, too, had heard such comments from time to time. But never had any of us been asked if we were a Jew boy or Jew girl in such a coarse and blatant way.

"You have horns?" John asked. Again, Daniel remained silent. "All Jews have horns," he continued. "They killed Christ. And they're cheap, and they lie, and they drink the blood of Christian children."

"How do you know?" Daniel asked as calmly as he could.

"My parents told me," John replied.

"Well, our horns only come out when we're really, really angry, or when we do something really, really bad."

"No kidding?" John's eyes opened wider. "Shoot! Then your parents will know when you do something bad! They'll see the horns. That sucks."

"No it doesn't. Because when they punish me, I just punch holes in the walls with my horns. So they stop! I always win. Every time."

"Really?"

"Yup. There are hundreds and hundreds of holes in my bedroom walls. Like pushpin holes, only a lot bigger."

Daniel knew that John was visualizing his description and enjoying the mental picture. In his way, Daniel enjoyed it, too, because he was now the one in charge, and he knew what he was able to accomplish with just his words. He stared at John so that he could remember what his expression was with every bizarre twist of the twisted tale.

"Do they punish you a lot?" John asked.

"My parents? Yup. There are holes everywhere. Not just in my room. Sometimes when I punch holes, I make them into shapes."

"Shapes? What kind of shapes?"

"Wine bottles. Poop in the sandbox. Titties. All kinds of things."

"Cool!" John's eyes glazed over, no doubt still imagining in his head what Daniel was describing. "Why are you here, anyway?"

"I have to have my tonsils out," Daniel explained. "What about you?"

"I have a blood clot in my neck," John said. "Did you really kill Christ?"

"My grandfather did. He had to," Daniel said.

"How come?"

"Because he found out that Christ was gonna kill everyone in Howard Beach so that they could become angels. But there was this guy in Howard Beach who didn't want to be an angel, so he paid my grandfather to kill Christ."

"Really? Wow!"

"Yup. Really."

John thought about the response long and hard. But then he realized once again who his roommate happened to be—a Jew boy.

"My uncle told me to make sure I'm not in a room with any niggers or Jews."

"Then I guess you should leave, because I was here first."

"But they told me I gotta stay here. And my parents said they'd punish me if I gave the nurses any trouble." John was torn. He thought hard. "Well," he finally said, "you don't seem so bad. I guess it's okay that we're in the same room."

"Do your parents punish you a lot?" Daniel asked, still intrigued with the one-sided game he played so expertly.

"Sometimes. But I just hold my breath when they do. That really scares the shit out of them. Once I passed out. It works, most of the time."

"Why do they punish you?"

"For doing things. Like smoking. Do you smoke?"

"Sometimes."

"Do you drink?"

"Yup."

"Do you steal?"

"Do you?"

"Just bikes, sometimes. Hey, did you see the radio on the desk where the nurses sit? Wanna sneak out and steal it?"

John got out of bed, walked to the door, and peeked out. "Nobody's there now. Come on."

Daniel was no longer certain it was just a game. But neither did he want to admit to any weakness or apprehension. He was too far invested. So he slipped out of bed and followed John into the quiet hallway. There was a steaming cup of coffee on the desk and a phone off the hook, with several blinking lights on the console.

"Better hurry," Daniel said. "Someone might come back soon."

John crawled under the desk and unplugged the small Philco radio.

Daniel pulled at the cord and grabbed the radio to his chest.

"Wait!" John whispered loudly. "Look—a pack of cigarettes. And a stethoscope."

John took the cigarettes, and Daniel grabbed the stethoscope with his free hand. They tiptoed briskly back into their room and closed the door behind them.

Daniel put the stethoscope and the radio under John's bed. "We'll play with them later," he said.

John went to the window and opened it.

"Come on," he said. "Let's have a cigarette. We'll keep the window open. That way no one will know." John had matches hidden in the little case his mother had brought along. After he lit one for himself, he offered a cigarette and the matches to Daniel. They stood by the third-story window, smoking like two businessmen on a lunch break.

"Where are your horns?" John asked. "You're doing something bad. Shouldn't they come out now?"

"They only come out at home."

"Oh. What about your parents' horns?"

"Their horns come out all the time. Especially when they lie."

"All Jews lie. My parents told me."

"Especially mothers and fathers and teachers. But not rabbis. They're not allowed to lie."

"Really?"

"Yup."

They took several drags on their cigarettes and blew the smoke outside. After a few more puffs, they tossed the butts out the window.

"Wanna throw some stuff out?" John asked.

"Out the window? Like what?"

"How about those stupid pictures on the wall?"

"There's glass over them. They'll break."

"So?"

John stood on his bed and took the picture down and then climbed on Daniel's bed to retrieve the other one. The window faced the rear of the hospital, where a path ran along the back facade of the building. Next to the path was a one-way road, although no cars were on it at the moment. Daniel knew that if John threw the glass-covered paintings out the window, anyone who walked down there could get hurt; but again, he was too deep into this baffling matchup of wits to simply end it. So he tried to furtively glance down to make sure the coast was clear. But John came over with the two framed paintings before Daniel even had a chance to look.

"Here." He gave one of the paintings to Daniel. "I'll go first," John said, and then he dropped his painting out the window. When it hit the path below, the glass shattered loudly. "Your turn. Try to get yours further out so that it goes onto the street. That way, if a car comes by, it'll get a flat tire. That'll be so cool!"

Daniel actually preferred that idea, since a flat tire was less egregious than a slashed person. So he gave the painting as much momentum as he could as he tossed it out the window so that it would land on the road and not on the path. It hit the road with an even louder burst of shattered glass, and that made John giddy, as if he had won some sort of prize. Just then, another nurse, a much younger one, entered the room pushing an empty wheelchair. The boys were startled.

"What are you two doing?" the nurse chided. "Get away from that window. Are you both crazy or something? Not only is it dangerous, but you'll catch pneumonia."

The nurse closed the window.

"Now, which one of you is John Waymire?"

"Me," said John.

"You have to go for a few tests. Hop into the wheelchair, and I'll take you for a ride. Do you want a blanket for your lap?"

"But it's so late."

"I know, sweetie. I'm sorry. But this is when your tests have been scheduled because your operation is so early in the morning. You'll get a good night's sleep afterward. I promise. Okay? And you—" she said to Daniel, "you get yourself back into bed." The nurse hadn't noticed that the paintings were missing.

As John was wheeled out of the room, Daniel got back into his bed and climbed under the sheets. He pulled the sheets tight against his neck. He felt cold and strange. A million thoughts went through his head. Or, as he also speculated, possibly no thoughts at all went through his head. He didn't even remember how much time had passed between the moment John was wheeled out and the moment someone else walked into the room. Five minutes? Ten? Fifteen? But someone else *did* walk into the room, and Daniel felt relieved simply not to be alone anymore.

It was Rabbi Sheldon.

"Hello, Daniel," the rabbi said as he approached the side of the bed. He wore a tan Polo shirt and white pants, and had it not been for the blue felt yarmulke on his head, he could have been on his way to a nighttime game of tennis across the street at Salisbury Park. "I know it's late, but I was out anyway, so I decided to stop in for a visit. Visiting hours are long over, but this—" he touched his yarmulke—"opens up doors for me that are sometimes closed to other people." He winked. "Hope you don't mind."

"No."

"Of course, you owe me a new tire now," he smiled. "There's a spot for clergy people in the back of the hospital. I was on my way there when all of a sudden—crunch!—I ran over something and got a flat tire. Glass, I think. Serves me right for taking advantage of special parking, huh?"

Daniel couldn't bring any words to his mouth.

"Well, Daniel, it's a year before your own bar mitzvah, and already you're a man—so calm and brave about this little operation." The rabbi's smile was reassuring. "You're not nervous, are you? Because there's nothing to be nervous about."

"No."

The rabbi looked around. "What—no instruments?" he asked.

"I'm only here for a day and a half."

"But the room needs a little something. It's so… antiseptic. There aren't even any pictures on the wall. It needs music! You know, Daniel, one day your words and music will make this world a beautiful place. I feel that in my heart, Daniel. Maybe not this year, maybe not next year, maybe not for many years. But soon. It's between you and the great conductor up there." He pointed to the ceiling. "Which is why I'm surprised that you let your mother and father take you here without so much as that little toy xylophone you used to drag to shul when you were four years old—interrupting my services something awful, by the way."

Daniel tried to smile; it was difficult because he sensed teardrops in the corners of his eyes.

"You don't even have a radio in this room? *Now* I'm worried!"

Although he didn't want to, Daniel found himself glancing at John's bed. The teardrops grew.

"What's the matter, my little mensch? You look sad. I can tell. You're crying."

What could he say to stop Rabbi Sheldon from digging deeper into his grief?

"You know, Daniel, we Jews don't have a monopoly on all the sadness in the world. But there sure as hell is a lot of it! And we rabbis are pretty damned used to it after all these years. It's one of my jobs to recognize when someone has something heavy on his mind—even just a schmear of something heavy—so that I can try to see how you and I together might lighten the load. Because you know what?"

"What?"

"Because whatever it is, I bet we can work it out. Look at our people over the last five thousand years. Hate, jealousy, persecution, pogroms, discrimination, the Holocaust… But we're still here. There's a reason for that. Because we never give up. We always have hope. So let's not give up. Vishtayst?"

Daniel wanted very much to abide by what Rabbi Sheldon said, to have hope, to never give up. But at the same time, the rabbi made him wonder if perhaps he committed the biggest sin of all just by feeling lost and dispirited.

"Your father still works too hard and comes home crabby," Rabbi Sheldon affirmed. "Am I right?" Daniel nodded. "Your mother still thinks the world is out to get her, and that only a quiet house will fix that. No? Steven still doesn't try hard enough in school and often has his head in the clouds. Lori still worries that the sky will fall down on her pretty little head and fears she'll end up with no job and no career. Your grandmother still kvetches up a storm about this, that, and the other thing. Yes?"

Rabbi Sheldon sat on the edge of the bed and stroked Daniel's hair.

"None of these are life-threatening diseases, Daniel. They are normal parts of this meshugener thing we call family life. It will all seem like bupkis later on. But that's not the only thing on your mind," he added. "I can see that. Tell me. What is it?"

He wanted to tell Rabbi Sheldon everything—but at the same time, he didn't want to say a word.

"I met someone," Daniel finally allowed. He had decided to share at least one story as a representative sample of the whole sordid affair. "A boy. He said horrible things about Jews. And I didn't say anything back."

Rabbi Sheldon nodded his head slowly, almost imperceptibly.

"I see. Well... this isn't quite the test of good or evil that sends some people up there and others to nowhere land," the rabbi said after a moment. "Not at your age. I think it's just a pop quiz—not the actual test. Sometimes God makes us learn in strange ways about people, about weakness, about regret, about all these things. It's a big world out there, Daniel. There's a lot to learn, a lot to take in. You're learning, and you'll use it wisely one day. You did nothing terribly wrong. Next time you'll want to speak up. How much you wanna bet? Besides, look at you—talented, kind, you don't smoke, you don't drink, you don't steal... you're a little mensch."

Rabbi Sheldon gently wiped away Daniel's tears with a tissue.

"Anything else?" he asked.

"No."

"My timing couldn't have been more perfect, huh?—stopping by just as the tears started to fall. I guess that's why I'm the wonderful rabbi and you're just the lousy kid." He playfully jabbed Daniel's shoulder with his fist. "So your tonsils come out in the morning, and you come home on Friday. That's good. That way you can come back to your bar mitzvah lessons next week. Cantor Goldstone is going crazy. He was with someone yesterday who sang like a gefilte fish. And did you ever hear a gefilte fish sing?"

"No."

"That's my point."

And with that, Rabbi Sheldon said goodbye and departed.

The following morning, at seven-thirty, a nurse wheeled Daniel into a room that was full of medical equipment. The nurse and another man in a white smock helped him into a long, wide, and deeply reclining cushioned chair. A masked doctor appeared as if out of nowhere and said hello. He placed a plastic cone over Daniel's nose and asked him to sing a song. Daniel began to sing "Yesterday," a new Beatles song that Cousin Brucie had introduced on his radio show just a few days before. Daniel already had it memorized.

"Yesterday..." His voice was weak and tired. "All my troubles seemed so far away. Now it looks as though they're here to stay..."

And that's how he fell asleep.

•　　•　　•　　•

Daniel came home on Friday afternoon but was so tired that he slept most of the day away. On Saturday morning, as I was about to leave the house, an ambulance could be heard a block or two away. It woke him up. Daniel came into the hallway and told me that for a moment he thought he still at the hospital. I assured him he wasn't.

The siren made me think back to the time, several years before, when early one day an ambulance pulled up in front of the Kelleher house across the street. That was when Doug's baby brother Michael had a terrible accident that severed one of his legs. Many neighbors came out onto their lawns. It was a frightening affair. An hour after the ambulance left the block, two men walked up the front steps of the Kelleher house. One was a priest, the other was Rabbi Sheldon. I remember thinking, Why not? After all, Glenn Sheldon was Doug Kelleher's friend, too. It was the right thing to do. I had already admired Rabbi Sheldon, but admired him even more after I saw him visit the Kelleher house.

Later that morning, when we finally learned what had happened, Grandma Rose wanted to know if she could cook something for the Kellehers, but Mom said they would probably prefer things other than what she would prepare. Mom decided to wait a day or two before she called on Delores Kelleher to offer prayers and best wishes. She said there was probably too much going on at the Kelleher house at the moment and that the family may not wish to be bothered.

When Daniel mumbled to me that he thought he was still in the hospital, I gently tried to push him back into his bedroom. I knew he could use another hour or two of sleep. But he told me that the sound of the ambulance reminded him, too—as it had reminded me—of the Michael Kelleher incident. I told him that was the same thing I had been thinking when I heard the siren.

"Great minds think alike!" he said. "But here's what's funny about it. When I heard the siren, I started thinking more about Doug than I did about Michael. I mean, Michael was the one who lost his leg—but I only thought about Doug."

"In terms of what?" I asked.

"In terms of remembering how I don't have any more friends on Pearl Drive."

Daniel walked back toward his bedroom. I followed. I had planned to study at the Adelphi library but knew that could be postponed for a half hour or so. Daniel sat on his bed as I stood in the doorway.

"I don't really miss him, you know," he said.

"Doug? You don't?"

"No. After Steven's bar mitzvah, we hardly saw each other anymore. It's actually strange when we see each other now outside. We don't know what to say. I just wish I didn't have to hear about him so much."

"You mean because of all the plays he's in?"

"Yup. He's playing Captain Von Trapp now in *The Sound of Music* at that camp he goes to."

"I know," I said. "I read about it in Newsday."

"Newsday! A Long Island newspaper! His dumb camp is in the friggin' Poconos, for crying out loud. Four hours away! And have you seen their living room window lately? They put up the album cover from the movie so that everyone who passes by can see it. Is Julie Andrews the Kelleher governess now?"

And with that, Daniel fell back to sleep.

•    •    •    •    •

I spent the afternoon at Adelphi. When I returned home, Dad was still at LILCO. He had been there since four-thirty in the morning and wasn't expected to return until seven-thirty at night. Mom and Grandma Rose argued about that. "I never heard such a thing," Grandma said, "a husband who works all day and all night. Oy gevalt. And on a Saturday yet. Not even in the window factory did we work that much." Mom said that it was a different world now. "Some world," Grandma countered.

Grandma's mood troubled me, so I knocked on Steven's bedroom door to see if he wanted to talk. Sometimes he had interesting things to say and funny ways of saying it. I peeked in. He had just put on his little league uniform.

"You're leaving now?" I asked. "Isn't it early for practice?"

"I'd rather play baseball with a bunch of cheerful Christians than be in a house with a couple of kvetching Jews!" he said.

Steven left the house.

Daniel had been working on some kind of story in his own bedroom. I knocked to say hello and to see if his throat bothered him. He said it was still a little sore. He, too, seemed to be in a sour mood, and I sensed he wanted to be alone.

Steven was right. It was difficult to be in the house. Between his sarcasm, Daniel's bitter mood, the constant sniping between Mom and Grandma, and Dad's perpetual absence (which made Mom and Grandma even more upset), it always seemed better to find an excuse to leave than to stay at home. I told Mom I had agreed to help organize a concert at the Jewish Student Union office. I didn't even belong to the Jewish Student Union—not yet, anyway. But it was the only good excuse that came to mind.

On Sunday, the phone rang at noon. It was the Logan Airport Transit Police in Boston. They had news about Steven. Daniel and I were home alone with Dad. Mom and Grandma Rose were at the mall.

Without permission, Steven and his friend Wayne from little league, along with several of Wayne's friends from another school, chipped in to charter a flight on a small Cessna airplane out of Republic Airport, which wasn't far from our house. Steven didn't think he'd get permission from Mom and Dad, which is why he kept it a secret. Wayne didn't tell his parents, either. Both Steven and Wayne thought they'd return home by late afternoon, and that no one would even know they were gone.

But there was a serious miscommunication among the boys. Steven and Wayne were under the impression that they would cross the Long Island Sound, fly over part of Connecticut and Massachusetts, then turn around and come home. But Wayne's friends had another plan, which they neglected to share: their plan was to land in Boston, attend a Red Sox game at Fenway Park, then fly home late at night. To make matters worse, the amount of money that Steven and Wayne were told to bring along was not adequate for a return trip, or even for a bus.

The other friends refused to help them out. Steven and Wayne were stranded at Logan Airport.

After a series of phone calls between Dad, Wayne's mother, the Boston transit police, and Greyhound Bus Lines, it was arranged that Steven and Wayne would take a bus to Garden City, where Dad would meet them, pay their fares, and drive Wayne home. Wayne's mother would reimburse Dad for her half. But just before he was about to leave for the bus depot, Dad received another phone call, this time from the Nassau County Police Department. Mom and Grandma Rose had been in a car accident and were at Meadowbrook Hospital.

Dad called Wayne's mother and asked her to pick up the boys in his place. He told me to keep an eye on Daniel. I was worried about Dad going alone to the hospital and thought it might be a good idea to accompany him, along with Daniel. Dad agreed, but Daniel said he'd rather wait at home alone. Dad didn't like that idea.

"I'm twelve," Daniel said. "I can stay by myself for a little while."

Dad had neither the time nor patience to argue. "Okay. But if Steven isn't home by eight," he said to Daniel, "go next door to Ashler's and wait there. No arguments. Lori will come home in a few hours. If I happen to come home with Mom and Grandma tonight, make sure the house is quiet. No instruments. Understand?"

Dad and I left for the hospital in separate cars. Daniel decided to take a walk down the block. He went slowly and kicked rocks along the way. He ended up at a small wooded field near the parkway, where neighborhood kids often hung out. No one was there. He looked for a cigarette butt in the dirt, found one, brushed it off, and took it home. In the basement, he lit it with a book of matches that was on Dad's work table, and smoked tranquilly for the forty-five seconds the butt stayed lit. Then he went back upstairs. Steven barged into the house at eight-fifteen and slammed his bedroom door. He didn't know that Daniel was the only one in the house.

As far as the two of them were concerned, it was one of the loneliest nights of their lives.

.    .    .    .    .    .

Mom and Grandma Rose had been at the Roosevelt Field Mall. They wanted to do a little more shopping at a small shopping center closer to home, where there was a fabric store they both liked very much. As Mom turned off Miller Avenue to drive into the parking lot, a man in a delivery truck rushed to get from one side of the lot to the other and smashed into Mom's car. Her car spun fully around. The front left side buckled like an accordion. All the windows were obliterated, including the windshield. The truck driver told the police that he hadn't rushed at all—that Mom didn't look both ways as she turned into the parking lot. One witness said the truck was speeding. Two lawsuits resulted from the accident; they dragged on for three years.

Remarkably, Grandma Rose suffered only minor bruises, but Mom was seriously hurt. Grandma's sister-in-law Yetta drove out to Long Island to take Grandma back with her to Yonkers, for despite being unhurt, Grandma was badly shaken by the incident. At first, she refused to go with Yetta because she wanted to stay home to take care of Mom. But Yetta and Dad insisted, and Grandma finally relented.

Mom returned from the hospital on Monday, two days after the accident. I hadn't actually seen her when I was there on Sunday. (Dad didn't let me; all I did speak with several doctors.) So it was quite a shock when I first walked into her bedroom. Her left cheekbone was broken and covered by a large bandage, her left eye was swollen shut, and she had a series of stitches that zigzagged across her entire face and forehead where glass shards from the windows had pierced the skin. She had black-and-blue marks all over her arms. Her right knee had been dislocated and was in a cast.

Steven and Daniel were as devastated as I.

"Go away," Dad said when he saw the two of them by the master bedroom door. "Don't stare. You can talk to her tomorrow."

"It's okay, Murray," Mom whispered. "They'll have to see me sooner or later. Might as well be sooner. Where's Lori?"

"I'm right here," I said. I was behind the boys. "She's gonna be perfectly fine," I assured the two of them. "I talked to the doctors."

"From your lips to God's ears," Dad said. "Steven, go tell that jerk Ashler to move his goddamn car. He's blocking the damn driveway."

"Okay. See you later, Mom," Steven said. "I hope you get better soon." Because of the accident, his little Boston adventure went unpunished.

"Thank you, sweetheart. I love you."

"Love you, too."

"Lori," Dad said when Steven had left, "take Daniel to buy school supplies." The fall semester was to begin in just over a week.

"I don't need school supplies," Daniel said.

"Oh no? You have everything you need? Notebooks, pencils, pens, erasers, a ruler. Everything? For Hebrew School too? I seriously doubt it."

"I'm not going back to Hebrew school."

"Yes you are," Dad snapped. "Your bar mitzvah is a year away. No Hebrew School, no bar mitzvah."

"I don't want a bar mitzvah."

"You don't want a bar mitzvah? Fine. Go tell Rabbi Sheldon that you don't want a bar mitzvah."

"Murray, please," Mom pleaded, "no shouting."

Dad's tactic worked: Rabbi Sheldon was the one person Daniel did not want to disappoint.

I drove Daniel to a stationary store a few miles away. It was late in the afternoon. A boy named Jeff Cohen was there. Jeff was a fifteen-year-old who had his bar mitzvah at Temple Beth Shalom and now attended post-confirmation classes. Daniel saw him many times at the temple. Jeff had always treated him nicely, even though Daniel was three years younger. They went off to the side to chat while I stood on line to pay for the school supplies.

"Hebrew school will sure be weird when it starts next week," Jeff said.

"How come?" Daniel asked.

"You didn't hear?"

"Hear what?"

"You didn't get the letter in the mail today?"

"I don't know. My house has been kind of crazy lately."

"Rabbi Sheldon."

Jeff said it as if Daniel should have understood what he meant—as if everyone in the world should have known.

"What about him?"

"Gone."

"What? He quit?"

"Quit? No. Fired."

"Fired?" Daniel said it louder than he should have. A few people in the store looked his way. "Why? Why the hell would they fire him?"

"He was caught doing it," Jeff said.

"Doing what?"

"*It*," Jeff said while he used the fist of one hand and the index finger of his other to demonstrate. "The Big F. The Unholy Semitic Screw. The thing you do to be fruitful and multiply, even when you don't want to multiply. With someone else's wife!"

At first, Daniel didn't understand what Jeff was talking about, but then it registered. He wanted to punch Jeff in the face. He refused to believe it. He wanted to shout, to lash out, to do something bad to show his anger, disappointment, and frustration. But he didn't. Not then. He simply remained quiet.

"They'll probably get some old, farty, smelly Polish guy with an accent from Brooklyn to be the new rabbi," Jeff said. "That's the rumor, anyway."

On the way home, Daniel asked me to take a slight detour and drive to the temple. He said he wanted to see if Ned Early had finally moved the piano back into the classroom. It had been a long time since it was taken out. The temple parking lot was empty. Beth Shalom was typically very quiet on Monday afternoons. Even Ned Early took off most of the day. Daniel asked me to wait, hopped out of the car, and went around to the back of the building, not far from the sanctuary, where there was a heavy metal door with a defective lock that could be jarred loose just by pulling hard on the door handle.

He didn't bother to look for the piano at all. Instead, he went directly to the sanctuary, hopped the three little steps to the bimah, and ripped down the red felt curtain in front of the cabinet in which the Torah scrolls were stored. The curtain came down, but its top horizontal panel remained attached to the rod. He left the curtain on the floor. Then he pushed one of the lecterns onto its side. When it hit the floor, its angled top dislodged from the base and tumbled down the steps at the front of the bimah. The top of the lectern hit a metal folding chair, and that chair knocked up against the chair next to it, and that one, in turn, crashed into a stained-glass floor-to-ceiling window. The glass shattered into thousands of colorful pieces, like a Marc Chagall painting.

Daniel screamed out God's name in vain. No one was there to hear him, which perhaps is why he yelled as loudly as he did.

He returned to my car as if nothing had happened. We drove home. When we walked into the house, Daniel glanced at the Chagall reproduction in our foyer and shook his head despondently. He looked as if tears were just a moment away. I know he liked that painting—I did, too. So I had no idea what conclusion to draw about his reaction, or how to try to reach one. On the other hand, I had had my share of inexplicable crying over the years.

Daniel went into his bedroom. I drove back to Adelphi.

# Five

Steven graduated from model rockets to radio-controlled airplanes, and from Honey West to Rachel Tanenbaum.

In the spring of 1967, Steven got a part-time job in the cargo department of a small, private airline based at Republic Airport. Rachel's father was an executive at a big leisure-products company in Manhattan and often flew in and out of Republic on business trips. Sometimes he took Rachel with him. That's how Steven and Rachel met.

By the time summer came around, Steven had earned enough money to buy himself a 1960 light-blue Dodge Dart. It ran fairly well, even though the seven-year-old car looked as if it had been driven through several wars. That's why it was so cheap. Since he was not yet seventeen, Steven had to get along with a learner's permit instead of a driver's license. But that didn't stop him from his attempts to impress Rachel with the Dart. He invited her over to the house as often as possible so that they could sit in it together.

With the job, the car, and a teenaged face that was astonishingly free of acne (which made me jealous, even though by this time I was finally acne free myself), Steven felt confident and mature enough to ask Rachel to go steady with him. She accepted. In anticipation of a successful driver's test, Rachel brought him an expensive radio-controlled airplane, which he adored. Mom said she was impressed with Rachel's maturity. Dad said he was happy that she was Jewish.

Rachel was one of the guests at the fiftieth anniversary party for Grandma Leah and Grandpa Jesse that Mom and Dad arranged at the beginning of September. Also in attendance were several dozen relatives from New York, New Jersey, and Connecticut, and some as far away as Florida. The party, on a Saturday afternoon, was held in our basement, which Dad had fixed up for the occasion, and which Mom and I had decorated with signs, old photos and dozens of colored helium balloons.

"Believe it or not, 'White Christmas' was my idea. Irving Berlin got it from me," Grandpa Jesse said proudly to Marty and David, two middle-aged sons of one of Grandma Leah's brothers. They hung onto his every word at the party. "Irving's office was on Madison Avenue and Forty-Third Street," Grandpa explained. "I was on my way to meet a friend for lunch. This was about forty years ago when I still played in a band and was writing songs for a living. It was November, but very warm outside. No snow, no nothing. So Irving comes out of his building. He sees me walking towards him—"

"Did you hang out by his office just so that you could bump into him?" one of the nephews interrupted.

"Sometimes," Grandpa admitted. "Especially when I was trying to get one of my songs published. He had his own publishing company, and he published other people's songs. He knew who I was. He knew I was in the business. So anyway, he sees me coming near and he says, 'This is winter? What kind of a winter is this?' So I says to him, 'Mr. Berlin, would you like to hear my new song? I've been having problems getting published lately. Listen to one verse, that's all I ask,' But he says to me, 'You think *you* got problems? *I'm* the one with problems. They want a song for Christmas. How the hell can I write a song about Christmas when the weather's so goddamned beautiful?' So I says to him, 'Well, I guess you can always dream about it, Mr. Berlin. Just like my dream that you'll publish my new song.' So he looks at me, right there on Madison Avenue, and he says, 'I *am* dreaming, kid. I'm dreaming of a white Christmas.' And then he turns around and goes down the block."

I stood with Dad and Steven several feet away, next to the two bridge tables upon which all the food had been placed on platters and in bowls.

"Why don't you go talk to Grandpa," Dad whispered to Steven. "Save my poor cousins from more of his fekakta stories."

"Why?" Steven asked. "They're having a good time. Anyway, it's Grandpa's party, and he'll cry if he wants to."

"What the hell does that mean?"

"It's from a song. It was big when I had my bar mitzvah."

"A song? Who are you, Daniel?" Steven glanced at me, but neither one of us was entirely certain if Dad's comment was meant to be complimentary or cynical.

Steven had no response to Dad's quip, probably because he didn't know how to respond. It had become pretty clear over the last few months that the boy Dad referred to—the Daniel who used to live and breathe music—had gone away. No one really knew where. He still took piano and guitar lessons at home (albeit just twice a month now), and saxophone lessons at school, but it was all rather mechanical now, without a sense of passion. That wasn't the only change: Daniel's grades fell, too. They didn't have to, for Daniel knew the work; he had just stopped trying. And then there was his appearance. Lackadaisical would be the best word to describe it. He resisted haircuts (in fairness, so did millions of other boys), and started to wear Steven's old, tattered blue jeans and flannel shirts. He slept most weekend mornings until eleven or twelve o'clock and took very long showers to get himself up and out. He spent a lot of time in his room and claimed still to not miss his friends—those who were still around, anyway. By this time, Glenn Sheldon and his mother had moved to Nevada; Doug Kelleher was a big shot in the Sacred Heart High School Drama Club with a group of followers wrapped around his finger, and Craig Stuart preferred to hang out in his own kitchen. As for the DePuzo twins, they stopped by our house to call on Daniel every once in a while, and he went to their house on occasion. But Mom and Dad kept a tight grip on their relationship ever since Joey was caught beating up a boy in school for having more baseball cards than he did. The boy had been knocked unconscious and spent three days in the hospital.

Grandma and Grandpa's anniversary party was the first time in a long time that Daniel had combed his hair, put on decent clothes, and tucked in his shirt. He was nice to everyone. He actually looked forward to it (as did I) because it gave him new things to observe. He studied Grandpa Jesse as he shared personal anecdotes, and took mental notes on how no one ever interrupted him when she was on a roll. He also watched how Grandma Leah commanded attention whenever she recounted family history, even if the people she talked to were personally responsible for creating that history in the first place. Both Grandma Leah and Grandpa Jesse were masters at their respective games, and they were very happy at the party, where they got to play their games over and over again.

Daniel observed Grandma Rose, too, which merely confirmed for him what by then we all knew far too well—that she was decidedly more crotchety than ever. She had been in and out of hospitals for the past six months with various ailments, and each time she went in, she was convinced she would never come out. She made sure everyone grasped that fact in no uncertain terms. I wondered if one of the reasons that Mom and Dad planned the anniversary party was to give themselves a diversion from Grandma Rose.

Dance music from the Forties was played on Dad's old stereo system, and several people danced, including Steven and Rachel. Many of the adults stopped whatever they were doing to watch the young couple, and those who watched smiled and said how cute they were.

Grandma Rose had planted herself on an old wingback chair that had been brought over from her Queens apartment. (Little by little her furniture and belongings were sold, thrown out, given to other relatives, or stored in our house. There really hadn't been a formal decision made about where she would live permanently. What *was* known, however, was that she couldn't live alone anymore. Dad had already turned a small, mostly-unused family room at the back of our house into a comfortable bedroom for her.) I went over to say hello to her.

"Who's that?" Grandma asked me. She pointed.

"That's Steven, Grandma. And his girlfriend Rachel." I wondered if she was starting to lose some of her awareness. That had not yet been a problem.

"No, not him," she said. "Behind him. By the Victrola."

"Oh—that's Alex Blaustein. He's one of Grandma Leah's relatives. The grandson of a cousin."

"A nice boy?"

"I don't know," I said.

I really *did* know, but didn't want to upset Grandma with the truth. Alex was a year older than Daniel, and he was an angel—only if you were to listen to Frieda and Leon Blaustein talk about their son. It was easy to see why the Blausteins were only too pleased to put Alex on a pedestal: Frieda and Leon were short and chubby, they stuttered and lisped, said dumb things most of the time, and weren't successful in any of their businesses. By contrast, Alex was tall and slim, courteous to adults (or at least pretended to be), always dressed impeccably, was known for his leadership role in many school clubs and activities, and used a vocabulary that gave him the impression of being a sophisticate.

But he was no angel.

Alex felt superior to everyone and tried to prove it at every turn. He impressed some people, but not me, and not my brothers, either. That's probably why Alex never seemed to like Daniel. The few times they had been together over the years during family occasions were not enjoyable for Daniel at all.

Daniel decided to go upstairs for a few moments, but just as he was about to climb the basement stairs, Alex grabbed his arm and took him over to a little table that had on top of it an ashtray and two glasses of liquor.

"Watch this, Daniel," Alex said.

Alex looked around, saw that no one was watching, and dumped the ashes from the ashtray into one of the glasses. Daniel merely shook his head.

"Let's retire to your room," Alex smirked. "Shall we?"

Daniel couldn't think of a good excuse, so he led Alex upstairs. At the top of the stairs, Alex stopped, took a balloon that was fastened to the end of banister with a ribbon, untied the end, and sucked in the helium.

"Ahhh—nectar of the gods," he said in a high Donald Duck voice. "You still play music?"

"Let me try that," Daniel said. He took the balloon from Alex and inhaled as much helium as he could. "Do I still play music?" Daniel repeated in a voice even higher than Alex's.

Alex laughed.

"Sounds like we're high," Alex said. "Would I be spinning my wheels in the wrong direction if I assumed that you were in possession of some cannabis?"

"What?"

"Do you have any grass? You know—pot? Weed? Marijuana?"

"No. But I know where we could get some."

"Really?"

The boys continued through the kitchen just as Frieda Blaustein took a sip of her drink in the basement and broke into a violent coughing spasm.

•     •     •     •     •

"Where in the hell of all the deepest darkest voids are we going?" Alex asked as he and Daniel crossed to the other side of Pearl Drive.

"The DePuzos. Johnny and Joey. They're twins. They told me they found some pot in their mother's boyfriend's car. And they have a pretty sister who I might do it with one day."

"Do what with?" Alex asked.

"*It*," Daniel said, using the fist of one hand and the index finger of the other to demonstrate. "The Big F. The Unholy Semitic Screw."

Alex smiled. For once, he didn't have a sarcastic comeback.

"Do these twins go to your school?"

"No. Joey beat up some kid and got sent to juvenile detention. It's like jail for kids. And they decided to send his brother with him, just for the hell of it."

"Awesome!"

The twins were in their backyard with a new stack of baseball cards. Both were chewing furiously on the gum that came with it, and also sweating profusely, although it was a cool September afternoon.

"This is Alex. He's sort of like a second or third cousin or something," Daniel said to the twins. "We snuck out of a party at my house."

Joey and Johnny mumbled a weak "Hi."

Joey looked up. "Is your Uncle Nat at the party?" he asked.

"No. Why?"

"Because my grandfather was just talking about him."

"Word has it that you are in custody of some reefer, my man," Alex said to Joey, who looked at him as if he had just heard a foreign language.

"What?" Joey asked.

"You have some pot?"

The twins looked at each other.

"Be right back," Joey said.

While Joey went into the house, Johnny led the other two to a small patch of woods behind the house. Joey returned with a rolled joint and a lighter. He lit the joint, took a hit, and passed it to Daniel. Daniel took a hit and passed it to Alex.

"We also found a box of rubbers in Frankie's car," Johnny said as the joint made its way around.

"Who's Frankie?" Daniel asked

"Frankie Russo. He's my mother's boyfriend." Johnny took a packet of condoms out of his pocket and showed it to Daniel and Alex. When the joint returned, Daniel took his third hit—an especially long one—then passed it to Alex.

After his fourth hit, Alex began to sing in a strange, wobbly falsetto voice, as if he still had a lung full of helium. *"Good, good, good, good vibrations,"* he chirped. Johnny and Joey looked amused.

"You sing like shit," Daniel said.

"You probably do too," Alex replied. "You're higher than a kite."

"Well, let's see."

Daniel picked up the verse:

*"I'm pickin' up good vibrations, She's giving me excitations..."*

The two boys sang together:

*"Good, good, good, good vibrations..."*

"What the fuck's an excitation?" Joey asked. Just then, Felice DePuzo called out to the boys from the back door.

"Johnny, Joey, are you's out there? You have to come in and help me move some furniture. Now!"

"We better go before she starts screaming her fucking head off," Johnny said.

Joey dropped what was left of the joint and stomped it into the ground. Johnny kicked dirt, rocks, and leaves over the remains, and then offered Daniel a stick of gum.

"Do you have one for Alex?" I asked.

Joey searched his pockets and found another stick of gum, which he gave to Alex. The twins went into their house while Daniel and Alex walked through the woods next to the backyard to get to the block behind Pearl Drive.

"You have quite satisfactory friends, my man," Alex said. "I never thought you were a cool kid. But you're okay."

"Thanks."

They walked to Miller Avenue. Daniel felt lightheaded. He tripped twice on the way and screeched the word "Excitation" in a falsetto voice over and over. Alex laughed. It was late in the afternoon. Most of the stores on Miller were closed or about to close. Miller Variety was a stationary store that sold candy and toys, and it was still open. It had been a favorite destination of kids all over Westbrook Hills ever since we had moved in, and even before that.

"Let's go in this fucking excitation place," Daniel said to Alex. Alex laughed again.

There were no customers in Miller Variety when they walked in. The proprietor, a gruff old man in a white smock who had worked there ever since I could remember, stood behind the counter with a broom. Daniel asked him where he kept the magazines.

"In the back," the man barked. "You've been here a million times. You have to ask where the magazines are?"

Alex lingered up front by the candy while Daniel went to the back of the store. On the way, he passed a display of miniature flashlights and, inexplicably, had a tremendous urge to own one. He continued on to the magazines but found nothing of interest. So after about a minute, he headed back to where Alex stood at the front of the store. Along the way, he let his right arm drop to his side and grabbed five of the tiny flashlights from the display. He slipped them into his pants pocket.

"You don't have Ukulele magazine?" Daniel asked the old man, trying to make himself sound angry.

"Never heard of it," he said. "Try the music store on Hempstead Turnpike. But they're closed now."

The boys went back to the house. As they walked through the front hallway, Alex turned the thermostat to ninety degrees when no one was looking and flipped on the heat switch. Several guests had already gone home, but about ten or so were in the living room. Mom and I were in the kitchen preparing two last trays of hors d'oeuvres.

"Hi, Aunt Beverly, hi Cousin Lori," Alex said. "Everything is very nice. It's so comfortable in your home. You throw a lovely party."

"Thank you, Alex," Mom said. "You're very sweet to say so."

Leon and Frieda Blaustein walked through the kitchen and chided Alex for not telling them that he had left the house. He apologized but said he was having a great time with Cousin Daniel.

"Can we stay a little longer?" he asked his parents. "I'd really like to get closer to Daniel. He should be more than just a distant cousin, and I'm not being fraudulent when I say that."

"We have a long drive home, Alex," his father said. "It's already getting dark. I don't want to get home too late."

"Just another hour. Aunt Beverly and Lori just put these delicious little hot dogs and egg rolls in the oven that I love so much. I think they did it just for me. Please?"

"Well… okay," replied his mother. "Half an hour. That's all."

Daniel asked Alex to follow him downstairs and to grab as many helium balloons as he could on the way down. No party guests were there. The boys went into Dad's workroom. Daniel found a spool of electrical tape and put it in his pocket. With more than a dozen helium balloons dragging behind them, they left the workroom only to bump into Steven.

"Come here," Steven said, his voice stern and severe. "Alone."

Steven and Daniel went over to a corner of the basement and left Alex by the workroom door holding six or seven of the helium balloons. Daniel had the other half. Steven stooped down and looked closely into his brother's eyes.

"Who are you," Daniel asked, "Dr. Lewis?"

Steven smelled his breath.

"We'll talk later," he said in an ice-cold voice, and then went upstairs to join Rachel.

Daniel and Alex left the house again and walked over to the elementary school. By the time they reached the empty softball field, it was nearly dusk. The only illumination in the sky was a yellow glow from the western horizon. The rest of the sky was a light charcoal gray. Daniel took the flashlights out of his pocket.

"Where'd you get those tiny flashlights?" Alex asked.

"I stole them," Daniel said. "From the candy store."

"Awesome!"

"Each one already has a little battery inside. They come that way."

Daniel turned on the miniature flashlights. He used the electrical tape to attach the five flashlight to five of the balloons, and then took the strings of all the entire bunch — about fifteen helium balloons in all — and tied them all together with an extra long length of ribbon.

"Let's see what happens."

Daniel let go of the gathered strings, and the balloons rose in the darkening sky. The tiny flashlights shone brightly through the multi-colored latex and made it appear as if an extraterrestrial craft floated in the sky — a colorful gauzy cluster of clouds in an otherwise cloudless horizon.

"Fucking goddamn cool," Alex cooed. "That is so fucking goddamned astounding! Jesus H. Christ! That's probably the sort of thing you see on acid." The balloons veered slowly to the north and settled into a steady horizontal course. "Ever do acid?"

Daniel stared up at the sky. He didn't answer.

"Daniel, can those twins get us some acid?"

They watched the balloons disappear. Daniel was completely lost in the visual drama.

When the boys got back to the house a few minutes later, Grandma Leah and Grandpa Jesse were on the front lawn. It was a little darker outside than it had been at the elementary school.

"Just in time," Grandpa said. He shook Daniel's hand.

"Bye, Grandma, bye, Grandpa. Happy anniversary."

"Thank you, sweetheart," Grandma said. "I'm always proud of you. You'll show them all."

Daniel and Alex went inside the house. All the other guests had gone, except for Alex's parents, and Rachel. They were all in the living room with Mom and Dad. Grandma Rose was napping in her room. I had been in the kitchen washing dishes but joined the others in the living room. Oddly, a breeze blew through the room; I looked at the living room windows and saw that they had all been opened.

"Someone turned the heat all the way up to ninety degrees," Dad said when he saw the puzzled look on my face. "Either someone was drunk, or someone's just a stupid idiot."

Alex laughed but quickly turned it into a cough. Daniel remained silent.

Frieda Blaustein came over to me.

"Lori," she said, "there was so much mingling to do today, I didn't even get a chance to talk to you. What are you studying in college?"

"She's studying psychology," Mom offered.

"Beverly," Dad interjected, "she can answer for herself."

"Bad habit," Mom said. "Sorry. I'll stop. From now on."

"From your mouth to God's ears."

"I'm not sure what my major will be," I explained to Frieda. "I'm taking psychology courses, an education course, and a religions-of-the-world course."

"And the rest of the time," Steven joked, "she takes drugs, protests the Vietnam War, burns pictures of LBJ and dreams of having Mick Jagger's baby."

Although by this time, I was able to respond to Steven's teasing better than I had been in the past, I was not yet as quick as I wanted to be. It was Rachel Tanenbaum who had a ready comeback in my defense.

"Steven!" she exclaimed, with just a hint of a smirk on her face. "First of all, Mick Jagger would never be able to hold up his end of a conversation with Lori. Second of all, if I remember correctly, you told me that *you* protested the Vietnam War and burned pictures of LBJ. So don't make fun of your sister."

The Blausteins were very impressed with Rachel, and it seemed as if Mom and Dad were, too. I'd be remiss if I didn't say that I liked her very much, as well.

"How long have you and Steven been seeing each other?" Leon asked Rachel.

"Just three months," she said. "But it seems like... oh, at least three-and-a-half."

"Oh—a real tummler you got there, Steven," Leon said.

"We saw something magical outside a few minutes ago, and we're taking it as a sign that we're supposed to be together," Steven said.

"A sign?" Dad asked. "What kind of sign?"

"We were in the backyard—I won't tell you if we were smooching or not—and up in the sky we saw these beautiful colored lights that were moving very slowly. Like in a dream."

"We were talking about whether or not we should get more serious," Rachel added, "and then we saw it. It was beautiful, and we decided it was a sign."

"Colored lights," Dad muttered skeptically.

"Are you sure *you're* not the one doing some of those drugs," Leon said, "—SLD or whatever..."

"LSD," Alex corrected him. He shook his head pitifully.

"Nope," Steven said. "I'm not saying it was a UFO or anything like that. Maybe it was, maybe it wasn't. I don't know what it was, but it was special. No matter *what* it was, it made us happy." He smiled. "See you guys later. We're going for a walk."

Steven and Rachel left the room and went out the front door.

"Well," Dad said, "you don't have to be a scholar to be a poet, so there's hope for my son yet!"

"Don't talk like that, Murray," Mom chided him.

"I can see those two getting married one day," Frieda said. "It will be a beautiful wedding. Beverly, you'll make the food, Murray, you'll set up the lights, Jesse will tell funny stories, Daniel will play the piano, and Lori... Lori, what can you do?"

"Maybe I'll conduct the ceremony," I said, surprising even myself with the swift reply. All the adults laughed (and so did Alex, to show he was adult enough to appreciate it). The burst of laughter on my behalf was sudden and unexpected, and I felt the kind of embarrassment I used to feel so easily. So I smiled but then excused myself to go to the bathroom.

Mom sat on the couch. "Well," she sighed, "it seems as if everyone in this family has decided to start talking a little bit strangely all of a sudden. Steven and his magical UFO, Murray and his nasty comments about his own son, Lori suddenly becoming a holy roller... Would you like to say anything strange of your own, Daniel?"

He thought about it.

"Excitations," he said. "How's that?" Then he went outside.

Alex joined him there, just ahead of his parents, who had decided it was time to leave. "How come you didn't tell Steven and his chick about the balloons?" Alex asked.

Daniel didn't answer.

The Blausteins got into their car and drove off. Mom and I started to straighten up the house. By the time Steven came home to have that little chat he had promised to have with his brother, Daniel was in bed pretending to be asleep.

•    •    •

The next day I asked Daniel if he had a good time at the party. He said he did and then asked the same question of me. I told him I did, and that everybody seemed to have enjoyed themselves, with the exception of Grandma Rose. We agreed there was little any of us could have done about that; it was becoming progressively more difficult to stay unruffled every time Grandma whined and complained. I tried to do my part (and then some, if I may be so self-righteous) by asking her to teach me some of her cooking tricks. I had, in fact, become quite interested in holiday-related dishes, and Grandma Rose was happy to oblige. That meant, of course, that I had to stay home more than I really wanted to, but it was a sacrifice I was willing to make.

Mom and Dad were pleased with how calm and composed I was lately. Steven noticed it, too. What they didn't know, of course, was that I was able to maintain that composure only because Dr. Yaccarini went above and beyond his call of duty to help me on an almost daily basis. I am more than certain that the war in Vietnam and the problems at home could very easily have sent me into a tailspin, for I had not yet tapped into all the strength of will and self-reliance that I needed. But Dr. Yaccarini didn't allow me to spin out of control. He insulated me by helping me focus on the topics in which I delighted, such as literature, history, religion, and dreams. One day he said to me: "Young lady, your biggest problem will not be a fear of never becoming an adult with a purpose. Your biggest problem will be choosing which purpose you're best suited for. Because there are so damned many!"

One day, while I cleaned up after a kitchen session with Grandma Rose, I thought about how Dr. Yaccarini, in his understated way, may have planted the seeds for the cooking lessons, which were both enjoyable for me and a wonderful diversion for Grandma. Daniel walked in, clearly in a disengaged mood.

"You'll soon be a nice diversion, too, " I said to him.

He had no idea what I was talking about, which was clear by the confused look on his face.

"Your bar mitzvah is coming up," I continued. "That will cheer Grandma up a lot. She's always been big on weddings and bar mitzvahs. I don't think that ever changes, no matter how crabby a person gets."

Although Daniel's thirteenth birthday had already passed, the bar mitzvah ceremony was planned for a month after the anniversary party because of the temple's busy schedule. There were far more thirteen-year-old boys at Temple Beth Shalom than there were weekends on the calendar.

"Well," Daniel said, "at least it will cheer *someone* up."

I did not like that remark. But he followed it up by grabbing a piece of bread that he said needed "a schmear butter," and that gave me hope.

* * * * *

But even with Daniel's bar mitzvah on the near horizon, Grandma Rose's habits at home rarely wavered. It was not uncommon for her to complain bitterly about all the noise in the house and then turn up the volume on *The Mike Douglas Show* so loud that we couldn't even hear the phone ring. In the Hillman house at that time, two things were always certain: one, we'd never know if someone was trying to call, and two, we always knew who was being interviewed by Mike Douglas.

Grandma Rose may have complained about the noise, but in actual fact, our house was no different than most typical suburban homes. Steven talked on the phone quite a bit, Mom loved her electric mixer, Dad occasionally did some work in the basement with power tools, and Daniel sometimes played records. (I was hardly in the house; when I was, I suppose I was the quietest one there.) But the entire family was mindful of Grandma's frail condition, so no one went overboard.

Still, she complained.

As far as Daniel's records were concerned, it wasn't necessarily the volume that bothered Grandma Rose as much as their alien nature. It was just a coincidence that she rarely heard him play his folk records, which she probably would not have considered so alien. Those groups and singers—Peter, Paul, and Mary, Joan Baez, Pete Seeger—were as enjoyable to Daniel as the rock bands. What Daniel particularly liked about the folk singers was that they were true storytellers who simply spun their tales on vinyl instead of paper.

But it was 1967, and if you were not into rock and roll more than anything else, you might be considered an outcast by your peers. So in addition to other styles, Daniel made a point to familiarize himself with the Jefferson Airplane, the Velvet Underground, the Animals, the Who, Procol Harum, Pink Floyd, the Rolling Stones, and some of the other rock bands of the day. Those were the sounds Grandma called alien—the ones she unintentionally heard more than the others.

Unfortunately, it wasn't just Grandma who urged a little more quiet time in the house. Mom's accident the year before (which was only just now going to court) had left her with a slight ringing in her left ear, and that ear, she insisted, was sensitive to loud noise. Dad also added to the censure, because too much racket in the house, he insisted, made him tense. He already had enough to be tense about, what with the imminent court case and Steven's grades in school, which hadn't much improved. Although Dad gave up smoking when I was born, he had recently picked up the habit again.

As a result of all this, music, which had once been such a comfort to Daniel—when it was actually something that gave him strength and purpose—was now nothing more than a source of anxiety. Both Daniel and I would have welcomed its return in some meaningful way, simply as a reassurance that not *everything* had to change. As it turned out, once the fall term got underway at Westbrook Hills Junior High, music *did* return for him—but that, in turn, kicked off a whole new set of little dramas.

The school had a highly regarded music program. Miss Gracely, the department chairman, knew of Daniel's musical reputation and urged him to join the chorus, which she also directed. Miss Gracely had a very long neck. She was known as the Giraffe by students who didn't like her and the Goose by students who didn't quite hate her. One day after school, Daniel met Miss Gracely in the hallway, and she whispered to him that the audition for the chorus was just a formality—that he would definitely be accepted. She even promised that he wouldn't have to attend every rehearsal if he had other important things to do. That's how much she wanted him to be in her chorus. Daniel was flattered but tried not to show it. That night he asked for my opinion. I told him to join. "What's there to even think about?" I said.

The first rehearsal was on a Wednesday afternoon in the band room. Halfway through, the Goose told everyone to take a ten-minute break.

A girl named Jen had been in front of Daniel throughout the rehearsal, and during the break he kept his eyes on her. Like Annette DePuzo, Jen was a tomboy. As much as Daniel had found Annette fetching, Jen was even more so. She kept her hair short, though the bangs fell into her large brown eyes, and she hummed to herself constantly. She smiled at Daniel when she saw him stare at her. When Jen went out to the hallway to get a drink of water at the water fountain, Daniel wandered around the band room and overheard two other chorus members harmonize with each other. Their names were Jerry and Doreen, and they sang a new Beatles song called "Hello, Goodbye." Daniel listened from afar and enjoyed what he heard. Then Jerry and Doreen discussed the new Beatles album that had just been released, but they couldn't remember its name.

"I think it has something to do with a general," Jerry said to Doreen. "And something about a broken heart. Whatever it's called, it's really weird."

Daniel thought well of Jerry and Doreen right away. Their harmony was accomplished, and he liked the way they looked. Jerry's hair was longer than most of the other boys, but not at all messy, and Doreen's hair, though wild and defiant, somehow flattered her. So he went over to them to start a conversation.

"It *is* a weird title," Daniel said, "—the new Beatles album. And you're pretty close."

"Close? What do you mean, close?" Jerry asked.

"Well, it's not a general, it's a sergeant. And it's not a broken heart, it's a lonely hearts club."

"What the fuck are you talking about?"

"It's called 'Sergeant Pepper's Lonely Hearts Club Band.' But you weren't too far off."

Doreen laughed. Jerry smirked.

"Like I said, it's weird," Jerry acknowledged. "But I'm getting the album this afternoon anyway. Hey—what a minute. Aren't you Daniel Hillman?"

"Yes."

"I heard about you," Doreen added quickly. "You play like a thousand instruments or something, and you've performed at all kinds of places. Right?"

"Only five instruments, and only at shitty places."

"You write songs?" Jerry asked.

"Uh huh. But I don't want to talk about me. I want to talk about us."

"Us?" Doreen asked.

"Yes. Us. Let's start a group. I heard you guys singing before. You're good. Let's form a quartet. Folk-rock. Like the Mamas and the Papas."

"Quartet? But there's only three of us," Doreen said.

"What about Jen?"

Just then, Jen came back into the room from the hallway, still humming. She already knew Doreen and Jerry, so Dan had to introduce only himself. They spoke for a few minutes about his idea for a quartet, and then the ten-minute break was over. The Goose tapped a music stand with her baton to bring the chorus to order. Rehearsal lasted another twenty minutes.

Afterward, the four of them walked together outside and chatted about school, parents, the Beatles, the Stones, Dylan songs, Dylan's voice, the Mamas and the Papas, and Miss Gracely's incredibly long neck. And also about themselves. Daniel successfully evaded most of the questions they asked about him; he really wanted to learn about the three of *them*, and made sure he did.

Jerry was an only child whose parents were divorced. He lived with his mother, who had a terrible temper. He wanted to live with his dad, but his dad had run off to Georgia with a younger woman. Jerry planned to join them down south in a year or two.

Doreen had no temper at all. That's what she said about herself after she heard Jerry describe his mother's disposition. Not much upset Doreen—not even her older sisters when they forced her to do work around the house that they themselves were supposed to do. She said it was a learning experience—and that her sisters would get punished for it one day.

Jen was a clown. A high-spirited clown. She loved to wear clothes that didn't quite match. She loved to drop her books so that she could ask a boy to pick them up, and when the boy picked them up, she would sit on his back and refuse to let him up. She was energetic, sarcastic, and confident.

The four of them walked home from school together every afternoon for the next two weeks, and worked out the harmonies for "Monday, Monday," "In My Life," "Blowin' in the Wind," and several other popular songs. Sometimes Daniel ran home to get his guitar and played softly behind the vocals as the quartet walked around the neighborhood. Mothers just returning home from shopping and fathers just returning home from work complimented them in their driveways whenever the group passed by. *"How many times can a man turn his head and pretend that he just doesn't see?"* was heard on more than a few street corners in Westbrook Hills on those chilly afternoons. People even came out on their lawns to listen. *"The answer, my friend, is blowin' in the wind. The answer is blowin' in the wind."* Jen would often bring maracas or a tambourine. Before the month was over, they were asked to sing at one school assembly, one block party, and two Sweet Sixteens. They never knew what to charge and eagerly accepted whatever was offered.

"We need a name," Doreen said as they sat in her basement one afternoon passing around a joint.

"Well," Jen said, "we're a folk group. Let's call ourselves the Little Folks."

"Sounds like a fucking kids' show," Jerry argued. *"Captain Kangaroo* at eleven, *The Little Folks* at twelve. Absofuckinglutely not. Let's think of something else."

"How about the Boys and the Girls," Jen offered. "Sort of like the Mamas and the Papas, only younger."

"The Boys and the Girls?" Jerry complained. "Why the fuck would we want to tell the whole fucking world that we're kids? No record company is gonna sign us if they think we're a bunch of fucking kids. Besides, the name should have something to do with music."

"What does the Jefferson Airplane have to do with music?" Daniel asked. "Or the Beatles?"

Jerry was stumped. But secretly, Daniel agreed with him; he thought a band's name *should* have something to do with music. They tried out several more, but couldn't agree on anything.

The next afternoon they practiced in an empty playground near Jerry's house. For a while, they sat on the swings working out harmonies to "Happy Together." Daniel asked Jen if she'd like him to push her on the swing (and hoped she would say yes). She said she didn't need anyone to push her. "I've been pumping on my own forever," she avowed.

Suddenly they saw two older boys from school behind the chain-link fence that surrounded the playground. At first, the boys seemed to be listening to the songs, but then they began to yell words like "fags" and "whores" and "retards" and threw rocks in their direction.

"Shouldn't we do something?" Jen asked

"Absofuckinglutely," Jerry yelled—and in a flash, he hopped the fence, chased the boys, caught up to them, knocked them down on the ground, and kicked them in their faces until their lips and noses bled and swelled up. The boys ran away. The next day in school, there were whispers all around about 'those four kids, Doreen, Daniel, Jerry and Jen,' who had beaten up the two older boys. Even though it was only Jerry who had meted out the punishment, the rumor about 'those four' picked up momentum throughout the day. So many times was it mentioned—'those four kids, Doreen, Daniel, Jerry and Jen'—that the name of the group suddenly crystallized in Daniel's mind: the DeeJays. It was short, clever, and had something to do with music. The other three liked it, too. So that was the day the quartet became the DeeJays.

"But we should really do more rock," Jerry said. "That's what will get us a record contract."

"The Mamas and the Papas is basically a vocal group," Daniel insisted, "not really rock, and *they* have a record contract. The Righteous Brothers is mostly soul, and *they* have a record contract. Herb Alpert and the Tijuana Brass is mostly jazz, and *they* have a record contract."

"So, what are you saying, Daniel?" Jerry asked. "That you'll get us a record contract?"

"Absofuckinglutely."

"How?"

"You'll see."

"Tell me! Because I don't believe you, you conceited little twerp."

Daniel didn't actually have a feasible answer, but it hardly mattered because he had grown to dislike Jerry and couldn't stand the thought of doing anything that could help him become successful one day. What's more, Daniel had to put the DeeJays on the back burner for the next two weeks because of the many last-minute bar mitzvah preparations with which he had to be involved.

There had been a time, of course, when Daniel would have been very excited about his bar mitzvah. But like Rabbi Sheldon, that time was long gone. Still, he felt the need to go through with it, a sentiment abetted by my own frequent encouragement. I told him on more than one occasion that it was a personal milestone that, because of his natural talent, stood an excellent chance of making him feel tall not only in his own eyes, but in the eyes of his family and in the eyes of God. I also told him that I was very much looking forward to it. To this day, I sometimes wonder if the only reason he went through with it was to avoid disappointing me.

. . . . .

Dad hadn't initially counted on the need to keep expenses down for the bar mitzvah. But as it turned out, that need did materialize. For one thing, when he first started making plans more than a year before, Mom had not yet been in the car accident. There were several fees related to the case for which Dad had to dip into the family savings. For another, Steven, who always needed at least one tutor to help him pass his classes, in recent months needed three. Between the lawsuit-related costs and the extra tutors, Dad had to cut back on the bar mitzvah budget, which affected everything from the place where it was to be held to the number of guests who would be invited.

Daniel played no music at the reception. Although Mom and Dad seemed surprised at his decision, they didn't argue with him. Daniel said that the three-piece band they hired would be more than adequate.

He also wondered how special the day could possibly be with Rabbi Mishkin in charge of the ceremony. Steven had once said that the new rabbi at Temple Beth Shalom had "teeth that are yellower than piss, and the personality of kosher linoleum, only less exciting," and while I certainly would not have gone down that impudent road, Steven's central theme was not entirely unfounded; Rabbi Mishkin was a slovenly man who lacked an engaging personality. To me, he was a living lesson on how *not* to be a good rabbi.

What family members and temple congregants saw on Daniel's face as he approached the bimah to chant his portion of the Book of Prophets was what I can only describe now as indifferent acceptance. Undoubtedly he felt conflicted emotions; after all, he was standing behind the podium that he had irrationally destroyed not too long before. The top had been reattached to the base with nails and duct tape. The temple's austerity budget permitted nothing more. Also, he was standing in front of the red felt curtain that he had ripped down and which had been repaired instead of replaced.

Daniel tried to concentrate only on the Hebrew words as he sang his portion. When he concluded the final passage, Rabbi Mishkin and Cantor Goldstone smiled and patted him on the back. That was all the recognition he received that day from the spiritual leaders at Temple Beth Shalom. Afterward, all the congregants and guests adjourned to the temple lobby for the conventional half-hour of wine, grape juice, breads, and cookies. Many people went over to Daniel to make all the traditional comments about his having become a man. Several asked what he wanted to be when he grew up, and whether or not he had any specific plans. (Most claimed to have already known the answer.) Daniel smiled and said he didn't know.

Elsewhere in the lobby, Mom talked with the temple president, an attorney, about her upcoming court case. Dad went off to a corner to smoke a cigarette. Yetta sat at the side of the room with Grandma Rose, whose legs were hurting terribly that day. Steven stood by the wall near the sanctuary doors to stare at the Tree of Life—the large three-dimensional commemorative plaque onto which little silver leaves were engraved with the names of deceased loved ones of temple members. Grandpa Jesse and Grandma Leah held court with various relatives near the lobby staircase.

I walked over to Daniel to compliment him on his recitation. Despite his indifference, he did an excellent job, and I told him so in no uncertain terms. Though I hadn't studied Hebrew, I knew that he pronounced every word properly and hit every note precisely.

"Are you taking up where Rabbi Sheldon left off?" Daniel asked.

"Maybe," I said. "And now I can't wait to light a candle at the reception."

"Fine. But I don't know what good it will do," he responded. I decided not to ponder the implications of his comment; instead, I went to find other relatives to greet. I'm fairly certain that Daniel was almost instantly angry with himself for saying it to me, but neither did he want to embarrass me by running to apologize.

But he *did* feel like running. Not out of the temple, but somewhere away from the crowd. He went upstairs to the hallway where all the temple offices are lined up one after the other. Rabbi Sheldon's name was still on the door of Rabbi Mishkin's study, even though the switch had been made more than a year before. No one was around, so Daniel walked in. It was basically the same as it had been before—a large, messy desk against one wall, and two other walls covered with floor-to-ceiling bookcases. The spines of the books on the shelves, with which both Daniel and I were familiar from the old days, made him think even more of our old rabbi. The family had hardly discussed Rabbi Sheldon's infidelity. It was regarded almost more as an accusation than a truth (which was encouraged by the fact that no details were ever leaked). On those few occasions when we did discuss it, we seemed to instinctively want to find extenuating circumstances rather than to lay the blame squarely on the rabbi's shoulders. Regardless of any speculations, Daniel knew that Rabbi Sheldon would have made him feel good about being there on his bar mitzvah day, which after all is *supposed* to be a special day. He might have dragged out of Daniel his disappointments, his ambiguous feelings about our mother and father, even his mixed emotions about forming what was now a popular vocal group called the DeeJays. Those emotions were mixed because he despised one member more and more each day, and was very fond of another who didn't return his affection.

There were hundreds of books in the rabbi's study. Some were about musical instruments in biblical days, others about famous Israeli musicians. Those were the ones that Daniel and Rabbi Sheldon had often discussed. Daniel had actually read many of them. On Rabbi Mishkin's desk were five empty Coke cans, each with a straw sticking out. A copy of Newsday was also on the desk. Daniel ripped up one page of the newspaper and made a dozen tiny spitballs. He took one of the straws and started to shoot the spitballs at the books, trying to get the projectiles in the center of the spines. It was a silly, juvenile act, but Daniel felt it was right to attack those books, even if in such a childish, meaningless way. Besides, the damage—if that's what spitball strikes could be called—was so visually slight that no one would notice it for weeks or months or even years. But Daniel would know, and for the moment that was good enough for him.

As he prepared to shoot a spitball at *The Music of the Jewish People, Volume One* on a shelf near the top of the bookcase, Daniel noticed a framed photograph next to it—a photograph of himself. It showed him playing the piano at a temple event in 1962. Rabbi Mishkin probably didn't even know it was up there. And since Rabbi Sheldon was gone, and since in a way even that eight-year-old piano player in the picture was gone, the photograph had to go, too. So Daniel went over to the wall, shoved some books aside on the bottom shelf to make room for his left foot, and stood on the shelf. Then, to make room for his hands to lift himself up, he shoved aside a small snow globe inside of which was a tiny fiddler on a shingled roof. Daniel raised his left leg to the second shelf. That's when the entire floor-to-ceiling bookcase came tumbling down. The fall and the noise seemed to last longer than they should have, as if a major earthquake shook all of Long Island at that very moment.

Miraculously, Daniel was unhurt, but he had to use all his strength to crawl out from underneath the shelving unit and the sea of books. It was difficult to do. He sprained a wrist and an ankle in the process. The top half of the bookcase had broken apart when it hit the edge of the desk. What had been one massive case was now two. Many of the books were still underneath the two sections, though several dozen flew into corners and onto the desk. There was not an inch of the rabbi's study not covered with part of the bookcase or with books. Daniel heard footsteps in the distance, coming up the stairs to the office level, no doubt drawn by the noise. So he stood up and tried to think quickly, to decide what to do in the mere moments available to him. He considered climbing out the window, even though it was on the second story of the building. He went over to the windowsill to see how far a fall it would be. There was a book on the sill called *My Bar Mitzvah*, which had a picture on its cover of a happy family—a thirteen-year-old boy, his older brother and sister on either side of him, and his smiling parents behind. Daniel muttered:

"Yeah. Right."

"Yeah. Right," someone else muttered.

Daniel turned around. By the open door stood Ned Early. He had a concerned look on his face, but it wasn't menacing.

Ned had on the outfit he wore during almost every temple event: a bright red vest over his blue work shirt, and dark blue pants that were clean except for the knees, which were threadbare.

"I don't rightly know if 'young man' is the right thing to call you today," Ned uttered in an annoyed sigh. "A man? Hmmm. Doubt that." He looked at the mess in the room. "This here's your bar mitzvah day. Why you sneaking in here to destroy the whole damn office, pardon my cuss words?"

"It's a lot better than being downstairs making believe it's the happiest day of my life," Daniel said.

"Well well well—looks like you decided that today is the day you git yourself a smart-alecky mouth," Ned responded as he started to pick up some of the books. "You're not the only person in the world, you know. You got a lot a people down there who love you and respect you and have high hopes for you—so you best git down there now for nobody's sake but theirs. Especially your parents."

"Why?"

Daniel averted Ned's eyes.

"Why? 'Cause they got you here, boy."

"What's so good about being here?"

"I don't mean here at the temple. I mean here on Earth. You like being alive, don't you?"

"Actually, I don't know."

"You're full of it, son," Ned said. He grabbed Daniel's arm and swung him around. It was a firm grab, and it hurt a little, though it probably could have been much more painful had Ned intended it to be. "I see the way you look at things. Girls, and books, and posters in the hallway. I can see you thinking. You don't look at them things the way other kids do, and you don't just think. You really *look*, and you really *think*. And whatever goes in here," he said, pointing to his eyes, "goes right up here," he said, pointing to his head. "And God only knows what it's gonna do up there one day. I used to hear the way you talked to Rabbi Sheldon when he was here. Not just 'yes, Rabbi' and 'no, Rabbi' and 'I don't know, Rabbi' and 'okay' and 'uh-huh' and stuff like that. You really *talked*. So don't you go telling me you don't know if you like being alive. I ain't just no stupid Negro handyman. I *know*. I know a hell of a lot more than you think I know, son. You're just a little angry now, for some reason. I don't know what it is. Maybe it's a bunch of things. And that's why you sneak around to smoke, and you cuss, and you look like you hate the whole damn world. I ain't saying they ain't good reasons—but they ain't life and death reasons, neither. You're being goddamn selfish—God forgive me for saying so in temple."

"*I'm* being selfish?"

"Yes, you are. Because unlike me, and this old Rabbi Mishkin, and Cantor Goldstone, and your good ol' grandpappy, you got your whole life ahead of you. So if you want to be angry, go ahead and be angry— but be angry at yourself for being angry." Ned was bent at his hips so that his eyes could be level with Daniel's. "I'm right, ain't I?"

Daniel didn't know what to say. He felt the tears coming up.

"I know I'm right," Ned continued. "You have to git up pretty early in the morning to fool ol' Ned Early."

"Do you know about the sanctuary?" Daniel asked—even though he hadn't planned on mentioning it at all.

Ned was quiet for a moment, then cocked his head and said, "I do now."

He continued to stare at Daniel and shook his head slowly.

"Lucky boy," Ned sighed.

Daniel was confused.

"Lucky?"

"Yup. You know that old bum with the white hair that wanders up and down Hempstead Turnpike? The cops were pretty sure it was him who broke into the temple. They almost arrested him. You're lucky they decided he was too weak to do all that ruckus."

He glanced at the wall where the bookcase used to be.

"The darn thing was always wobbly," Ned said quietly. "Bound to happen one day. Probably all the ruckus downstairs finally jarred it loose. Just glad Rabbi Mishkin wasn't here when it happened."

Ned gently pushed Daniel out the door.

• • •

The reception, originally planned for the Westbury Manor, had been switched to a restaurant in Bethpage called The Olde Village Inn. Despite Daniel's objections, Doug Kelleher and Craig Stuart had been invited. Mom never considered inviting the DePuzo twins. "I'd rather invite Leopold and Loeb," she said. Rachel Tanenbaum wasn't invited either, much to Steven's chagrin.

"She'll think you don't like her," Steven said to Dad.

"She'll understand," Dad insisted. "And if not, what will be, will be."

At the reception, Mom and Dad, as the bar mitzvah hosts, walked around the room together many times trying to be as gracious as possible. Grandma Rose was well attended by her relatives from Queens, Yonkers, and Pompano Beach. She sat the entire time, and people were more than willing to come over to her. She became very animated when she told horror stories of her recent illnesses and hospital visits.

Grandma Leah had with her photos of her family's 1906 arrival in New York, which she shared with her cousins to prove how much I looked like her mother Libke, after whom I was named. She also described for them the ocean journey in dramatic detail. Grandpa Jesse recounted for several other relatives how it was a campaign song he wrote for Franklin Delano Roosevelt that helped FDR get elected to his first term as president in 1932.

Dad had hired a young trio—a piano player, bass player, and percussionist, all in their mid-twenties—to provide the music. Steven went over first to the photographer and then to the bandleader to talk to both of them because he had noticed stickers on their equipment trunks for Carnegie-Mellon and Cornell. College was on Steven's mind; at the end of his junior year, his high school guidance counselor hinted that his mediocre academic record would mean he'd have an uphill climb getting accepted into anything other than a community college. But as Steven liked to point out, he always did pretty well climbing up hills.

Daniel and I had an interesting conversation with Aunt Paula—Mom's sister-in-law—about the Six Day War that Israel fought with Egypt, Jordan, and Syria just three months earlier. Aunt Paula talked to me as if she were talking to an adult in her own peer group, and I was very appreciative of that, particularly since most relatives spoke to me as if I were still in junior high school. Aunt Paula, who was a high school social studies teacher, mentioned that my opinions on the conflict in the Middle East were sensible and well thought out and that I should consider becoming a college history professor. She told Daniel that while he should keep up his music, he should also consider other fields.

Aunt Paula was married to Mom's brother, Milt. We didn't see much of Uncle Milt and Aunt Paula as we grew up because they live in Michigan, where Milt still owns an office supply store. Aunt Paula was always very nice to us during the few times our families got together.

She admired the little gold Jewish star around my neck, which I had purchased the week before at Adelphi during the Hillel Club's 'Chotchke Fair.' She told Daniel that he looked debonair in his new suit.

Daniel tried to be friendly to all the guests. He talked to relatives, smiled during the cutting of the challah and candle-lighting ceremonies, and even danced with Mom. Several people asked him to play the piano, but he politely refused.

Doug and Craig played mostly on their own. Doug found a small empty porcelain vase on a table in the lobby and went around the dining room pretending to be Major Anthony Nelson from *I Dream of Jeannie* on television. Most people were entirely confused by it. Mom saw him do the routine at two tables and shook her head. "It's just not right," she said. Craig Stuart snuck into the busy kitchen and, when caught and asked to leave, said he was just trying to learn something new.

As the final hour of the reception approached, I heard a wave of whispers roll over the room and wondered what it was about. At first, I thought it was because Mom and Dad were dancing to the trio's rendition of "Sunrise, Sunset." But when I looked around some more, I saw that Uncle Nat had arrived.

Uncle Nat discreetly stayed off to the side of the room. Even then, with his shiny brown suit and a crisp gray felt fedora that he held in his hand, he was a presence that could not be avoided. Some people went over to him to shake his hand and ask how he was.

Grandpa Jesse and Dad finally approached him.

"Nu? How's my kid brother?" Grandpa asked.

"Good, kinahura. Busy. Sorry I'm late, Murray. I hit traffic on the Cross Bronx."

"That's all right," Dad said. "You're good?"

"I'm good."

"Good."

Dad and Grandpa went to talk to other people and left Uncle Nat to make his own decisions on where to mingle and with whom to chat. I sensed that he was looking not only to say hello to the bar mitzvah boy, but also to Steven and me. Steven, who had just finished another conversation with the photographer, was nearby. Uncle Nat walked over to him, reached into his breast pocket, and then handed him a small pamphlet called The Pilot's Pocket Handbook, which he said he requested from a friend at the FAA. Uncle Nat told him it was a little present for the older brother on the younger brother's bar mitzvah day. But Dad interrupted them to inform Steven that Grandma Leah wanted to tell him something. I don't think that was true.

Uncle Nat saw Daniel standing alone and walked over to him.

"Kids get allowances," Uncle Nat said. He put his hand in his pocket. "But you're not a kid anymore, are you? Today you are a man. So today it has to be a little more than an allowance. Vishtayst?"

His hand came out of his pocket with an envelope.

"Mazel tov, kid."

"Thank you," Daniel said as he took the envelope.

"Can I ask you a question, Daniel?"

"Sure."

"Why do you look like you don't want to be here?"

"Because I don't."

"Sure you do. First of all, being here means you're older, and the older you get, the closer you are to going off on your own." Uncle Nat winked. "Second of all, today's the only day you get envelopes like this, at least before you get married. Don't give the money to your pop. He'll want to put it away for college. Not that there's anything wrong with that. But I know it ain't easy being a kid, and you should be allowed to reward yourself every once in a while. Go to the city. See a show. Buy an instrument. Whatever."

"I *have* to give all the envelopes to my dad," Daniel told him. "He already said so. God forbid I do something *I* want to do."

Uncle Nat looked around.

"It's cash, kiddo. And not too chintzy, if you know what I mean. Which means that you can take out a little to keep for yourself, and no one will be the wiser. The rest you can give to your pop. Understand?"

"Yes."

"Good."

Dad ambled over to them and told Daniel that Uncle Milt wanted to tell him something. I'm pretty sure that wasn't true, either.

Then Uncle Nat came over to me. He put his fedora on a nearby table and placed his hands on my shoulders.

"Lori, Lori, Lori," he said. "Whenever I see you I'm reminded of just how special this family really is. You and your brothers. How are you?"

"Fine, Uncle Nat," I said. "How are you?"

"Always trying to be better. Is everything all right with you?"

"I guess."

"You guess? I want you to *know*! Come on now. The power of positive thinking. Don't they teach that in college? 'Yes, Uncle Nat—everything is going to be so wonderful that soon I'm gonna plotz from my own nachas.' That's what I want to hear from you, Lori."

I smiled and said okay. He kissed me on the forehead and held me at arms' length.

"Beautiful!" he said. "And such a pretty little Star of David. Remember a few years ago I told you that's what you needed? You listened! Though I was thinking something a little more… shall we say, generous. Who got that for you?"

"I bought it myself. It was cheap. I really can't afford—"

"When it comes to the right thing to do, you can't put a price on it. Am I right?"

Uncle Nat reached into his jacket pocket, took out a little box, and handed it to me. I opened it. Inside was a gold chai on a chain, with a tiny diamond in the middle of the two Hebrew letters.

"Oh! Thank you, Uncle Nat," I said. "It's absolutely beautiful."

"You deserve it, Lori. What can I say?"

Dad stepped up behind me and whispered loudly that Mom needed to talk to me about something. Again, it was undoubtedly a ruse to end my conversation with Uncle Nat. But I did as he asked because I didn't want to give Dad any reason to get upset.

Out of the corner of my eye, I noticed Uncle Nat meander around a bit and speak with three or four other guests. But after a few minutes, he left The Olde Village Inn for good.

"Interesting character, that Nat," Aunt Paula said to me when I returned to her table. Daniel was there now, too.

Even though Uncle Nat was on the other side of the family, Aunt Paula knew all about him. "I know all the Nat stories," I remember her saying at a party at our house a few years earlier. Daniel and I knew most of the stories, too, but Aunt Paula's versions, which over the years she recounted at various functions, were particularly intriguing to hear. According to Aunt Paula, Uncle Nat developed a nasty temper early in life because he knew he was an unplanned and unwanted baby. He always got in trouble. No one knew how to handle him. He dropped out of high school and couldn't hold a job. But he had a charismatic personality that, in Aunt Paula's words, "he wore like a velvet glove, and he knew how to use it better than anyone." Nat laughed easily, his eyes sparkled when he spoke, and he seemed able to connect with whomever he was speaking, almost as if that person was the most important person not just in the room, but in the world. Anyone who met Nat Hillman instantly liked him. At least at first. But girlfriends left after a few months, and bosses fired him after a few weeks. He spent some time in jail for business deals gone bad on which he couldn't make good. He once got into a fight with a coworker who accidentally fell off the roof of an eight-story building where the two of them had been scuffling. Nat disappeared for many years after that. When he reappeared, in his late thirties, he was a successful businessman, although no one knew exactly what successful business he was in. As Aunt Paula put it, Nathan Hillman was gregarious but secretive, intimidating yet refined. He came to very few family events, and apparently that was because he had sense enough to know that his presence was rarely welcomed, and he didn't want to hurt the family more than he already had. He had a bad soul but a good heart. "Yes," Aunt Paula conceded, "perhaps it is indeed possible to have both." Whenever Nat went to family events, he never stayed very long.

I appreciated more than enjoyed the stories; Daniel was truly enamored of them. He always asked for a few additional details, but this time Aunt Paula said that she didn't want to spend his bar mitzvah telling Nat stories. Daniel said he understood.

At that point, Uncle Milt asked Aunt Paula to dance, so the two of them walked to the dance floor. I went to sit with Grandma Leah, and Daniel headed for the bar to ask for a glass of soda. When the bartender put the soda in front of him, Dad turned him around by the shoulders.

"You should spend more time with your friends, Daniel," he warned, "not walking around all by yourself."

"There are only two of my friends here, and they're doing fine on their own," Daniel said. "And I'm talking to relatives!"

"Talk to your friends, too. Go find them. I'm paying for them to be here, so you better play with them."

"I don't want to play with them. They're really not my friends anymore."

"This party cost a lot of money, Daniel, and I won't have you moping around by yourself. It's your bar mitzvah, for Christ's sake. Go!" He said the word 'go' with a little more force than he probably had expected to use.

"No!" Daniel said, with an equally harsh edge to his voice. "My friends don't even like me."

"Now!" Dad shouted.

"Why?"

"Because that's the way it is." His voice was once again louder than it needed to be.

"Why are you yelling at me? Leave me alone."

"Who's paying for this, dammit?"

"Who the fuck asked you to?"

Dad slapped Daniel's face. Without even thinking about it, Daniel threw the glass of soda against the wall. It shattered into dozens of pieces. The dark soda stained the light tan wall-covering. Most people looked to see where the commotion was coming from. Some gasped, others covered their mouths. Grandma Leah, very much engaged in a story of how Daniel bore a striking resemblance to her father Label, didn't even hear it, so I pretended not to have heard it, either.

Fortunately, it was late in the afternoon, and two dozen or so guests had already left the party. About twenty minutes later, Mom, Dad, and Steven drove back to Westbrook Hills, and I took Daniel and Grandma Rose home in my own car. That night, Daniel apologized to Dad, with few words and even less conviction. As he told me the following morning, he didn't believe he had done anything terribly wrong. Perhaps that's why Dad, too, apologized, albeit with nearly the same number of words and level of sincerity.

Later that afternoon, I asked Daniel if he wanted to take a drive with me to Adelphi. He liked that idea; he needed to get out of the house. We walked around the campus. It was mild as the afternoon turned into evening. There was a comfortable breeze, and before long, a million stars lit up the pitch-black sky. The air smelled good.

"It's an almost spiritual feeling, isn't it?" I said to Daniel. "The sky, the air... Nature is a sort of nondenominational house of peace."

"Did you make that up?" he asked.

"I guess so. Why?"

"Can I borrow it?"

"Sure. What for?"

"I have no idea. I'll think of something."

•　•　•　•　•

A few days later, the owner of a new bookstore on Miller Avenue hired the DeeJays to sing at his store's grand opening. A week after that they were asked to play at a block party near Jen's house, and then at a charity carnival at the United Methodist Church, a block away from Temple Beth Shalom. The group was on a roll. The Westbrook Hills Times printed an article about them. But as much as they were proud of their accomplishments, they were also very frustrated. They had just fifteen songs in their repertoire, but had neither the time nor, quite often, the space in which to work out harmonies to new ones. They felt stuck. With colder weather on the way, playgrounds wouldn't cut it for much longer. They needed a new place to rehearse. Preferably inside.

Jerry said his house was smaller than his cat's litter box and that his mother would never allow it. Doreen told the group that her house was out of the question because her mother hosted a different club every afternoon and evening. Jen knew that her parents would say no because she was still being punished for sitting on a freshman for ten minutes, making him miss an extra-help class at school.

So one Thursday night while the family was having dinner (I was at a concert at Adelphi, or at least that's what I told them), Daniel asked Mom and Dad if he could have his band over to rehearse a few songs.

"Grandma gets headaches when things are loud," Dad said.

"We're not loud. It's just singing. Is it okay, Grandma?"

"Every band is loud," Dad said, disallowing Grandma to speak for herself. "I hear kids practice in garages all over Levittown, Bellmore, Bethpage… all the time. It's always loud. Louder than it has to be."

"Ours isn't like that."

"That's what they all say."

"It's not. I swear."

"Eat your food," Mom said

"He's eating his food," Steven yelled. "Why do you tell him to eat his food when he's already eating his food? Say what you mean. If you don't want his band to practice here, just say no, you can't practice here. But don't tell him to eat his food."

"Oy gevalt," said Grandma Rose.

Dad turned to Steven. "What's the hell's the matter with you?" he asked.

"Nothing," Steven said.

"Well?" Daniel asked again, confused at the exchange but unwilling to try to make any sense of it. "Can we rehearse here? It'll just be for two or three nights. It's just four of us."

"No!" Dad shouted. "No bands in the house. Stop asking. Steven has to study, Mom's ear hurts, Grandma gets headaches, I'm working my goddamn tail off..."

"Oy gevalt, Murray," Grandma said, "the language."

"What does working your goddamn tail off have to do with having a few kids over to sing?" Daniel asked. "You're not even home most of the time."

"Don't argue."

"And Steven studies in his room with the door closed. It's just a couple of friends singing in the basement for an hour or two. Steven won't even hear us! No one will. Not even Grandma."

"Do it at someone else's house."

"Nobody else's parents will let us."

"Oh!" Dad said, believing he had stumbled onto a sudden unplanned victory. "No one else's parents will allow it, huh?—but I have to be the schmuck that does? In that case, absolutely not."

"But Dad—"

"Suddenly you're so interested in music again? You didn't even want to play at your bar mitzvah."

"What's that got to do with anything?"

"Bands don't lead to anything good."

"Murray—" Mom began.

"Don't Murray me, Beverly. That's not just me talking, and you damn well know it. You've said the same thing yourself a hundred times."

"It's a little different, Murray—"

"This is so fucking stupid," Daniel said, and then quickly pushed himself back from the table while Grandma uttered another and much more disgusted "Oy gevalt."

"Don't you ever talk like that again," Dad shouted.

"Why do you hate me?" Daniel yelled as he left the kitchen. "Why does everybody in this stupid house hate me?"

Daniel went to his bedroom and slammed the door. When I arrived home half past midnight, he was in the kitchen filling a glass with water from the sink. I asked him why he wasn't in his pajamas, but he merely grunted and went back to his room. On Friday morning, before anyone else was up, he left the house without bothering to get washed, change his clothes, or have breakfast. Nor did he take a coat with him. He went to the baseball field at school and sat on the bleachers in the chilly pre-dawn darkness. He found five cigarette butts in the dirt and smoked them all.

•　　•　　•　　•　　•

Mom called the main office at Daniel's school during homeroom period to make sure he was there. The school secretary walked into his homeroom class, looked at Daniel, then departed. Nothing else of note happened that day at school. But when it was over, things took a sudden and unexpected turn, ostensibly for the better: the DeeJays found an impressive place to rehearse.

The moment Daniel arrived home from school, the phone rang. He picked it up. On the line was Steven's friend Billy, the musician from Hicksville. Billy said he needed to ask Steven a question, but Steven wasn't home. Daniel and Billy talked for a few minutes on the phone about the DeeJays and the music scene on Long Island. Billy, a pianist, singer, and songwriter, knew quite a bit because he had been performing at clubs since he was fifteen. His current band, which he said he had just formed but wasn't sure would last, rehearsed almost every night in his Hicksville basement. They had plans to rehearse there that evening. When Daniel mentioned his own group's rehearsal problems, Billy offered to let them use his basement for an hour or so before his own rehearsal began. He said to come by at about six-thirty.

"But Steven doesn't get home from baseball practice until seven-thirty," Daniel said.

"So? Come anyway," Billy responded.

Daniel knew that Mom would question why he was going to the house of one of Steven's friends, so he told her that he was going to a chorus rehearsal at school. She asked why there was a nighttime rehearsal, and Daniel explained that the Goose had insisted on it. Mom was so preoccupied with Grandma's kvetching that she simply let the comment pass. (That night, though, she asked me if I knew a teacher named Mrs. Goose.)

Daniel called Jen to tell her the good news about Billy's basement, and he asked Jen to call the others. They all met at the bookstore on Miller Avenue and walked together to Billy's house.

Billy loved the DeeJays. He listened to them sing two songs and was very impressed with their four-part harmony. Even though he was only five years older, Billy acted like a seasoned pro who had taken the group under his vastly more experienced wing. He even accompanied them on "Monday, Monday" and "Windy" on the upright piano in his basement, and helped them work out interesting new harmonies for "Happy Together." Jerry tried to sound more knowledgeable than he really was and asked Billy some silly questions about recording studios. Billy answered honestly, but all that did was make Jerry feel foolish for having asked the questions in the first place.

Billy's bandmates arrived shortly before seven-thirty. The members, who ranged in age from seventeen to twenty, mumbled irritably to each other, unable to understand why Billy would want to hang around (in the words of the drummer) with little kids. But after they heard the DeeJays sing one final song, the Beatles' "In My Life," all but the drummer seemed to have a much better idea. The drummer, however, was an angry, moody young man who continued to remain wary of the DeeJays' presence in the basement.

"Daniel is Steve Hillman's brother," Billy explained to him.

"I don't care if he's John Lennon's fucking brother," the drummer said. "Are we gonna rehearse or play ring around the rosy?"

"Don't pay any attention to that asshole behind the curtain," Billy said to Daniel. "He's always like that. Always wasted, too."

As Billy's band set up their instruments, Doreen went to the bathroom, and when she came back she had a sickened look on her face.

"I don't like it here, Daniel," she whispered anxiously. "Look at all that stuff on the sink in the bathroom."

Daniel peered inside. On the rim of the sink was a pipe, an ashtray overflowing with cigarette butts, a bottle of Jack Daniels, and a pornographic magazine. Inside the sink was what appeared to be vomit. A slow stream of water flowed steadily from the faucet.

"Don't worry," Daniel whispered to Doreen. "Billy is my brother's friend. I'm sure we'll be okay."

Billy looked over a piece of sheet music. The drummer let out a series of belches so deafening that Billy's mother called down to ask if someone had gotten hurt. The bass guitarist walked over to Jen, and when she smiled at him he pointed the neck of his guitar in her direction, then slowly lowered its angle toward her crotch. Jen was too stunned to make a decisive move—until the tip of the instrument actually touched the zipper of her blue jeans. That's when she moved away with two determined steps, one backward, one sideways. She flashed the bass guitarist an angry, disgusted look. Billy's mother called downstairs once again to say that someone was on the phone for Billy. Billy went upstairs, and when he returned he said that it was Steven on the phone.

"Did you tell him I was here?" Daniel asked.

"Yeah. Why?"

"Nothing. I think we should go. Thanks for letting us rehearse."

Daniel motioned for Jerry, Jen, and Doreen to follow him upstairs. They walked back to Westbrook Hills. There wasn't much talking on the way.

The next morning, when my brothers left the house to walk to their respective schools, Steven stopped Daniel on the front lawn.

"Don't you ever, *ever* go over there again—especially not without me!" he said sternly.

"Why not?"

"Because."

"What kind of stupid fucking answer is that?"

"Where'd you pick up that filthy mouth, Daniel?"

"What century are you living in, Steven?"

"Just don't hang out there. It's not a good idea. I'm older. I know better."

"*You* hang out there."

"I just help them out and they pay me for it. And I know how to stay out of trouble. I can't talk about it now, Daniel, but just listen to me. Do you understand?"

"I like Billy. And he likes me."

"You like him because he's a real musician. But don't hang out with the group unless I'm with you. Got it?"

"What are you, my father? My rabbi? My goddamn guardian angel? Just shut your fucking mouth and leave me alone."

"Don't ever talk to me like that again, you little bastard. I'm trying to help you."

"I don't need your help. I know a lot more than you do. I don't have any tutors."

"And there are still a few things I know that *you* don't."

"Not according to your piss poor grades."

For a moment, Steven was speechless.

"You've really become an idiot," he finally said. "You know that?"

"Good," Daniel replied. "That's what I've always wanted to be. An idiot."

"Then I won't help you anymore."

"Good. Because I don't want your fucking help."

They walked on opposite sides of the street toward Miller Avenue. The high school was to the left, the junior high to the right. On Miller, they went their separate ways.

After that, Steven and Daniel rarely spoke to one another.

# Six

Steven received his draft notice in the spring of 1968. It arrived on the first day of his final semester of high school.

Mom, who knew quite a bit about local politics by reading Newsday voraciously and attending many town council and county government meetings over the years, called a few officials to ask why Steven was not told about 2-S deferments for college students, from which so many others benefitted. Just days before the draft notice arrived, Steven had been accepted to Nassau Community College. But mom was told that regional draft boards were not legally obligated to defer college undergraduates, and that because of Steven's grades, his acceptance to a two-year community college, and his lack of a declared major, the draft board would stick by its decision to move ahead with his draft notification. Mom cried and pleaded into the phone, but to no avail.

She and Dad had tried several maneuvers to keep Steven out of the army. First, they asked Rabbi Mishkin to devise a story that he had decided to study privately with him so that he could eventually apply to rabbinical school, and that the lessons would have to begin that winter. They thought that would get Steven a deferment. Rabbi Mishkin did indeed write a letter, but it was weak and unconvincing, and it didn't work. Then Mom and Dad contacted several Long Island senators and representatives, but after the politicians reviewed Steven's academic record, no firm commitments were made. A move to Canada was considered, but Dad was mortified at the prospect of finding a suitable job, and he had read a story in Life magazine about families who moved to Canada only to discover that their other children rarely fared well north of the border.

Steven had actually looked forward to starting at Nassau Community College in the fall (even though he would still have to live at home). During the last week in June, he graduated from Westbrook Hills High and resumed his job with the private airline at Republic

Airport on a full-time basis. He told his boss at the airline that he would have to quit in the middle of October to report for basic training at Fort Jackson, in Columbia, South Carolina. His sympathetic boss, who had a son in the Navy, allowed Steven to earn overtime pay even when there was no overtime work to be done. Steven was also obligated to inform Nassau Community that his college career would have be delayed by at least two years. Rachel Tanenbaum had recently left for Cornell University, hundreds of miles away in upstate New York, and by mutual understanding their relationship, like Steven's college career, was put on hold.

I chatted with a few friends at Adelphi who had brothers facing the same situation. I was told by various people in various ways that some draft boards were far less sympathetic than others, and that ultimately young men either had break the law by ignoring the draft notice and hope for the best—or go where they're told to go and *still* hope for the best.

In mid-June, Dad requested to meet with the president of LILCO, a man who had many friends in powerful positions. The president was sensitive to Dad's concerns, but the best he could do was arrange for Steven to be assigned to a special transportation corps that would never actually fight on the front lines. Steven would work at a base in South Vietnam helping to maintain jeeps, helicopters, motorcycles, and as rumor had it, a top-secret experimental Air Force glider. While still very nervous about the future, Steven said he was excited about the assignment.

Although Mom and Dad always tried to put a hopeful, optimistic spin on Steven's upcoming tour of duty, I knew they were worried sick over it. So was I—though Dr. Yaccarini did all he could to allay my fears with stories of veterans he knew who returned home even stronger and with more determination to make a difference in the world. My own resolve to keep the anxiety at bay, however, did not go very far at home, for my parents were still worried about *me*. I was hardly at the house, and when I was I almost always hid away on the phone. I also saw Mom and Dad look dubiously at my tie-dyed tee-shirts emblazoned with flowers and peace signs. I know for a fact (having overheard a few conversations in the kitchen) that they wondered if I had finally succumbed to the counterculture they had read about in newspapers and magazines. Did they speculate that behind my pleasant, modest exterior I was a drug-worshipping, orgy-loving hippy? (Thinking about that now still makes me laugh.)

As for Daniel, he started to consider himself a fantastic actor because of how successful he was making believe that everything was fine. Whenever he was at home, he disguised his sloppy appearance with combed hair and a tucked shirt. He effectively hid two bad school grades from Mom and Dad by intercepting the notes that were sent home and skillfully forging their signatures on the response. He became an expert at masking the odor of tobacco and marijuana.

It all seemed to have worked. Then again, Mom and Dad probably weren't paying much attention.

•   •   •   •   •

One day that autumn, Daniel began to write a poem called "Dandelion Wishes" (which I still remember to this day, even though he never completed it). The theme posed the question of whether it was wise or foolish to depend on luck for anything good to happen. But after he jotted down several lines, his pencil broke. He couldn't find a sharpener, and all his other pencils seemed to have disappeared. So he knocked on my bedroom door to ask to borrow one. I was by my dresser getting ready to go out. On my desk was an essay I had written for one of my classes. It was called "Nature's Irony, God's Deception." Without my knowledge (for I was desperately trying to get my hair to cooperate), Daniel started to read the essay. Since my penmanship was large and clear, he had no need to bend down and put his face close to the paper. That's why I didn't know he was reading it.

"How can there be death in the air when everything is so incredibly beautiful outside?" he read silently to himself. "It always strikes me as one of nature's wildest ironies, as one of God's craziest deceptions, that the crisp, rainbow colors of autumn foliage results from the slow death of the leaves that fall from their branches. The leaves lose all their strength because they are starved of photosynthesis. The green goes out, they fall off their branches, they turn brown, they die, and they make autumn look like autumn. So in effect, life goes on, even though a major player is dead."

Finally, after giving up on my hair, I noticed in my dresser mirror that Daniel was reading the essay. My expression—which he saw in the mirror—gave it away.

"Holy crap!" he smiled before I could speak. "You write beautifully, Lori. This is gorgeous. I wish I could write as good."

"*Well*," I said. "You wish you could write as *well*. And you do write well, Daniel. I've seen some of your book reports."

I'm sure he expected me to be embarrassed by his invasion of my schoolwork, but I wasn't embarrassed at all.

"That essay is for a new course called The Co-Existence of Human Psychology and Religion in American Society," I explained.

"Jesus! That's a long name for a class."

"I know. Most of us call it Lord Psych to save time. Vincent told me that he got the idea for it after one of our discussions."

"Vincent?"

"Dr. Yaccarini. My psychology professor. I talk to him a lot about religion. He believes that priests and rabbis and ministers and imams and all other spiritual leaders tackle psychological problems far better than psychologists. He says they use less science and more human connection. He says that the best spiritual leaders are the best psychologists because they're not burdened by seventy-five years of ridiculous scientific surveys and studies. That's what the course is about. Partially, at least."

"You like him, right? Vincent?"

"Just as a friend and a mentor, Daniel."

"What else does he say?"

"He says that people should not be allowed to become priests or rabbis until they reach at least fifty years of age, after they've had a chance to live many lives with their congregants and *through* their congregants."

"I think I can become one now," Daniel said.

"A rabbi? How come?"

"Because I've already lived fifty years in just the first fourteen."

"Sometimes I feel the same way," I said.

I decided to confide in Daniel the fact that my talks with Vincent Yaccarini had prompted me to look for my own apartment—and that I had found one, a block away from campus. I had actually signed the lease earlier that morning and had come home just to pick up some of my clothes.

"How are you gonna pay the rent?" Daniel asked. "Mom and Dad will probably say—"

"I also got a part-time job," I explained. "I start tomorrow. I'm an administrative assistant at the Kings Park Psychiatric Hospital. Vincent helped me get it."

"That's great. What made you think of autumn leaves, anyway?"

"When Vincent walked into the classroom one morning, he said, 'Oh, what a beautiful morning.' First, I thought about you. When you were little, you used to sing that song from *Oklahoma!* And you also used to sing that song with the line 'All the leaves are brown, and the sky is gray...' Remember?"

"'California Dreaming.' The Mamas and the Papas. Good song. The DeeJays used to sing it."

"I remember. Anyway, I thought about the leaves on the ground, all over campus. I remember learning about leaves and photosynthesis in high school, and... I don't know—it just made me think about the whole process and the beauty, and... well... when we were assigned the essay—"

"It just all came together," he finished for me.

"Yes."

"Well, remember how everyone used to ask you what you wanted to be when you grow up," Daniel said, "and how nervous you used to get because you had no idea what to say?"

"Yes."

He held up my essay.

"Easy answer, my child. How about a writer?"

"Easy answer for you, too," I smiled

"For me?" he asked. "What?"

"How about a rabbi?"

•   •   •   •   •

Between Grandma Rose's worsening health, Steven's impending departure for South Vietnam, and the mystery over my exploding social life, Mom and Dad simply had no patience for Daniel's piano, guitar, saxophone, and xylophone. He hardly played anymore. The real question was whether or not he really missed the instruments all that much. So many other intriguing thoughts and captivating ideas played freely in his mind that there may have been little room left for ivory keys, nylon strings, and wooden reeds anyway.

He wasn't at home a lot, either. Often Daniel told Mom that he was at a band rehearsal at school or practicing songs at someone else's house because he didn't feel like trying to explain his state of mind. Most likely, he barely understood it himself.

Daniel stayed away on the weekends, too, and continued to use music as the excuse. The specific explanations he concocted varied: sometimes he was visiting a new music store two towns away; other times he was playing his guitar for kids in the playground or listening to a barbershop quartet at Salisbury Park. Once or twice it was true, but mostly he sat hidden within a cluster of trees at the park smoking cigarettes or a joint he had purchased from older kids in the neighborhood with some of his bar mitzvah money. When I'd stop by the house (about twice a week), half the time he wasn't there; the other times he was by the kitchen table reading a novel or skimming through Newsday.

I once stayed overnight to help Mom and Grandma Rose tidy up the house—a little bit one night and a little more the following morning—because it hadn't been cleaned in weeks. There was a mahogany liquor cabinet in the living room, fully stocked for the occasional party or visits from friends or relatives. I opened up the cabinet to dust inside. I went back to it the following morning because there were new fingerprints on the mahogany that hadn't been there the night before. I opened it again and noticed that a bottle of whiskey was missing. As I learned much later, Daniel had poured a little bit of the liquor into his old Beatles thermos from elementary school and brought the thermos with him to the park. No one in the house ever suspected anything (Mom and Dad don't drink alcohol), which simply enhanced Daniel's desire to do it; he reasoned that if no one really cared what he did to get out of a rut they didn't even know he was in, then why shouldn't he just continue doing it? It seemed somehow more productive to him than simply rotting in place.

One Sunday afternoon, at the beginning of October, Daniel walked over to Salisbury Park. The DeeJays had rehearsed there a few times, but the group was now defunct. Daniel thought about that as he passed through a gated entrance on Salisbury Park Drive. He and Jerry had had many fights, some of them fierce, usually about the direction they each felt the quartet should take. That wasn't the only reason the group fell apart. Jerry had been caught with marijuana at school and was expelled, and Jen fell in with the football crowd and completely lost interest in the DeeJays. Doreen was the only one with whom Daniel remained friendly, although she had very little time for the friendship because her parents and older sisters had increased the amount of work she had to do at home. Daniel started to call her the Suburban Cinderella, though Doreen never quite understood what he meant.

At Salisbury Park, Daniel met a young man named Gary. He was Steven's age. Gary sat on the hill near the lake strumming his guitar, and when he saw Daniel he called him over. He said he had once seen Daniel sing with the DeeJays at a block party. Gary was in a band called Frozen Flame that played all around Nassau County, including many parties at Hofstra University, where he was a freshman. He said he had just bought the guitar with money his father had given him for books.

Daniel and Gary talked about the Beatles, Cream, the Doors, the Rascals, Simon & Garfunkel, Peter, Paul and Mary, the Mamas and the Papas, Miles Davis, John Coltrane, and many other groups and performers. Gary had a transistor radio that he said he bought with the money his aunt had given him for college clothes. For a while, Daniel and Gary listened to songs on the radio. Gary offered a cigarette, and together they smoked lazily under a tree. Daniel even let on about the whiskey in his thermos and permitted Gary to take a few sips. They discussed the music business, politicians, and the war in Vietnam. Gary said his car had eight anti-war bumper stickers on it, including Impeach LBJ and Hell No, I Won't Go. He bought the car, he said, with the money his grandparents had given him to put away for graduate school.

Gary accompanied himself on the guitar as he sang a song he wrote called "Bye Buy," which he said was his anthem against commercialism.

"A little ironic, isn't it?" Daniel said. "I mean, you bought all that personal stuff with the money people gave you for your education, but you're bitching about commercialism."

Gary shrugged.

He asked Daniel if he wanted to play a song or two. With Gary's guitar, Daniel performed a song he wrote for the DeeJays called "Around the Block," which was a different kind of anthem—about learning life's lessons by being knocked around by it.

"Cool lyrics. Nice tune. Good picking. Interesting concept," Gary conceded. "But I wonder if *you* see the irony."

"What irony?" Daniel asked.

"I really don't think you've been knocked around too much, kid. Figuratively speaking. You're only fourteen. *I've* been knocked around.

Not you."

"You're only eighteen."

"Seventeen, actually. I'll be eighteen next week. Same day as my parents' twenty-fifth anniversary."

They continued to chat, laugh a little, and celebrate their assorted angers and miseries.

"You're a pretty cool kid," Gary said, "for a fourteen-year-old."

"I'm not a kid," Daniel corrected him.

"Oh yeah. I forgot."

Gary took him to a thick cluster of trees and bushes on the other side of the lake.

"Here," Gary said. "Take these."

He gave Daniel two pills.

"What are they?" he asked.

"The songwriter's narcotic of choice these days. Like speed, but it's not speed."

"How dangerous?"

"Now you *do* sound like a kid."

"I just don't want to OD before I get laid, that's all."

"Fair enough," Gary laughed. "Not dangerous at all. Listen. This world is morally and culturally bankrupt. Agreed? It fucks up our brains. So these little pills take care of that. They make you feel creative. Even spontaneous. Trust me. Sometimes they even make you forget that none of your fucking wishes ever come true."

"Dandelion wishes?" he said.

"What?"

"Nothing."

Daniel pretended to pop both pills into his mouth but actually swallowed just one and flicked the other into the woods when Gary wasn't looking. Gary ingested both, then wandered off on his own, guitar in hand. After a few minutes, Daniel started to feel dizzy. He went deeper into the woods and made himself throw up. But he immediately felt silly for throwing up, as if it confirmed what Gary had said—that he *was* still a kid. A goody-two-shoes. Although he already smoked cigarettes and grass and drank whiskey, he wondered what it would take to completely eliminate the possibility of ever being called a kid again. *More* drinking? *More* smoking? That was his mindset at the time. And his plan.

Daniel went home and grabbed more of the bar mitzvah cash that was buried in a desk drawer. Within the hour he purchased a hundred dollars worth of pot from a neighborhood connection and thirty-five dollars worth of whiskey at a liquor store in Levittown. (He could have taken another bottle of whiskey from the liquor cabinet at home, but apparently it slipped his mind.) He told the liquor store proprietor that it was for his parents' twenty-fifth anniversary, and the weary man simply accepted the explanation.

There was an abandoned warehouse at an industrial park two blocks from Temple Beth Shalom. Everyone knew about it since it was bright yellow and clearly visible from the major thoroughfare beyond it. That's where Daniel went. The metal door at the back of the warehouse was unlocked. He spent the night inside that empty building. It was a miserable, self-pitying, and very puzzling night—but not exactly a solitary one, for several rats shared the warehouse with him. Daniel wasn't scared, even when the rats passed perilously close to his legs on their way from one end of the dark, cavernous room to the other. With the pot and the whiskey playing upon his mind, conventional awareness was noticeably absent, and hyper-awareness, which took its place, was strangely calming.

He awoke at four-thirty-five in the morning thanks to a radio in a delivery truck that had parked at an active warehouse next door. The deejay on the radio announced the time relentlessly. Daniel had a massive headache, threw up on the metal door, walked home, let himself in, took a shower, brushed his teeth, and went into his room to sleep for a few more hours.

Apparently, no one in the house knew he had been gone all night.

•　•　•　•　•

I suppose we've all had at least one lousy math teacher and one lousy foreign language teacher in the course of our school careers. The three of us—Steven, Daniel and I—had high school teachers under whose guidance, for one reason or another, we did poorly, even if we tried hard. I usually cried. Steven usually cursed. Daniel got lucky.

His grades started to fall, and Mom and Dad finally began to pay a little more attention. At first, they attributed his academic plunge to the fact that the first year of high school is always a bit of a challenge. But another explanation came to light. There had been two classes offered at Westbrook Hills High School in which Daniel had been very interested, Mass Communications and Film History. His guidance counselor explained to him that those two classes were offered only to juniors and seniors as electives. Daniel complained about it for weeks. Mom visited his guidance counselor, who speculated that Daniel's performance in school was a protest of sorts to what he considered a gross injustice. Mom and Dad were pleased that there seemed to be a logical explanation, which made it easier for Daniel to walk away unscathed from his first-ever lousy report card.

But then two letters were mailed home, which almost reversed his good fortune. One note was from Señora Marrano, his Spanish teacher, and the other from Mr. VanBrink, his math teacher. Daniel had been caught passing notes back and forth to other students in each class.

Señora Marrano was fluent in eight languages, but English wasn't one of them. She had trouble communicating with the class, and most lessons took twice as long as they should have. One day, while waiting for what seemed like an eternity for Señora Marrano to write an assignment on the board, Daniel and another student named Ray created their own little diversion to pass the time. Using a sheet ripped out of a workbook, they wrote music without lyrics and passed the paper back and forth between them trying to guess the song each had written down. Apparently, Señora Marrano saw them with the incredible peripheral vision that all teachers profess to have.

Mr. VanBrink, rumor had it, became a math teacher after nine years of abject failure as an actor. As a teacher, he was a great success—if success were to be measured by how many students feared and hated him. If you received a lousy quiz grade on a test, Mr. VanBrink would write it on the blackboard for all to see. He made sarcastic comments about more than just a few students. A boy named Jamie, a guitar player, had heard about the musical pastime created under Señora Marrano's nose and initiated the same game with Daniel in VanBrink's class. VanBrink had just written Daniel H / 59 / FAIL on the board. He turned around and saw the boys passing a note between them.

Daniel tried to intercept the letters sent home by Señora Marrano and Mr. VanBrink before Mom retrieved the mail. But he was too late. Mom told Dad about the letters when he came home from work. Dad said that he'd talk to Daniel later in the evening.

I came home for dinner that night. Grandpa Jesse called on the phone just as we began to eat to inform us that Grandma Leah had been rushed to the hospital with trouble breathing. She'd have to stay there for an indeterminate length of time. Dad decided that while Grandma Leah was in the hospital, Grandpa Jesse would stay in Westbrook Hills. Despite the added pressure on him, Dad agreed to drive Grandpa to the hospital to visit Grandma Leah at least once a day, either before or after work. Grandma Rose had already moved into my old room since I had an apartment of my own. Grandpa Jesse would sleep in Steven's room, and Steven would move into the basement for the few weeks he had left in the house before basic training. By the end of the night, the letters from Señora Marrano and Mr. VanBrink were completely forgotten.

Lucky Daniel.

* * *

I'm sure Dad felt that the word "okay" was the only sensible response he could give when Daniel asked if he could go to the Long Island Autumn Carnival with Craig Stuart and his family. After all, our house was a cauldron of tension. And clamor. Mr. Ashler's driveway was being ripped up and repaved, and Grandma Rose complained bitterly about the noisy machines. Also, Grandpa Jesse screamed into the phone at least ten times a day to discuss Grandma Leah's condition with the doctors who were treating her at Coney Island Hospital. Between Grandma Rose's kvetching, Grandpa Jesse's shouting, and Ashler's driveway construction, there was hardly a quiet moment in the house. (It was the same sort of lackluster "okay" that I received from Dad when I told him that I wanted to take my old bedroom desk to my apartment.)

Mrs. Stuart, Craig's mother, saw Daniel walk home from school one day and called out his name. She felt bad that he and Craig had lost touch, and thought that inviting him to go with the family on their annual outing to the carnival at the Roosevelt Field Raceway might rekindle the friendship. Although Daniel no longer felt any connection with Craig (all Craig ever wanted to do after school was watch *The Galloping Gourmet* on television), he accepted Mrs. Stuart's invitation. After all, she told him that Linda, Craig's pretty sister, would be joining them.

"Okay," Dad said. "Anything's gotta be better than staying here in this noisy fekakta house."

Linda Stuart was now a junior at Saint John's University and seemed to have gotten sweeter and prettier as she got older, even as her mother, father, and brother (and I do feel bad for saying so) got fatter and duller. It was sad, yet true.

The Stuarts, with Daniel in tow, drove to the carnival in Mr. Stuart's old, rusty Chevrolet. I remember that car from when I was a child. It was more or less the same on that carnival day as it was when Daniel was an infant, albeit a little rustier, and the old Goldwater/Miller bumper sticker from 1964, which back then had covered a Nixon/Lodge bumper sticker from 1960, was now covered over by a Nixon/Agnew bumper sticker.

Daniel sat next to Linda on the ride to the raceway. She told him that she looked forward to hearing him sing and play a few songs one day soon. "When you sing, you make people think you're singing only to them," she smiled. He said he'd love to.

A graceful letter L hung around Linda's neck on a delicate chain, and it glimmered brightly for a moment when the car turned a corner and a ray of sun burnished its gold.

"That's very pretty," Daniel said to her. "The golden L. Almost sounds like the name of a novel."

"The golden L!" Linda repeated. "A novel—or a song. It's so poetic, Daniel, and very sweet of you to say. Maybe you could write it one day."

When they arrived at the racetrack, Mr. Stuart parked the car on a large grass field on which there were hundreds of other cars. The carnival atmosphere was strong, even back there on the grass: the grinding organs of merry-go-rounds, the yapping of game barkers, the screams of children on rides, the smell of cotton candy and hot dogs... It all added to the anticipation in the air, although Daniel really didn't anticipate all that much, other than the pleasure of walking side by side with pretty Linda Stuart.

Mr. Stuart said that he and his wife wanted to take a leisurely stroll on their own and that Daniel, Linda, and Craig should visit any rides or attractions they wished. Linda asked the boys if they wanted to stop at some of the tents where the sword swallowers, bearded ladies, muscle midgets, and fortune tellers held court. Craig said he wanted to find out what he would be when he grew up, so Linda put her arms around the boys' shoulders and led them to the tent of Pandoro the Magnificent. On the way, she bought Craig a large pretzel. Daniel politely declined.

Daniel had had a growth spurt since his bar mitzvah and was taller than Craig—almost as tall as Linda, in fact. That made it easy to imagine himself walking arm in arm with her at the carnival. Suddenly he had the urge to be anywhere *but* the carnival; carnivals were for kids, and Daniel (as he had decided at Salisbury Park with Gary) was a kid no longer.

Daniel, Craig, and Linda arrived at Pandoro's tent. They could barely fit inside, but managed to squeeze into three hardwood chairs that were placed around a small, square table in the middle of the tent. Linda sat between the boys. Craig's face showed a little concern. "Don't worry, Craig," Linda whispered. "I'm right here." There was a metal cistern in the middle of the table, next to a cardboard sign that said 25¢ Each Guest. Two tall lamps stood against two of the canvas walls; the bulbs in each lamp were extremely muted. Linda put three quarters in the cistern. After the coins clanked and settled down, Pandoro the Magnificent stepped out from behind a black curtain and sat in the fourth chair. He was a massively built man, with a high forehead, bulging nose, and thick lips that looked almost blue in the shadowy atmosphere of the tent. Slowly, he removed the cistern and sign, put them under his chair, and replaced them with a large crystal ball that had been under the table. The crystal ball reflected the dim bulbs back into the room as colorful beams of light. Craig still looked frightened; Daniel enjoyed it. He imagined Pandoro the Magnificent as a larger-than-life character in a grand literary epic of good and evil and about the inevitable confusion between the two. He stared at the giant man with a look of amused curiosity.

"Welcome," the giant fortune teller said in a deep, booming voice. "I am Pandoro the Magnificent. Who shall be first?"

"I guess me," Craig said nervously.

"Your name is Craig. Yes?"

"Yes!" Craig responded. He looked surprised and amazed.

Pandoro stared at Craig and then looked into the crystal ball.

"You will own a fancy restaurant when you grow up," he said. "You like restaurants, yes?"

"I *love* restaurants!" Craig exclaimed loudly, having lost every ounce of fear.

"Your restaurant will be very special and very beautiful. In a tall building in a city."

"New York City? The Empire State Building?"

"No. Not in New York."

"Albany? Where my cousins and uncle and aunt live?" Craig asked excitedly.

"Yes… yes… Albany. And it will be part of a hotel."

"I *love* hotels."

"Yes, you do. Your restaurant will be part of a big, fancy, glorious hotel in Albany, and it will be run by you and your wife."

"My wife?"

"Your wife Melissa. Melissa will love to cook as much as you do. You will meet her in Paris, France, where you will study cooking. You will study there for three years."

"Will Melissa be French?"

"No. She will be from England. But you will not meet her until you are twenty-two years old… No! Twenty-three. She will be lovely. She will have black hair and brown eyes. Very beautiful."

"Wow."

"Who's next?" asked Pandoro.

"Would you like a turn now, Daniel?" Linda asked.

"No. You go first."

Pandoro gazed at Linda for a very long time, and then consulted his crystal ball.

"Your name is… Laura," Pandoro began.

"It's Linda."

"Yes, Linda—of course. Although there are many times when people call you Laura by mistake. Am I right?"

"Well… I don't really—"

"You are in college now, Linda. A college not too far away. And you study cosmetology."

Linda looked surprised. "No, but I *am* taking a dermatology course right now. That's funny," she said, turning to Craig. "Uncle Joe made the same mistake last week. He said cosmetology when he meant dermatology."

"You will become a very successful doctor—"

"A doctor?"

"Let me see… No…. I am sorry. No, not a doctor. A nurse."

"Yes. That's what I'm studying. Nursing. That's true!"

"A nurse in a famous hospital in… let me see… Yes! Right here on Long Island. The head nurse. And patients will be enamored of your charm and grace, and they will buy presents for you and sing songs for you."

Linda blushed.

"I am sorry if I embarrassed you," Pandoro said.

"That's okay," Linda replied. "Is there anything else?"

"You will have four children, and they will all become doctors because they will be very proud of their mother and will want to be just like her. They will all be successful. As successful as you, Linda. That's what I see. And now you," Pandoro said, as he turned to Daniel. "Are you ready?"

Daniel shrugged. Pandoro stared at him and then looked into his crystal ball.

"Your name is Daniel. You want to be a writer. You have many ideas in your head for stories, and sometimes," he added, wagging his finger suspiciously, "sometimes that gets in the way of studying for school."

"I'm not a writer," Daniel said.

"But you *are* creative," Pandoro replied quickly. "If not writing, then something else."

"Music!" Linda offered.

"Yes," Pandoro agreed. "That's right. Music. But…"

"But what?" Daniel asked.

"But the music may not last forever. There are other things."

"He must have been in my house lately," Daniel whispered to Linda. She smiled sympathetically and put her hand on his shoulder. "Anything else?" he asked Pandoro.

"Yes. You have problems at home. You wish people acted differently. You feel as if you don't really know who you are, or who anyone really is. Things aren't going the way you thought they would. They've gotten harder over time. Darker. Each year a little darker than the one before. But it will change, Daniel. Things will change for the better. It's true. You'll see."

"When?"

"Soon. But remember, things get more complicated before they get easier. Don't be in a hurry. Sometimes it's easier to go through a storm when you're still young. There will be storms, Daniel. But someone will be there for you when you need it most, maybe even someone unexpected, and then things will get better."

"Who will be there for me?"

"That I cannot say. But it will happen. You will see."

Linda thanked Pandoro the Magnificent and then led the boys out of the tent. The three of them remained very quiet as they shuffled along the crowded walkways.

"Let's ride that kiddie roller coaster," Linda said. "Just for fun."

Daniel was less than thrilled with the idea, initially. He sat on one side of Linda in the coaster seat, with Craig on the other—and once the centrifugal force of the ride caused Daniel to lean in toward Linda or she toward him, suddenly he was in heaven.

After the ride, the three of them rejoined Mr. and Mrs. Stuart under a large, tin awning, where dozens of families and couples sat on aluminum benches to watch various musical and dance performances. There was a portable stage in front of the awning, bookended by two trailers. According to the billboard nearby, the afternoon was to feature a dance troupe from New York City, a folk singer who went by the single name of Bethany, a country quartet that featured unusual instruments like washtubs and gallon jugs, and a rock band called Frozen Flame. Daniel remembered that name; Frozen Flame was the band in which Gary from Salisbury Park played guitar.

The country quartet performed one final tune, which Mr. Stuart seemed to particularly enjoy. Then Frozen Flame took over the portable stage. The first song they played was a loud, raucous piece called "Cambodian Rhapsody in Black and Blue." Mr. Stuart looked away and made a sour face for most of it.

"This is music?" he asked Linda when the song had ended.

"I know you don't like it, daddy, but I do," Linda said. "So just be patient."

"You don't like it, either," Mr. Stuart insisted.

"Yes I do," Linda protested. "It makes you think."

"Think about what?" her father asked. "Ripping your ears off?"

"The war. It's an important topic. Anyway, I like many different kinds of music, daddy. I wish every band played every kind of music there is. Wouldn't that be great?"

"Wait a minute, sweetheart. Let me get this straight. Are you saying you'd like it if those beatniks up there played, say, a little Glenn Miller?"

"Sure! Why not?"

"It'll never happen," Mr. Stuart said, waving off the idea as absurd. "Not in a million years. What next—the Rolling Stones playing 'Hello, Dolly'?"

"Why not? It could happen." Linda looked at Daniel. "Don't you think it could happen?"

"Well," Daniel said, "the Beatles recorded 'Till There Was You' from *The Music Man*, and Jay and the Americans recorded 'Some Enchanting Evening' from *South Pacific*."

"You see?" Linda said to her father. "I knew Daniel would support me." She patted his knee and smiled.

Daniel basked in Linda's approval. As a byproduct of that basking, he glared at Mr. Stuart. Mr. Stuart caught the glare and seemed quite displeased by it.

Then someone tapped Daniel's shoulder. It was Gary from Frozen Flame.

"I thought that was you," Gary said. "I saw you from the stage. How you doing?"

"Good. How are you?"

"Can I talk to you for a minute? Over there?"

Daniel went off to the side with Gary. Mr. and Mrs. Stuart continued to look around. Craig had gone to a nearby food concession to buy a cupcake. (The sign above the concession announced "Oversized Cupcakes For Oversized Appetites.")

"Our bass guitarist just barfed behind the stage," Gary told Daniel. "I think he's sick. He's in that trailer over there, trying to stay alive. We've got four songs to go. Can you fill in?"

"I don't really play bass," Daniel said. "I never took lessons."

"Pretty standard stuff. If you're as good as I think you are, and as everybody says you are, you'll be able to fake it pretty good. And the choruses are pretty easy. I'm sure you'll be able to harmonize after about two-and-a-half friggin' seconds. I told Lou you could probably help us out."

"Who's Lou?"

"Lou's the guy who started the band. A real asshole—but a nice guy. Anyway, he said I could ask you to do it, and he said we can throw you a couple of bucks. Okay? Do you have to go ask your parents or something?"

"I'm not here with my parents." He looked at the Stuarts. "I'm here with my girlfriend. Let me just go tell her. I'll be right back. I'll meet you behind the stage."

Gary departed. Daniel went over to Mr. and Mrs. Stuart and Linda and told them that he was asked to fill in for a sick musician for just four songs. Mrs. Stuart said, "Oh! Okay," but Mr. Stuart looked a little doubtful. Linda said it was very exciting.

Daniel didn't wait for a reply from the elder Stuarts (which Mr. Stuart didn't seem to appreciate, either) and instead simply walked off to meet up with Gary behind the stage. They climbed the short stairway to the platform. The bass guitar was on its stand, plugged into an amplifier and ready to go. Lou introduced a song called "The Gables of My Heart," and Daniel joined in at the third measure. Gary was right; it *was* easy for him to keep up. His few experiences with a bass guitar over the years (combined with his lifetime of observation) helped him play to the point where no one suspected he had never had a formal lesson. Gary was right about the lyrics, too; after the first complete verse and chorus, Daniel had the chorus committed to memory and was able to harmonize flawlessly. With the first number complete, he looked at the audience and saw Linda applaud.

Lou announced the next song, which was called "Longitudinal Attitude." Daniel listened to the first few bars to concentrate on the rhythm and lyrics, and just as he was about to join in, he glanced up to see Linda with a young man who wore a Saint John's University sweatshirt. It threw him off a bit. Daniel missed a note or two when Linda started to laugh at something the Saint John's boy had whispered in her ear. The lyrics of the chorus repeated several rhymed words—fly, high, why, bye—but when Daniel looked out again and saw Linda hug the Saint John's boy, he unintentionally sang the wrong words, and he sang them off-key. Gary and Lou glowered at him. Daniel tried to concentrate. Linda wasn't even listening anymore.

"Daniel!" Lou called out.

He started to play the proper notes again and even sung the correct words when the chorus came around. But then he saw Linda and the Saint John's boy walk away, their arms locked around each other's backs. For the last thirty seconds of the song, Daniel didn't even bother to play.

Gary walked away from his microphone and Daniel stepped back from his.

"What the fuck happened?" Gary barked, with his back to the audience for extra protection against being heard by anyone in the crowd.

"Nothing," Daniel said. "Do you have any pot?"

"No. We have a little coke, but—"

"But nothing. If you want me to do a good job on the last two songs, don't give me any money, just give me some of the coke."

"Have you ever done coke? It's pretty heavy-duty stuff," Gary said. "I don't think—"

"I don't care what the fuck you think." The words just poured out, as if they came from a fictionalized, highly dramatized alternative Daniel who simply needed something dramatic to happen. But it wasn't fiction; it was all too real, and there was no way to turn back. He was unable to stop his mouth from saying whatever his mind told it to say, no matter how ridiculous. "Just give me the goddamned coke, or I'll call the cops and tell them you have it."

"Sorry, Daniel. The stuff ain't mine," Gary said. "It's Gene's. The guy who got sick. And I don't think he'll want to share it with a kid."

"I'm not a goddamned fucking kid. Remember?"

On the microphone, Lou announced to the crowd that there would be a five-minute break before Frozen Flame played its final two songs. Daniel returned the bass guitar to its stand, climbed down the stairs, and walked to the trailer. There was a handwritten sign taped to the door that said Frozen Flame Members ONLY. PRIVATE. Keep OUT. He walked in. It was dim inside. Someone was doubled over on the floor. Daniel assumed it was Gene, the sick bass player. There was a thin line of white powder on top of a wooden stool beside him, and a tiny metal spoon on the floor.

"Didn't you see the fucking sign?" Gene coughed.

"No. I can't read," Daniel said.

"Ever hear of knocking, asshole?"

"Ever hear of sharing, asshole?"

"Not with a kindergartner. Who the fuck are you, anyway?"

"I filled in for you. And if you want me to save your ass for the last two songs, you'll give me a little."

"Get out of here, you little shit-head."

"No."

Daniel reached for the spoon. Gene grabbed his arm and pulled him down. They struggled like two children in a playground. The stool fell to the ground. The white powder was so broadly dispersed that there was hardly any trace of it at all. Gene had murder in his eyes.

"Do you know how much you just cost me, you fucking bastard?" he screamed.

Daniel didn't stick around to find out. He ran out of the trailer and back to the Stuarts, who were still under the awning with Craig. Daniel told Mr. and Mrs. Stuart that he was anxious to see the World's Smallest Strong Man. Linda was nowhere to be seen. Mr. Stuart led the two boys and his wife to another part of the carnival. Daniel wasn't sure whether or not Frozen Frame ever finished its set. Meanwhile, Mr. Stuart paid a quarter for each of the four of them to glance behind a canvas wall, where there was a midget flexing his bulging, blue-veined biceps.

Linda finally joined them for the ride home. She asked Daniel if he had a good time at the carnival. He said yes, and knew that out of courtesy he should ask the same of her. But he didn't. What's more, he stayed completely silent on the ride home.

A few days later, I showed Daniel an article I had read in Newsday about the Long Island Eight to Eighty Talent Contest. Frankly, I was no longer certain if a music event was something that would get him out of his slump, but I also felt that he was mature enough to make that decision on his own. That's why I shared the article with him. Besides, the contest could serve as a way to give the family something to do together for the first time in a very long time.

The talent contest was to be held the second Saturday of October at Salisbury Park. The article was really just a promotion for the contest, not a call for contestants since the contest had already been announced in the newspaper two months earlier. When I showed it to him, Daniel decided to walk over to the park to find out more about it. "I'm bored anyway," he said to me as he left the house. "Maybe it could shake things up a bit."

The woman behind the administration desk told Daniel that although the event was just five days away, the deadline to sign up was the afternoon before the contest date. He filled out a form.

Later that day, Daniel mentioned the contest to Mom and Dad, but made sure to stress that it wasn't terribly important and that they didn't have to attend if they had something else to do that day. Mom said she'd try to go, as long as both grandmas were okay. Dad said he'd try to go if there weren't any problems at work. Daniel also told them that he'd mention the contest to Steven later in the day and that he didn't have to mention it to me since I already knew about it.

As it turned out, Mom had to rush Grandma Rose to the doctor the day of the contest, and Dad had to attend to an emergency LILCO meeting in Riverhead. Daniel never did tell Steven about it. As for me, I had been selected that morning to provide the convocation at the Sabbath service for my school's Jewish student organization. I accepted the challenge with the hope that I'd be able to leave in time to see Daniel in the talent show. By the time I was ready to leave campus, however, the contest had already begun. By the time I arrived, it had just ended. What I didn't know until later on was that I hadn't missed a thing.

On the morning of the contest, Daniel grabbed his guitar case and walked over to Salisbury Park. It was a gorgeous fall day. He passed the tennis courts, the playground, the first-aid office, and the boathouse. He started to walk up the grassy hill in front of the band shell, where dozens of people were spread out on blankets and beach chairs. Halfway up he saw Craig Stuart and Doug Kelleher on the grass. As he approached, the boys barely acknowledged him.

"What's the matter with you guys?" he asked.

Craig cleared his throat—and then hesitated.

"My mom and dad are over there," he finally said.

"So?"

"They sort of said they don't want me to hang out with you anymore."

"Why not?"

"I don't know. They said you acted strange at the carnival."

Daniel turned to Doug.

"What about you?" he asked.

"Nothing's the matter," Doug muttered. "I'm in the talent show. I'm just going over a song in my head. I'm pretty sure I'm gonna win. So don't get jealous. I know how great you think you are."

Daniel walked away.

Moments later, he saw Jerry and Jen at the top of the hill. They were harmonizing to "Scarborough Fair." When they saw him, they stopped.

"Not bad," Daniel said.

"Not bad, or pretty damn good?" Jerry said in a highly cynical tone.

"What's that supposed to mean?"

"Nothing."

"Want to form another group?" Daniel asked, trying to remain upbeat—or at least as upbeat as he was able to feel at the moment. "It's a shame we broke up. We could've done something with it. We were pretty good."

"We *are* another group," Jerry said "We're Double J. Me and Jen. We're in the talent show."

Jen looked uncomfortable. She bent down and pretended to tie her sneaker.

"If you're wondering," Jerry said, "you're not invited to be in it. You wanted to be in charge too much. You thought you were better than everyone else. So thanks, but no thanks."

"Just because we had a few arguments—"

"Fuck the goddamn arguments. Fuck the DeeJays. And fuck you. Come on, Jen."

Jerry grabbed Jen by the elbow and pulled her away.

Daniel was stunned. Dazed. Instead of going back down the hill, he wandered over to a bench that was just beyond the concert field. He leaned his guitar case against the bench and sat down, mentally and emotionally spent. He began quietly to warble the words of a song the DeeJays had had in their repertoire. Despite the beautiful weather, it seemed appropriate:

*"All the leaves are brown, and the sky is gray.*
*I've been for a walk on a winter's day..."*

It brought a tear to his eye—but he sensed that someone was standing to his right and slightly behind him, so he tried to hold it in.

"When the Lord closes a door," the still-faceless and nameless person said, "somewhere he opens a window."

Daniel turned halfway around. There was a gentleman there holding a silver-handled cane.

"You seem to have the weight of the world on your barely broken-in shoulders," the man said. "And you have a lovely singing voice."

The man was a little older and heavier than Dad. He wore a three-piece suit. He looked out of place at Salisbury Park—he was more the type to be at home in Manhattan's Central Park instead. His voice had an accent, although Daniel wasn't quite sure what kind of accent it was. Something European, he guessed.

"Are you talking to me?" Daniel asked.

"I am indeed," the man smiled. "Why such a glum face?"

"I don't know. It's a long story."

"Are you here with your family?"

"No."

"Friends?"

"No."

"Ahh—that must be part of the long story." The man sat down on the bench next to Daniel and put his cane on his lap. "I see you have a guitar. Are you performing in the talent show?"

"Maybe."

"Hmmm... If I were directing a stage production right now, I would ask you to repeat the word Maybe with more motivation. Perhaps with the accent on the second syllable. 'May*bee*.' Or preceded by a deep sigh and a long, weary 'Ohhhhh,' as in 'Ohhhhh, maybe.' You see?"

The man's strange, impromptu performance made Daniel smile.

"Good, good. A smile," he said. "I like that. It becomes you. Now suppose you tell me what the problem is."

"It's personal." Daniel hoped that didn't sound rude.

"Of course it is. If it were public, you would shout it out at the top of this hill for all to hear. Is it because no one came to see you perform today?"

"Well… it's not like I really made a big deal about it."

"And now you regret that. You're having an internal tug of war, my young friend. Can I tell you a story? I once did a show in Vienna. I wasn't very happy about it. I wasn't comfortable with my character. So I went out of my way to make sure my family and friends did not come for the first two weeks. Well, the joke was on me. You see, the first two weeks were absolutely the best of the entire run. Fabulous notices."

"You're an actor?"

"It is my privilege, and an honor, to be able to wear many hats in the entertainment realm. I am quite a lucky man."

Daniel looked at him closely and was almost certain he had seen his face many times on television.

"Do you play any instruments other than the guitar?" the man asked.

"Piano."

"And?"

"Saxophone."

"And?"

"Xylophone."

"And?"

"Drums. A little."

The man smiled and nodded.

"I see. I see," he said. He tapped his cane twice on the ground. "And I know you sing. You write songs, too?"

"I used to. Are you in the talent show?"

"A judge. A favor for an old friend who lives nearby. May I ask your name?"

"Daniel."

"I'm Theodore. Pleased to meet you, Daniel. It makes perfect sense for you to have that name, Daniel," he declared. "Whatever troubles you have today will be solved with a little bit of faith." He looked at the clouds and recited the lyrics from a Broadway show:

> *"Wonder of wonder, miracles of miracles,*
> *God took a Daniel once again,*
> *Stood by his side and, miracle of miracles,*
> *Led him through the lion's den."*

"I know that song!" Daniel said. "It's from *Fiddler on the Roof*. I saw it on Broadway."

"When?"

"A few years ago."

"Ahhh. Join me."

Together they sang:

> *"When Moses softened Pharaoh's heart,*
> *That was a miracle,*
> *When God made the waters of the Red Sea part,*
> *That was a miracle, too…"*

"You're a very special young man, Daniel. Try not to let the world get in the way of your dreams. Make your dreams get in the way of the world—any way you can. And if one dream doesn't open the window, pull another one out of your closet."

"My closet?"

He pointed to his head.

"I call it the closet. You see—"

Just as Theodore was about to explain, he was interrupted by an announcement over the loudspeaker requesting all judges to assemble behind the band shell.

"Goodness," he said, "I lost all track of time. Tell you what, Daniel. After the show, let's meet right here, and we'll make plans for a little more mutual discovery and see how we might help each other. Yes?"

"Okay."

Theodore man stood up and began a slow descent to the band shell at the bottom of the hill, using his cane to help him navigate around the spectators.

Daniel grabbed his guitar case, stood up, and walked around the outermost part of the field at the top of the hill. He couldn't decide what mood he was in; it seemed to change by the minute. He looked up at the clouds but found no answers there. He looked down at the lawn. Still nothing. Then he saw a single cluster of dandelion seeds wedged between two blades of tall grass. It was stuck in place. He gently scooped it into his free hand, clenched his fist around it, made a wish, and blew it into the air.

"Shithead," someone called from the distance. Daniel turned around but saw no one. "Shithead. Over here." The voice came from a patch of woods close to where he and Gary had taken the pills a few weeks before. Daniel walked over. Just inside the woods, next to a big tree, was Gene, the bass guitarist from Frozen Flame.

"Remember me?" Gene sneered. "Do you know how much you cost me at the carnival? Two hundred fifty fucking dollars. Do you have two hundred fifty bucks to pay me back, asshole?"

"No," Daniel said. He smelled marijuana in the air and saw five beer cans on the ground.

"What are you gonna do about it?" Gene asked.

"I don't know."

"You don't know? Well, I do."

"What?"

"I'm gonna beat the fucking crap out of you."

Daniel started to back away, but Gene leaped and grabbed him by his hair and dragged him farther into the woods. The guitar case fell to the ground. Gene punched the side of Daniel's head, and then attacked his stomach. He punched fast and furiously. He kicked Daniel's shins and ankles, then grabbed his left arm and twirled him around until his shoulder hit a tree trunk with such excruciating force that he fell helplessly to the ground. Gene dropped onto Daniel's chest with his knees, with all his weight, and knocked the air out of him. He punched the side of Daniel's head and scraped his face into the dirt until his nose and mouth bled. Daniel's ribs throbbed. He could hardly breathe. One eye was swollen almost entirely shut. Huge lumps grew on his forehead and pulsed with pain.

It could have been mere seconds or perhaps more than a minute between the time of the final punch and the time Daniel realized that Gene was no longer there; he was unable to tell because he had lost all sense of time. Without an ounce of strength to stand, Daniel remained on the ground. There was blood on his nose, his cheeks, his lips, and on the ground. Finally, a young couple noticed him and helped him to the first-aid office, which was a two-minute walk. The nurse in the first-aid office wanted to call the police, but Daniel pleaded with her not to. He told her that most of the injuries were the result of an eight-foot fall from the bleachers at the park's athletic field. Apparently, the nurse didn't realize that Salisbury Park had no bleachers.

•　　•　　•　　•

As bad as Daniel looked, in terms of his overall health, I knew he was in no serious jeopardy. There were many patients at the psychiatric hospital where I worked part-time who got hurt all the time (a lot of it self-inflicted), and it was usually a lot worse than swollen eyes and bloody lips. I told this to Grandma Rose when she saw Daniel for the first time the day after the incident at Salisbury Park. She sat in the kitchen with a cup of tea, having just returned to Westbrook Hills from a short stay at the hospital. She gasped when Daniel walked in.

"What happened to your face?" she shrieked as if he had turned into a monster.

"I fell off the bleachers," he said indifferently.

"Bleachis? What's a bleachis?" Grandma asked.

Daniel went to his room and left it to me to explain.

"Bleachers," I said to her slowly. "Where people sit to watch football games. He said he lost his balance and fell off."

"Oy gevalt. Football. I never liked the football."

"He wasn't playing football, Grandma. Anyway, it could have been much worse. He could've broken his arms and legs, or he could've gotten a concussion. He was lucky."

"Oy. That's lucky? A face like that. His forehead out to here?"

I left her to her cup of tea, knocked on Daniel's door, and stuck my head in his room.

"I told Grandma that you were lucky. And I think you were," I said.

"So now you're a doctor?"

"Don't be sarcastic, Daniel."

I made a close visual check of Daniel's facial wounds (as I had been taught at the Kings Park Psychiatric Hospital) and told him to stay home from school on Monday.

He returned to school on Tuesday. That was the same day that Grandpa Jesse went back home to Brooklyn to be with Grandma Leah, who was discharged from the hospital that morning. I was back at my own apartment. When I called Daniel to ask how he felt, he told me that his swelling had already subsided and that his black and blues had begun to fade. I told him to take that as a sign of good things to come.

.    .    .    .

Steven left for basic training in South Carolina on the twentieth of October and was flown to Southeast Asia on the eighteenth of December. Two weeks later, we all received letters from him. Mom and Dad's letter was mostly about the conditions of the camp, which Steven said were actually quite comfortable. He also talked a little about how most of the men in his platoon felt about the recent presidential election. The majority, he said, were glad that Nixon triumphed over Humphrey. "They think Nixon has the balls to get us out of this crazy war," he wrote. "Sorry for using the word balls." The letter I received, which he sent to the house because he had lost the address of my apartment, was short. He said that on the day he arrived he had been reassigned to a transportation depot in Cambodia because of some sort of administrative foul-up. He said he really didn't mind because there were even more jeeps, tanks, and "really cool choppers" there than there were where he was originally stationed. He asked me about Adelphi and what it felt like to be a college senior. He said he couldn't wait to come home to hang out in my apartment.

The letter he sent to Daniel was the longest:

*I know we hardly spoke to each other for almost a year, except when we had to, and I bet you can't even remember why. It was all because of that time I screamed at you for going to Billy's house without me. I was just looking out for you, believe it or not. I don't really expect you to understand right now. One day you will. Anyway, it all seems so stupid now, so let's just forget it.*

*When I get back home, the first thing we'll do to make up for lost time is go see a Broadway show. I'll drive. (Is Dad taking good care of my car?) Then we'll head out to Jersey to ride in a hot-air balloon. I met a guy here at the base who has two older brothers who own a hot-air balloon company, and they give rides, and he said I could look them up and that they'll give us a free ride. Okay?*

*By the way, it's no time for another lecture right now (which is how our stupid little fight started in the first place), but don't forget—I may not be an A student but I'm not stupid, and I know you like I know the back of my hand, and I know some of the things you're doing back home, things you shouldn't be doing, although I know most kids do it from time to time. All I can say, Daniel, is that it won't lead to anything good. There's a lot of that crap going on where I am now, <u>a lot</u>, and it really screws you up bad. We'll talk about it more when I get home if you want, but just promise me you'll be smart about things.*

*Anyway, write back if you get a chance. I'll tell you more about the choppers they want me to work on in my next letter. I'm learning about them now and got to ride on one yesterday. It was <u>so</u> cool.*

*Love, Steven.*

Daniel folded the letter and kept it in his pocket for the next few days.

•　　　•　　　•

Back at school, Daniel joined the theatre club's Tech Squad. He had first considered auditioning for the musical combo that was to play in the pit for the annual spring musical, *Oliver*, but opted for the Tech Squad instead. It was well known that the Tech Squad had a reputation for fun and hijinx, and those were two things that appealed to Daniel a little more than they had in the past. Tech Squad members got to play with all sorts of sophisticated sound and lighting equipment, smoked cigarettes in a storage room under the stage, and had what many students considered to be the most modern and liberal faculty advisor in the entire school. His name was Mr. Bragglia. He taught art, photography, and printing, was known to tell jokes about sex and prostitutes, invited students to his house to smoke pot, and kept a stack of Playboy magazines in the projection booth behind the auditorium.

There was a faculty-wide effort at school to get all students involved in *Oliver* in one way or another. The administration wanted to keep the students occupied with the musical so that attention could be drawn away from the rest of the world—hijackings, college protests, drug overdoses, Vietnam... Social studies teachers spent time in class discussing turn-of-the-century London and concentrated on some of its more salacious (and therefore intriguing) aspects. Science teachers worked with their classes on dry ice experiments to use as a special effect in the show. English teachers turned Charles Dickens into a pop star, and art teachers ran poster and flier contests.

Daniel was the only freshman on the ten-member Tech Squad. His initiation was held after school on the first day back after the Christmas and New Year's break. At the initiation, all the squad members sat on the dusty floor backstage. Mr. Bragglia wasn't there yet. A senior named Paul oversaw the rite of passage. He demanded that Daniel empty his pockets. Apparently, most initiates had items in their pockets that embarrassed them and provided a source of amusement for the other members. But all Daniel had in his pockets were a few dimes and quarters, a house key, and a pen. He also had Steven's letter but managed to leave that hidden. The group was disappointed that their new pledge had provided no bawdy diversion.

Mr. Bragglia arrived backstage and sat on the floor.

"Daniel," he said, "we have a lot of work to do to properly light the show, so help us out by cleaning a blue gel. Then we'll teach you how to put the gel over one of the Fresnel lenses. Use the bathroom in the band hallway. Come back when you're done."

Daniel didn't know what a blue gel was, so he asked. Mr. Bragglia explained.

"The gels are on the shelf next to the control panel. They're stacked by color. You can't miss them. Take a blue one and clean it in the bathroom sink."

Daniel went to the control panel and grabbed a square acetate gel from the blue stack, took it to the sink in the boys' room, turned on the faucet, and put the gel underneath. Instantly, the blue dye ran over his fingers and into the sink.

He didn't panic. Instead, he realized that it was a second initiation rite—that he had been tricked. The intention, he assumed, was to scare him into thinking that he had just ruined some delicate, expensive school property. But he didn't clean up with soap and water and rush back to apologize; instead, Daniel rubbed his palms on the remaining blue dye and threw the useless gel into the garbage can. Then he joined the others backstage, with his hands behind his back.

"Well?" Mr. Bragglia asked.

"It worked," he said. "Do I shake your hand for scaring the crap out of me?"

"Yes, you do," Mr. Bragglia smiled proudly. "I started the tradition four years ago when I first got here. Never fails."

In a quick gesture, Daniel offered his hand to Mr. Bragglia, who shook it and immediately sensed that something was amiss. Mr. Bragglia took back his hand, looked at it, and saw that he, too, had a blue palm. All the Tech Squad members broke into laughter, and Mr. Bragglia managed a half-smile.

"Hmmm," he said, "I see we have ourselves a real pisser, gang." He looked at his palm again. "Welcome to the Tech Squad, Daniel. I'll be right back. I need to wash up."

Mr. Bragglia stood up and exited through the backstage door. Daniel sat on the floor and began to chat with the other Squad members. Paul asked about his bruises. In this rendition of the story, Daniel said he fell off the bleachers at a rock concert in Queens. Another boy asked why he didn't want to play in the *Oliver* combo since he was such a skilled musician—but before Daniel could answer, Dr. Carnivale, the school's assistant principal, opened the backstage door and peered in. He was tall, and stooped, and held himself in such a wooden way as to appear to be in constant grief. The veteran Tech Squad members stiffened up, for they sensed that something was wrong; school administrators hardly ever came backstage unless there was a very good reason or a serious problem.

"Is Daniel Hillman here?"

Daniel raised his hand.

"Come with me, please."

Daniel stood up and glanced briefly at the others. Some of them shrugged. Others had blank faces. He wondered if Mr. Bragglia had turned on him; did the hip, cool Tech Squad faculty advisor suddenly go establishment? Did Daniel's little practical joke, which was simply a response to a practical joke played on him, backfire?

When they arrived at the Main Office, Dr. Carnivale turned around, stooped down even lower than he was already naturally stooped, and put his hands on Daniel's shoulders.

"You have to go home," he said. "Now."

"Why? The gels?"

"Just go home. It will be explained there."

"But the show—"

"Don't worry about the show. Mr. Bragglia has everything under control. Walk carefully," Dr. Carnivale said. Daniel backed up and left the office.

The first thing he noticed when he approached the middle of Pearl Drive was that there were many cars in front of the house. When Daniel walked in, the foyer was empty, but there were whispers and whimpers coming from the kitchen. He closed the front door. Dad came to the foyer, took him in his arms, kissed his head, then bent down to his ear.

"Steven is dead," he whispered slowly.

"What?" Daniel was certain he had misheard.

"He…" Dad cleared his throat quietly, "… he and another boy were in a field near the base where a helicopter was having trouble. He stepped on a landmine. He's dead."

Daniel looked up. Dad was crying.

"I need you to be strong," he said through his tears. "For everyone. As strong as you can possibly be. For Mom. For Lori. Grandma. Everyone. It won't be easy. It will be very difficult, in fact. *Very* difficult. But you have to try."

"Where's Lori?" he asked.

"She doesn't know yet. I left word for her where she works to come home as soon as possible." (By choice I will not share exactly how I took the news; suffice it to say that Vincent Yaccarini, two of his colleagues, and three new Adelphi friends did all they could to help me deal with it at the time. Though I was able to move on after a few shaky months, there were many times when I wasn't so sure.)

"Mom's in the den with a few people," Dad said to Daniel. "Rabbi Mischkin is here. Uncle Milt and Aunt Paula are on their way." Dad noticed Daniel's blue palms. "What happened to you?"

"It's nothing," Daniel said. "Steven was wrong."

"About what?"

"God isn't a lot of fun…Do I have to go in there now?"

"No. Not if you don't want to."

Daniel went to his room instead, took the bottom drawer out of his desk, turned it upside down, and dumped the contents on the floor. He rummaged through and found the stub of an old joint. Dad's words—*It won't be easy. It will be very difficult*—ran through his head as he attempted to hold and light the tiny joint. That was difficult, too. But he managed to do it anyway.

# Seven

As in a dozen Decembers that came before, the Kelleher house across the street was a winter wonderland of decorations throughout the entire final month of 1969. It had white, red, orange, blue, yellow, and green lights strung across the front gutters on both levels, a giant green wreath on the front door adorned with tiny bells and sparkly ribbons, a five-foot-tall plastic Santa on the lawn surrounded by clay bunnies and sheep, three wooden flying reindeer fastened to poles stuck into the garden under the master bedroom window, and an evergreen tree to the right of the steps covered with clusters of tinsel, candy canes, electric candles, little ceramic carriages and, at the top, a big silver star, illuminated by the porch light above the front door.

For Chanukah, the Hillman house had an old, tarnished menorah in the living room window, and that was it.

Chanukah was never meant to be a major holiday. It is really just the simple retelling of the story of a miracle—one in a long line of miracles in Jewish history—in which the Hebrew people resisted annihilation yet another time. A Jewish freedom fighter named Judah led his army of rebels against the evil King Antiochus, who trapped and surrounded them inside a temple and hoped to drive them out, slaughter them, and destroy the holy site. The Jews had enough oil to last just one night—oil they needed for light, heat, and cooking. But they prayed for a miracle, and the oil lasted for eight nights. By that time, Antiochus and his men had given up and departed.

In the old days, Jewish families merely retold the story, lit a menorah for eight nights in a row (to represent the eight nights that the oil had lasted), ate a hearty meal, and that was that. But because Chanukah falls in the middle of the winter doldrums, and because it is always so close to the magic of Christmas, it had developed into something far more significant. It became a major holiday.

In many ways, this particular Chanukah at the Hillman house, a year after Steven's death, was a throwback to the way it used to be far back in history—the way it was *supposed* to be. There may be an interesting irony in there to explore one day.

Daniel and Dad were the only ones home that first night of Chanukah. Mom was in Florida with Grandma Rose. I was in Manhattan, where I now lived and worked.

Grandma Rose had taken over her sister-in-law Sophie's condo in Pompano Beach shortly after Sophie passed away in the fall. Grandma had grown weary of the winter cold and the occasional snowstorm. Sophie's sons, both attorneys, offered the condo to Grandma Rose and arranged the transfer with virtually no red tape at all. Mom traveled to Florida every few months now. Ever since Steven's death, she found it comforting to be able to leave the house for extended periods of time. She couldn't even look at Steven's closed bedroom door without weeping. She placed a picture of Steven beside a picture of her baby brother Howard on the night table by her side of the master bed at home, but frequently put them both face down. Despite Grandma Rose's worsening health, she was the stronger of the two; it was Mom who needed the most care, emotionally speaking, and it was Grandma who provided it, usually through heavy doses of tough love. She yelled at Mom often and told her to get on with her life, that there was nothing to be done, that the memories could help heal and sometimes even comfort.

As for me, I had graduated from Adelphi in May with a degree in sociology and accepted a position as assistant dean of student activities at Yeshiva University in Washington Heights, in upper Manhattan. Vincent Yaccarini had an acquaintance at the school who arranged the initial interview. The school made an attractive offer, allowed me to take some classes at no charge, and even let me move into a school-owned apartment on West One Hundred Eighty-Fourth Street for a small monthly fee. The job didn't actually begin until late August, so I had the summer free to hang out with friends from Adelphi. The group of us had huddled together in one of their living rooms to watch Neil Armstrong walk on the moon on the twentieth of July. That was a sad event for me, for I knew how Steven would have been riveted to a television set making plans for his own lunar stroll one day. A month later I went to a music and art festival in Bethel, a small town in upstate New York. They called it Woodstock. I didn't tell Daniel or anyone else in the family too much about it, other than the fact that I steered clear both of the drug scene and most of the mud. I had also started to date a young man named Jonathan, who had been in several of my classes at Adelphi. It rose to a new level after Woodstock. But in September, Jonathan was offered a job at a social research firm in San Francisco. It was exactly what he wanted to do. So he and I planned a farewell in Manhattan. First, we had dinner at a restaurant on Eighth Avenue, and then we saw the musical *Promises, Promises* on Broadway. I thought of Daniel the entire time we watched the show.

I had originally planned to drive to Westbrook Hills to be home on the first night of Chanukah, particularly since I knew that Dad and Daniel would be alone. But there had been a blizzard two days earlier, and most of the roads were still impassable. So I was stuck in Manhattan. Miraculously, there were very few power outages across Long Island, so Dad wasn't called in to handle any emergency situations. He had found an old menorah on a shelf in the basement. It was dusty, battered, and encrusted in wax, but he put it on the living room window sill. He also put a shoebox on the kitchen table. He called Daniel, who was in his bedroom, to come to the kitchen.

"Well," Dad said, "I don't know how to make potato latkes, and I don't know how to wrap presents, so this will have to be our Chanukah."

"That's okay," Daniel said. "I didn't have much money, so I couldn't—"

"You're not supposed to buy gifts for us," Dad interrupted. "We're supposed to buy gifts for you. Of course, your mother usually does it, so—"

"It's okay."

Daniel opened the shoebox. Inside were five twenty-dollar bills.

"Buy yourself whatever you want. You're too old for toys, and what do I know from clothes. Personally, I wish you'd get a haircut, but we'll talk about that another time. Get yourself whatever you have in mind. I thought maybe some kind of tape recorder, better than that little one you have, to record songs or something. I was gonna look for one, but then the storm came and, well, you know. You still write songs, don't you?"

"Not really. But thanks for the money. I'll buy something. Actually, I have a present for Lori. A book about getting around Manhattan. But—"

"She'll probably be able to make it here by tomorrow," Dad assured him. "Definitely by Friday. I'm sure she has something for you, too. Why don't you go get the menorah from the living room window? You can say the prayer."

"We can do it without the menorah. 'Baruch atah….Chanukah,'" Daniel said—skipping the eleven or twelve important words in between.

"Good enough," Dad smiled. "Happy Chanukah."

"Happy Chanukah."

And that was the extent of their celebration that year.

In his room, Daniel pretended to make a spiritual gesture with a sip from a little bottle of whiskey that he kept hidden in his closet. When Dad fell asleep, he went outside in the backyard and smoked a joint.

The roads were cleared by Thursday afternoon, so I was able to drive to Westbrook Hills. I gave Dad a flannel shirt, the kind he liked to wear at home in the winter months, as well as a coffee mug with a cartoon rendering of the history of Thomas Edison's inventions. To Daniel I gave a little silver harmonica and a music book called *One Hundred Hits from Broadway*. I stayed for two days and slept in my old bedroom. I cleaned the house, which was a mess, did a couple of loads of laundry, and prepared a few meals. Dad went to work both days. I chatted with Daniel from time to time, but mostly he stayed in his room. That was a bit upsetting, but I let it pass.

As I put on my coat for the drive back to the city, Daniel knocked on my bedroom door and asked to come in to wish me a safe trip back to the city. I was happy about that, though I chose to downplay my delight. I did, however, feel compelled to share a few thoughts.

"Daniel," I said, "I was at Woodstock. I know what it smells like. I smell it on you all the time. And in your room when I was cleaning."

"You smell what on me?" he asked. "English Leather?"

I tried to remain straight-faced; I suppose I wasn't entirely successful.

"Don't worry, Lori," he said.

"I *do* worry," I let on. "I've seen where it can lead. I've been to college. I'm older than you—and right now it's not like you have much of a mother or father, so—"

"You don't have to be my mother and father, Lori, and you don't have to worry. I'll stop."

"Is that all you've been doing?"

"Yes."

"If you tell me you're telling the truth, I'll believe you. Listen, I won't lie to you and make believe you don't have a few good reasons to almost justify whatever you *are* doing. But believe me, there are more justifications for *not* doing it. You just have to trust me."

"You sound like a therapist," Daniel said. "Or a motivational speaker. You know what, Lori? *You'll* be the Hillman who makes it."

"Makes it? Makes what?"

"Something of yourself."

"Daniel—"

"Don't worry. I'll stop. I promise."

With that, I drove back to Manhattan.

•   •   •   •   •

Another snowstorm swept over Long Island, but this time the temperature dropped to eighteen degrees, which made the roads slick and driving treacherous. Utility poles and power lines were turned into ice sculptures. Wires snapped, which caused blackouts in dozens of towns. Even the utility poles that weren't affected by ice were in jeopardy because of the thousands of cars that skidded off the roads and crashed into them. Dad had to supervise repairs for the next five days, from early morning to late at night. Daniel was off from school that week, and Dad asked me if there was any way I could stay at the house for a while. When I called Daniel about that, he swore he was perfectly capable of being home alone, and that I shouldn't take a chance on the roads. I wanted to trust him—so I did. After all, Daniel's grades, while certainly not as exemplary as once they had been, were fairly decent when the first-semester report card came home, and Dad was pleased about that. Also, despite his unruly hair and unkempt appearance, Daniel was quiet and respectful in the house. So with all that in mind, Dad finally consented to let him stay in the house by himself. Dad insisted, however, that he go next door to Mr. Ashler's house if he had any problems. Daniel said he would, but never did. Instead, he went to Mr. Bonomo's house a few times, ostensibly to play with Joey and Johnny DePuzo, but really to play the ukulele for Sal Bonomo and flirt with his granddaughter Annette.

Meanwhile, Daniel's piano and guitar lessons came to an end. Mom and Dad were supposed to call his private music teachers to discuss new times and rates, but both forgot to do so, and both teachers just stopped coming to the house. When the fall semester had started, Daniel rejoined the school band as a saxophone player and continued on with the chorus. But after just three weeks he said goodbye to both, having decided that it was too hard to concentrate on music or songs to which he had no emotional attachment. As Daniel saw it, the compositions selected for the band and the songs selected for the chorus were chosen solely to make mothers and fathers believe that their school taxes were being put to good use; the music had little to do with a true exploration of the art. It had been the quirks and peccadilloes of the band and chorus members that initially had much more of a pull on Daniel, not the prospect of being in concerts. But whenever he tried to engage the members in thoughtful discussions, most of them usually just wanted to be silly.

Nor did he rejoin the Tech Squad—although the Squad members liked him and urged him to reconsider. Daniel felt that plugging in lights and flicking on switches accomplished nothing useful. Again, he was far more interested in the Squad members and their personal stories than in the actual procedures of putting on a show. But *they* were far more interested in seeing how many behavioral lines they could cross with their hijinx.

As an unfortunate result of all this, Daniel made very few new friends in his sophomore year at Westbrook Hills High. Instead, he spent a lot of time alone in his room after school. One reason was strictly academic: he had signed up for two courses that semester, American Literature and Modern Drama, which required quite a bit of reading. He enjoyed both classes very much, and read far more than the teachers required. That, though, merely added to his growing reputation as a loner. In fact, when I drove him to the mall one weekend to buy new sneakers, we overheard two older students talking about him. One called him a prodigy who had turned into a hermit. Later that day, at Howard Johnson's, he told me that he had heard similar things at school, and also that some people believed he had become imbalanced because of his brother's death. I asked him how he handled those whispered comments. He said that he handled it mostly by ignoring it.

•  •  •  •

The Tech Squad invited Daniel to a New Year's Eve party, even though he was no longer a member, but he declined and opted to stay home. Mom was still in Florida. Dad had agreed to supervise the midnight shift on New Year's Eve, which paid triple overtime, and I planned to go to a party in my building in Washington Heights. Daniel swore that he didn't mind being alone. Once again, I wanted to believe him.

An hour before midnight, a gust of wind knocked over the metal trash cans at the side of the house and blew them toward the street. Daniel heard it from his room and looked out the window. Both cans were in the middle of Pearl Drive. So he threw on his coat and went outside. As he began to drag the garbage cans up the driveway and back to the house, Mr. Kelleher came down the block in his car and slowed as he began to swing into his own driveway across the street. The headlights shone on Daniel for a moment. Mr. Kelleher stopped the car and rolled down his window.

"Daniel," he called out, "is that you? You're alone tonight?"

"Sort of," he said. He had no time to think of a better response.

"Sort of? Your mother and grandmother are in Florida, right? And a little while ago I passed a LILCO crew out in Plainview and could swear I saw your dad there. You shouldn't be alone on New Year's Eve. Come over to our house. We're having a little family party. I had to find an open drug store for my mother. She's with us tonight. Anyway, I won't take no for an answer, Daniel."

It was futile to lie. Mr. Kelleher, as nice as he was, nevertheless had a stern, forthright way about him. To lie and reject the invitation might only open up a bigger hole into which Daniel might eventually fall, a hole much bigger than the lie itself.

So he went back inside, grabbed his house key, locked the front door, and walked across the street to the Kelleher house. When he arrived, he saw Alexis, Bridgett, and Caroline—the twenty-four, twenty-one and nineteen-year-old Kelleher sisters—on the floor of their living room watching television. Daniel put his coat on a tall wooden rack by the front door. Mr. Kelleher was on his way into the kitchen with the small paper bag he had with him from the drug store. Twelve-year-old Michael was in the corner, near the Christmas tree, in his wheelchair. A large, colorful afghan covered his lap. Daniel wished him a Merry Christmas. Doug was nowhere to be seen.

After a few minutes, Mr. and Mrs. Kelleher and Mr. Kelleher's mother came from the kitchen and joined everyone in the living room. Mrs. Kelleher asked Daniel how Mom was, and he explained that the Florida trips seemed to help her.

"How's your sister Lori?" Mr. Kelleher asked.

"Good. She has a nice job at Yeshiva University in the Bronx, and she has her own apartment there, too."

"The Bronx?" Mrs. Kelleher repeated, a bit hesitantly.

Michael wheeled himself over to the television set and switched the channel several times. Periodically, one or two of the sisters would go to the kitchen to check on the snacks that were still heating in the oven. Frequently they asked Michael and Daniel if they wanted anything to eat or drink.

Michael settled on a television channel and backed his wheelchair away from the set.

After she watched silently for about a minute, Alexis, the oldest sister, asked Daniel if he still played all the instruments he used to play and if he still wrote songs. But Daniel never had a chance to reply because a television show came on at that moment which all the Kellehers seemed intent to watch. Almost in unison, everyone shushed everyone else.

Caroline Kelleher, the youngest daughter, sat on the floor next to Daniel and dropped popcorn on his legs every few seconds.

"Wait till you see," she whispered to him.

"See what?" he whispered back. "Where's Doug, by the way?"

"Watch," Caroline said.

The show was called "The WPIX Second Annual Eight to Eighty New Year's Eve Party." It was on channel eleven, a local station. The man who usually did the weather on the WPIX news was the host.

"Ladies and gentlemen," said the host, "the top ten winners of the annual Salisbury Park Eight to Eighty Talent Contest held in October are happy to perform for you tonight, live from our studio right here in midtown Manhattan."

"Such a garish suit he's wearing," Mrs. Kelleher observed.

"Shush," her elderly mother-in-law said. "I'm listening."

"Later on," the host continued, "our last performer will be eighty-year-old Sam Hunter, who is one of the funniest men you'll ever meet. Sam will perform for us five minutes before midnight, and then after that, all of us—our television audience, our performers, and yours truly—will count down the last fifteen seconds to 1970."

"Why fifteen seconds?" Caroline complained. "Why not a whole minute, like they do on channel two?"

"Shush," her grandmother chided. "I'm listening."

"But first things first. Ladies and gentlemen, to start us off, help me give a warm welcome to adorable little eight-year-old Becky Gruber from Queens, who will dance as an angel from the famous ballet, *The Nutcracker*. Take it away, Becky Gruber."

Becky danced to a recording of one of the Nutcracker movements and then ran off the stage.

"Why didn't she take a bow?" Bridgett wondered aloud.

"Because," Mrs. Kelleher explained sternly, "no one taught her the right thing to do."

"Shush. I'm listening."

The host came back on.

"And now," he said, "from Westbrook Hills, we have talented fifteen-year-old Douglas Kelleher, who will sing 'Happy Together,' which as you know was a hit by the Turtles. Douglas, are you ready?"

"See?" Caroline said to Daniel as she picked up some kernels of popcorn from his legs.

"How come you didn't all go down to the studio to see him?" Daniel asked Caroline.

"Because we wanted to see him on TV."

Their grandmother asked everyone to be quiet with another loud "Shush."

Doug sang "Happy Together," accompanied by a pianist who was off to the side, unseen.

"I'm pleased they gave him such a good piano player," Mrs. Kelleher said.

"He sings like a real pro, doesn't he?" Mr. Kelleher pronounced.

"He looks so comfortable on stage, doesn't he?" said Alexis.

When the song was over, Doug took a bow and left the stage. Both Mr. and Mrs. Kelleher said he was wonderful.

"Shush!"

"It's over," Bridgett said to her grandmother.

"I'm surprised you didn't audition, Daniel," Mrs. Kelleher observed. "Or did you?"

"No," Daniel said.

"Too bad," Bridgett said. "Because you never know what could happen. I bet someone will see Doug on TV and ask him to be on another show."

"And then," Caroline added, "he might even get a record contract. Or his own program."

Mrs. Kelleher, who rarely smiled, finally smiled.

Daniel told the Kellehers that he was tired and also wanted to be home when Dad returned from his LILCO assignment. He thanked them all, retrieved his coat, and went to the front vestibule. Caroline followed and opened the door. As Daniel left the house, the Kellehers were still talking about Doug's amazing future as a Hollywood star.

•    •    •

"Make you a deal," Dad said to Daniel the next day. "If you agree to come with me to Brooklyn, I'll tell Mom that you actually ate something healthy while she was in Florida."

Grandpa Jesse was still in good health, but Grandma Leah now suffered from emphysema, swollen legs and ankles, and various other ailments. That made it difficult for her to take care of the two of them and still keep up the apartment. As a result, Grandpa Jesse was now almost always nervous and befuddled. It was the first day of 1970, a Thursday, and a rare day off for Dad. Since most of the roads had been adequately cleared, he decided to visit his elderly parents. He wanted some company for the ride, and he also knew that Daniel's presence would be a welcome surprise. (Mom was scheduled to fly home from Pompano Beach two days later.) Daniel didn't need much convincing; he wanted to get away from the block anyway (or at least from his view of the Kelleher house across the street).

So he put on a clean pair of jeans and a fresh button-down shirt for the visit to Brooklyn.

Even when Grandma Leah had been in good health, the one-bedroom apartment she shared with Grandpa Jesse was always in a bit of disarray simply because Grandpa had collected paraphernalia over the years with which he refused to part. Now that she was in *bad* health, the apartment seemed almost like a hoarder's paradise. Grandpa Jesse's "damned chotchkees" (as Grandma called them) were all over the apartment: musical instruments, papers, framed photos, unframed photos, newspaper clippings, back scratchers, tiny bronze busts of nine U.S. presidents, metronomes, discarded street signs, old telephones and old telephone books, sheet music, records, eyeglass cases (without eyeglasses in them), TV Guides from as far back as 1959, empty bottles, microphones, torn boxes of rubber bands (held together by rubber bands), and much more.

While Dad and Grandpa spoke in the living room, Daniel went into the bedroom to talk with Grandma Leah. She was in bed, under the covers, with a smile on her gaunt face. Her spotty hands, up by her chin, held onto the edge of the blanket. Her yellow hair looked clean and neat for a woman in her condition. That was not unlike Grandma. She always took great care to present herself in the best possible light, regardless of the circumstances.

Daniel kissed her on the forehead.

"It's okay with me," she said to him, "but your mother lets you wear your hair long like that?"

"Well, she hasn't been home since November," Daniel replied. "She's been in Florida."

Grandma closed her eyes.

"Stupid fekakta war," she mumbled painfully. "How are you, Daniel?"

"Holding up. Okay, I guess."

"I'm not surprised."

She closed her eyes again, for a longer period of time, then opened them.

"You were always a strong boy," she said.

"Me? Strong?"

"I don't mean you can lift a house. I mean your mind. You were always strong up there. A thinker."

"Is that good?"

"Yes, darling. It's very good. You don't just *do*. You *think*. Your brother, may he rest in peace, just *did*. And sometimes he got in trouble for just doing. Am I right? Your father, too, sometimes, when he was young. Even your grandfather. Too many mistakes that way. Am I right?"

"I don't know. I guess."

"If your grandfather thought things out a little more, he could have been a famous musician today. But he was too impatient."

"I'm impatient too, Grandma."

"You're so young. What's to be impatient about? What you think is impatient is really just being a boy."

She closed her eyes again, then opened them after a few seconds.

"Also, you like people, and that's important. You like them, and you look at them, and you listen to them, and you get to know them."

"I don't like *all* people," Daniel said.

"Of course not all people. Who does? But most. No? That's a good quality. I saw it since you were a baby. Which is why people always liked you. That's why you'll be the one, Daniel."

"The one what?"

"The one to make us all shep nachas. Not that there's anything wrong with what your father does and what your grandfather did. They've always supported their families, kinahura. But the Hillman men, God bless them all—Hillman men never seem to reach their full potential. You will. I know it. I feel it in here."

Daniel looked down—not to avoid Grandma's eyes, but to search for something in his mind that he sensed was there, somehow buried.

"When I was little," he finally said, "I thought the Hillmans were God's gift to the world. Like we were all blessed or something."

Grandma Leah smiled.

"There are gifts, and there are gifts," she said. "Your grandfather— he never trusted anyone. Your Uncle Jack… very smart, but he never looked like he wanted to have a good time, and I don't think he ever did. Your father? Smart too, but he was too easy to accept things the way they were, to let people pressure him too easily. He accepted whatever they said like it was his destiny." She dabbed her nose with a crumbled tissue she had in her clenched fist. "My brother-in-law Nat… oy, Nat… Angry at the world. Takes out all his anger on himself by being such a nogoodnik."

"I always liked Uncle Nat," Daniel said. He knew that if anyone would handle the news well, it would be Grandma Leah.

"Of course you did. There's a word that explains it. Charisma. Moxie."

"That's two words."

Grandma laughed lightly through her nose. To do otherwise probably would have been painful. "You're a tummler. Just like your grandfather, except without the chotchkees. But you trust people, no?"

"Most. Not all."

"And you don't get scared too easily."

"Sometimes I do. But not too much, I guess."

"And you like to have fun."

"I guess."

"And you're not angry."

"Well..."

"And you don't just accept things the way they are."

"Well..."

"And you have a strong mind. You're all these things. Which is why you can be whatever you want to be, Daniel."

Grandma's words soothed and hurt him at the same time.

"How come you never told me any of this before, Grandma?"

"Because they always yell at me when I talk like this, your father and your grandfather. Who knows why? Maybe they're superstitious. I'm not superstitious. They've got maybe one-tenth the confidence I have. I only wish I was a little stronger to help you. But now that my mind is racing, my body is giving up."

Daniel looked down again, this time to hide a tear.

"Listen, sweetheart, you won't mind if I rest a little bit, no? I'm suddenly very tired." Grandma closed her eyes and seemed to almost instantly fall asleep. The body under the covers seemed smaller than ever, and her breathing more labored.

Daniel left the room but caught a glimpse of himself in the full-length mirror on the back of the bedroom door. He thought to himself, Great—the one person who has undying faith in me is dying right in front of my eyes.

Back in the living room, Dad and Grandpa Jesse were in a tense conversation about home care, nursing homes, finances, and maid services. There was some yelling, even though both of them had earlier promised to keep it down for Grandma's sake. Dad smoked several cigarettes in just the forty minutes they were there.

"What will be, will be," he said two or three times.

"Everything will be all right," Grandpa insisted.

"From your lips to God's ears."

In the car on the ride home, Dad repeated the word 'stubborn' several times and grabbed the steering wheel so tightly that his knuckles turned white. He smoked two cigarettes before they were even out of Brooklyn.

"Is the smoke bothering you?" he asked as the Belt Parkway turned into the Southern State in Nassau County.

"No. Can I have one?"

Dad shot him a look.

"Daniel," he said, "I know you kids like to do things you're not supposed to do. I did too when I was your age. Just don't go overboard. Okay?"

"Okay."

"There's something else," Dad continued. "These are crazy times we're living in. The war, the hippies, the drugs. And I know things haven't been easy for us, with Steven, and Mom, and Lori, both grandmas... All I'm saying is….well… just…"

"Don't worry, Dad."

"Okay. I won't worry."

He turned on the radio. A song with a strange vocal sound effect played on WABC.

"Another stupid song," Dad said. "Isn't this the same crazy thing we heard on the way here?"

"That was 'Dizzy,'" Daniel said. "This is 'Crimson and Clover.'"

"There's a difference? Dizzy schmizzy. A song called 'Dizzy' can only make you dizzy. The songs you used to write were a thousand time better."

That caught Daniel off guard. He thought about what that dapper man with the cane at Salisbury Park had said to him that afternoon: When God closes a door, somewhere he opens a window. Daniel wondered if Dad and Grandma Leah had been attempting to open windows. For the first time in a long time, he actually looked forward to sitting at home to watch an old Bowery Boys movie on television with Dad, like they used to do when he was little. But as soon as they walked into the house, the telephone rang. There was a fire at a LILCO substation in Uniondale. Several pieces of important equipment were destroyed. Dad had to leave in a hurry.

•　　•　　•　　•　　•

When Dad wasn't working on his regular shift, he was called upon to supervise and support crews at substations either because of bad weather, an excessive number of worker absences, or accidents and catastrophes like the Uniondale fire. Mom, with her frequent trips to Florida, was also somewhat of a stranger on Pearl Drive these days. I stopped by once a week on average. Since I had no more possessions in the house to bring back with me to the city, few meals to help prepare, and little cleaning to do, my visits were mostly to check up on Daniel.

One morning when Daniel was home alone, Dad left a note for him before he left for work to apologize for all the long hours he had been away on the job. "At least these extra hours at work are helping me put away some money, and maybe we can use some of it for piano or guitar lessons again. I haven't heard you play in months," he wrote.

Daniel made himself breakfast, watched television, put on a coat, then went outside. The block seemed empty. No one appeared to be home. He knocked on Johnny and Joey's door, hoping that Mr. Bonomo might want to chat for a few minutes. Joey answered the door and invited him in. There was no indication that Mr. Bonomo was home, so Daniel resigned himself to having to watch Joey and his brother work on a science project for school. They had built an ant colony out of balsa wood and were attempting to train two dozen ants to crawl in a counterclockwise pattern through its miniature hallways. None of the ants cooperated, so Johnny stepped on almost all of them.

When Daniel asked why the house was so quiet, Johnny told him that his mother and her boyfriend were looking at a store in Merrick that they wanted to buy and that their grandfather was at a meeting on Staten Island. Annette, he said, was in her bedroom. Daniel decided to leave the twins alone because they began to fight about the ant massacre. The boys were now without a science project.

Annette was in her first year at Hofstra University, which was a few miles away from Westbrook Hills. I had seen her a few days earlier when I drove down Pearl Drive for a visit home; she had blossomed into a curvaceous young woman, and of this Daniel was well aware. When Annette heard him say goodbye to the twins on his way out of their house (which I'm willing to bet he said extra loud on purpose), she came out into the hallway.

"Hi, Daniel," she said. "I was just getting a glass of water."

"Hi," he smiled.

"Playing with my stupid brothers?"

"No. They're doing something for school. With ants."

"Ants? If I find one ant in my room," Annette snarled, "those idiot twins are dead."

"So are the ants."

"And after I kill them, you'll only have *me* to play with."

Daniel didn't know what to say.

"Where you going now?" she asked.

"Home, I guess."

"Wanna see some college catalogs? I'm going over a bunch in my room. I'm transferring out of Hofstra. Aren't you going to college soon? You might as well get a head start looking around."

"I'm only in tenth grade."

"You seem a lot older. At least a lot older than my dumb-ass juvenile delinquent brothers. Come to my room."

Daniel followed Annette into her room. She never did get the glass of water she had mentioned only moments before. Daniel asked what college she wanted to go to.

"Fashion Institute of Technology is my number one choice," she responded. "It's called F.I.T. I actually already applied, and I'm sure I'll be accepted."

"Why are you so sure?"

"Because I am. I got into Hofstra pretty easy, and it's kind of competitive. But I'd really like to be in the city."

"F.I.T.'s in New York City?"

"Yup. Manhattan. I'm going there tomorrow after my classes to look around."

"By yourself?"

"Unless you want to come with me." She paused. "Want to?"

Although Annette had no way of knowing, Daniel did want to go into the city. He had an audiocassette tape recording of five of his original songs that he had made two years earlier, and he had toyed with the idea of somehow delivering it to the WABC radio station as a last-ditch attempt to see if music still held the appeal for him that it once had. He wanted to explore whether or not music was still what made him special, as he (and almost everyone else) used to think. He needed to find out if his goal to be the first *something* required music for its fruition. He longed to make Grandma Leah proud. Although his voice was lower now than it had been two years before, he felt that the songs were fairly compelling and that the recording turned out surprisingly well. If he went to the city with Annette, he reasoned, he might have an opportunity to deliver the cassette right into the hands of WABC's most famous deejay, Cousin Brucie. "You'll do something, you'll try something, you'll ask something, you'll give something to someone" Grandma Leah had said to him a long time ago. Maybe, he wondered silently, this is what she meant.

"Is anyone else going with you?"Daniel asked.

"Nope," Annette responded. "Just you. I get home from Hofstra at one. I'm leaving for the city at two. I can pick you up at the high school. A few minutes after two. In the parking lot next to the football field. We'll drive to the Westbrook Hills station and take the two -fifteen train. I'll buy your ticket. Okay?"

"Okay."

"You won't be bored seeing F.I.T.?"

"Maybe while you're at the school, I'll do something else in the city that I want to do."

"Okay. That sounds good."

He went home.

"Dad. Forgot to tell you," he wrote on a piece of note paper. "School field trip tomorrow. Museum in NYC. Mom signed the permission slip before she went to FL. Will be home at night, not too late. Daniel." He left the note on the kitchen table. Then he found an index card in his desk drawer, cut it in half, wrote his name and address on it, and put it in the little clear-plastic case in which he also secured the audiocassette.

Daniel woke up to a clear and crisp mid-January morning and went to school wearing a light spring jacket. At a few minutes after two, Annette's red Chevette pulled into the parking lot next to the football field just as Daniel slipped out of biology—his last class of the day— without being noticed.

"Nice car," he said as he hopped in.

"A birthday present from my mom's boyfriend."

That's when Daniel noticed that Annette, too, was all in red—a red wool coat and a red beret—and that struck Daniel as a distinctive touch. He said he liked her outfit even more than he liked her car. She laughed.

Annette drove to the Westbrook Hills Long Island Rail Road Station, where she purchased two round-trip tickets to Penn Station. The train arrived, and they boarded. They sat opposite each other on two facing seats that were otherwise empty. Annette began to flip through her F.I.T. catalogue. Dan touched the small plastic case tucked into his pants pocket to make sure the audiocassette was secure.

"You're staring at me," she said.

"Sorry," he mumbled.

"It's okay. I know I'm beautiful."

"Actually, you are," Daniel said.

She continued to read her catalog. The train left the station.

"You've been over our house so much," Annette said a minute later, "that sometimes I feel like you're another brother."

"Mostly, I hang out with your grandfather, not your brothers."

"I know. That's smart. But I'm glad you're not."

"Not what?"

"Not another brother. Because then we wouldn't be able to screw one day."

Daniel swallowed hard. Annette noticed and chuckled. The train suddenly swayed to the left sharply, diverting Annette's attention, which gave Daniel a chance to regain his composure.

"My grandfather likes you," she said

"He makes me play music. No one in my house listens to me play anymore. But your grandfather—"

The train swayed again, this time to the right, which cut him off mid-sentence. The lights went off, then on again.

"What if you don't get accepted to F.I.T.?"

"I'll be accepted."

"Steven wasn't accepted to four of the five colleges he applied to."

Annette bit her lip. She reached her arm across the space between their seats and touched Daniel's knee. She left her hand there for several moments.

Forty-five minutes after they had departed Westbrook Hills, the train arrived at Pennsylvania Station in midtown Manhattan, below Madison Square Garden. Daniel and Annette briefly discussed where and when they'd meet for the return trip. Although the discussion was impersonal and businesslike, Daniel knew that there was always the train ride home, where things could get personal once again.

Cousin Brucie's show always began at six o'clock in the afternoon. Daniel made the assumption that Brucie would be in his studio at least an hour-and-a-half before that—but it was only three-fifteen. He had more than an hour to kill. So he decided to walk down Seventh Avenue, toward Greenwich Village. The sun was already starting to set, and the neon signs on all the stores and restaurants began to buzz brightly.

Daniel turned right at West Twenty-Third Street and walked down to Eighth Avenue. At Eighth and West Nineteenth there was a crowd of people gathered on the corner to watch some police action unfold several yards up the street. Two uniformed officers held a man against the façade of a building that had its metal security gate down and locked in place. The man's arms and legs were spread. A third officer who was in plain clothes and had a badge pinned to one his belt loops went through the man's pockets and took out an assortment of little packets, vials, syringes, and containers.

"Jesus," the plainclothes officer said, "this guy's a friggin' drugstore."

Daniel watched with great curiosity but then continued down Eighth Avenue. When he noticed the time on a clock-radio inside a store window, he decided to head back to midtown. At the Penn Plaza complex, he was confident he knew which building was home to the WABC-AM radio station from having once seen photos in a magazine. He walked into one of the buildings. The lobby seemed at least three stories tall, and all the voices, footsteps, sneezes, and coughs echoed one after the other off the marble walls and down from the ceiling. There was a row of elevators, although Daniel didn't know which one would take him to the radio studio. A pretty woman by the elevator buttons must have assumed by the look on his face that he was uncertain about his destination.

"Where do you want to go?" she asked.

"WABC," he said.

"Twenty-third floor. Take that one," she said as she pointed to an elevator door. "Do you have an appointment?"

"Yes."

"Did you check in with the guard?"

Daniel looked back toward the main part of the lobby, and for the first time saw a desk with a guard behind it. The guard seemed to be addressing several people at once. Either he didn't see Daniel when he first walked through, or Daniel's brisk pace made the guard think that, as young as he was, he did indeed have an appointment and knew exactly where he was going.

"Yes," Daniel said to the woman. "I talked to the guard, but he didn't tell me what floor."

"Oh, that figures. Oscar's nice, but sometimes he's forgetful."

Daniel took the elevator to the twenty-third floor. The elevator door opened into a small, carpeted lobby with a highly-polished dark-wood table in the middle. There were several music magazines on the table, including Billboard and Variety; Daniel was familiar with both from the

Westbrook Hills Public Library. At the moment, no one sat behind the reception desk. A disc jockey named Dan Ingram was currently on the air; his wise-cracking banter could be heard from speakers hidden somewhere in the ceiling.

Two hallways spread out from either side of the lobby. Daniel randomly selected one of the hallways and began a slow journey toward the unknown. There was another reception desk at the end of that hallway. Just before he reached it, a woman came out of a door. She looked puzzled when she saw Daniel. She had wavy gray hair and a pair of eyeglasses that hung on her chest from a thin gold chain around her neck. The woman rounded the desk and sat down.

"Happens to me all the time," she said. "I take just two minutes to get a cup of coffee, and someone comes in. I'm so sorry."

"That's okay," Daniel said.

"How can I help you?"

"I'm here to see Cousin Brucie."

"Do you have an appointment?"

"He knows my grandfather." In his head, Daniel was able to justify the claim by assuming that Cousin Brucie had once seen Grandpa Jesse's name on a big band album from the old days.

"Who's your grandfather?" the woman asked as she put on the glasses.

"Jesse Hillman."

"Well, I'm sorry, but I'm afraid your name would need to be on this list here, and I don't—"

"I came all the way up here on the train. I had to skip some classes today, and I might even get in trouble unless I can prove that I actually spoke to Cousin Brucie."

The woman took off her glasses. "I don't understand. You mean—"

Just then, another door in the hallway opened up, and two people stepped out, a man and a young woman. They walked toward the reception desk. Daniel knew instantly that the man was Bruce Morrow—the famous Cousin Brucie—because his face was thickset and ruddy, as in all the photographs he had seen over the years in Billboard and Variety. The young woman he was with looked to be not much older than Annette. She had straight black hair, broad shoulders, and dark, expressive eyes. Somehow, though, her eyes also seemed cautious and ill at ease.

"I'm sorry, Bruce!" the receptionist said. "I don't know how this young man—"

"Hi there, little cuz," Cousin Brucie said to Daniel, completely disregarding the receptionist.

Daniel said hello and then said hi to the girl next to him.

"This young lady is gonna be a big star one day," Brucie said in his animated way. "She has one heck of a voice—"

"You have to listen to my tape," Daniel interrupted, ignoring his words the way Cousin Brucie had ignored the receptionist. "I write songs."

"Hold on there, fella," Brucie said. He turned to the young woman.

"I'll see what I can do, Karen. No promises. I'm not as powerful as everyone thinks."

"Okay," the young woman smiled bashfully. "Thank you. It was very nice meeting you. And you, too," she said to Daniel.

The young woman went to the elevator, which had just arrived to let off two other people. Then she disappeared.

"Karen and her brother just signed with a big record company out on the coast, and they're hoping for a few plugs on my show to help get them rolling," Brucie said. "She's only nineteen! Can you believe that?"

"I'm only four years younger than her," Daniel said as if it were an earth-shattering revelation of which Cousin Brucie needed to be aware. "Listen to my tape," he urged. "You have to."

"I do?"

"Yes. You'll like it."

"I'm sure I will," Cousin Brucie said. "But the thing is, little cuz, there are rules and regulations. Copyrights. Protection. All kinds of things to protect me and the radio station. It's the legal people, you know? Not me. They're real nervous types, if you know what I mean."

"You helped Paul Anka when he was a kid. I read about it."

"Yes, but—"

"And you're helping that girl with the black hair."

"Yes, but she's already—"

"I have to do this."

"Do what?"

"They're good songs," Daniel said. "Good songs make people happy. And everyone wants to be happy?"

Cousin Brucie laughed.

"Yes. I like to be happy," he said. "What's your name?"

"Daniel Hillman."

"Well, Cousin Dan, I'd really like to help you out, but if my boss finds out I took a tape from a kid off the street—"

"My grandfather was in the music business. My father played trombone in the army. I've been playing music since I was two. I've written about thirty songs. I've performed at about a hundred weddings, birthdays, bar mitzvahs, and Lebitz Family Circle meetings. I'm not just a kid off the street."

Brucie was a little more pensive now.

"Lebitz Family Circle meetings, huh? So we're members of the same tribe! You're a lantsman?"

"Yes. I am. Maybe we're even related. From way back. In Poland, or Romania."

"You're a real pisher, kid. Well… I can't promise anything, but I'll see what I can do. Okay? Give me the tape."

Daniel reached into his pocket and handed the plastic case to Cousin Brucie.

"But let's keep it just between you and me. Vishtayst?"

"Vishtayst."

"Okay. So long, little cuz."

Cousin Brucie walked down the hallway, whistling. Daniel went back to the elevator. The receptionist, who had witnessed the entire conversation, watched as he left. Her mouth hung open, and the expression on her face was clearly one of bewilderment. That made Daniel laugh inside. He decided to never forget that face. For some reason, he thought it would come in handy one day.

* * *

"Something good happened," Annette said to Daniel as soon as she met him under the giant Penn Station marquee. "I can tell on your face."

"We'll see," he said. "How'd your tour go?"

"Good. I like the school a lot. I can't wait to get my acceptance letter. I guess we both had a successful afternoon. And it's not even over yet."

"I know."

"This is weird, isn't it? You and me in the city?"

She slipped her arm through his, and that's how they walked into the train station.

"It's not weird to me," Daniel said. "It's nice. I mean, some of my other friends have sisters, but you're a lot nicer than all of them put together. You're a lot nicer than my friends, too, come to think of it."

"Even Doug Kelleher? I thought he was your best friend."

"He was once. But he was always too bossy. He always had to prove that he's better than everyone else."

They went from one escalator to another, still arm in arm, as they made their way to the tracks on the lowest level of the station.

"How did he boss you around?" Annette asked.

"Well, when we were kids and played spies, he always had to be James Bond, and I'd have to be just some stupid assistant who usually got killed. That kind of thing."

"James Bond is handsome, and Doug Kelleher isn't. He's goofy looking. So don't let it bother you. Actually, I already know how he shows off," Annette said. "Remember at Joey and Johnny's last birthday party, when he did that scene from the stupid play he was in at his church?"

"No," Daniel said. "I wasn't there."

"Oh, that's right. How come you weren't there?"

"That was the day of Steven's unveiling."

"What's an unveiling?"

"Something Jewish families do a year after someone dies."

Annette stopped, looked his way, and hugged him. Despite all the people and all the noise down there on the train platform, it was a quiet and comforting moment for Daniel.

The train arrived, and they boarded. They sat side by side.

"You've been through a lot," Annette said. "Your mom's accident. Steven in Vietnam. Lori always being a little strange." The train entered the dark tunnel underneath the East River, and Annette put her head on his shoulder. "You do grass, don't you?"

"Yes."

"I guess you have to, huh? *These* days. What about coke?"

"Coke?"

"Cocaine."

"Not yet."

"It's good. Makes you forget all your troubles, and you don't even barf afterward. I have some at home. In my secret place. Want to do it with me?"

"I guess."

"And maybe we'll do some other stuff, too."

"Okay."

•       •       •       •       •

Dad's car wasn't in the driveway when Annette's red Chevette passed by, but that hardly mattered since she intended to drive to her own house anyway. Daniel followed her out of the car and into her garage.

We had never had a garage at our house. We had a shed. One of my friends had a garage, but we never went inside. I'm willing to bet that Steven had been in more than his share of garages, given his affinity for cars and trucks. But I'm not certain how much Daniel knew about garages. So when Annette said that she had a secret hideaway in the garage under the rafters, maybe Daniel knew what she was talking about, or maybe not. In any case, he followed her lead. (What happened next is a little difficult for me to pass along; I am, after all, his sister. In retrospect, it makes the story of when Steven urinated in the snow seem as innocent as *Green Eggs and Ham*.) Annette took a wooden ladder from the corner of the garage and put it in the middle of the floor. She stuck the top of the ladder through a square opening in the flat, unpainted plywood ceiling. The opening looked big enough for one person to fit through. Annette climbed the ladder. Daniel followed slowly. He wasn't used to climbing ladders—especially almost straight up. There was a room above the flat ceiling—a big, empty space. It was very dark. The only illumination came from the garage light below that filtered up through the small square opening. When Daniel arrived at the top of the ladder, he saw the rafters—a series of A-frame wooden beams that supported the roof of the garage. A small mattress covered with a flowered sheet was in the middle of the plywood floor, next to the square opening. A big black trunk was at the foot of the mattress. By the time Daniel made it entirely through the small opening, Annette had already removed her coat and opened the trunk. Out of it she took a small mason jar with a silver cover, a miniature spoon, a tall, skinny candle in a small gold candleholder, a book of matches and an ashtray. She closed the trunk, set all the items on top of it, and lit the candle.

Daniel took off his coat and watched Annette carefully. She seemed to know exactly what she was doing, and her take-charge attitude mesmerized him, as did the shadows cast by the flickering candle. Annette kneeled on the floor, opened the mason jar, took the small spoon, and filled it with the white powder. She put the spoon to her nostril and inhaled with one long breath. She handed the spoon to Daniel. He kneeled down beside her, collected the powder from the jar into the spoon, and mimicked exactly what she had done. After a few silent seconds, Annette positioned herself cross-legged on the plywood. Daniel imitated the move opposite her, and they sat that way, staring at each other for a long time. They giggled. They talked about the sensations they suddenly began to feel. Daniel felt both nervous excitement and hyperawareness of everything around him—not the least of which was Annette, less than an arm's length away from him. Her perfume, which he hadn't noticed before, suddenly seemed very potent, and very intoxicating. Then, once more with Annette's silent prompt, they moved to the mattress. They sat side by side with their feet on the plywood. Annette removed Daniel's shirt and pants, then removed her own blouse and skirt.

"Now the rest," Annette said.

She pulled down his underpants, then took his hands and guided him to remove her bra and panties. When he saw her breasts and long, bare legs he trembled severely—but felt fortunate that he was able to stop the trembling as both more confidence and alertness kicked in. Whether or not that was fueled by the cocaine he didn't know. From an emotional standpoint, all Daniel had to measure this sudden and bewitching encounter against were daydreams and Playboy; he had no physical perspective with which to compare it, so he had no idea how he was really supposed to feel. He just let the experience take him wherever it wanted, with neither preconceived notions nor expectations. Perhaps that's what helped him at least *seem* prepared for the task at hand. Annette told him what to do, and he did whatever she asked. Some moves he repeated a second time, and there were a few he explored on his own without being told. Annette seemed more pleased than surprised at anything he attempted. And then, with what seemed like prudent timing, they finished what they had begun.

Afterward, they sat across from each other on the mattress for quite some time, with the sheet bunched up around their bodies. That made it seem almost as if they were skinny dipping in a pool with waves splashing all around. From time to time, Annette swooshed the sheet playfully with her hands to further heighten the effect. That, in turn, created a little breeze that made the candle flames jiggle.

"What are you thinking about?" she asked Daniel after a brief silence.

"Stuff," he said.

"Me too," she responded. "Like what?"

"Like what I did in the city. And what we just did. And me and you."

"Nice surprise, huh?"

"Yes. I loved it. You're beautiful."

"I know."

Annette blew out the candles. They got dressed, and she kissed him on the lips. Then they climbed down the ladder. By the back door of the garage, Daniel, with complete poise and conviction, kissed her on the lips once again and said goodbye. Annette smiled impishly. They stepped outside. She went into her house. Daniel walked home.

Dad was back from work, and when he inquired about the school trip, Daniel almost asked what school trip he was talking about. But he caught himself and said he enjoyed it. Dad said he was exhausted and went to bed, even though it was only eight-fifteen.

When Dad closed his bedroom door, Daniel went to the phone in the kitchen and called Grandma Leah.

"Grandma? It's Daniel," he said when she answered the phone on the fourth ring.

"Daniel, darling — is everything all right?"

"You won't believe what I did today."

He told her about his visit to WABC, and how he handed a cassette of songs to Cousin Brucie, who promised to listen to it.

"You see!" Grandma said, "that's chutzpah. That's what I mean. You've got it more than anyone, and I'd say that even if Grandpa wasn't hard of hearing and snoring like a bear in front of the television."

"Thanks, Grandma."

"What else did you do today? Did you have school?"

"Yes."

"And then? After the city?"

"I made a new friend."

"Good. Friends are good. Family and friends. Without them there's nothing. You've got friends and chutzpah. You've got it all, kinahura."

"Thanks."

"Where's your father?"

"Sleeping already."

"And your mother's coming home soon?"

"Yes. Tomorrow."

"You have homework yet?"

"Yes. I better go do it."

"Go, darling. Thank you for calling. I love you."

"I love you, too."

They hung up. Although Daniel considered it a good conversation, he went to bed feeling somewhat bewildered.

·   ·   ·   ·   ·

I supposed it's no surprise that Daniel had an urge to see Annette again not long after their garage encounter. But most of the time she was at Hofstra or out with her college friends. The desire was so great that Daniel literally ran home from school for the next few afternoons to see if Annette's red Chevette was in her driveway.

There was another reason, too, why he hurried home the moment the final bell rang: he wanted to check the mailbox before Mom had a chance to do it. If a note arrived from Cousin Brucie, he wanted to be the one to retrieve it.

After a full week of running, checking, and longing, Daniel turned into what could probably best be described as a nervous wreck; he bit his nails, scratched his head, smoked too many cigarettes, and stole too many sips of whiskey from his elementary school thermos, which he still hid in his room. It was easy for him to hide the nicotine smells and the cigarette butts because Dad's smoking had increased so much lately that it was impossible to tell where his habit ended and Daniel's began. Whenever he was finished smoking, Daniel simply discarded the butt in one of Dad's ashtrays.

The mail arrived at noon on Saturday. Mom was at the beauty parlor, and Dad was out with a LILCO crew. There was an envelope with WABC-AM MUSIC-RADIO printed on one side. Daniel opened the envelope in the kitchen. Along with the audiocassette was a note:

*Dear Sir/Madame:*

*Due to potential legal ramifications we cannot accept your material(s) and are returning it/them herewith. No one on our staff has read/viewed/listened to the enclosed material(s). Thank you very much for your interest in WABC-AM*

*MUSIC-RADIO. We wish you the best of luck in placing your material(s) elsewhere.*

Daniel stared at the note paper for a long time, then crumbled it up and threw it into the kitchen garbage, along with the cassette. He sat by the table and thumbed listlessly through Newsday. On the eighth or ninth page of the newspaper was a large head-and-shoulders photograph of Doug Kelleher. Underneath it was a caption that looked more like a headline. It said:

*Westbrook Hills Teen Tapped For Supporting Role
in Hollywood Television Show*

"When the Lord closes a door..." Daniel remembered Theodore saying in the park. He decided to end the saying on his own terms: 'Sometimes you have to look for another door to walked through—even when you're not expected.'

Without grabbing a sweater or jacket, Daniel left the house and jogged down the block to the DePuzo house. The red Chevette was in the driveway, but no one answered when he knocked, so Daniel went around to the rear of the house. The back door to the garage was open. He went in. The ladder stood against the square opening in the ceiling. That meant Annette was in the hideaway. Daniel climbed up. The candles were lit. There was a joint in the ashtray on top of the trunk. There were two bodies on the mattress. Annette and Doug Kelleher were naked, side by side, facing one another. The sheet was scrunched up by the bottom of their legs.

A strange, severe, invisible force pushed Daniel backward, wiped the image from his mind, and propelled him down the ladder. His heart pounded. He found himself standing on the cement garage floor in a desperate search for the back door. When he found it, he scurried through and ran back home. As he approached the front lawn, he saw Mr. Ashler looking out of his living room window.

Inside the house, Daniel went directly to the liquor cabinet in the living room and grabbed as many bottles as he could at once. He didn't bother to look at the labels. He carried the bottles into the kitchen, set them upon the table, took a coffee mug from the drain rack in the sink, filled it halfway with rye, and swigged it. Then he poured from a bottle of vodka and swigged that, too. Then rum. The iron will to inflict emotional if not physical pain no doubt is what enabled Daniel to get all of it down his throat—though he quickly found out he had neither an iron throat nor an iron stomach; both burned with intensity as the liquid went down. Tears poured out of his eyes. His iron will, with a fair measure of foolishness and perhaps a little temporary insanity, encouraged Daniel to persist in the craziness. He took three large gulps directly from a wine bottle and followed it with two large gulps out of a bottle of cognac. There was vomit low in his throat. He managed to hold it in. He refilled the mug with more rum and took it with him around the house in search of a cigarette. But he found no cigarettes, nor remnants of any that had already been smoked. Dad must have finished his last pack before he left for work, and Mom must have emptied all the ashtrays before she went to the beauty parlor.

Daniel then considered the basement workshop. Dad often smoked down there when he tinkered around, and the workroom ashtray was almost never emptied. Mom never liked to go in there since Dad picked up the habit again because she said it was like walking into a nicotine tent—and this despite the fact that Dad kept the little window near the ceiling partially open at all times, even during the winter. How Daniel navigated the basement steps without falling as he made his way downstairs will forever be a mystery. In the workshop, he put the mug of rum on the worktable, but did so with more force than he had anticipated, and some of the liquid spilled onto the table and formed a clear pool around the mug. The ashtray was full of butts, as Daniel knew it would be. He grabbed the ashtray with such a brutal swipe that he spilled the entire contents onto the floor. He picked a butt off the floor, put it in his mouth, and looked for something to light it with. Suddenly the room seemed much smaller than it really was—although it was already very small—and ice cold. Daniel held his arms in close, kept his legs pressed tightly together, and turned in quick, furious motions in search of a book of matches or a lighter. Among Dad's tools was a soldering gun, which he used from time to time to fuse electrical circuits or metal pieces together for projects in the house. It hung from its electrical cord, which was wrapped around a nail that stuck out of the side of the worktable. Daniel unwrapped the cord, plugged it into an outlet, and squeezed the trigger. The coil on the soldering gun turned red almost instantly, and a little ribbon of smoke rose from the tip. He touched the tip to the end of the cigarette butt to light it and took a deep drag. What he thought would be a soothing sensation was one only of more pain and soreness. He put the soldering gun on the worktable, unintentionally into the clear pool of spilled rum. The pool of alcohol flamed up like a magician's trick, accompanied by a large, sizzling pop. Daniel froze with fear. Though the worktable had a metal covering that was not flammable, the little eruption of fire began to consume a pile of sawdust that sat alongside the liquid. Then the fire spread across the tabletop, fed by the sawdust which ran in an almost straight thin line to several small cardboard boxes of nails, screws, and washers. The boxes caught on fire. The smoke was suddenly very thick. The fire grew.

Daniel looked around frantically—although for what he was searching he did not know. He considered throwing all the power tools he could find on top of the flames to try to smother them, or maybe a tablecloth or an old quilt, which he thought might be found somewhere in a closet or a drawer in the basement. But he realized that if he left the workroom for even a second, the fire would most certainly get out of control; yet if he stayed, it would get out of control with him still in the room. He turned around. Black rubber hoses hung down from hooks on the back wall of the workroom. He grabbed one of the hoses but had no idea what to do with it. If only those hoses had been attached to the water pipes that he knew must run along the basement ceiling somewhere nearby... But no—the hoses just hung there on the wall, useless, in big upside-down U's, each end pointing to the floor. Then, suddenly, from somewhere, water *did* come into the workroom, from the small open window near the ceiling. Someone outside had stuck a garden hose through the window and had turned on the backyard spigot. The heavy spray of water doused the flames on the worktable. After about a minute, the fire was completely out, the garden hose was off, and smoke swirled ominously along the edges of the ceiling. Daniel stood in a puddle of water, soaked through to his skin. He looked toward the window and saw Mr. Ashler's wearied face glaring in. After another moment, Mr. Ashler disappeared.

A minute later, he walked into the workroom, grabbed Daniel by the arm, pulled him upstairs, and pushed him into the bathroom. He turned on the cold water faucet full blast and shoved Daniel's head into the sink.

"I had to do this to both of my idiot sons at one time or another," he grumbled.

Daniel didn't fight him. After Mr. Ashler dunked Daniel's head into the sink five or six times in a row, he took a towel from the rack and wiped his face. He reached into the medicine cabinet, found a bottle of mouthwash, and made Daniel take a mouthful.

"Swallow it," Mr. Ashler barked. Daniel looked at him in horror. "Swallow it!" he repeated, even louder.

Daniel swallowed it.

"Why?"

"Because I don't have time to make coffee and I don't think kids should drink coffee anyway. When will your mother and father be home?"

"I don't know."

"Get out of these wet clothes, then get into bed and stay there."

Daniel shuffled into the hallway, turned around and said,

"Why?"

"Because. Just do it," Mr. Ashler said.

"No—I mean, why is everything so fucked up?"

"Maybe you expect too much. Or the wrong things. Who the hell knows?" Mr. Ashler began to wipe down the bathroom vanity with the towel. "And watch your filthy mouth. I'm gonna put away all those goddamn liquor bottles I saw on the kitchen table. And then I'm gonna clean up the basement as much as I can and try to make it look like you just had a little accident so that your old man doesn't beat the living crap out of you. Although in my opinion, he should."

Daniel went to his bedroom, shut the door, pulled down the window shade, curled up on the bed, and shut his eyes. Nineteen Seventy had only just begun. There were still eleven and a half months to go. Daniel was sick of it already.

# Eight

Grandpa Jesse stood between two cemetery plots and said,

"For fifty-five years I slept on her left. Soon I'll have to sleep on her right. Oh well…"

One of the two plots in front of him was still covered with grass; a coffin was suspended over the other. When Grandma Leah died, Daniel and I felt we had lost someone who was as much a friend as a grandmother. She was shrewd, levelheaded, and entirely devoted to the family. I could not even begin to try to calculate the number of conversations I had with her over the years in which her wise, proud, and gentle comments made me think that not only was I okay, but better than okay. I know Daniel felt the same way.

In December 1970, Grandma Leah took ill with a fever and a "virus of unknown origin" that affected her lungs and kidneys. She had been taken to a hospital in Baltimore where there was a physician who specialized in just that—viruses of unknown origin. Grandpa Jesse, in a moment of unruffled confidence, insisted on the phone that she'd be all right.

The day after she was transported to Maryland, I visited the house in Westbrook Hills and sat for a while in the living room to watch television with Dad and Daniel. (Mom was in her bedroom; she stayed there quite a bit in those days.) I asked Dad how Grandma Leah ended up in Baltimore.

"What's the difference?" he said between cigarette puffs. "She's there. That's all."

"The difference is I'd like to visit her," I said, "and it's so much better when you're not in the dark about things. Sometimes confidence is more than half the battle. I don't want to be ignorant and uninformed where my sick grandmother is concerned."

Dad looked at me through an oddly serene corkscrew ribbon of cigarette smoke.

"I thought you graduated college," he said. "You're talking funny again like you used do to when you were studying that psychology stuff."

"Uncle Nat arranged it, right? Frankly, I don't think that's a big issue—Uncle Nat's involvement—if you were wondering."

"I wasn't wondering."

Other than that, Dad refused to talk about it. We watched television instead. I left shortly afterward, determined to drive to Maryland, whether I was armed with good information or not. First, I drove to my new house in Morristown, New Jersey to check my schedule for the week, just in case I decided to stay in Baltimore an extra day or two. I still had a job at Yeshiva University in the city, and I also took post-graduate courses at a school closer to home. Daniel called me just as I was about to leave and asked if he could come with me to Baltimore. I gently turned him down. The logistics would have been too complicated, plus I wasn't certain that Daniel was emotionally prepared for what likely would be a very difficult visit.

I was right. As I told Daniel when I stopped by Westbrook Hills a few days later, Grandma Leah was sicker than we had been led to believe.

"I wasn't expecting that," I told him as we sat together in the kitchen.

"What did you two talk about?" Daniel asked.

"A little bit of everything. It was hard to find the right words to answer her questions so that I wouldn't upset her."

"You probably didn't have to," he said. "She's very smart, you know."

"I know."

"What did she ask about?"

"Well," I said, "first she asked if Grandma Rose was happy living in the house." (Grandma Rose had moved back to Westbrook Hills since she no longer had any living relatives in Florida.)

"What did you say?"

"I told her that everyone was doing whatever they could to make things work out."

"Very diplomatic," Daniel said. "Maybe you should work for the U.N."

"Then she asked about you. She wanted to know if you still play music."

"What did you say?"

"I said I really didn't know since I live two hours away now. But I said I couldn't imagine you'd ever give it up entirely."

I made myself sound uncertain on purpose; I, too, wanted to know.

"Will I ever give it up?" Daniel said as if I had asked the question myself. "I really don't know what to say, Lori. I'm sort of..."

"Seeing where things lead? Looking for your passion?"

"I suppose."

"I understand, Daniel. But I do feel bad that you don't take lessons anymore. If it's just the money, I'll pay for them."

"It's not the money, Lori," Daniel insisted. "Not at all."

"Then what is it?"

"I really don't know. The words prodigy and fate don't always go together, I guess. What will be, will be."

"Now you sound like Dad," I said to him.

"I smoke like him too," he answered.

"That's just not right."

"Now you sound like Mom."

We looked at each other and smiled. Relatively empty smiles—but smiles nonetheless. It gave me hope.

"Listen," Daniel finally said, "I'm fine. Really. Just be happy that you're sixty miles away in New Jersey. I'm happy for you. Maybe I'll join you one day."

Later that day, I overheard Daniel talking on the phone with a friend from school who had plans to drive to the University of Baltimore to tour the campus. Daniel asked if he could tag along and make a stop at the hospital. But Grandma Leah died the day before they were supposed to go.

As 1970 turned into 1971, Grandpa Jesse also moved into the house in Westbrook Hills. Unruffled confidence turned into forgetfulness and befuddlement after his friend, lover, and partner of fifty-five years passed away. He no longer even had the impetus to sing a song or tinker on an instrument, as he used to do all the time. So even with Jesse Hillman living in the house, still there was no music.

• • • • •

In a way, Pearl Drive had died, as well. Felice DePuzo and the twins had moved to Florida. She and her boyfriend bought into a string of hair salons in West Palm Beach. Annette was in Florida, too, now at the University of Miami, where she lived on campus. Mr. Bonomo was alone in Westbrook Hills with his marble lions. The Kelleher house had been leased to a young couple with a toddler while Mr. and Mrs. Kelleher rented a house of their own in Los Angeles, where Doug pursued a television and movie career. Craig Stewart, now a junior at Holy Name High School, put on another ten pounds, but he did have his teeth fixed and was in the care of a popular dermatologist. All of this was thanks to his sister Linda, who was engaged and working as a nurse at St. Mary's Hospital in Waterbury, Connecticut. She arranged the dental and dermatological care through connections at the hospital. Mr. Ashler now had one of his sons living with him. The son was thirty-five, unmarried, had a huge beer belly and smoked a cigar. If not for his beard and moustache, it would have been impossible to tell the younger Ashler from the older one. At first, they fought a lot, but then it became eerily quiet at the Ashler house, and neither of them was seen outside very often.

As for Mom and Dad, they seemed to live comfortably, if languidly, within their own impenetrable shells and convenient clichés. Daniel went about his business and shared little with them. By April he had been late to school eight times since the second semester began. With both Grandma Rose and Grandpa Jesse living in the house, mornings were chaotic, and Daniel's tardiness was not always his fault. Mom had promised to write a note to the principal to explain, but never got around to it. Dad said it wasn't a father's place to write a note to the principal. No one questioned Dad's strange logic, for just questioning it made him tense and prompted him to raise his voice.

One day Daniel was called down to the principal's office just as school was letting out. There was a copy of the Village Voice on the table in the outer waiting room. Daniel thought it was odd for a high school principal to have a copy of the Village Voice, but he let it pass for the moment. He read the cover story about Bob Dylan, the famous songwriter and troubadour often cited as one of the most passionate voices of his generation. Coincidentally, I had read about Dylan myself just a day or two earlier in a Yeshiva University magazine, where I learned that he was born Robert Zimmerman and had belonged to the

Jewish fraternity at the University of Minnesota when he was a student there. The DeeJays had played two or three songs written by Dylan, such as "Blowin' in the Wind" and "Mr. Tambourine Man." Both had been audience favorites. Daniel had always been interested in Bob Dylan, but as much from a historical perspective as a musical one. According to the article in the Village Voice, Dylan was scheduled to play a solo show at The Bitter End, a club in Greenwich Village, in the middle of April. Daniel flipped through the magazine and also saw a small Bitter End advertisement for the show. Something compelled him to rip the page out of the magazine. He folded it and put it in his pocket.

When Dr. Monaco came out of his office, he saw Daniel reading the magazine.

"My son gets that at home," Dr. Monaco said, almost apologetically. "He recently got his first job at a public relations agency that has a lot of clients in the entertainment business. He brings that home. I accidentally put the darn thing in my briefcase this morning." Then he brought Daniel into his office and told him he would have to stay late for detention for two weeks because of the sizeable number of unexplained and unexcused late arrivals at school. Daniel nodded, said okay, and went home.

•    •    •    •    •

Passover was a little more than a week away. I had already decided to spend two or three days and nights in Westbrook Hills, even though that was never easy for me to do, what with both Grandma Rose and Grandpa Jesse now in the house. But I did have several reasons to make the effort. For one thing, Grandma Rose was always a little calmer whenever I asked her about cooking and sewing. For another, Dad smoked just a little less because of my constant gentle lectures about its ill effects on everyone else in the house. Finally, I had heard about Daniel's long-term detention and thought he could use a sympathetic ear.

Before the holiday arrived, Daniel walked home one afternoon after detention and heard his name called out before he got to the house. Mr. Bonomo had just taken his garbage can to the curb and saw Daniel from half a block away.

"Come by whenever you want. Okay, Daniel?" he called out.

Daniel said he would.

Although Mr. Bonomo lived alone now, sometimes there were other men there with him, usually just standing around laughing, cursing, and spitting. Some of them wore fancy dark suits, and others were in tee-shirts and sneakers. Some were rail thin and others obese. (Daniel once confessed to me he enjoyed the sight of it; he called it "flamboyantly dramatic" and even admitted to passing the house two or three times in a row just to observe the group of men a second and third time.)

Mostly, though, Mr. Bonomo was alone, and Daniel did indeed stop by to chat on a number of occasions. Often the old man would ask him to bring his guitar, and Daniel would play Dean Martin and Perry Como standards for him. Other times he would harmonize to Frank Sinatra records. Mr. Bonomo enjoyed it all very much, and Daniel enjoyed the approval. Mom and Dad never knew about those visits.

One afternoon in the middle of April, in his last period of the day at school, Daniel fell into a daydream and didn't respond when his chemistry teacher, Mrs. Frome, asked him a question. In addition to the daydream, he had been very tired because both Grandma Rose and Grandpa Jesse hadn't felt well the night before and the house was awash with loud chatter and kitchen noises until two in the morning. Daniel hardly slept. When the teacher called on him to explain his silence, he rubbed his eye with his finger. Apparently, it was his middle finger, and Mrs. Frome thought he was sending her a vulgar message. She sent him to the principal's office with a note. As a result, another week of detention was tacked onto his punishment. As he walked home, Daniel purposefully sought out some students who were known for their drug use. He saw a senior who everyone called Sonny and asked to speak with him. Daniel had only four dollar bills and a few nickels in his pocket, but talked Sonny into giving him a joint and a pill for just three of the bills. Sonny called the pill a Black Beauty.

At home, Mom, Grandma Rose, and Grandpa Jesse were in their separate rooms. Daniel went into the basement to smoke the joint, then into his bedroom to swallow the pill. He stayed there for two hours. He completed ninety minutes worth of homework in the first hour. One assignment, for his mass communications class, was to write an essay in the style of a newspaper article based on notes his teacher handed out. His notes, which came with an accompanying photo, was about a feminist activist named Gloria Steinem who at the time was in the news quite a bit. When he was finished with his homework, Daniel paced his small room like a caged animal for almost another hour, mulling over dozens of topics in his mind. For a while he couldn't get the picture of Gloria Steinem out of his head. That was following by thoughts and images of Linda Stuart and Annette DePuzo.

Finally, as the second hour drew to a close, Daniel felt the need to leave the house. He walked over to the Bonomo house.

"Isn't Passover next week?" Mr. Bonomo asked.

"I think so," Daniel responded.

"You *think* so? Shouldn't you *know* so? Isn't it an important holiday?"

They sat in the living room. Mr. Bonomo was in an easy chair. Daniel sat cross-legged on the carpet.

"Yom Kippur's the really big one," he said. "In the fall. That's when you ask God to forgive you for all your sins. I guess that's why it's important. Especially for me lately."

Mr. Bonomo laughed. As he sat in his blue stretch pants and oversized black and white polka dot shirt, to Daniel he looked like a jolly old man who was entirely at peace with himself. What's more, his laugh was comforting, particularly since there was hardly any laughter in Daniel's own life anymore.

"I guess I could use a Yom Kippur, too," Mr. Bonomo said.

"Don't you have something like that?"

"Confession. But you gotta schlep to church for that. At my age, I'd rather schlep to this chair and listen to you sing. When I listen to you, I can say a prayer of thanks."

"How come?"

"Because it makes me realize that God made a few good people. You're a good boy, Daniel Hillman."

Joey and Johnny once told Daniel that no man in the Bonomo family had ever wept, so Daniel was not about to shed a tear—but he did feel like crying. So he said he had to go home to do an assignment for school. It was the only way to get out of it.

A few days later, after his next-to-last school detention, Daniel stopped at Mr. Bonomo's house once again for a visit. As Mr. Bonomo poured himself a glass of prune juice in the kitchen, he called out to ask Daniel what was on his mind, for he sensed that his young guest was in a pensive mood.

"I hate school and everyone in it," Daniel called back.

"I hate drinking this shit," Mr. Bonomo responded from the kitchen, "but if it gets me where I have to go, I'll put up with it. And so should you."

"What do you mean?" Daniel asked.

Mr. Bonomo came back into the living room.

"I'm seventy-three years old," he said. "If drinking this purple shit gets me to seventy-four, which my doctor says it will, I'm happy to drink it. You're in high school. You hate the son-of-a-bitch school. But if going through high school gets you out into the world to do what you want to do, then be happy to do it. Do it and be done with it."

"I don't know what I want to do when I get out of school."

"No? Well, you'll figure it out one day," he said. "And whatever it is, it will be good. And whatever it is, don't ever give up trying. Kapish? It can take time. But you'll find it. Trust me."

Daniel went over to the old man and put his arms around him. Without a moment's hesitation, Mr. Bonomo hugged him back and kissed him on the head.

"You know," Mr. Bonomo said, "my own grandsons never gave me this much affection." He took another sip of his prune juice. "They hate school, too, by the way. Down in Florida. But they just beat up the kids and the teachers they don't like. You don't do that, I hope. There are other ways."

"I used to write songs to get out my frustrations. But I don't do that anymore."

"Why not?"

"I don't know. I just don't."

"Daniel," Mr. Bonomo said, "go home and get your guitar. Come back and write a song for me. Right here in my living room. I'd be honored."

"I'll be right back," Daniel said without a moment's hesitation.

He had to wait to cross the street while two shiny black cars passed by. When he arrived home, he didn't believe his eyes when he saw what was on the curb in front of our house, just past the tailfins of Mr. Ashler's Cadillac. It was his drum set and his xylophone. The drums were piled one on top of the other, and the xylophone was on its side.

The front door of the house opened. Dad, who happened to be home that afternoon, came out onto the stoop.

"What the hell are you doing?" Daniel called out.

"Watch your language," Dad said. "Lori's gonna stay with us for a few days during Passover. Grandma Rose will have to sleep with Mom, and I'll have to sleep in the basement. I have to put a cot down there, and these things are in the way. You haven't used this stuff in years, anyway."

"They're in a corner of the basement! You can't even see them."

"The basement is too crowded already. Besides, noise makes Grandma nervous. She gives me a headache with her goddamn oy gevalts all the time."

"But it's *my* stuff, and I don't want to get rid of it—"

"Daniel, please. I have a migraine. I don't want to argue. I have problems at work, Mom is giving me hell about the house, which is why I came home early from work… there's no end to it."

"But—"

"No buts. Grandma Rose likes to sew down there. You don't need all this damn stuff."

"Yes I do," Daniel screamed. "I fucking do! There might be some important sheet music stuffed into one of those books. Some of my songs are in there! And I still want my instruments because I might start to play again one day. It's *my* stuff, goddammit."

"Watch your mouth," Dad yelled back. "And it's *not* your stuff. My money paid for most of it. Money I worked my ass off to earn and which we don't have a lot of anymore, by the way. So it's really *my* stuff. And if you're not using it—"

"But why the fuck do you have to throw it out? Why can't we just—"

Dad, in what certainly seemed a spontaneous act, hurled the music stand toward Daniel's feet. It missed him by an inch and caused him to back up over the curb and nearly fall into the street.

"Don't you ever talk to me like that again," Dad screamed. "Who do you think you are?"

"Go to hell. All of you."

Dad turned around to go into the house, and Daniel ran across the street to go back to Mr. Bonomo's house. When he got there, the two shiny black cars that had passed by him before were now parked out front, and four men in blue windbreakers were escorting Mr. Bonomo out the front door. Two of the windbreakers said FBI in big yellow letters on the back, and the two others said Nassau County Police in smaller white letters. Mr. Bonomo was handcuffed.

"Mr. Bonomo—"

An FBI man held up a finger to tell Daniel to be quiet. Mr. Bonomo glanced at him, but then quickly looked down. One of the Nassau policemen put his hand on Mr. Bonomo's head and pushed him into a stooped position to get into the car. Then all four men got into the two cars and drove away.

There was sweat on Daniel's forehead. His neck was hot. His arms felt cold. His head throbbed.

Instead of going home, he walked briskly down Pearl Drive. The walk turned into a jog when he rounded Miller Avenue. He stomped down hard on the sidewalk to get his legs and ankles to hurt so that he would think of nothing but the pain. When Miller Avenue intersected with North Country Boulevard, he got his second wind and turned the jog into a run.

North Country Boulevard led to Church Lane, a side street that parallels the Westbrook Hills Long Island Rail Road station. As Daniel ran, he wondered if maybe in some strange way everything had led to this day, to this moment. It happened to be the day that Bob Dylan was scheduled for an evening performance at The Bitter End; maybe Manhattan was where he had to go, to find his way to The Bitter End, to meet Bob Dylan... and then what? Maybe the answer would present itself when he got there. Maybe this was the last clue, the final test, the right place at the right time. Maybe Bob Dylan would be the one to help him figure things out. Maybe in some way music was always supposed to be the key to open whatever door Daniel was supposed to walk through next. As he ran, he wondered if he should find a way to tell Dylan how the DeeJays played a few of his songs and how they were always among the most popular in their repertoire. Maybe it was Dylan all along he needed to recruit to his cause. If not for the tardiness in school, and the drum set at the curb, and the FBI agents at Mr. Bonomo's house, maybe Daniel would never have realized where the right place was to try to get to at the right time.

Daniel had just a dollar bill and few nickels left in his pocket. Creativity was imperative. Because most people at this late afternoon hour were on their way home from the city instead of going the other way, it was fairly easy for him to elude the conductor, who was already dead tired after a day-long shift.

It was six o'clock when the train pulled into Penn Station. Daniel quickly made his way to the street by hopping several steps at a time up the series of stairways that led to Seventh Avenue. From the Village Voice article, he knew that The Bitter End was on Bleecker Street in Greenwich Village. He made a right turn outside of Penn Station.

As Daniel kept his eyes focused ahead of him, he wondered once more what he should say to Bob Dylan when he met him (if indeed he was able to engineer an introduction). He wondered, too, if he should just stop thinking about it at all. Maybe he should just let whatever was going to happen simply happen. After all, isn't that what Dad had always said—that what will be, will be? And if *nothing* happened, well, would that be much of a surprise? Probably not.

When the street numbers finally dropped to single digits—West Fourth, West Third—Daniel asked an old man in a suit how to get to Bleecker Street. Once he arrived on Bleecker Street, Daniel put his head down to catch his breath after the long walk. When he looked up again he saw the long red awning that stretched over the width of the sidewalk, with the words The Bitter End printed in white script along the side. A small crowd was gathered out front. Daniel approached a lady with short curly hair and asked for the time. She said it was almost seven o'clock. The show was scheduled to begin at eight.

He ran to the side of the building, to a door with the words Club Personnel Only stenciled in the center, and rapped loudly five times with his fist. There was no response. He did it again. The door opened, and Daniel pushed his way in, neither looking to see who opened it nor thanking whoever it was. He walked down the hall. A short, stocky man in a blue shirt and untied yellow tie—he may have been the one who had opened the door—called out from behind:

"Hey, you can't go down there," he shouted. "Who the hell are you, anyway?"

It was dim in the narrow hallway. The air was thick with haze and with the combined scents of cigarettes and marijuana. The stocky man hustled down the hall in pursuit.

"You can't just walk in here like that, kid."

"I have to see Bob Dylan," Daniel said.

"Just wait here, and I'll check. What's your name?"

"Daniel Hillman."

"Okay. Stay here."

The stocky man disappeared down the hall. Daniel followed two or three moments later, even though he was told not to. He came upon a row of doors. Each one was closed, at least partially. Randomly, he selected one door and pushed it open. Two men sat on a low, sunken couch. One had long hair and headphones that hung around his neck; the other had short hair and looked over a clipboard.

"I need to see Bob Dylan," Daniel said.

"Who the hell are you?" asked the man with the clipboard.

"Daniel Hillman."

"What do you want to see him about?" the other man asked.

"He's gonna help me."

"How old are you?"

"Sixteen."

"Bob's not here yet."

"When will he be here?"

"Probably two seconds before he's supposed to go on stage."

"How can I get him to see me?"

"Hmmm... let me see... well, he just finished recording 'Watching the River Flow' and he really likes it a lot. He thinks it's gonna be a hit. Why not bring him a good luck present? Maybe he'll see you then."

The other man smiled. Daniel was frustrated because he didn't know if what he was told was real or completely fabricated.

"Is that true? About the song?"

"Yes. Absolutely," said the man with the clipboard, still without looking up. "It's Dylan sounding like Dylan again, thank the Lord above." He chuckled.

Daniel knew many details of Bob Dylan's career but was unaware of the specific things of which the man was speaking. All he knew in his addled and manic state of mind was that a suggestion had been made to buy Bob Dylan a present to celebrate his new recording. Nor could Daniel at the moment recall too many details of Dylan's personal life — although he assumed his indulgences may not have been dissimilar to many other famous musicians. But what kind of present? And how would he pay for it?

"Drugs?" he asked out loud.

"Excuse me?" asked the man with the headphones.

"Does he do drugs?"

The man smirked and warbled in a lazy voice:

*"Take me on a trip upon your magic swirling ship,*
*All my senses have been ripped,*

*And my hands can't feel to grip,*
*And my toes too numb to step..."*

The other man shook his head pitifully at the off-key rendition. Daniel recognized the lyric from Dylan's "Mr. Tambourine Man," but was unable to guess the meaning behind the smirk and the head-shaking. So he turned around and left the room.

It was a certainty in Daniel's mind that there were plenty of drugs to be found in the area; there was that street corner—the one from the afternoon with Annette—where a man was frisked by the cops. As Daniel recalled, one of the cops had called that man 'a friggin' drugstore.' If only he could find that corner again, or one just like it, maybe there'd be a good-enough present to buy for Bob Dylan. The problem, of course, was that he needed a way to purchase something without actual money. If somehow he was able to pull that off, then perhaps Dylan would help him figure out what was supposed to come next.

The stocky man in the blue shirt was by the back door, and when he saw the uninvited and unwelcome intruder, he tried to grab him. Daniel began to run around him, but the big man's girth worked to his advantage because Daniel got caught between the wall and the man's flabby thigh. The man grabbed Daniel's arm. With his other arm, Daniel pushed him away and slid behind him. There was a bulge in the big man's back pocket, which Daniel assumed to be his wallet. With his brain on irrational overdrive, Daniel screamed as loudly as he could, having sense enough to know it would create an effective diversion. It worked; the man didn't realize that his wallet had been taken out of his pocket. Stealthily, Daniel put the wallet into his own pocket and bolted away.

He put out his hands and burst through the door into the alley behind the building with such tremendous force that his palms stung. It seemed a bit darker outside than it had been before. Despite a few stares and jeers, no one on Bleecker Street appeared to be terribly concerned that a teenager was running along the sidewalk with a crazed look on his face. The corner of West Nineteenth Street and Eighth Avenue was the corner he needed to find—though he felt too possessed to ask for directions.

Daniel continued to run, turning left here and right there, and somehow after an amount of time that to his flustered mind could have been five minutes or twenty-five, he found himself closer to his destination than he thought was possible—the corner of Eighteenth Street and Ninth Avenue.

Several men were huddled together in front of a storefront; to Daniel, it seemed to be an urban sidewalk version of the kind of touch football game he used to play with Steven when they were little. There were six or seven of them, all different shapes and sizes, divided almost evenly between white, black, and Asian. Without an ounce of fear or trepidation—at least none that he can remember—Daniel walked over to the men.

"Got any stuff I can buy?" he asked no one in particular.

The men looked at each other.

"How old are you?" a short white guy asked.

"Sixteen."

"Got any dough?"

Daniel took the fat man's wallet out of his pocket, removed the bills, and counted them as quickly as he could. There were several twenties, two or three tens and a few singles, though he wasn't entirely certain if he counted correctly. He may even have counted a ten as a twenty—or vice versa.

"About a hundred twenty-two," Daniel said.

The men looked at each other again.

"We'll see what we can do," said the Asian. "Stand over there."

The men huddled closer.

"It's important," Daniel called out. "All I got is a hundred twenty-two—but it has to be good stuff."

Without breaking from the huddle, one of the men lifted his head and said,

"You disrespecting our supply, my man?"

"What?"

"Sounds like you're saying our shit ain't no good."

"No. I'm not. I swear."

The tallest of the gang, a lanky, swaggering black man, walked over to Daniel, and in one swift movement shoved a pill into his mouth and said,

"It *is* good stuff. You'll see."

Daniel was so shocked at the sudden action that he swallowed the pill without saliva. It scratched his throat on the way down.

"A hundred twenty-two, huh?" repeated the short white guy. "Won't get you much. But enough for the night, maybe. What you just got was a freebie. Marvin here's got some stuff that you can have for the dough."

Daniel handed the money to the black guy, who held his hand out for it, and the short guy handed over a small brown paper bag, which Daniel folded and put in his pants pocket.

"Is this shit for you, son?" the black man asked.

"No. It's a present."

"For who?"

"Somebody who's gonna help me."

"Help you what?"

"Figure things out."

"Only you and God can do that, son. And God ain't paying much attention lately."

"What will be, will be."

The short guy smiled.

"I guess you're right, my man. What will be, will be. Now don't go hallucinatin' all over town. Keep your mind on figuring things out." He giggled and high-fived the Asian man who stood next to him.

Daniel was dizzy and had the urge to vomit, but he didn't want to do that in front of the men and valiantly managed not to.

"What will be, will be," the black man repeated.

A return to The Bitter End was now Daniel's mission, and he used whatever concentration he could marshal to do just that, which meant steering clear of people along the way. He was just barely successful. His heart pounded. When he arrived at West Nineteenth and Broadway, two police cars turned onto West 20th, but kept going. There was also a policeman on foot talking to a newsstand vendor. Daniel slowed down and ambled closely beside a young woman who was walking a dog. The policeman didn't look his way. But when he parted company with the woman and her dog, he bumped into a street sign with such force that he fell onto the sidewalk. As he stood up, he touched his head and felt a lump. Two or three people came over to see if he was all right. Daniel smiled to the best of his ability, and the people scattered.

He continued along the sidewalk, slowly, staring intently at the cement in front of him. As he got closer to The Bitter End, he picked up the pace. His goal was to get to Bob Dylan before too many other people surrounded him. Daniel wanted to be the one to stand out. It was *his* night. *His* time.

The club finally was in sight. Daniel rocketed through the back door, just like before, and collided with the fat man, also like before—but this time the fat man used all his corpulent strength to prevent Daniel from getting any farther. The fat man said he had called the police when he realized that his wallet was missing and that another quick phone call would bring two or three officers directly into the club, instead of out on the streets where they were already looking for him.

"But I have to see Bob Dylan," Daniel shouted. "He's waiting for me."

"The only one waiting for you is the warden at Rikers Island," the fat man said as he squeezed Daniel's arm harder than before. "Tommy," he called out, "call the cops. That kid is back."

"You don't understand. I'm Daniel Hillman."

"I don't care if you're John Lennon. You're a crook. Ever hear of grand larceny?"

"I have to see him. I *have* to."

Daniel kicked the fat man between his legs. As the man doubled over in pain, Daniel ran down the hall in search of the room where Dylan might be and hit the jackpot with the first door he opened. Inside the small, dimly lit room were three people on a shag rug. There was a man with short red hair on the left and a woman with a flowered skirt on the right. In the middle was Bob Dylan. All three were smoking cigarettes. Daniel walked into the room and closed the door behind him.

"Mr. Dylan," he said, breathing heavily, "they said you'd help me."

The singer lifted his head.

"Who said?" he asked.

"I was a child prodigy once. But—"

"But what?" Dylan asked. He did not seem to be ruffled that a total stranger had barged into the room.

"But no Hillman ever tried hard enough. I want to be the one."

"The one what?"

"I don't know."

"Either do I."

The man with the red hair looked up.

"I really don't think you should be here, son," he said quietly.

"I *have* to be here," Daniel said. Suddenly he was aware of how his body was covered in sweat. There was also a loud buzz in his ears and a sharp pain in his stomach. "Please. I have a present for you…"

Daniel took the brown paper bag out of his pants pocket and handed it to Dylan. Dylan opened the top and peaked in.

"Is this… What is this?"

The woman stood up. Slowly she made her way to the door and slipped out of the room.

"What's your name, son?" Dylan asked. "Maybe we can get you some help. You don't look too good. I want to help you, man."

Daniel heard heavy breathing from the doorway and sensed that the fat man was in the hallway. The woman who had just left stood cautiously behind him.

"Should I call security?" she asked the fat man.

"The cops are on the way. This fucking kid stole my wallet, and then he assaulted me," he explained.

The fat man stood in the doorway to trap Daniel inside. But Daniel wedged his way through the small opening by bulleting between the man's right leg and the door jam. The sudden blitzkrieg startled the fat man; he smashed his shoulder against the door jam and let out a wail.

Daniel ran out of the club—a near carbon copy of his first exit thirty minutes earlier. His hands stung again when he barged through the back door. He crossed Bleecker Street to the other side, which was slightly less crowded, and ran in the direction of Penn Station. He stayed close to the façades of the shops and restaurants. But this time it was different because now many customers were leaving the retail shops and entering the restaurants on the block, and he bumped into quite a few of them, which had not been the case before. Suddenly he thought of those people not as strangers, but as enemies, and he imagined they were after him. He zigzagged from one side of the street to the other, which actually made him all the more conspicuous, although that hadn't been his intention. He had trouble breathing. His legs were weak. He may have called out Steven's name, anxious to ask his brother if this was what imminent death felt like. People stopped, stared, and pointed; Daniel yelled at them to leave him alone. The neon signs hurt his eyes. He heard police sirens in the distance and covered his ears. He closed his eyes, too, and ran that way for a few seconds, into the middle of the one-way street. He wondered if perhaps that was the best way—to let blindness and deafness do whatever it wanted to do to him on the streets of lower Manhattan. He thought bitterly: Maybe I *will* be the first something—the first teenager to successfully commit suicide right in the middle of Greenwich Village, with hundreds of people watching. But the ominous sound of a car screeching to a halt startled him out of that bizarre fantasy. He uncovered his ears and opened his eyes. Someone called out,

"Daniel! Get in the car."

The passenger door opened to let him in. In the driver's seat was Uncle Nat.

．　．　．　．　．　．

"I almost killed you, kiddo," Uncle Nat said as he sped away. "Good thing I just put in new brakes."

As Uncle Nat swerved his car around a corner to go down another one-way street, Daniel uttered a few garbled half-questions. But each time he tried to say something, Uncle Nat simply put up his right hand and said, "Shush. Not yet."

After a few minutes, they pulled into an outdoor parking lot on West Broadway and got out of the car. Uncle Nat flashed a twenty dollar bill at the attendant, who accepted it, nodded, and drove off with the shiny Buick Riviera.

Daniel followed Uncle Nat to an old, dilapidated building halfway down the block. The bottom store was an abandoned Chinese restaurant; a sign that said Far East • Dine In • Take Out hung lopsided on the wall, held by a rusted chain. The painted letters on the sign were faded almost to the point of obscurity. Daniel and Uncle Nat went to the side of the building, where there was a fire escape. The bottom rung was just three feet from the sidewalk. Uncle Nat made Daniel go first so that he could keep an eye on him as he climbed. They went to the second floor. With a key he took out of his pocket, Uncle Nat opened the black metal door on the landing, and they went inside.

Even in his poor condition, Daniel knew what kind of room he was in.

"Is this a shul?" he asked Uncle Nat.

"Yup. Only has a few congregants left. Fourteen or fifteen, maybe. The rest are dead. No one will be here tonight, though. Some people joke around and call this place Temple Egg Foo Young because of what used to be on the ground floor. Pretty silly, huh?"

It was a tiny sanctuary no larger than a high school principal's office. There were a dozen or so metal folding chairs scattered around the yellow-tiled floor. Almost all of the tiles were cracked. The small, rectangular windows along one wall were filthy, though one was made of stained glass and still had brilliant blues, greens, yellows, and reds that were illuminated by lights from a neighboring roof.

In place of a raised pulpit, like the one at Temple Beth Shalom, there were two shabby lecterns on the floor, about four feet apart, connected with a green velvet rope—the kind used in movie theatres.

"A bargain basement temple," Uncle Nat said, as he saw Daniel look around.

On the wall behind the lecterns hung a three-dimensional, brushed-metal rendering of two tablets with the Ten Commandments etched upon them in Hebrew. Below the metal sculpture was a tall, battered locker—similar to a gym locker—with a large Jewish star made of wood hanging from a chain hooked over its two top corners.

"Yup," Uncle Nat said, "that's the ark, believe it or not. The Ark of the Covenant, where they keep the Torah."

Daniel lowered himself into one of the folding chairs and stared at the locker.

"How do you know about this place?"

"There's a guy I do business with, works across the street. He mentioned it once. Sometimes I come up here just to hang out."

Uncle Nat took off his black coat and draped it over a chair. He had on a brown suit underneath. It looked new.

"Just sit," he said. "You got a nice bump there on your forehead. Are you okay?"

"I completely forgot about that," Daniel said, touching the bump gently.

Uncle Nat chuckled.

"I'll get you a glass of water," he said. "There's a water fountain on the floor above that actually works. With cups. Clean cups, believe it or not. Better than what comes out of the sink in the bathroom. I'll be right back."

Uncle Nat passed through the metal door and climbed the fire escape to the floor above.

As ill as he felt, Daniel was also aware of his own sense of whimsy. So he slid off the chair, got on his knees, and began to pray. He didn't know what to say, but he prayed anyway. Moments later, Uncle Nat returned with a cup of water. Daniel sat on the chair just as he came into the room.

Daniel took the cup and drank the water in two enormous sips.

"How did you find me, anyway?" he asked. "And who told you to look for me?"

Uncle Nat sat in the chair next to his.

"Well," he said, "from what I understand, your mother saw you running down the block after a little argument she says you had with your pop. She was watching from the living room window. When you didn't come back in an hour, she started to worry. She called all your friends. Nobody knew where you were, but somebody's father was coming home from work on the train and saw you at the station. Your mom got really scared. So she called me."

"On the telephone? She had your number?"

"Your mother's not stupid. She called around. She found out that I'm staying at a hotel in New York for a few days and got my number. First time she ever spoke to me on the phone, by the way."

"Did you say this place has a bathroom?" Daniel asked.

"Ten old men davening for three hours? There'd *better* be a bathroom. Over there." He pointed to a door at the back of the room. Daniel visited the bathroom and threw up three times in the toilet. When he was finished, he washed his face and hands in the rusted sink and went back to the sanctuary.

"And then what," he asked as if he had never left, "after my mother called you?"

"I told her to look in your room and tell me everything she found that's not usually there."

"What did she find?"

"An ad ripped out of a magazine. For a show tonight at The Bitter End."

"Oh."

"And the rest," Uncle Nat continued, "was just luck. I stopped at The Bitter End, and a bunch of people were looking for a kid who, in their words, mind you, not mine, was 'fucked up, acting like an asshole, and making lots of trouble.' That's a direct quote. Cops were there, too. So I figured you might be somewhere in the neighborhood."

Daniel put his head down. He tried to let it all sink in.

"Will you be able to get us out of here?" he asked.

Uncle Nat smiled.

"I think so," he said. "We'll stay a few more minutes."

They sat in silence.

"Listen, Daniel… You don't have to tell me what happened if you don't want to. Or why. At least you're okay now. And safe. That's what's important. The rest is up to you."

Daniel began to cry. He saw no use in hiding the tears.

"I guess this is a pretty good place to think about it, huh? Whatever *it* is," Uncle Nat grinned. "With the Torah in that locker right over there, and the Ten Commandments above it." Daniel looked up at him. "Hey, I may be a nogoodnik," Uncle Nat added, "and the black sheep of the family. But I *do* know what the Ten Commandments are. And I know how to recite the blessings over bread and wine. And I know who Abraham, Isaac, and Joseph were. You think I don't know?"

"I know you know."

"Doesn't mean I'll get to heaven. But it couldn't hurt. Am I right? What about you, Daniel? Still a good little Jewish boy, despite the fact that you're not a little boy anymore?"

"I guess I've broken a few Commandments lately."

"You haven't killed anyone, have you?"

"No," I said. "But I feel like I have."

Uncle Nat stood up and grabbed his coat. "Listen, kid," he said. "Don't take the blame for all the crap that happens. That makes absolutely no sense when you really think about it. And don't hand off all the blame, either. Things happen. Life's complicated. Sometimes you just gotta make the best of whatever you got. Vishtayst?"

He rubbed Daniel's head gently.

"What do you say we head out now?" Uncle Nat said softly. "I think it'll be okay."

"I don't really want to," Daniel said.

"Not ready to honor thy mother and father?"

"I just can't go home yet. Why can't I just stay with you for a while?"

"The thing is, Daniel, I've been accused of a lot of things in my day, and I'd rather not add kidnapping. I gotta take you home, kid. Besides, I don't think I'd be a very good guardian. I tend to move around a lot."

"But… me and you… in a place like this… after what happened… after the way you found me… I mean, it's almost like a novel or something. A movie. I want more of that."

Uncle Nat chuckled.

"Believe me, I'm one character you don't want more of in your life," he said. There was a look of sincerity on his face.

"But I don't want to go home."

"I'm sorry, Daniel, but—"

"How about Lori? She's only an hour from here. In New Jersey. Maybe we can go there instead. I know her phone number."

Uncle Nat thought about it for a moment.

"I guess that would be all right. Next of kin and all that. And an adult... Okay. Then, after I drop you off, you and Lori can decide what to do, as far as your mom and pop are concerned."

He helped Daniel stand up.

"We'll call her when we're on the other side of the Holland Tunnel. In Jersey. You're okay to be in the car for an hour? It's relatively new, if you know what I mean."

"I'm fine."

"Okay."

"Thanks, Uncle Nat. Thanks for..."

"Knowing how to find people?" he said with a grin. "You're welcome."

Daniel looked up at the Ten Commandments, then followed Uncle Nat down the fire escape to the side of Temple Egg Foo Young. I received a phone call fifteen minutes later.

# Nine

Yesterday afternoon I felt compelled to go over *The Mystery of Jewish Mysticism* once more. It was the fourth or fifth time this month I had reviewed the essay—but that's how important it is to my upcoming exam. Daniel walked into the kitchen just as I reached the last page. He had with him a thick stack of papers, three-hole-punched, with gold clips through each hole binding the stack together.

"Again?" he asked when he saw the essay I was reading.

I reminded him that the test was tomorrow. He sat down at the opposite end of the table.

"What's that?" I asked. "Can't be college catalogs or anything like that, can it?"

High school graduation is just a week away. All the seniors at Governor Morris High School have already made their college decisions. Daniel plans to spend the remainder of 1972, and perhaps one additional year, exploring other options before he decides where he wants to go to college. That's how I knew his stack of papers had nothing to do with colleges or universities.

What he had in his hands was the final galley proof of a new novel written by a friend of his English teacher. As Daniel explained, he had a discussion about the publishing industry with the teacher, Mrs. Newlin, who knew that Daniel would appreciate seeing what galleys look like. She managed to get a copy for him.

"Now one day in the future, when the galleys of your own novel arrive in the mail," Mrs. Newlin had said to him, "it won't be a complete surprise. You'll know just what to expect when you open up the package!"

"That was very nice of Mrs. Newlin," I said to Daniel. He agreed.

It has been a little more than a year since Daniel came to live with me. He likes my house. He likes Morristown, too, as well as New Jersey, despite the teasing the state always seems to get on television and the jokes that Dad always used to make whenever we visited relatives here. Whatever New Jersey is or is not, it is a world and a lifetime away from Westbrook Hills. It even looks completely different. Despite its name, Westbrook Hills had no hills; by contrast, this part of New Jersey has a landscape that can sometimes pass for Kiamesha Lake in the Catskill Mountains.

Daniel has been at Governor Morris High School for a full school year. Longer, actually, since he also had to finish off the final two months of his junior year. Fortunately, most of the courses and requirements were similar to those of his old school, which enabled him to complete those two months with remarkably few problems. Certainly there was much red tape involved, but I managed to handle that fairly easily. (My background both at a psychiatric hospital and a university office prepared me well.) The beginning of his senior year was a little difficult for Daniel, emotionally speaking, but after just a few weeks, the transition was by all accounts entirely successful.

Further proof is the fact that his senior year went very well, academically and otherwise. He made friends. He and Marissa have been dating for a few months now. They walk home every day and hang out in the house at least twice a week. Other than an embrace or two in plain sight (with an occasional passionate kiss thrown in), they really are quite modest in their public behavior; what they do in private is something I'm ready neither to discuss nor consider. I do know, however, that the two of them talk for hours on end about more topics than I can even imagine. Marissa wants to be a musician, preferably in a Broadway pit orchestra. Daniel recently took her to see *The Rothschilds* at the Lunt-Fontanne Theatre in Manhattan for her eighteenth birthday.

Daniel's other friends include the Feingold twins, Eli and Zachary. They remind us of the DePuzo twins, Johnny and Joey, with five major differences in the Feingolds' favor: the way they look, the way they talk, they way they dress, the way they smell, and the way they think. In short, the Feingolds are wonderful boys. They love photography, and sometimes Daniel goes with them on what they call their 'landscape journeys' all over northwestern New Jersey, particularly by the Delaware River. Their photographs are very beautiful. I may ask to purchase a few. I'll keep one or two in the house, and if I'm lucky enough to have an office one day soon, I'll put a few there, as well.

Daniel likes all his teachers—except Mr. Gerlach. Gerlach is a tough physics teacher with very little humor and even less hair. Daniel calls him the BQN—short for Bald Quantum Nazi. I told him to be careful. "You can be saying 'Bald Quantum Nazi' to someone in a hallway at school when Mr. Gerlach is actually standing right behind you," I warned him.

"From your lips to God's ears," Daniel responded.

Mom and Dad plan to attend Daniel's high school graduation. Grandma Rose and Grandpa Jesse probably won't join them, since neither take well to long car rides. Grandma is now in a nursing home in Queens, and Grandpa is in a similar home in Brooklyn. The few trips they made to New Jersey with Mom and Dad were marred by traffic jams on one or both of the bridges they have to cross to get here.

We've seen Mom and Dad about once a month since the decision was made for Daniel to live here. Sometimes they drive out to New Jersey, and sometimes we go to Long Island.

Mom sees a therapist twice a month and belongs to a woman's group that deals with family issues, and that seems to help her stay positive. She even started a newsletter for parents of slain soldiers from Long Island; it's small and loses money, but she loves working on it.

Dad was given a desk job at LILCO headquarters, which has resulted in much less stress and anxiety. His last physical exam had turned up dangerously high blood pressure and an irregular heartbeat, so he put in for a new position. The LILCO bosses, very pleased with him all those years, gave it to him without hesitation. He's already led some very important corporate initiatives from a big desk in a little office at the corporate complex. He usually works from nine to five.

Our recent visits with Mom and Dad have been peaceful.

There were many arguments, both on the phone and in person, that preceded the decision to allow Daniel to stay with me. Mom and Dad had a dozen or so criticisms and called it everything from an unconventional idea to one fraught with too many unknowns. Even when they decided to seriously consider it they complained there would be too much paperwork. Daniel and I had dozens of frustrating conversations with them. We even sought the opinions of Aunt Paula, Vincent Yaccarini, and a few other people. There was the occasional long, awkward silence on the phone, and a number of gut-wrenching tears. But we got through it. While all this was going on, it became clear very quickly that Daniel was far more relaxed and upbeat at my house than he had been in Westbrook Hills. He found it easy to open up to me, and I seemed to instinctively know when to ask or when not to ask questions in order to get him to talk about things that weighed on his mind. Daniel told me many stories over the past year, added quite a bit of commentary, and almost always asked for my opinion. I enjoyed those talks immensely and encourage them even to this day. Sharing them gives Daniel a sense of serenity, and gives me a sense of relief to know that everything has a reason and that most of the time, things work out the way they're probably supposed to.

"I think I know what led you to be such a good storyteller," I told him a few days ago. "A bisl of fate mixed with a schmear of luck."

"Thanks, Grandpa Sol," he said.

. . .

Daniel likes all the books in my house. There are many. More than half are Hebrew books and biblical texts. He says that he's entirely comfortable around those, even though he's forgotten much of the Hebrew he learned in Hebrew school. Besides, he wouldn't dare criticize my book selections because he knows that much of my limited shelf space must be reserved for those particular volumes since they are compulsory for my rabbinical studies. He takes one out from time to time to see if in his mind he can update a biblical story to make it interesting and relevant as a modern-day parable.

He also enjoys giving me quizzes as the date of my ordination draws nearer.

If all goes well, a few weeks after Daniel graduates from Governor Morris High School, I will walk across a stage at the Rabbinical College of America to become the first ordained female Conservative rabbi in the United States. We are both very proud of that. So are Mom and Dad, although I still sense a bit of uncertainty in their reactions. They don't quite know what to make of it. I was told by someone at the seminary that it will be a milestone in Conservative Jewry that may have worldwide implications and spark a considerable amount of interest and publicity. When I heard that I decided not to think about it. All I really want to know is where my first congregation will be and what my congregants will be like. I'm anxious to get to know them, care for them, encourage them, and listen to *their* stories the way I've listened to Daniel's.

Two days ago, Daniel overheard me talking to myself in the kitchen. (I didn't know he was in the house.)

"I hope I'm a good rabbi," I had said aloud.

"You will be," he called out from the living room. It startled me. He walked into the kitchen. "You're smart, and you're confident. Just like that girl at the airport."

"What?" I asked. "Who?"

"And you're good with people."

"Well," I said, "rabbis become good rabbis when they have good people around them."

"You heard that from Rabbi Sheldon, didn't you? He said the same thing to me once. A million years ago. I thought he was talking about himself. But maybe he was talking about you."

"No, Daniel," I said. "He was talking about you."

•    •    •    •    •

The Rabbinical College campus is just a few miles from my house, and it's become almost a second home to me because of my busy schedule of classes, lectures, and seminars. It's probably not a stretch to say that Daniel takes care of my house more than I do during a typical week. I'm on an accelerated program, partially because that's my preference and partially because the college is anxious for the publicity it will likely receive once I'm ordained. That, I'm told, could translate into increased enrollment and more grants.

Daniel has an open invitation to visit me on campus whenever he wants. They have several pianos there, and it pains me a bit to know that the one thing still missing in his new and more contented life is music. At Governor Morris High he had joined the school newspaper and the history club, but neither the band nor the chorus. I choose to believe that Daniel will always love music. To me, it's a foregone conclusion. I even mentioned that to him a day or two ago.

"There are no such things as foregone conclusions," he said back to me. Fortunately, he smiled when he said it.

Last night I reclined in the easy chair in my living room to study a book on Bible interpretations. Daniel was on the couch and used the coffee table as a desk to write an extra-credit essay for his English class. It was about Scout, the narrator and one of the main characters in Harper Lee's *To Kill a Mockingbird*.

"Anything can be turned into a novel," Daniel said at one point. "Isn't that cool? If it's done right, that is. Happy things, depressing things, strange things, even Bible stories, and childhood memories like Scout's."

"Childhood is always good for novels," I said. "I wish the Bible had more stories in it that kids could relate to, that they could enjoy."

"Maybe I'll write that version one day. By the way, you know I wrote a novel, right?"

"I had my suspicions," I said. "I'm sure that's one of the things you've been doing in your room every night."

"Actually, that's *all* I do in my room," he acknowledged. "Except when Marissa's there. But I'm sure you don't want me to talk about that."

"If you don't mind... no."

"I also wrote two short stories that are coming out in the literary magazine at school this week."

"What are they called?"

"One is called *The Little Girl in the Chapel*. The other one is called *The Golden L*. And I just submitted a one-act play to a playwriting contest in Cincinnati. Five winners get flown to Cincinnati to see their plays performed, and they also get a little bit of money to use for college."

"What's the play about?"

"Ned Early."

"Ned Early? From Temple Beth Shalom? That's fantastic! What's it called?"

"Don't laugh," he urged. "It's called *You Have to Wake Up Pretty Early in the Morning to Fool Ned Early*. I like long titles."

"Wow! Daniel! Tell me about the novel. Have you done anything with it? What's it called? What's it about?" I was truly excited.

"It's called *The Sidewalks of New York*," he explained. "There are two parallel stories in it that come together halfway through, one about a guy like Yussel Hillman, and another about a guy like Salvatore Bonomo."

"Yussel Hillman? Grandpa Jesse?"

"Yup."

"And Joey and Johnny's grandfather?"

"Uh-huh."

"Nonfiction?" I asked. "Fiction?"

"A little of both. Did you know they both came to Ellis Island in 1907, and they both were forced against their will to walk around the streets of New York City? But both ended up loving the fact that they had to do that because it led them to being able to figure out what they wanted to do with their lives. Of course, things didn't always work out the exactly the way they had hoped. But if they did, there'd be no story. Right?"

"And both of them would have become entirely different men. Do they meet in the story?"

"You'll have to read it," he smiled.

"I want to. Did you tell Mom? She'd be interested."

"Not yet. I have to think about that. If by some miracle it's published, I don't want her to worry about me being called some kind of literary prodigy."

"When can I read it?"

"Well," he said, "I can show you my typed copy—but wouldn't it be cool to wait for an actual book?"

"When will it be an actual book?"

"That part's out of my hands, Lori. We'll see.."

Daniel told me that Mrs. Newlin had given him a long list of the names and addresses of literary agencies, and that he had already put a dozen copies of the manuscript in the mail.

"I'm hoping for you," I said. "And praying. And believing. God, Daniel, you must be on eggshells waiting to hear. You should work on another project while you're waiting, to get your mind off of it. Are you? Do you have any ideas?"

"Are you kidding me? Tons!" he said. "Books, plays, movies... You name it. I'll never get around to them all."

"You have time. You have your whole life. What are some of your other ideas?"

"Well, I have a ten-page outline for another novel. It's about this kid growing up. People come and go, things happen, life changes—but for him, the passing of time has nothing to do with clocks and watches. It's all about feelings and emotions that change. Does that make any sense?"

"I'm sure it will—once I read the novel," I assured him. "Does he learn any important lessons along the way?"

"You mean, does he come to understand what life is all about?" Daniel asked.

"Well, I don't think *anyone* can ever understand what life is all about," I admitted. "Not rabbis, not priests, not shrinks. No one. But I think you can learn to understand *yourself* a little more. About your own purpose in life."

"Maybe. But in this story, the kid learns that there's almost no use trying to understand anything because nothing's up to him anyway. There are no foregone conclusions. But the thing is, he also learns that that's okay. That it's normal. Perfectly natural. That whatever happens, happens, and what will be, will be. I guess Dad was right all along. Some things are meant to be, and some things just aren't meant to be, and there's no blueprint you're born with to let you know which is which. You just gotta let it happen."

I thought about that for a moment. It was a weighty topic, but he seemed to be balancing it well.

"So does that make it a little easier for this kid to face the future?" I asked.

"I honestly don't know yet," Daniel answered pensively—and with a smirk. "I haven't gotten that far. I mean, in a world where there are no foregone conclusions, you really can't depend on wishes, and you can't really depend on luck. Wishes and luck just don't exist. You know—wishing on stars, throwing coins in the fountain, all that kind of stuff—it's all meaningless bullshit. So if that's the case, I'm not sure what this kid will end up doing in the last few chapters. To tell you the truth, I can't wait to find out!"

We both chuckled.

"There's only one thing for sure," Daniel continued. "Destiny. But destiny has a big catch. The catch is that no one knows what their destiny is."

It was a lot to take in, and I'm not certain if I was more surprised than confused by it all. But no matter what, seeing how dynamic and poised Daniel was as he talked about it made me know that it was my job to keep the conversation going.

"It's such a fascinating topic," I said. "Difficult—but fascinating. Do you have a name for this novel yet?"

"I thought about *Time* for a while, but people would probably think it's just a boring history of the magazine. Then I thought about *In My Life*, or *Nowhere Man*, but the Beatles would probably get pissed at me and sue my ass off, and since you're not becoming a lawyer, I have no one to represent me. Then I jotted down *One More Darker*, which is something I once said to Glenn Sheldon." Daniel sighed, shook his head, then continued. "I also considered *Beth Gevalt*, but then it would have to be a satire, which I don't want it to be since there's nothing satirical about it. Same thing for *As the World Kvetches*."

"How about *Yellow Circles in the Snow*?"

Daniel shot me a look that I can only describe as startled. Or maybe amused. Probably both.

"Seriously, though," I quickly added, "how about calling it *To Be Continued*?"

"That's not a bad idea," Daniel acknowledged. "That would make a sequel a foregone conclusion—even though there are no such things as foregone conclusions."

"Well, whatever you decide, let me know if there's anything I can do to help."

We sat for a few minutes in silence.

"God, I miss Steven," he said.

"I miss him too."

"I miss Grandma Leah and Grandpa Sol."

"And many others, I bet."

"Harry Houdini. Ella Vayda. Rabbi Sheldon. Carol. Ned..."

"Some of them," I said as I pointed to the phone, "are right there. And others," I added, pointing to Daniel's head, "are right there."

It was late, and I had an early class. I stood up, grabbed the essay, and prepared to leave the kitchen.

"Lori," Daniel said, "thank you. I love you."

I went over to him.

"I love you too, Daniel."

I put the essay back down on the table and hugged him. We held each other for a long time. I think he was crying. I know I was—and I didn't mind at all.

•  •  •  •  •

Early this morning, about five minutes before I had to leave for campus, and a half hour before Daniel had to walk to Governor Morris High, I glanced out the living room window and saw him standing on the front lawn. I had already noticed a wet towel in the bathroom hamper and a clean dish in the kitchen dish rack, so I knew he had showered and eaten breakfast. I assumed he just wanted to relax before heading off for school. Maybe he was waiting for Marissa. I suppose he could have been thinking about Mom and Dad, or about his future plans. Perhaps he just wanted to think about *The Sidewalks of New York*, or the literary agents on whose desks the manuscript now sits, or any number of novels, shorts stories, plays, and movies he plans to write one day. After all, the conversation from the night before was no doubt still fresh in his mind. I'm not sure. I can only speculate.

Daniel stopped in the middle of the lawn, which hadn't been mowed in about two weeks, and sat down. I watched as he played with a few blades of tall grass. He pulled them out slowly, apparently in an attempt to see if he could free them wholly from the ground without snapping them in two. There were a few little twigs that school kids snapped off from the Weeping Cherry tree by the sidewalk and had thrown onto the lawn. Daniel picked up a twig and tried to balance it on his finger. Suddenly, a white cluster of dandelion seeds flew by in front of him. He stood up, and as he did the delicate seeds shifted away from him. But the cluster moved so slowly that he was able to catch up to it with a single step. He reached out and grabbed it. I thought back to what he had told me last night about *Nowhere Man* or *One More Darker* or whatever he might ultimately call his latest project. I knew exactly what he was thinking—that he did not want to make a wish on that little white cluster and send it up to the sky by blowing on it. That he was determined to abandon the childish idea of yearning for something simply by running it through his imagination—while at the same time sending the seed of a weed into the air. How silly! What foolishness. He wanted to get that crazy notion out of his head forever. To make a wish would be a ridiculous waste of time, and utterly unnecessary.

But he did it anyway.

# END

# Yiddish/Hebrew Glossary

Baruch atah . . . *Blessed are you*

Bimah . . . *elevated platform at the head of the temple sanctuary*

Bisl . . .*a little bit*

Boychick . . . *nice little boy*

Bupkis . . . *nothing*

Chai . . . *life*

Challah . . . *braided loaf of egg-based bread*

Chazzan . . . *singer; cantor*

Chotchke . . . *trinket*

Davening . . . *praying*

Fekakta . . . *something ridiculous, senseless*

Gelt . . . *money*

Good Shabbos . . . *Good Sabbath*

Hazzor i-yim bed-heem ah-berinnah yiktsoru . . . *Those who sow in tears will reap with songs of joy*

Hillel . . . *Jewish student union*

Kinahura . . . *an expression of thankfulness (usually translated as "You should never get the evil eye")*

Kinderlach . . . *children*

Kreplach . . . *meat-filled dumpling*

Kvetch . . . *complain*

Lantsman . . . *countryman, in a religious sense*

Latke . . . *a small fried potato pancake*

Mazel tov . . . *congratulations (translated as good luck)*

Mensch . . . *a real man*

Meshugener . . .*crazy*

Nachas . . . *enormous pride*

Nu . . . *So?*

Oy . . . *an expression of dismay*

Oy gevalt . . . *an even stronger expression of dismay than oy*

Oy gut . . . *oh God!*

Pisher . . . *someone you find amusing, or admirable, or annoying*

Plotz . . . *collapse*

Potchkee . . . *to play or tinker around*

Punim . . . *face*

Schmear ... *to spread*

Schmutz . . . *dirt, grime*

Shabbos . . . *Sabbath*

Shayna punim . . . *pretty face*

Shepping nachas . . . *feeling a lot of pride*

Shiva . . . *Jewish ritual period of mourning*

Shtetl . . . *small (and usually poor)Eastern European village of mostly
  Jews*

Shul . . . *temple*

Torah . . . *the books in which the laws of Judaism are written*

Tuchis . . . *rear end*

Tummler . . . *joker*

Vey is mir ... *woe is me*

Vishtayst . . . *understand*

Yarmulke . . . *religious head covering for a Jewish man*

Yiddishe Mama . . . *Revered Jewish mother or grandmother*

Zaida . . . *grandfather*

# NOTE FROM THE AUTHOR

If you enjoyed *Blowin' in the Wind*, please consider leaving a review online—either on Amazon, other bookseller sites, or even on your own social media platforms. In today's digital world, word-of-mouth advertising, hastened by the internet, is one of the most powerful tools for promotion. That's just what my fellow authors and I need in order to validate what we enjoy doing for the reading public. It would be much appreciated.
Thanks.
Joel

# ABOUT THE AUTHOR

Joel began writing professionally at the age of 17 as a stringer for his hometown newspaper. After studying journalism, communications, and theater at Hofstra University, he began his career as an assistant editor on several trade magazines, then moved into public relations and marketing communications. As a journalist his work has appeared in more than 20 magazines. He is the author of five nonfiction books, including "Some Kind of Lonely Clown: The Music, Memory & Melancholy Lives of Karen Carpenter." As a playwright, two of Joel's plays have been brought to life on stage. He has also been a guest commentator on several documentaries and radio programs.

Professional website: JoeltheWriter.com
Novel blog: https://blowin-in-the-wind-novel.blogspot.com
Facebook page: facebook.com/joel.samberg.1
Literary blog: Hey-You-Never-Know.blogspot.com

Thank you so much for reading one of our **Literary Fiction** novels.

If you enjoyed our book, please check out our recommended title for your next great read!

*The Five Wishes by Mr. Murray McBride* by Joe Siple

## 2018 Maxy Award "Book of the Year"

"A sweet...tale of human connection...will feel familiar to fans of Hallmark movies." *-KIRKUS REVIEWS*

"An emotional story that will leave readers meditating on the life-saving magic of kindness." *-Indie Reader*

View other Black Rose Writing titles at www.blackrosewriting.com/books and use promo code **PRINT** to receive a **20% discount** when purchasing.

www.ingramcontent.com/pod-product-compliance
Lightning Source LLC
Chambersburg PA
CBHW011129100726
47898CB00009B/2917